Praise for
Jodi Ellen M

T0017759

THE PROTECTOR

"Readers will love this book from the very beginning! The characters are so real and flawed that fans feel as if they're alongside them. Malpas's writing is also spot-on with emotions. 4½ stars!"

—*RT Book Reviews*, Top Pick

"A joy to read...This is the first book I've read from Jodi Ellen Malpas, but she has become a favorite in one read." —Night Owl Reviews

GENTLEMAN SINNER

"Malpas's sexy love scenes scorch the page, and her sensitive, multi-layered hero and heroine will easily capture readers' hearts. A taut plot and a first-rate lineup of supporting characters make this a keeper."

—*Publishers Weekly*

"A magnetic mutual attraction, a superalpha, and long-buried scars that are healed by love. Theo is irresistible." —*Booklist*

"Filled with raw emotions that ranged from the deepest rage to utter elation, Jodi Ellen Malpas wove together an incredible must-read tale that fans will certainly embrace." —Harlequin Junkie

WITH THIS MAN

"Super steamy, emotionally intense."   —*Library Journal*

"The raw emotion and vulnerability is breathtaking."
                                                        —*RT Book Reviews*

"Unpredictable and addictive."   —*Booklist*

"Devoted fans of Jesse and Ava will eagerly devour every word from this book."   —Harlequin Junkie

THE FORBIDDEN

"A brave, cutting-edge romance."   —*Library Journal*

"A gut-wrenching tale full of passion, angst, and heart! Not to be missed!"   —Harlequin Junkie

LEAVE ME
Breathless

Also by Jodi Ellen Malpas

LEAVE ME
Breathless

JODI ELLEN MALPAS

FOREVER

New York Boston

Forever
Hachette Book Group
1290 Avenue of the Americas, New York, NY 10104
read-forever.com
twitter.com/readforeverpub

First Edition: November 2019

Forever is an imprint of Grand Central Publishing.
The Forever name and logo are trademarks of Hachette Book Group, Inc.

The publisher is not responsible for websites (or their content) that are not owned by the publisher.

The Hachette Speakers Bureau provides a wide range of authors for speaking events. To find out more, go to www.hachettespeakersbureau.com or call (866) 376-6591.

Library of Congress Cataloging-in-Publication Data

Names: Malpas, Jodi Ellen, author.
Title: Leave me breathless / Jodi Ellen Malpas.
Description: First edition. | New York : Forever, 2019.
Identifiers: LCCN 2019017664| ISBN 9781538745212 (softcover) | ISBN 9781478995722 (audio download) | ISBN 9781538745229 (ebook)
Subjects: | GSAFD: Romantic suspense fiction. | Love stories.
Classification: LCC PR6113.A47 L43 2019 | DDC 823/.92--dc23
LC record available at https://lccn.loc.gov/2019017664

ISBNs: 978-1-5387-4521-2 (pbk.), 978-1-5387-4522-9 (ebook)

Printed in the United States of America

LSC-C

10 9 8 7 6 5 4 3

For my readers.
Without you, I am just a woman with a crazy,
overactive imagination.
Thank you for being in my world.
JEM x

CHAPTER ONE

RYAN

Something isn't right. I left MI5 ten years ago, but my sixth sense is still as strong as ever, a kind of danger detector, and I'm detecting danger right now. My skin is prickling. Adrenaline is starting to pump through my veins.

I scan the vicinity outside our client's house, seeing nothing un-usual. There's been nothing unusual since our personal security agency accepted the contract two weeks ago. Our client, a model from Canada with a devoted stalker, leaves for the airport any minute with her six-year-old daughter. It would be a fucking travesty at this point to run into a threat.

My partner, Jake, is tense, too, his big shoulders high as he scruti-nizes the street beyond the iron gate that separates this house from the rest of London. He's quiet. I'm quiet.

"Yo, Jake," I call, watching as the big guy leisurely takes backward steps away from the gate until he's at the door with me.

"There's a black Audi across the street." He goes to his phone. "Blacked-out windows. It's been there for over an hour and the driver hasn't gotten out."

I fucking knew it. "You checked with Lucinda?" I move to the gates to take a look, seeing the RS 7 parked up the road, the passenger window open a fraction.

"The plate's a clone." Jake confirms what I feared.

I check left and right casually. "And here I was thinking how easy this job had been." I back away, feeling the weight of my Heckler pushing into the base of my spine. Fucking hell, I haven't had to draw my gun in years. Yes, this job has been boring as shit, just like every other in the ten years I've served at the agency, but boring is safe. Boring means I make it home to Hampton.

Jake looks over his shoulder as the front door opens and our client emerges with her daughter. "Miss Warren, we're going to have to ask you to step back inside for a few minutes," my partner says coolly.

She blinks, surprised. "But my plane leaves in two hours." There's panic in her voice, and she scans the street beyond. "Is there a problem?"

"Let's just get you back inside," Jake says softly, walking toward her and taking the little girl's hand, leading her back into the house with her mother.

Miss Warren's eyes flick between mine and Jake's, clearly trying to find an answer to her question. Then she opens her mouth to speak but quickly thinks better of it, turning to her daughter and crouching. "Darling, I think I've left Paddington on the couch. Why don't you run along and fetch him."

"Okay." The little girl dashes back to the living room, and Miss Warren stands, turning toward us. "Please, tell me what's going on."

"There's an unidentified vehicle across the street that we need to check out," I explain.

Her eyes immediately widen, her inhale loud. "Oh my God, it's him."

I look to Jake, wondering if he's sensing what I'm sensing. "Him, as in your stalker?" he asks, confirming he's suspicious, too.

She starts blinking rapidly, her hands shaking as she tucks her hair behind her ear. "Yes." She looks away, and I can no longer keep my thoughts to myself.

"Miss Warren, is there something else we should know?"

"I don't have a stalker," she more or less whispers, her eyes clouded as she finds it in herself to look at us. "I have an ex-boyfriend who's a less-than-desirable character and would do anything to hurt me."

I recoil. "Why?"

"Because I left him."

"Name?" Jake demands, going straight to his phone. I watch as she breathes in, as if bracing herself to tell us. Nothing about this is boding well.

"Corey Felton."

"What?" I blurt, hoping I heard her wrong. Jake curses under his breath, smacking at his phone with his thumb. "The drug trafficker?"

She can only bring herself to nod, and I see a million apologies in her eyes. Jesus Christ, Corey Felton is wanted in ten countries for various crimes. But he's elusive. Untouchable. And judging by the fear I can see in Miss Warren's eyes, he's just as nasty as the whispers suggest. "The police wouldn't help me unless I assisted with their inquiries," she rushes to explain. "I just need to get back to Canada, and I know he'll do anything to stop me." Miss Warren peeks past us to the gates again.

"We'll get you and your daughter to the airport safely, don't you worry." I give her my best reassuring smile, and she nods, backing up and shutting the door.

"What's the deal?" I ask as Jake stares down at his phone.

"Backup's on the way. If it's him, we'll need it."

If it's him? "Of course it's him." My blood sizzles with adrenaline. "You ready to dance?" I ask as we walk back toward the gate.

"If I don't make it home to Cami and Charlotte in one piece, she'll be coming after your blood, you know that, right?"

"I know," I say quietly, my eyes set on the black Audi across the street. Jake and I go way back, though it's only been the past couple of years we've worked together on assignments. Jake taking a partner was a condition laid down by his wife if he wanted to remain in the business. I was the perfect man for the job.

I slip out onto the pavement—just as our backup truck skids into the street. "Subtle," I mutter.

"He's been underground for years," Jake says, joining me. "Every police force from here to the States wants him."

Just as I start striding toward the RS 7, reaching back to pull my Heckler, the growl of the Audi engine starts up. A buzz of excitement that I haven't felt in years comes over me, no matter how hard I try to push it back. He's about to make his getaway.

Just let backup deal with it, I tell myself. *No need to go all Jason Bourne in the middle of London.* But my legs move faster of their own volition, my jog turning into a full-on run. I race across the street toward the Audi, hearing car horns blare and the screech of tires as it tries to pull away from the curb into oncoming traffic. It doesn't get very far, wedging its front end in between a bus and a BMW. But the bus starts to reverse to give the Audi space to pull out. To escape. *Fuck no.*

The damn fucking suit they insist I wear hindering me, I sprint into the road, spotting a black cab heading straight toward me. The driver catapults back in his seat, bracing for impact. "Shit, shit, shit."

"Ryan, what the fuck are you doing?" Jake booms behind me. I keep my eyes forward, watching as the cab gets closer and closer and closer, the screeching of its tires deafening. "Ryan!"

At the last second, the driver turns the wheel, and the loudest bang erupts when it slams into the Audi just as it breaks free through the line of traffic, blocking it in between the BMW and the bus again. Without even pausing to think about it, I pull open the back door of the cab and slide through to the other side, ignoring the stunned face of a businessman in the back with his phone to his ear.

The Audi begins to reverse, ramming the parked car behind it, but comes to a screeching stop when the backup team pulls up alongside us. "Going somewhere?" I yank the door open, grab the driver, and haul him out, my gun immediately wedged under his chin.

"Fuck," I hear Jake say from behind me, just as I register that the man I have pinned to the side of the mangled Audi isn't Corey Felton.

Realization hits me like a brick. "It's a decoy!" I yell, releasing him and throwing myself over the hood of the car. The second I land on my feet, I break into a sprint, my focus set. *The fucker.*

I'm back at the house in seconds, kicking the front door open, my arms at full length before me, my gun steady in my grip.

Miss Warren runs into the hall, frantic. "What's going on?" She comes to a startled stop when she sees me. She's in one piece. Still here. So . . .

"Where's your daughter?" I ask.

"Oh my God." Her hands go to her mouth, her eyes wide. "He'll take her. He'll use her to keep me."

My jaw tenses as Jake appears, and I give him the nod, telling him to get Miss Warren out of here just as the thud of a door shutting sounds from the back of the house. I'm flying down the hallway, and the moment I enter the kitchen I feel something push into my temple. I freeze.

"Drop the gun," he says calmly, and I immediately lower the weapon to my side, seeing the little girl out the corner of my eye, held to his front. My brain works fast, noting her position, his position, his hold, her fear.

It's now or never. *Drop the gun, Ryan!* But I know the second my gun is out of my grasp, I'm out of the game, and that little girl will be gone. I feel my muscles twitch. My heart rate increases. My eyes refocus. *Now or never.*

My arm flies up fast, hooking back and knocking the gun aside as I turn and grab his arm, freeing the girl before I thrust him up against the wall, slamming his hand into the plaster so he drops the gun. God, there's nothing I'd love more than to tear him a new arsehole . . . but the girl. So I reluctantly kick his feet from under him and take him down to his front, immobilizing him with his arms up his back. He whimpers like a fucking baby as I look up at the little girl, giving her my most dashing smile. "Baddies always get caught," I whisper, and she grins, filling me with relief as I glance to the door, willing backup to hurry the hell up. "Did he hurt you, sweetheart?"

Her little head shakes from side to side, and she presents me with a bear. "But he stomped on Paddington."

"He did?" I shudder for effect just as Jake bowls into the room, looking ready to attack. He soon finds me on the floor. "Hi," I say, grinning up at him. "Got any cuffs?"

He visibly relaxes and shouts down the corridor for backup, and we're quickly joined by six more men, all kitted out in armor, all armed. "What took you so long?" I ask drily, letting them claim my prey. I get up, dust myself off, and slip my gun into the waistband of my trousers. "Come on, you." I scoop the little girl into my arms. "Let's get you and Paddington back to Mummy." I pace out the kitchen and hear Miss Warren before I see her, crying her heart out.

"Oh, thank God!" She charges for me and grabs her daughter, squeezing her tightly.

"She's fine."

She smiles up at me through glassy eyes. "Thank you."

"All in a day's work," I lie, heading through the crowds to find some air. I make it outside, hearing the angry yells of Corey Felton as I go, and prop myself up against a fence, my heart still going ballistic in my chest.

"What the fuck were you thinking?" Jake bellows, stomping toward me, and just like that my adrenaline drains from my body and I blink a few times, checking myself over. "You should have let backup deal with it, for fuck's sake, Ryan."

"Yeah, yeah," I retort for the sake of it, not needing Jake to kick my arse. I'm suddenly doing a damn fine job of that myself. Fucking hell, what *was* I thinking?

Jake must notice my sudden shakiness, because he wraps an arm around my shoulder on a sigh and starts walking us to the gates. "You're such a fucking maverick."

He's right, I am. "Guess it never leaves you, huh?"

"And stupid. You could've gotten yourself killed."

"I'm breathing, aren't I?"

"Yep. And now you're gonna get a severe headache from the top."

I snort. Coming from Jake Sharp, that's fucking rich. Besides, it's not my damn fault we weren't furnished with the whole story. "I can deal with a headache." What I'm struggling to deal with is how fucking stupid I've just been. Damn instinct. I need a drink.

"You of all people know that when you care about shit, you look after yourself," Jake reminds me.

"All right, you can stop lecturing me now."

He releases me when we get to the gates. "It's not only yourself you're putting in danger," he mutters moodily.

Guilt. More of it sweeps right on in and punches me in the gut. Jake's wife is heavily pregnant, and now she's worrying even more every time he leaves for work. "How's Cami?"

"Ready to pop." His cheeks inflate, and I laugh a little. "Three weeks left."

"Excited?"

He's quiet for a second, and I know why. He was a lone wolf for so long, swamped by his demons. He's had it tough. I've spent so much time with Jake over the past couple of years, we've had no choice but to get along. He's talked. I've listened. He deserves his happiness. "Yeah," he eventually says, looking across to me. "I'm looking forward to doing it right this time."

And there's me putting us in unnecessary danger. I reach up and slap his shoulder, all manly, as I always do when things get a little deep from time to time. "Beer later?" I ask, nodding to the pub over the road.

"I'm game."

We both slow to a stop when we see Lucinda's car screech around the corner. Fuck me, that car sounds angry. I look at Jake as Jake looks at me. "Beer now?" I ask, heading away from our fiery handler who is about to go fiery on my arse.

Jake's with me, both of us backing up. No one wants to be around Lucinda when she's after blood, and she's currently after mine. So I'm running scared.

* * *

We enter a quiet space, with only a few patrons scattered around. "Two Buds, thanks." I toss a note on the bar and pull up two stools. We're both silent as the barman gets our drinks, reflective, and we chink bottles and slurp together, releasing appreciative gasps at the same time. I haven't even placed my bottle down before Lucinda stalks in and scans the bar. Oh boy. She finds us, and I recoil somewhat, her formidable glare making me shrink.

"Should've known." She strides past us toward the back of the pub. "Come."

I look at Jake, who's in the middle of an epic eye roll. "If I wasn't so fond of her, I'd tell her to fuck off at least ten times a day." He slips down from his stool, and I follow on a light chuckle.

Taking a seat on the opposite side of a booth from her, we sit like good little boys and wait for her to rip our balls off. After all, we deserve it. Or at least, I do. Jake's got nothing to do with my momentary lapse in focus.

Two minutes later, our handler's still doing something on her phone, and Jake and I still have our balls. I look at Jake. Jake looks at me. I shrug. "Drink?" I ask her.

Lucinda fires me a filthy glare, and there go my balls. "Don't test me, Ryan," she snaps. "You've already given me a fucking headache today."

I sit back, getting a safer distance away as I hear Jake laugh. "I only asked if you wanted a drink. Besides, who knows where that girl would be now. I had to act fast."

"What?" Lucinda says with a laugh. "By going on a rampage in the streets of London brandishing your firearm?"

"I'm sure the official big-bods will be easy on you, since one of your men caught a man they've been tracking for years." I smile sweetly, and she rips her fire stare from my wilting six-foot-three-inch form, holding her hand in the air for the attention of the barman.

"Flat white," she calls. And then silence falls, neither Jake nor I willing to fill it, as I spin my bottle slowly on the table.

Lucinda eventually pushes a file across the table, and I look down at it. "What's that?" I ask.

"Your next contract."

"Time off," I remind her. "I'm going home for a few weeks."

"Home? It's in the middle of nowhere." She laughs. "Boring as shit. Two hundred residents, a few stores, a pub, and a school. Why the hell would you want to go back there? What will you do?"

"That's none of your damn business," I spit, feeling Jake's eyes fall onto my profile. He knows what I'll do. And he's the only one. That's what happens when you spend so much time with one person. You tell them shit. "I'm going home, and that's it," I say with fierce finality, and Lucinda slumps back in her seat as her coffee lands on the table.

With no thanks to the waiter, she pours in a healthy dose of milk, picks it up, and downs it in one fell swoop, never once taking her lethal glare off me. She can go to hell. I'm going home to Hampton and that's it. She can find someone else to do the next contract. And at that very moment, she turns her eyes onto Jake.

He immediately starts shaking his head. "Forget it. I have a baby due in a few weeks."

"It's a two-week contract."

"Nope." He swigs from his bottle of beer. "I promised Cami this was the last job."

"What if I told you I'll kick your stupid arse into shape?"

"You did that years ago. Now I'm more scared of Cami's wrath than yours, so go to hell, Luce." Jake toasts her on a sarcastic smile as she snorts her disgust. I find myself grinning. Lucinda loves Cami. Jake's wife is the only woman on the planet our handler actually likes.

"Guess you'll have to find someone else," I muse, clinking my bottle with Jake's. "We're out." I watch as she inhales, her eyes narrowing to scary slits and slowly dragging onto me. My grin drops as she hands me another file. "What's this?"

"You said you're going home for a few weeks. This is your job when you're back in London. A nice, boring, low-risk one-man affair."

"You said Miss Warren was low-risk," I point out as I stare at the paper file, my mind replaying the past hour. I wince as my heart pounds a little bit faster. Wince harder when I see Alexandra's face in my mind's eye. "I'm passing," I declare, looking up at Lucinda. As I expected, her face is a picture of shock. "I'm taking a career break."

"What?"

I can feel Jake's stunned stare on me, too. "I'm done with this game," I tell her. It doesn't matter how careful I am. It's been proven today that danger has an uncanny ability of finding me, and clearly my instinct to dance with it hasn't left me. I'm aware this contract could have ended very differently.

Lucinda's nostrils flare as she withdraws the file. "I'll call you when you're thinking straight." She gets up and stomps out of the bar, and I can still feel Jake's eyes on me. "What?" I ask without looking at him.

"Are you serious?"

"Deadly serious." I take a swig of my beer.

"What will you do?"

"Work on my house. Maybe build a few more." I shrug to myself. I'm good with my hands. Built my own place in the woods from scratch. I've always thought about buying some land and building a portfolio of properties. Now's the time to do it. I've worked in some form of protection for nearly twenty years. I'm done.

"Sounds kinda good," Jake says as his phone rings and he answers. "Hey." I can tell by the tone of his voice who it is, and I smile to myself. He's a mean bastard at work, moody and difficult to read for most, but he's mush when dealing with his wife and daughter. "No, you can't be." Jake's arse is up from the chair fast. "Fuck, Cami, I'm on the other side of London. I'm having a beer. And it's too fucking soon! We're supposed to be going to the country place."

"Sorry." I hear her breathe. "I'll just tell this baby to hold off until Daddy's finished his pint, shall I?" A few rushed pants. "The midwife is five minutes away."

"Fuck," he curses, turning and running out of the pub.

"Jake!" I yell, going after him, abandoning the two beers we very nearly got to finish. "Jake, wait."

"Cami's in labor," he yells over his shoulder, breaking out in a sprint across the road. "I've got to get home."

"I'll drive you. You'll get yourself killed the state you're in."

He throws me an indignant look. "I'm fine."

"Your forehead disagrees." I point up, and he reaches to wipe the sweat away. "Get in the truck. I'm a better driver than you, anyway."

"Fuck you."

I chuckle, falling into the driver's seat. "Is someone with her?" I pull out of the space fast and zoom down the street, weaving in and out of the traffic.

"A friend. Heather." He goes straight to his phone, and a few seconds later he's talking again. "I'm on my way. How is she?" Jake's quiet for a few moments, and my attention splits between him and the road. The guy has always been tense, but he's off the charts at the minute. "I should be half an hour, depending on traffic. Can she wait that long?"

I take a sharp right and sail through a red light.

"Make that twenty minutes," Jake adds. "Put her on."

Another sharp corner, and Jake motions up ahead to another set of lights that are currently on amber. I take his hint and swerve around a few mopeds in front, putting my foot down.

"Hey, angel," he breathes, and I smile, the softness in his voice making my big body melt a little. "Ryan's driving perfectly sensibly," he assures her, turning his eyes onto me. "Yeah, I'll tell him. Just breathe like we practiced, okay? You can do it. Where's Charlotte?" His smile is epic as he listens to Cami. "Sounds like you're in good hands." He jumps in his seat as the sound of a monster scream fills the truck, and I look his way, eyes wide. "Focus on the road," he grunts, putting his phone on speaker. The sound of Cami's wail fades, and I hear her start panting.

"Ooh, that was a sharp one," she sighs.

"Dad!" A little girl's voice comes across the phone, sounding excited as opposed to anxious.

"Hey, princess." Jake's tone has gone even softer, and his body virtually dissolves into the seat beside me. "You taking care of Cami for me?"

"Yep. She's sweating really bad, though. And she's really red."

"She'll be fine. I'll be there as quick as I can, okay?"

"You better hurry, Dad."

"I'm hurrying, princess." He falls into the door when I skid around a corner, cursing when he hits his head on the glass. "Trust me, I'm hurrying. See you soon." Jake clicks off the call and rubs at his forehead, bracing his other hand on the dashboard. "Put your foot down, Ryan," he mutters sarcastically just as I whiz past a fancy Ferrari, the driver flipping me the finger. I honk my horn in reply and focus on getting my mate to his wife before his baby arrives.

I can't claim Jake's not without his own trauma by the time I pull up outside their house in West London, but I do know he won't have missed the birth. Jake hops out after giving me his customary manly slap of appreciation on the shoulder. "Thanks, mate."

"Call me!" I yell as the door slams and he runs up the path. "And good luck, buddy," I say to myself, watching him fall through his front door.

I sit there for a few moments, idle by the curb, just reflecting on a few things in my own life. Not that there's much to reflect on. Just one thing. I smile and pull away, ready to get my arse out of the shitty apartment I've been crashing in for too long and go home.

Chapter Two

HANNAH

Bullets of amber lights dance across the dirt track before me, jumping as the wind rustles the canopy of trees above. I look up, squinting, letting the sound of the breeze in the treetops hypnotize me. The sway of the branches, the creak of old wood, the apricot glow trying to fight its way through the leaves. It's all so damn perfect.

It's home. At least, it is for now.

I edge toward the tip of the hill, pushing my bicycle along with my feet until the front wheel dips ever so slightly. Then, kicking my legs out to the sides, I throw my head back and let gravity take over, speeding down the hill with a laugh, the sounds of my delight echoing around the woods. The wind in my face is glorious, the whoosh of air passing me purifying.

I'm approaching the bottom of the slope far quicker than I'd like, kicking up clouds of dust in my wake. The basket on the front of my bike jumps as the dirt road meets the paved section, sending a few of the raspberries I've picked catapulting into the air. "Oh shit." One hits me square in the forehead, the ends of my head scarf whipping at my cheeks. I quickly pull it free, stuffing it in my pocket before the wind whisks it away.

"Afternoon, Hannah," Mrs. Hatt calls as I hurtle past her toward the small bridge that crosses the river toward town. Cats circle her feet as she walks down the brick path to the front door of her cottage, weighed down with shopping bags.

"Afternoon!" I yell, quickly reclaiming the handlebars with both hands when I hit a divot, causing me to wobble. I lose some speed as I roll up the slight incline of the old stone bridge but regain it after breaching the summit. Passing the town church, I see Father Fitzroy in the small graveyard that circles the ancient building, dusting off the headstones with a broom. "Afternoon, Father."

He swings around, turning to follow me on my bike as I pass. "Afternoon, Miss Bright." He holds up his broom before going back to his task.

I'm forced to use my brakes when I approach a group of school-children waiting to cross the road, and I slow to a stop, smiling as they're herded to the other side by their teacher. "Afternoon," she sings, pulling a stray child back into the line.

"Hi." I wave, laughing as the stray kid goes astray again. There are just ten kids, and that accounts for twenty percent of the school's students. That's what I love about this town. It's small. It's also cozy, friendly, and safe.

As soon as the children are across, I push off and start pedaling leisurely once again toward the huge pond that marks the beginning of the high street. The pub is the first building on the left, followed by a row of small chocolate box cottages, and then a gas station at the end. And on the right, a row of shops, starting with the town store—which sells everything from milk to screwdrivers—and ending with a post office. And in between, Mrs. Heaven's café and, finally, my shop. My gorgeous, cute little arts-and-crafts store.

I roll to a stop outside and throw my leg over my bike, leaning it against a nearby lamppost, and stare up at the new sign that was recently installed. I smile.

"There's not much call for art around these parts, love," someone says from behind, and I turn to find an old man with gray wiry hair and a long beard to match. His green-checkered shirt hangs out of his brown cords, his hands resting on the handles of a cart. He's staring up at my shop's new sign.

"I'm sorry, I don't think we've met," I say, approaching him.

"The name's Cyrus." He removes the toothpick from his mouth and points it at my shop. "I hope you're not planning on making millions."

"Not millions," I assure him. "Just enough to live on." I'll be okay for another year or two, but the money I left with is running low. So it's time to start making some for myself.

Cyrus eyes me, looking me up and down a few times. "You look like the creative type."

I laugh as I feel at my haphazard bun. "And what does the creative type look like?"

"Messy." Putting his stick back between his teeth, he pulls a broom from his cart and starts brushing at the pavement. I frown and look down at my dungarees, spotting a few blobs of paint. And then I pull at my white T-shirt. More paint spots. "It's even on your flop-flips." Cyrus chuckles, sliding his brush back into the cart and taking the handles.

"You mean flip-flops?"

"I mean what I mean." He starts pushing his cart up the street, the wheels creaking as he goes, and I pull my red scarf from the pocket of my dungarees, reaching up to put it back on, tying a big bow tightly on top.

"Hey, Mrs. Heaven," I call when I see her come out of her café.

"Hello, Hannah." She follows me into my store. "I brought you a muffin."

"You'll make me fat," I say as she hands it to me, and I take a bite, moaning a little. Mrs. Heaven's blueberry muffins really are heaven.

She chuckles and wipes her hands down her apron. "You could do with a bit of meat on those bones of yours."

"Are you kidding?" I say through my mouthful. I'm the curviest I've ever been. Long gone are my days of watching what I eat. Or being told what I can eat.

"A few pounds won't hurt you." She winks on an impish grin. "How are you settling in?"

I wander over to the last of my boxes of stock and pick the edge of the tape. "Great, thank you. Only a few more boxes to unpack before I officially open." I get on with pulling out the brushes, slipping them into pots on the nearby shelf in order of size and type.

"How exciting for you, Hannah," she chirps. "I'll be sure to tell all my friends about your work." Mrs. Heaven walks the length of one wall, where many of my landscape paintings hang. "Such a talented young lady. Have you always painted?"

I step down off the stool. "Yes," I say, because it's the easiest answer to give.

She hums, cocking her head from one side to the other. "I love this one."

I make my way around the cashier desk as she studies my latest creation, an oil on canvas of a nearby valley that I painted last week. "It would look lovely on the wall of your café," I hint, not so subtly.

"Well, when I have some spare cash, I might buy it from you."

"I'll do you a special deal," I say as I follow her to the door and open it for her. She chuckles as she chucks my cheek. She's always chuckling or smiling. She's the sweetest lady. "See you later, Mrs. Heaven."

"Bye-bye, Hannah."

I head out into the sunshine with her and tuck my hands into my pockets, watching as she dips and collects up a candy wrapper. "I don't know," she sighs, dropping it in a nearby bin. "Why do people insist on littering our lovely little town?"

She's right. It truly is a lovely town. It's almost a shame I can't stay here forever. I breathe in the clean spring air and wedge the door open, then get back to unpacking.

* * *

By five o'clock, I'm done, and I stand gazing at the splashes of color on every available space. It's cluttered, a charming kind of messy, just as planned. Just how I always dreamed my own art store would be. "Perfect."

With celebrating my achievement in mind, I lock the store door and head to the kitchenette to collect the bottle of wine I bought earlier, before I go upstairs to my apartment and chill out. Pulling open the mini fridge, I seize the bottle of cheap white...and nearly drop the damn thing when a loud crash has me jumping out of my skin.

I whirl around. What was that? "Hello?" I call, blindly placing my bottle of wine on a nearby counter. No one answers, and I damn my pulse for thumping so hard. Edging toward the doorway that leads back into the shop, I swallow and gingerly peek around the corner.

No one.

I pass the cashier desk, scanning every corner of my store, and stop moving when I see a pile of mini paint pots scattered across the floor, fallen from the shelf I just meticulously stacked. "Shit!" My hand shoots out toward the wall, knocking a painting askew, my heart stopping in my chest.

Meow.

"Jesus," I breathe as a monster tabby cat jumps onto the display table in the center of the store, knocking a few pots of brushes over. The clatters mingle with the pounding of blood in my ears, and I stagger back, my hand resting over my pumping heart. "Just a cat. It's just a cat." I force my muscles to relax while I repeat the mantra over and over out loud. "Where did you come from?" I exhale, just as an almighty bang sounds behind me.

I'm jumping out of my bloody skin again, more pots of brushes toppling on the table as the cat, obviously startled, too, jumps off and darts toward the door. I look across and see a woman on the other side, peeking in, her hand on the handle.

I'm safe, I tell myself. *No one knows I'm here. No one knows I'm anywhere.*

I hurry over and open the door for her, at the same time letting the huge tabby cat out. "Hi," I say as both our gazes follow the speedy getaway of the cat.

"Sorry, did I frighten you?"

I laugh under my breath as I turn and dip to collect up the brushes scattered all over the floor. "The cat scared me more than you did," I say, scolding myself again for being so unreasonably jumpy.

The lady comes to join me on the floor, helping me. "That's Timmy." She smiles at my frown as we both stand, both our hands full of various paintbrushes. "The cat," she confirms, nodding her head toward the door. "Belongs to Mrs. Hatt. If a door's open, he'll invite himself in."

"I'll remember that," I reply with a smile.

Resting the brushes on the table, she offers me her hand. "I'm Molly. I teach history at the town school." Off-loading my brushes, I shake her hand with a smile. "Well, I teach English and math, too." She shrugs. "Small school."

"Nice to meet you, Molly. I'm Hannah."

"I've been meaning to come introduce myself since I saw you moving in a couple of weeks ago." Molly takes a peek around, looking impressed. "How's it going?"

"Great, thank you." I head for the shelves and collect up the paint pots that Timmy knocked off. "I showcased some of my work at a show yesterday, and my online store is up and running now, too."

"Oh, good luck with that! There are some beautiful places around here to paint."

"There are," I agree. "It's a lovely little town. Have you lived here long?"

"Oh, I'm a lifer." Molly laughs as she approaches, helping me to restack the paint pots. "I love it here." Her brown eyes are big and round, a friendly twinkle in them, and her hourglass figure must be the envy of women near and far. She's got to be a few years younger than me, maybe late twenties, and her mousy-brown hair is pulled into a low, loose ponytail. "You'll never want to leave."

I smile, making sure it's not too tight. I might never want to leave, but I'll have to eventually. "I don't already."

"Where have you come from?" Molly asks casually as we finish arranging the shelf together.

I automatically clam up, but quickly work to shake off my awkwardness. I can't turn into a nervous waif every time someone asks anything about me. "I've lived abroad for years. Decided it was time to come home." An image of my mother flashes through my mind, and a lump forms in my throat. *Saturday*, I tell myself. *I can see her again on Saturday.* I blink and look up at Molly.

"Well, welcome back to England."

"Thank you."

I don't know whether she senses she shouldn't press me for more, or whether she's oblivious to my struggle, but I'm grateful all the same for her lack of prying. Wandering over to the opposite wall, she scans the paintings. "So I'm hoping you can help me."

"I'll try."

"The art teacher is off sick, so I'm covering her class tomorrow. But we never got the supplies we were expecting this week." She turns toward me. "The kids will be so disappointed if they can't paint their papier-mâché models."

"You need paint?" I ask, and she nods.

"Enough to paint various giant planets for their solar system project." She shrugs when I frown. "The art teacher is also the science teacher. Small school. I went to the town store and all they have is various shades of cream and white. That's the bands on Jupiter covered." Her expression turns somewhat awkward as I laugh.

"I only really stock oils and watercolors," I say as I gesture to the shelf. "They're expensive and you'd need a hell of a lot to spread over a solar system."

"Crap. I'm on a budget." Molly deflates. "Never mind, I'll just—"

"Wait, I have an idea that might work." I head for the kitchenette, and Molly follows. Opening the top cupboard, I start rifling through, pulling down various bottles of food coloring. "Would you pass me that bowl?" I ask as I grab the flour and salt from another cupboard.

"I'm intrigued," Molly says as she watches me tip two cups of each into the bowl, followed by two cups of water. I add a few drops of red food coloring and mix it all up with a wooden spoon. "That's Mars sorted." I grab a container and tip in the homemade paint.

"You genius," Molly sings on a clap of her hands. "Where'd you learn that?"

"When I was a student and money was tight." God, those days were so carefree. I was so happy. And now I can be happy again. "You just need a lot of flour, salt, and time, but it's cheap."

She looks at her watch, and I see a small flinch pass across her face. "I have to shoot to the vet to pick up my dog. The town store will be closed by the time I'm done."

"I don't mind going to the store," I offer, more than happy to help. "And I'll mix the rest of the colors up, if you're short on time."

"Oh my God, would you? I would be eternally grateful."

"Of course." I shrug off her appreciation. "It won't take me long. I hope your dog is okay."

"Oh, nothing major. Well, I say that. I'm sure Archie wouldn't agree when he's just had his balls cut off."

I laugh, wincing for effect. "What breed?"

"A Labrador. You a dog person, or a cat person?"

"A dog person." My smile falters as I go to the sink and rinse the bowl of red paint. "I used to have a cockapoo."

"Oh no, did she die?"

I nod, because, again, it's easier. She didn't die. I was told my life wasn't suitable for a dog. So she was taken to an animal shelter. "Candy. She was a crafty character. But loyal to the bone." And that loyalty turned out to be the cause for her having to leave me.

I set the clean bowl on the drainer and dry my hands with a tea towel as I face Molly, pulling my smile from nowhere. The sympathy emblazoned across her face stabs at my heart. "I'm sorry, Hannah. I can only imagine how you felt. They become a part of the family so quickly."

I bet she can't imagine at all. "Anyway." I toss the tea towel aside. "I'd better get to the store before it closes. Would you like me to drop off the paints once I'm done?"

"Would you?"

"Of course. I'm sure you'll have your hands full with Archie." I collect my keys from the counter. "Where do you live?" We walk out of the shop together, and I lock the door behind me.

"If you head past the school, past the church and Mrs. Hatt's, and over the bridge, you'll see a little cottage set back from the road. That's mine." Molly surprises me with an impulsive hug. "Thank you so much, Hannah. We'll have to have a drink together. My treat."

"That'd be lovely." I can't remember a time when I went for drinks with girlfriends. I haven't had any friends for years.

Molly breaks away and heads for her car, waving as she goes. Feeling happy and useful, I head for the store to stock up on flour and salt, and spend the next hour mixing paint until I have a stack of tubs in various colors to cover all planets. I also have various-colored smears of homemade paint all over my face. I look in the mirror and smile. Then I stack the containers carefully in a box, set it in the basket of my bicycle, and get on my way, leaving my cheeks sporting every color of the rainbow. Because having to be perfect isn't a problem anymore.

CHAPTER THREE

RYAN

With my elbow resting out of the window, I turn the wheel with one hand as I weave through the familiar windy roads of the Peak District. The sun is low, the glare brutal, but it's fucking glorious. I inhale the smell of nature and the great outdoors.

Home.

I reach forward and turn on the radio, and All Saints' "Pure Shores" joins me. I smile and relax back, tapping the steering wheel as I negotiate the snaking roads through the fields. Now, this is me. Nature. Clean air. Simple living. It's good to be back.

As I breach the threshold of town, I take my foot off the accelerator and slow to a crawl, surprised to see something unfamiliar. "Bright Art?" My truck slows to a stop as I take in the new store where a florist used to be. I laugh sardonically. "Good luck with that around here."

I put my foot down and carry on up the street, and as I drive over the bridge across the river, I spot Mrs. Hatt trimming her hedges. I honk my horn, and she swings around with her garden shears, her face a picture of pleasure. "Ryan!" she sings.

"Hey, Mrs. Hatt," I call as I slow to a crawl again. "Anything new to tell me?"

She chuckles, dipping and shooing away one of her cats. "Oh, you know Hampton. Nothing changes."

Yeah, nothing changes. Which means Darcy Hampton is still the mega bitch from hell. Can't wait to bump into her.

I honk my horn in goodbye and take the next right onto the dirt road that leads to my sanctuary, and I once again find myself breathing in the fresh country air, my eyes closing briefly in bliss as I let my contentment breeze out on a long exhale. "Fucking perfect."

I open my eyes.

And jump out of my fucking skin.

"Shit!" I swerve to the left, feeling something catch the side of my truck. "What the fuck?" I fight to gain control, yanking the steering wheel to the right as I hurtle toward a gigantic tree trunk. "Oh, you fucker."

Bang.

The impact jolts me in my seat, the hood of my truck flying up, the air bag inflating with a boom. It takes a few seconds for me to grasp my bearings, my hands tussling with the balloon in my face. "Shit." What the hell was that?

Jumping out, I ignore the steam billowing from the engine and race around the back, scanning the area. Nothing. Was it a rabbit? No, too big. "A deer?" I say out loud, just as the air is pierced with a high-pitched curse.

"Fucking hell!"

I swing around and see the bushes across the road rustling, and then a woman staggers out. "You fucking wanker!" she yells, falling to her arse and rubbing at her knee. "You should watch where you're damn well going."

Whoa! "Are you okay?" I ask, a little warily, gingerly stepping closer.

She looks up at me, her hand pausing in its rubbing of her knee. Her face deadpans for a second as she takes me in from top to bottom, before her scowl returns. "No." She pulls the leg of her dungarees up and hisses at what she finds. A huge, bleeding scrape. "Ouch."

I blink, a little taken aback, but now for other reasons. With her rainbow-streaked face, she's just about the most adorable thing I've ever laid my eyes on. From her dungarees to the cute scarf that she's got knotted on her head, she's stunningly pretty, even with twigs and leaves stuck all over her. Where did she come from?

I watch, still as can be, as she struggles to her feet and limps a few paces away from me. "Oh God, that hurts."

I come to life, snapped into action by her pained voice. Shooting over, I take her arm. "You came from nowhere," I explain. "There's never anyone on this road."

She shrugs me off, annoyed, and tries to straighten. "Get off, you oaf."

Yikes. She's seriously pissed off. I raise my hands in surrender, backing away as her hard stare slowly drops, being replaced with...

Oh shit. Her eyes well. Her lip wobbles. Her paint-covered face twists a little. "Ouch," she croaks again, rolling her shoulder and hissing in pain. God damn, have I ever felt like such an arsehole?

I move in quickly, unable to stop myself. "Here, let me help."

"I don't want your help."

Rolling my eyes and disregarding the fact that I'm about to be smeared in rainbow paint, too, I swoop in and scoop her from her feet before she tries some heroic move to decline my help again. I carry her to a nearby fallen trunk, holding her tighter when she struggles in my arms, hissing in pain between her protests.

"Quit wriggling," I order sternly, trying not to lose my patience. She eventually submits and stills in my arms, and I peek out the corner of my eye to find her staring at me, her eyes a little wide. "Bad day?" I ask flatly.

Her expression changes in a heartbeat, going from stunned to angry. "It was fine until you ran me down." She looks away, a little snootily, and I see her teeth sink into her bottom lip. She's not just still now, she's tense, too, and when she snatches a quick glance at me again, finding I'm studying her, she huffs and looks away.

"Then I'm sorry for ruining it," I say quietly.

"So you should be."

I lower her to the tree trunk and drop to my haunches before her, breathing in patience as she fights to focus on anything other than me. She'll struggle; I'm no small guy, and I'm crouched in front of her.

"Seriously, are you okay?" I soften my voice and dip to get myself in her downcast vision, forcing a small smile that I hope makes her feel better.

She lifts her eyes but not her head, as if afraid to look me in the eye. Her forced angry expression softens a little, and I take a moment to marvel at how blue her eyes are. "Well?" I prompt, realizing that I've been staring for a little too long.

She shrugs, more placid now. With her hand on her shoulder, she rolls it a little. "A bit sore."

"Can I take a look at your knee?" I motion to the area where the leg of her baggy dungarees is pulled high up her rather lovely thigh, exposing the grazed, bleeding mess.

"You can see it, can't you?" she asks a little sardonically, and my lips straighten in natural displeasure without thought. Is she going to continue to be difficult for the sake of it? Noting my annoyance, she waves a hand dismissively. "Go for it."

Dropping to my knees, I take her slender ankle and rest her foot on my thigh. "Relax," I order gently, feeling her stiffen at my touch. "I'm not a mass murderer." I peek up, and for reasons I can't explain, I savor the sight of her trying so hard to hold back her smile.

"How would I know?" she asks.

"Well, if I wanted to kill you, I could have done it within a second of seeing you." I inspect her knee, seeing bits of dirt and gravel in the cuts.

"What are you, a hit man?"

I laugh lightly and pull my T-shirt up over my head, then use it to dab away the trails of blood down her leg. "No, actually. Ex-MI5. Now I'm in protection. Or I was," I correct myself, seeing astonishment on her face, but she doesn't say anything. I'm not sure if she's stunned by the information, or by my chest. Could be both. I don't know, but something tells me to move things along quickly. She appears to be in a bit of a trance. "This needs cleaning up." She just nods, suddenly mute. "My place is just up the track. You happy to go there?" She shakes her head. "Lost your voice?"

Looking away as she blinks repeatedly, she clears her throat. "I can clean myself up when I get home."

She's wary. I can't blame her, really. I'm a six-foot-three-inch bloke with a scar on my lip and a bent nose from endless breaks. Hardly a comforting sight. Suddenly bothered by this, I force a smile again, knowing it's crooked from that scar. Her eyes drop to my mouth, and she swallows. The atmosphere shifts. The silence is awkward. My skin tingles unstoppably.

"My..." She seems to lose her voice as she shakes her head, looking past me, and I follow her stare to the bushes, seeing the wheel of a bike poking through the branches.

Oh.

I quickly rise, giving us both space, and pace over to tug the bike free, standing the mangled mess on the road. The bush is a vibrant mix of every color under the sun, and I notice various containers scattered everywhere. Paint. I go to ask what it's for, but when I look back, I find her pouting solemnly at her ruined bike. She shouldn't pout. She definitely shouldn't pout. Those lips...

"I loved that bike," she murmurs.

My admiring is interrupted, and I quickly feel like even more of an arsehole. Being a knight in shining armor isn't usually my style. Then again, I've never nearly killed a woman. Though I can't deny I've imagined strangling some. Or *one* in particular.

"I'm sorry," I say sincerely, feeling like total shit. "I'll replace it."

"You don't have to do that."

"But I want to."

Her head cocks as she studies me, like she's trying to figure me out. And silence falls again. Awkward, *again*. I lay her bike—which is certainly dead—on the ground and head over to my truck to escape the odd atmosphere. The smoke has calmed, no longer billowing up from the engine.

"Is it bad?" she asks, joining me. I tense, her arm nearly touching mine where she stands beside me.

"Just a popped valve." I pull down the hood, grimacing at the tidy dent on the bumper. "I think the tree took the worst." I collect her bike and put it on the back, then open the passenger door. "Hop in."

She's hesitant, looking back down the road. "No, it's fine, I'll walk." Approaching my truck, she reaches for her bike, and I immediately step in to help. And quickly pull back when she jumps out of my way like a skittish kitten.

I motion to the bicycle and slowly reach for it. "I was just going to help you get it down." As I set it on the ground for her, she closes her eyes briefly, exhaling, and I'm sure it's to gather herself.

"Thank you," she breathes, claiming her bike. She offers me a small smile, one I can tell is forced.

This isn't sitting well with me at all. She's bleeding, she's clearly hurt her shoulder, her bike is obliterated, and it's getting dark. Hampton may well be the safest place on earth, but an injured woman shouldn't be roaming around on her own. Not anywhere. And especially when I've offered to give her a ride. And especially when I'm the damn fucking cause for her having to walk home in the first place. I move forward but come to an abrupt halt when she takes a step back.

"I'd feel a lot better if you let me drive you home," I tell her.

"Honestly, I'm really fine."

"Your knee disagrees." I point to the bloodied mess, and she peeks down. "Let me at least clean it up."

She doesn't answer this time, and instead turns quickly and pushes her bike down the track a bit too hastily for my liking. "I'll be fine," she calls as she goes.

I step forward, instinct telling me to go after her and insist on sorting that knee and taking her home, but I stop myself. She doesn't want my help, and I'm not the kind of man to force myself on anyone.

So reluctantly, I let her go, watching as she tries to disguise her limp in a lame attempt to convince me she's okay. "Nice to meet you," I say quietly, slowly reversing my steps and ripping my gaze away from her fleeing form.

Let her go.

I head for my truck, looking over my shoulder a few times, seeing her getting farther away, until I glance back for the last time and find she's gone. I stop, laughing under my breath. Well, that was...weird.

Shaking my head clear, I realign my focus, grimacing when I take in the damage. "Motherfucker," I breathe, kicking the tire. "Welcome home, Ryan." I jump in and take it steady up the rest of the dirt road, trying to ignore my whirling thoughts. *Let her go. Let her go.* I press the brake and come to a stop, my fingers tapping on the wheel, my mind tangled. But it's getting dark. She's hurt. "Fuck it." I quickly turn my truck around and race down the road to find her, dead set on taking her to wherever she's going. Where was she going? And where the hell did she come *from*?

I scan the darkening road in front of me as I drive, searching for her. Nothing. "Where'd you go, sweetheart?" I muse, pulling to a stop when I reach the junction that'll take me back to the main road into town. I look up and down. It's empty. And I sit there for a few minutes, thinking. *Who is she?*

"What do you care?" I say quietly, slamming my truck into reverse and turning, heading home.

I park under the tree, and as soon as I make it into my cabin, I fling open all the windows and head straight for the fridge, finding a beer and twisting off the cap, relishing the hiss of gas. That first glug is like no other. I head back out to the yard and straight to the hammock, dropping in, kicking my feet up, and relaxing back, staring at the treetops.

Home.

As I lie, lightly swinging, sipping my Bud, I wonder how Jake is doing, but the mystery woman whom I nearly flattened quickly takes up first position in my mind space. Has she made it home okay? Speaking of which, where does she live? And again, who the hell is she? I've lived here my whole life; there isn't one person I don't know in Hampton. Or there wasn't. I close my eyes and see a rainbow of colors dancing in my darkness, and I hear the sharpness of her potty mouth.

And I'm smiling again. *Who are you?*

Chapter Four

HANNAH

It takes me a stupid long time to get home. My knee hurts, my shoulder hurts, my ego hurts. I'm cursing under my breath as I yank my broken bicycle through the front door of my store, the wheels creaking as I push it through the shop. I unbolt the back door, unlock it, and pull it open, more or less tossing my bike into the small courtyard. "Stupid," I pout as I wriggle my toes in my Birkenstocks, feeling blisters. God, I'm a walking disaster.

After dropping the blinds, I make my way upstairs to take a shower. And when I see myself in the bathroom mirror, I am utterly appalled. "Oh, Hannah," I sigh. There's not one inch of my body not covered in paint. Every color you could imagine, and a few new shades, too, not to mention all the dry leaves and twigs stuck to me. I am a multicolored mess of a woman. Wrinkling my nose, I reach up and pull my head scarf free, pointlessly poking at the pieces of hair sticking out everywhere. "A bloody mess."

After stripping down, I hop in the shower and wash the day away. I also shave, something I've recently let slip. And I leave a deep conditioner in my hair for three minutes while scrubbing my nails of all the dirt beneath them. Then clean and fresh, I slap a bandage on my grazed knee, hissing and wincing while I do, before crawling into bed.

Of course, my thoughts soon go back to the dirt road I was lost on, and I chide myself for being so damn rude to a man who was only trying to help me, even if he was to blame for my brush with death. But at least it was an accident. At least he didn't hurt me on purpose. And at least he was genuinely remorseful.

Who is he?

* * *

I wake with a start, bolting upright in my bed. Sweat pours from my brow, my mind working fast to remind me of where I am. *You're safe, Hannah.* I swallow and spend a few moments gathering myself. *Breathe, breathe, breathe.* Once my stupid hands aren't shaking too much, I reach for my iPad, load Facebook, and type in my sister's name. I won't be able to see any of her statuses, since we're not Facebook friends—we can't ever be friends—but I can see a photograph of her. I can look at her face. I *need* to see her face.

"Oh my God," I whisper when I see she's uploaded a new profile picture. "Oh my God, oh my God, oh my God." I smile like crazy as I stare at my older sister, Pippa. This is such a treat, because not only do I get to see my older sister, I get to see my niece, too. The little girl cuddled into my sister's lap looks more like her mum each time I see a picture of her. Dark hair, blue eyes, a beautiful heart-shaped face. She's the spitting image. "Look at you, Bella," I say, tracing the edge of her cute chin. "You got so big." She's seven now, and in this photograph they're at some kind of party. I can see a bouncy castle in the background and a hot dog stand. My niece's face is painted, too, beautiful butterfly wings spanning each cheek.

Paint.

"Oh shit," I blurt, tossing my iPad to the bed and jumping up. I pelt into the bathroom. "Shit, shit, shit." I scrub my teeth, throw on a loose black long dress, shove my feet into some flip-flops, and dash downstairs. I skid to a stop at the mirror by the door, quickly and clumsily knotting my hair on top of my head. Then I'm out the door and rushing up the street to the general store. My heart sinks when I see it's not open.

I peek through the glass, hoping to see Mr. Chaps, who owns the shop. Nothing. "Your sign says you open at six thirty," I mutter to the window. "It's six thirty-two, for crying out loud." Resting my forehead on the glass, I curse myself to hell and back. Molly was depending on me for paint, the paint that is now splattered over a lovely rhododendron bush thanks to a huge man in a huge truck.

My whole body goes heavy, and I jump a mile in the air when something lands with a bang at my feet. "Jesus," I breathe, seeing a stack of newspapers on the ground. Won't people stop making me jump out of my damn skin?

"Morning," a man chirps as he makes his way back to his van.

"Morning," I mumble with my palm on my chest, looking back into the store. My fright is forgotten, and I nearly kiss the glass when I see old Mr. Chaps wobbling toward me. "Oh, thank God."

I barely let the poor old man move from my path before I barrel through the door. "Morning, Mr. Chaps," I call over my shoulder as I rush to locate my wants and stack them into my arms until my chin is resting on top of the bags of flour.

"Morning, Miss Bright. You're nice and early today." He passes me with his stack of newspapers, heading for the checkout desk.

"I have an emergency," I call, struggling my way to the next aisle to find salt.

"Here." I turn and find him holding out a basket to me. "You'll drop all that and make a mess of my store."

"Thank you." I let him help me transfer my bags of flour into the basket before I continue on my way. I find the salt and throw a few bags in, and then I'm in the bakery section. I snatch a croissant from the shelf and start nibbling at the corner as I head to the end of the aisle and take a left to the checkout. And stop dead in my tracks, my croissant hanging out of my mouth, my abruptness causing the heavy shopping basket to clang against my shins. I don't even feel the pain.

I feel...

I swallow my mouthful, dropping the half-eaten pastry into the basket and quickly wiping the flakes away from my mouth. I don't know his name, but he's standing in front of the fridges. And he's shirtless. *Shirtless?* I grimace, not because it isn't a lovely sight—it's a *very* lovely sight—but because every mortifying moment from last night has just come flooding back to me. The paint, my awkwardness, my rudeness, my inappropriate ogling. I'm ogling now, the weight of my overflowing shopping basket forgotten. He's sweaty. His chest is glimmering. He has earbuds in. What's he listening to? What kind of music does he like? Does he run every morning? How's his truck? Should I talk to him? Thank him? What, for running me off the road? No, silly, for trying to tend to me after. For obviously forcing himself to smile in an attempt to ease me. He doesn't smile often. I can tell. He has no wrinkles at the corners of his eyes, and every mature man has those. How old is he?

My brain spasms, and I laugh out loud. *What's with all the questions, Hannah?*

Then he turns away from the fridge, and his eyes land on me. I snap my mouth closed, dip my head, and scuttle off, probably walking like I'm harboring forty pounds of potatoes in my knickers. And yet again, I'm mortified. I heave my basket onto the checkout desk and give a meek smile to Brianna, the store assistant. She looks a lot more awake and chirpy than I do, and when I notice her attention isn't on me, I turn and see that the guy at the end of the aisle is walking away toward the freezers.

"Does he always strut around in just his shorts?" I ask, returning my eyes forward and pulling some money from my pocket.

Brianna is now scanning my items, her eyes preoccupied, oblivious to what she's actually scanning. "Yeah," she sighs dreamily.

I take a bag and start to pack my shopping. So I should expect to be rendered stupid often, then? Great.

Brianna finishes up, I hand her my cash, and she gives me my change, all without looking at me. "He's a bit old for you, isn't he?" I say, probably inappropriately, as I slip my change into my pocket.

"I'm nineteen."

"And how old is he?" I should be ashamed of myself.

"Late thirties, I think. But he looks better each time he comes back to town."

I try not to be curious. I really try. "When he comes back to town?"

"He's been gone a month. And now he's back." Her eyes dance. "I have to ogle him as much as I can *when* I can. Who knows when he'll leave and when he'll be back."

"Ogle?" I say on a little laugh, ignoring the fact that I have also definitely been ogling. He's rather easy to ogle. And there's a lot to ogle, too. "He should wear a T-shirt when he's shopping for groceries," I mutter stupidly, earning a well-deserved snort of disgust from Brianna. "Who is he, anyway?"

"Ryan Willis. And he's the only beautiful thing around these parts, so don't say silly things like he should wear a T-shirt when he's shopping." Suddenly her eyes widen, and she's looking at me for the first time since I arrived at the checkout.

I'm about to ask her what's up when a basket lands on the counter beside me with a thud. I startle a little and snap my mouth shut, watching as Brianna virtually melts all over her cash register.

"Hi, Ryan," she coos, her head tilting, her eyelashes fluttering. He's a step behind me, and I can't seem to see him no matter how much I strain my peripheral vision. So I check out his basket instead. Sparkling water. Beers. Milk. Bread. My forehead wrinkles. Ice cream? His big hand wraps around the tub of Chunky Monkey, and I see him move forward. Unable to stop myself, I peek up, having to go past his sweaty chest as I do. Our eyes meet. His face is stoic. My blood heats.

"Hi," he says, his voice as rough as I remember. Gravelly. Low. Manly.

I stare at him like a freak, stuck for words. And struck by the sheer magnificence of the man before me. I blink and quickly swing my eyes to Brianna. "Thanks," I squeak, dragging my bag off the counter and making a swift exit. I'm sweaty now, too, and I pull at the front of my dress to circulate some air. For God's sake.

"You forgot your croissant," he calls, and I freeze by the door, my grip tightening around the handle as I close my eyes and fight to get some stability into my voice.

"You can have it." Pulling the door open, I hurry out of the shop and scuttle back to my store, cursing myself the whole way. *You can have it?* What the hell is he going to do with a half-eaten pastry? "Urhhh." I drop my head back as I traipse down the street. I'm pathetic. Say hello. That's all I needed to do. Smile. Be polite.

Having a stern word with myself, I let myself into my shop, going straight to the kitchen to mix up more paint. *You can have it?* I slam the door of the cupboard hard and slap my palm into my forehead. *Lame, Hannah. So damn lame.* The man must think I'm a total weirdo. And I hate that.

* * *

I have no idea how, but I make it to Molly's before she leaves for work at eight, and thankfully all the paints are still in their containers. Mrs. Hatt was kind enough to point the way when I passed on foot, and I found Molly's little cottage set back from the road with ease. She's eternally grateful as I stack the pots on the side while she gets her coat on, showing her all the colors before apologizing for leaving it so late.

"Oh, please, Hannah. You've saved my skin." She throws her arms around me and squeezes, and I can't deny it feels good. There's just something so warm about Molly. "We must do drinks tomorrow night."

"Sure." I accept easily. Because...why not? "I'd love that."

"Give me your number."

"Oh yes." I pull out my phone from my pocket.

"Jesus!" Molly blurts. "Are you planning on murdering someone with that thing?"

"What thing?"

She laughs and takes my mobile from my grasp, turning it in her hand. "It's a brick."

"It makes calls and receives texts." I shrug. "That's all I need it for."

"And could be used as a lethal weapon."

I chuckle, because she's right, and snatch it back playfully. "Take it easy on the phone. What's your number?" She reels it off, and I call her so she has mine. "Done."

"Seven tomorrow at the pub?"

Perfect. I know I'll need a drink tomorrow evening, something to take my mind off the predictable low mood I'll be in after my usual Saturday morning since I moved to Hampton three weeks ago. "See you there."

After checking that her dog is fine, I leave Molly searching for her work bag and wander down her cobbled footpath to the pavement. I pull the gate shut behind me and stare up the street, seeing the start of the dirt road in the distance. That track road led me to somewhere unfamiliar last night. Not just unfamiliar surroundings, but unfamiliar feelings.

It's been years since I've looked at a man in that way. But something about Ryan Willis didn't give me much choice. He was worried about me—a woman he doesn't know. He cared that I was hurt. He tried to help, to make it better. And while bamboozling me with his attention, he knocked me back with his rugged handsomeness, too. He's a nice guy. A stand-up, decent man.

My feet move without me telling them to, and I'm suddenly at the dirt road, staring past the low-hanging trees to the curve where I was taken out by his truck. The trees sway. The birds tweet. The morning sun beats down between the gaps in the dense canopy. *Peace.* I feel, see, and hear only peace. He said he lived there. He lives in the woods?

I take one more step forward and stop sharply when a rabbit dashes across the road.

Back away, Hannah.

Nibbling my bottom lip, I turn with effort and start my walk back into town. But I'm constantly looking over my shoulder as I go. Curious. Wondering about him.

* * *

When I get home, I have the shower I missed in my haste this morning, before throwing on a red sundress and tying a bright-blue scarf in my hair. I slip on my silver Birkenstocks and head downstairs just before nine thirty, unlocking the door to my store and propping it open with a stone statue of a Highland terrier. Then I put myself behind the counter.

And I sit there. And I twiddle my thumbs. An hour later, I tidy a shelf of brushes that doesn't need tidying. And an hour after that, I sweep the floor that's already clean. I see people passing by, people I recognize from the town—some by name, some by face—but none of them come in. I don't let it dishearten me.

When it reaches noon, I pop to Mrs. Heaven's café next door to buy myself a sandwich and one of her famous blueberry muffins. As I'm wandering back, I notice Molly by the lamppost outside my store. "Hi," I say as I approach, craning my neck to see what she's doing. She has a roll of tape in her mouth, her hands on the lamppost.

She smiles through the roll and finishes taping a piece of paper to it. "Hey." Stuffing a few bits in her purse, she nods toward my shop door. "How's business?"

"Quiet," I reply, though I suspect she has seen that for herself. Everyone around here must have. "I'm hoping my online store will pull the art lovers in."

Molly smiles and takes the tape from her mouth. "Thank you so much for helping me out this morning."

"My pleasure." I toss the remnants of my sandwich in a nearby bin. "How's the solar system looking?"

"Colorful." She laughs, but then she's quickly wincing, looking at my legs. "What happened to your knee?"

"Oh." I wave my hand flippantly. "I fell off my bike last night." I won't go into details. "It's just a graze." Diverting my attention to the poster she's just stuck to the lamppost, I go for a quick subject change. "What's this?"

"The town's annual fete." She reaches forward and pats down the tape. "A kind of celebration of the founding of Hampton. We close the high street and put on a bit of a party."

"Sounds great."

"Yeah, it's good fun. Mrs. Heaven sells her famous cakes, the pub landlord brings barrels of cider out onto the street, and Mr. Chaps sets up a toffee apple stand. Country dancing, a beauty pageant, that kind of thing."

I read the poster. "Hosted by Lord and Lady Hampton?" I say as I return my attention to Molly. I just catch her eye roll before she can hide it. I haven't had the pleasure of meeting them yet, but I've heard all about the richest family in town who live in the mansion on the Hampton Estate.

"Their ancestors founded Hampton centuries ago. This annual event is really just so they can bask in the glory of the oh-so-wonderful town we live in, thanks to them." Another hugely sarcastic eye roll. "We only have to stroke their egos for a day. It's no hardship, and everyone has fun." Her eyes suddenly light up. "Hey, you're good with paint, right? I mean using it, not making it."

I laugh a little. "Why do you ask?"

"We need something else for the kids. We only have the usual games and the beauty pageant."

"Like a painting competition?" I don't know where that came from, but Molly seems to love the idea if her bright smile is anything to go by.

"Oh yes! I was actually thinking more face painting, but a painting competition sounds perfect."

I shrug, pushing back the image of my niece's butterfly cheeks. How I'd have loved to be the one who painted those wings on her cute little face. But that can't happen. Ever.

Molly's smile brightens some more. "Can I put your name down?"

"Sure," I answer, happy to help. I love this town more and more each day—the community, the friendliness, the beauty of the countryside. Though I really shouldn't get too used to it. It'll only make it more difficult to leave when the time comes. This is a pit stop. A temporary home until I can move on to somewhere even farther from London. Maybe Ireland. Ireland's pretty. There will also be plenty for me to paint. England is risky. Being here is risky; I know that. But I need to see my mum.

I smile as Molly starts backing away, taking another poster from her purse. "I'd better go, I have another ten of these to put up before my lunch break is over. Thanks, Hannah."

"No problem at all. I'm looking forward to it." I slip the key in the lock of my door. "And if you need any help with the planning, you know where I am."

"You're a gem. See you at the pub tomorrow. We can talk more then."

As simple as our plans are for a drink together, I'm excited. I'm making my own plans with someone I actually want to spend time with. I can be myself. Drink wine to my heart's content without worrying I might say the wrong thing or upset someone.

*   *   *

The next day, I do what I've done every Saturday since I arrived in Hampton. I take an hour's taxi ride to Grange Town and visit the park. I sit on my usual bench, and I wait, feeling something between excitement and apprehension.

It's exactly five past ten when I see them, and my heart speeds up, my spirits lifting high. "Hey, Mum," I whisper, watching as Pippa pushes her down the path toward the lake. They stop in their usual spot where the swans always seem to congregate, and I laugh a little when Pippa pulls out a bag of seeds and drops it, sending the bird feed scattering everywhere at her feet.

"Always so clumsy," I muse, thinking of all the times as kids when we used to wreak havoc with our accident-prone chaos. Like that time Mum asked Pippa to rinse the pasta and she dropped the pot halfway to the sink after tripping over nothing. I laughed until my sides felt like they could split. Then Pippa laughed, too. Then she slipped on a piece of pasta and took me down with her. Mum screeched, Dad smiled fondly, not looking up from his newspaper, and Pippa and I rolled around on the floor. We had beans on toast for dinner that night.

And there was that time when we were teenagers and I was working on my final piece for my art examination. Pippa kicked the leg of my easel as she passed, sending my canvas face-first to the dining room rug. I remember staring at it, my paintbrush hanging limply in the air. Pippa cursed. Spewed her apologies fast as she scooped up my piece from the rug. Looked at it in horror. And I laughed because it was crap, anyway, and I was stalling starting from scratch. Pippa thought I'd lost my mind. Mum told us she hated that rug. And Dad was smiling again. Dad was always smiling. We were *all* always smiling.

Then I went to the university, got a job in a gallery, and met...

I quickly shake my thoughts away and focus on my mum and sister, starting to laugh again when Mum, looking rather lucid today, points around her wheelchair where all the ducks and swans have descended, pecking up the feed. It's chaos, wings flapping, Pippa shrieking, Mum laughing. It's a good day for her. She looks so beautiful when she smiles, always has, though her smiles are not as frequent these days.

My stomach starts to ache from my laughing as Pippa waves her arms around like a madwoman, trying to scare the birds away. It's an ache I remember fondly. Because Pippa and I were always getting into scrapes and laughing our way through them. And Mum and Dad always seemed to take pleasure from that. My sister and I were the best of friends, only two years between us. We were joined at the hip. Peas in a pod.

I sigh, and the inevitable wave of sadness I was trying to avoid comes over me. I wish I were over there with them. I wish they could know I'm here. I wish I could laugh with them. And more than that, I wish I could once again be the cause for their laughter. When I left home, I no longer made them laugh. I made them worry. And then I broke their hearts.

A tear falls, and I rush to wipe it away as I watch my sister push Mum out of the park, back toward the care home. I didn't want to leave the park feeling sad, and yet my mood is flat as I head back toward the main road to get a taxi back to Hampton. "See you next week, you two," I say, looking back. But they're gone.

Another week to wait. Another lifetime. How long will it be before I'm left sitting on the bench, hoping to see them, and they don't show up for their Saturday-morning walk around the park? What happens when Mum's too ill to go out?

I can't bear to think about it.

* * *

When I make it back to Hampton, I open the store for a few hours, if only to try to occupy my mind with something other than my relentless sadness. I check my online store, seeing that people are starting to view my work. It lifts my spirits, but just a fraction. There's only one thing that will help.

When you feel low, get your palette and let your imagination run riot. Painting was Mum's answer for everything. Sad? Then paint. Annoyed? Then paint. Bored? Then paint. *When things feel dark, lose yourself in color*, she always told me. *Lose yourself in what you love.* She taught me everything I know.

I grab a blank canvas, an easel, my paints and brushes, and I head outside. I need to lose myself in that one thing that always settled me. For so long, I was without this sense of peace. For so long, I was kept from my passion. It's funny that during those dark years, I needed my escape the most. But he wouldn't let me have it.

* * *

I close the shop at five and go upstairs to shower, washing the paint from my hands, my face, my…everywhere. I rough-dry my hair, skip brushing it, and add a peach head scarf that clashes terribly with my orange shift dress. I don't care. There's no one to tell me what I can and cannot wear. I head for my living room to get my phone, frowning when I find it's not where I left it. Or where I *thought* I'd left it. The next ten minutes are spent pulling all the cushions off the couch and searching my apartment. No phone. I glance at the clock. "Shit." I'll find it later. It's not like I need it. Because who's going to call me?

At seven fifteen, I make my entrance into the town pub. Father Fitzroy is propped up at the end of the bar, a pint in one hand, a newspaper in the other, and he tips his head as I pass him. I smile a hello and spot Molly at the table in the window.

I hurry over and perch on the hard wooden bench next to her, accepting the glass of wine she holds up. "Hey, sorry I'm late. I couldn't find my phone."

"You mean you lost the brick?"

I roll my eyes on a smile. "Good day?"

"Yes, and the school committee *loves* your idea of having a painting competition for the kids." Molly toasts the air and sips. "Do you need anything from us?"

"Maybe stools for the kids to sit on?" Taking my first sip of wine, I smile around my swallow and get comfortable.

"I'll bring stools. What are they going to paint?"

I look behind me, out the window and across the road to where I sat this afternoon outside my store and painted a lovely street scene. "Seems only right they paint Hampton when we're celebrating Hampton. How about the high street? It's so pretty."

"That's perfect! And there'll be bunting zigzagging the lampposts, food carts, and stalls. The perfect view." Taking the bottle from the middle of the table, she tops up both of our glasses. "Now, enough about business. Tell me about yourself, Hannah."

Her friendly smile makes it all the more difficult for me to lie. I lose myself in my wine as I try to remind myself of the story I've rehearsed a hundred times. "I had a crappy breakup with my boyfriend and was done with the rat race of the city." Simple as that. "So I got out while I could." I smile brightly, albeit forced. "I moved abroad for a few years, but it didn't suit me. You can't beat the English countryside, so I came back." Molly seems to buy my pack of lies easily, and it's a relief.

"Then cheers to fresh starts."

We clink glasses and drink to just that.

* * *

An hour later, we've nearly worked our way through the whole bottle of wine and we've not shut up. We've laughed so much, and it's taken me back to times gone by when I used to giggle constantly with my sister.

Molly is a little like Pippa—jumping from one topic to the next in one big jumble. It's easy to love her. And it's been a pleasure to talk because I just want to...talk. Not because I feel I have to. Speaking from the heart about my passion for painting instead of hiding it has lifted me. Molly's listening because she's interested in what I have to say. It's a novelty. The past four years I've spent being rather lonely, keeping everyone at a distance. Not letting them get too close. I'm feeling more like my old self, the young, carefree, giggly young woman I used to be before my life turned ugly. Before I became a completely different woman.

"More?" I ask, snagging the empty bottle from the table and standing.

"Why the hell not?" Molly drains the last inch of her glass. "And get some peanuts, too."

I laugh and make my way to the bar, where the owner, Bob, is leaning against the counter chatting to Father Fitzroy, another pint in his hand. "Same again, please." I set the empty on the bar.

"And a Budweiser," says a voice from beside me. I recognize it immediately, and my carefree smile drops like a rock. Ryan Willis. My hand freezes in midair as I release the empty bottle, my chest immediately throbbing. "Hi," he says, but I keep my eyes on Bob, searching my brain for a simple reply and finding nothing. No words, no instructions, no bloody anything.

Bob slides a bottle of Bud across the bar as he reaches for my bottle of wine. "You okay there, Miss Bright?" he asks, a little concerned. I'm concerned, too. I lose the ability to function like a normal, rational-thinking human being each time I'm in Ryan's presence. What the hell is wrong with me?

"I'm fine," I murmur as I grab our new bottle of wine and throw the money down. "Thanks." I beat a hasty retreat back to the table, cringing to myself the whole way.

"You okay?" Molly asks, holding up her glass for me to fill.

I force a smile and nod as I take my seat, desperately trying not to look toward the bar as Molly starts chatting again. I see her mouth moving, her hands gesturing, though I have no clue what she's saying. I'm too busy fighting to keep my eyeballs forward. But when she suddenly declares she needs the ladies', I'm left with no one to focus on. I look down at my grazed knee. And, damn me, peek over my shoulder.

He's sitting at the bar watching a football match on TV. His beer sporadically rises to his lips, and his throat stretches each time as he drinks. He's alone, quiet, seemingly happy in his own company. Then he looks back, and I fly around on my chair and focus on my wine.

Good God, I'm a loser. Say hi. Smile at him. He's just being friendly, for Christ's sake. But no matter how hard I try, I just can't bring myself to face him.

I gulp and look up when Molly comes back from the toilet. "Hey, did you get peanuts?" she asks as she scans the table.

I'm up from my stool quickly, being presented with the perfect opportunity to fix my recent blunders and hopefully show Mr. Cool that I'm not a total weirdo. "I'll get them." I go to the bar quickly before Molly can offer. "I forgot peanuts," I say to Bob as I turn toward Ryan, pulling a smile from nowhere.

His bottle pauses at his lips, his eyes turning to me but not his head. I have every intention of introducing myself officially, of holding my hand out and putting my silly awkwardness behind me, but then he lowers his bottle and turns a fraction toward me on his stool. He cocks his head. His eyes twinkle, just a little, and he gives me a crooked half smile.

And my plan turns to shit, my smile drops, and I'm mute once again. And my stupid body responds in a way it has *never* responded, catching me off guard. God, I'm *really* attracted to him. Fancy the absolute pants off him, in fact. He's rough, rugged, and handsome, even with his bent nose and crooked smile. I reach up to my own nose, feeling the tiny bump on the bridge. Did he break his nose, too? Or is his naturally bent?

He watches me as I stroke over the lump, his smile becoming faint. I quickly pull my hand from my face. Suddenly wary of my body's reactions, and honestly not knowing what to do with them, I back away, blindly snatching the peanuts off the bar.

"That's a pound, please, Hannah," Bob says, and I look at him like he's just asked me for a million.

"I'll get them." Ryan slips a coin onto the bar, and I'm positively dying on the inside as he watches me retreat, his smile now soft.

"Thanks," I more or less whisper, turning and heading back to Molly. I should avoid him forever, since I'm not myself when I'm around him. But there's just something about him. He's knocked me for six. He's kind of warm, without really being warm. He's kind of cute, without really being cute. And he's kind of familiar, without being familiar at all.

What is happening?

God, I don't know, but I do know that he must think I'm a total nutcase. Maybe I am. Or maybe I'm broken beyond repair. Maybe I just don't know how to act in front of a man anymore.

I squirm my way back to the table and take refuge in my wine.

"Are you hot?" Molly asks, pointing her glass at my flushed cheeks. I reach up and pat at them.

Yes, I'm burning up. Hot and bothered.

But obviously still broken.

CHAPTER FIVE

RYAN

My outside shower is one of the things I love most about being home. The mornings are cool this time of year, but that cool air mixed with the heat from the spray is an unbelievably amazing feeling on my skin. Steam from the hot meeting cold. Invigorating.

I grab a towel and wrap it around my waist as I head back inside my cabin to make a coffee. Sitting down at my desk, I check my emails, deleting most, then send a message to Jake for an update. My phone rings almost immediately after I've clicked SEND.

"Hey," I answer, leaning back in my chair. "I assume the baby has arrived."

"Oh, he's arrived all right." Jake laughs, though it's tired, and I suddenly hear the piercing cry of a newborn. "Caleb Sharp is most definitely here." He sighs, now sounding fucking exhausted.

I can't help my small smile. "Congratulations, mate."

"Thanks. How's things up there?"

"Peaceful." I get up and wander to the freezer, grabbing the Chunky Monkey and cracking off the lid.

"I can relate. I'm getting ready to take Cami and the kids to my country place. No neighbors. No noise. Just me and them in the middle of nowhere."

I smile. Hampton is in the middle of nowhere. No one comes here. No one leaves here. I momentarily reflect on the time I left town years ago with no plans of coming back other than to visit Mum. I soon did come back, though. Wild horses couldn't have kept me away. And then I'm thinking again about that paint-splattered woman. No one comes here. But she has.

"Anyway..." I get a spoon and hold my mobile phone to my ear with my shoulder as I dig into the ice cream. "You enjoy your sleepless nights." I grin when he snorts, hearing a sound from outside. I glance to my open door. "I've gotta go. Someone's here. Love to the family."

"Sure. Keep in touch, bud." Jake hangs up, and I throw my phone on the couch and move to the window, looking out as I take the first mouthful of my vice. It's silent, perfectly silent... until I hear the sound of branches cracking. I take the few steps to the front door, alert but by no means concerned by the sounds of someone on my property. I'm in Hampton. Nothing ever happens in Hampton.

Leaning my shoulder on the doorframe, I wait for whoever it is to show themselves, my eyes trained on the track where it disappears around the corner. And while I wait, I carry on slowly spooning some ice cream into my mouth.

Then I see something.

"Well, well," I say to myself, slowly swallowing. She rounds the corner, and even from here I can tell she's fighting with her instinct to retreat. Every time I've encountered this woman, she's been like a rabbit caught in the headlights. The first time, I get it. I'd run her off the road. She must have been shocked. But in the store? And in the pub the other night? She's a scared little thing. Or is it something else? I raise my eyebrows to myself. Do I want it to be something else?

She's gazing around, her awe obvious, as I start munching my way through my Chunky Monkey again. I can't blame her for being so enthralled. My place is pretty enthralling.

Then she spots me in the doorway and stops dead in her tracks. Her eyes are glued to my chest, and I peek down with my spoon hanging from my mouth, reminding myself that I've just gotten out of the shower and have only a tiny towel covering my dignity. "You going to bolt again?" I call softly, digging my spoon back into the tub.

She blinks and looks up from my bare torso. "Pardon?"

I smile and take the three steps down from the veranda to the lawn. "You have a habit of running in the other direction whenever I've seen you."

Her eyes close, embarrassment tingeing her checks. Or maybe the heat is caused by something else. A little flash of satisfaction courses through my veins.

"That's what I came about," she says. "I'm not usually such a weirdo." She can't look at me now and is playing with a frayed bit of fabric on the bottom of her denim shorts. The long-sleeved baggy sweater she's wearing swamps her small frame, and the blue scarf in her hair nearly covers her whole head. She's chic, in a cutesy kind of way.

I approach her, but slowly, mindful that it's taken all her courage to come here. Her shyness, while almost painful, is quite endearing. "I don't think you're a weirdo." I pop a big spoonful of ice cream in my mouth and relish the small smile she points at the tub in my hand.

"Chunky Monkey for breakfast?"

I flash her the inside of the tub. "What about it?"

The small laugh she allows to escape lights up her face, and it's truly a sight to behold. "Well, I just wanted to break the ice." She waves a hand between us. "I didn't mean to be rude on Thursday night, or in the store Friday morning." She frowns. "Or in the pub Saturday night."

"I didn't think you were rude. Shy, maybe."

"I'm not shy," she retorts, far too quickly. Defensively.

"Okay." I plunge my spoon in the tub and set it on the picnic table next to me. She's definitely shy. And maybe awkward. "How's your knee?" My eyes drop down to her leg and find a pretty pathetic dressing covering it.

"Fine." Her stare is back on my chest, her nervous fingers twiddling. Then ... silence. And it begins to get awkward again.

So I intervene. "Hello?"

"Hi," she says, looking up at me as she blinks rapidly. "I think I need some abs."

I choke on nothing. "Sorry?"

"Water!" she yells, taking a blind step back as she proceeds to laugh, a little deranged.

She's not looking where she's going. She's flustered. Embarrassed. I can see what's about to happen, all so very clearly. "Hey, watch the—"

I'm too late. Her foot lands on the branch, her arms begin to flail, and she starts to fall backward. Fucking hell, she'll be injured again, and once again it'll be my fault.

"Shit," she yelps. I lunge forward and catch her hand in the nick of time, hauling her forward with a little too much force.

Mistake.

Now she's flying toward me, and when her body crashes into mine, I stagger, catching my own damn foot on a branch and falling to my back on the dirt. I wince at the impact, leaves and dust wafting up around me, twigs digging into my skin.

"Fuck," I curse, my eyes squeezed shut. And when I open them, I find her plummeting face-first toward me. Oh shit. My muscles lock naturally, bracing for impact.

I note her wide eyes. I note the mortification on her face. I note my blood warming.

She lands right on top of me with a thud, and I grunt before forcing myself to be still, mindful there is only a tiny towel around my waist. Good God. I gulp and breathe in, slow and controlled, as she remains with her face squished into my chest.

"Water," she murmurs eventually. "I meant to say I need some water." Placing her palms into my pecs, she pushes herself up and looks at me, her face crimson, her fingers flexing a little into my flesh.

And I find myself laughing on the inside, though I keep my face straight. "You're feeling me up, and I don't even know your name."

Cringing all over me, she quickly removes her hands and sits up. She cringes harder. "And now I'm straddling you," she sighs, her shoulders slumping, though I get the feeling she is past being embarrassed. "My name's Hannah," she mumbles.

"I'm Ryan."

"I know." She shrugs when I cock my head in question. "The girl in the store told me."

Interesting. Is that because she asked? Quite unexpectedly, my thoughts go into overdrive, thinking how good she looks straddling me. Adorable, messy, and good. I find my arms lifting and folding back under my head as I admire her. "Nice to meet you, Hannah," I say flatly, and she rolls her eyes dramatically.

"I would say the same, but..." She drifts off as her eyes drift, too, roaming the lengths of my arms until she finds my eyes. "Nice to meet you, too." And she chuckles, her head shaking in dismay. The sound is clean, pure, and if I don't remove myself now, she'll find out that it's also gotten my blood pumping. So begrudgingly, I engage my muscles and she takes the hint, lifting her arse from my stomach. Though she flinches as she stands, prompting me to rush to help her with the one hand that's not holding my towel in place.

"Okay?" I ask, running my eyes over her gorgeously bedraggled body.

She nods and steps away. "I caught my knee on the way down."

I quickly find the graze, noting that the bandage is hanging off and the scrape is bleeding again. She reaches down and pats around the edges of the dressing, trying to refix it. "Damn it." Giving up, she lets the dressing flop down, and I wince when the wound comes into view.

"Did you clean it?" I ask, taking her arm and leading her to a nearby log.

"Yes." Her arse drops to the wood, and she gazes up at me.

Her impossibly big blues are wide in surprise as I lower to my haunches before her, getting a better look. "What did you clean it with?" I reach forward and dab at the edge, not liking the sight of raw flesh.

"Warm water."

"That's it?" My alarm can't be hidden. "Just water?"

She looks timid now as she nods her confirmation.

Exasperated, I rise. "Wait there," I order, pacing back to the house to fetch my first-aid box. "It needs seeing to before it becomes infected." I ditch my towel and drag on some jeans before opening a few cupboards in search of my supplies. As soon as I lay my hands on the box, I fill a bowl with some warm water and antibacterial liquid, and head back outside. She's still perched on the log, gazing around, and I have to stop myself from taking a moment to admire how fucking lovely she is.

I set down my things as she straightens out her injured knee. "How's your shoulder?" I ask. "You were rolling it the other night." I bend and wring out the cloth, taking it to the graze and dabbing gently as I wrap my hand around the back of her knee to hold her still. Her leg tenses.

"Stiff," she whispers.

Stiff. I shift in my crouched position, trying in vain to make room in my jeans, my eyes firmly rooted on her knee. Until they're not, my gaze dropping down the length of her shapely leg. My hand jerks, as well as my dick. I'm breaking out in a sweat. "Hold still," I order, a bit harsher than I meant to.

"I didn't move a muscle. *You* moved." Her hands push into the tree stump on either side of her body as I realign my focus and continue cleaning her wound. "Ow, ow, ow."

"You've got bits of gravel in it." I reach for the tweezers and get closer, unreasonably annoyed. I shouldn't have let her refuse my help the other night. I would have removed all the dirt and dressed it properly, and it would be healing by now. "Don't move."

"Shit, shit, shit."

"Shh," I hush her, picking out the small stones and flicking them away.

"You shush," she retorts through gritted teeth, and I can't help but smile down at her knee, trying to concentrate. "I haven't seen you around here," she says, her teeth clenched as I work on her wound. "Not before you ran me over, anyway."

I ignore her dig, since I suspect it won't be the last poke I receive about that. "I just got back to town after finishing a job." I lift a small flap of skin to get to a larger piece of grit.

Her leg jerks, and I force it still again. "Youch!"

"Got it." I toss the tweezers aside and grab the cloth, wiping away the rest of the blood.

"You said you work in protection."

"I *did* work in protection," I reply.

"And you don't anymore?"

"No."

"Why?"

I look at her on a smile. "Anyone would think you want to get to know me." Does she? Do I want to get to know her?

Her cheeks flush again. "Just trying to make conversation."

Intrigued by her apparent interest, I decide to feed her curiosity. "I joined the army when I was eighteen. I was pulled from the ranks at nineteen and put through a grueling recruitment process. By the time I turned twenty, I was working for MI5."

"Oh my God, were you a spy?"

I laugh a little. "No, I wasn't a spy." I'm not lying. I wasn't. I was an intelligence officer. So what if it's technically the same thing. "I worked in protection." Not lying again. I was protecting national security.

"So why'd you leave?"

"Change in circumstances," I say, looking up at her, not feeling the need to tell her about Alex. God, I can't wait to see her. "I started working for a private protection agency."

"And now you've left there?" she asks, and I nod, seeing the desperation in her to ask why that is, too.

But before she can, I point to her knee. "Does it sting?"

"Not too much."

"You're so brave." I peek up at her, seeing her nose wrinkle. That's cute, too. She's just too damn cute. "So I haven't seen *you* around here before." I throw her words back at her.

"I moved into town a few weeks ago." She gingerly flexes her knee when I prompt. "I have an art shop in town. It's kind of a gallery, but I sell craft stuff, too."

Ah, the new store. She looks like the creative type. But if anyone was going to set up a new business, especially in such a niche field, why on earth would they do it in Hampton? We're miles from civilization.

I don't have the heart to rain on her parade, though. Not after spotting the extra glow in her face when she mentioned her store. "I wondered where that store had come from," I say, reaching for a bandage. "What's your area of expertise?"

She laughs a little, and, God damn me, it stirs my dick to the point I cringe at my body's reaction. "I wouldn't say I have a specific area of expertise. I just have a passion for painting. I'll paint anything."

I smile as I rip a bandage open, remembering the paint splatters all over her the other night. "Then tell me, what's your favorite thing to paint?"

"I love the outdoors. Color, nature." She smiles, lighting up her face some more. "So landscapes, mainly. Things of natural beauty." Listening to her talk about something she so clearly loves is...enjoyable.

Hannah's eyes glisten as she stares at me, and suddenly the easy atmosphere shifts, the air thickening. The bandage sits in my useless hand, her foot on my knee, and I've completely forgotten what I was doing. Her tongue wets her lips. Oh shit. Adorable and effortlessly sexy. Desire races through me with a vengeance. "Things of natural beauty," I say quietly, and she nods slowly. "So you want to paint me, right?"

A grin slowly forms, and she breaks out in laughter, her head thrown back. My eyes lock on her throat, the smooth lines down the column positively begging for me to put my mouth there. *Fucking hell, Ryan. Sort your shit out.*

I slap the bandage on her knee a bit heavy-handed, and she yelps, her laughter gone in a second. Hannah looks at me, startled, and despite knowing I should apologize, I don't. I place her foot on the ground, then rise to my feet. I'm uncomfortable with how comfortable this woman makes me feel. She's like a precious box of adorableness. Her blond hair is a mass of messy waves pinned up haphazardly, her dark roots bold and undoubtedly meant to be, and the scarf knotted on her head is the brightest of blues you could find. And don't get me started on her big, sapphire eyes. They're hypnotizing. She's so slim, I want to feed her. Does she eat? Look after herself? I should cook her a burger. A big one. And watch her eat it. *Whoa!* I clear my throat and back away.

"So you live here?" Hannah stands, aware of my sudden withdrawal.

"Home sweet home," I say quietly as she gazes around. She's impressed, and I don't know why that pleases me. The only other woman I've ever so much as touched in Hampton hates this place. Hannah isn't like her. *Nothing* like her. I push away thoughts of the woman who is the epitome of high maintenance. A woman who has an exceptional ability to make everyone feel beneath her. A woman who tried to take away the one thing in this world I adore. A woman I fucking hate.

"Is that an outside shower?" Hannah's question yanks me back to the here and now, where a woman stands before me looking at my sanctuary like it's the most amazing thing she's ever seen. She's not appalled in the least bit. Just awed. It feels…nice.

"Yes, it is."

"And a hammock?"

I nod as she continues to take in my land, from the barbecue to the veranda circling my cabin. She turns and walks over to the shower stall and peeks around the wooden slats, up to the spray. "We're in England. It must be freezing most of the time."

"It's heated," I explain, joining her and flipping the lever. "Connected to the cabin's central heating system." The water hits the polished concrete slabs and splashes up our legs, and she nods with a thoughtful smile, gazing around again while I turn off the shower, wandering here and there, looking back at me every so often.

"You built all this, didn't you?" she asks, and I nod my confirmation. "So you're good with your hands?" My eyebrows shoot up without thought, and she laughs a little. Fuck, that sound. "It's wonderful here," she says. "I love it." And why does that make me so happy? Since when have I cared what a woman thinks of me and my way of living? My mind is going off on a tangent, and I look back at my outdoor shower. A woman has never been in that shower. What would Hannah look like in it? I jolt, kicking myself into line, finding that Hannah has put herself in my hammock. She's swinging back and forth, looking up at the treetops. I let her have her moment, not prepared to interrupt her when she's clearly so serene. Peaceful suits her. And she looks damn good in my hammock. Now she's humming, too. I smile to myself, though it's curious, and watch her for a while, my head whirling.

"Comfortable there?" I ask as she lifts her head and squints to see me.

"I'm moving in."

I laugh under my breath, unable to stop myself. "You sure do move fast. You only straddled me ten minutes ago."

Her eyes drop to my chest, reminding me that it's still bare. "Yeah," she all but breathes, struggling to sit up. The hammock swings precariously, and she yelps, forcing me to dive forward and steady her. Though I make damn sure we don't end up in a messy pile of bodies this time. "I'm not usually this clumsy," she blurts, holding my forearms and throwing her legs over the side.

Her clumsiness is quite endearing, yet I refrain from telling her so.

I help her down, ensuring her stability before I release her, though it's only when I try to step back that I realize she's the one clinging to me. She's looking at me again, her blue eyes ridiculously large and beautiful.

I look away. I need some breathing space. Weird shit is happening in my veins, my heart, my head. "Excuse me," I say, forcing myself from her hold and heading back to my cabin, scrubbing my hands down my face and breathing out. For a man who's content on his own, a man who's not interested in getting involved with a woman, this one sure has my blood hot. No woman has ever done this to me. Stirred my interest. Gotten me so curious. Made me laugh. Stoked desire.

I splash my face with cold water, if only to bring myself around from this . . . oddness. Only once I've composed myself do I head back outside. And stop dead in my tracks at the threshold when I see no sign of Hannah. Where'd she go? "Hannah," I call, taking the steps and scanning the area.

"Yeah?"

She appears from behind a tree, and my muscles relax. That's fucking weird, too. "I thought you'd gone." And so what if she had?

She blows a strand of hair from her face, trudging toward me. "You'll have to tell me how to get out of here." She gestures around to my hidden sanctuary. "I just followed my nose."

Followed her nose, huh? Should I read more into that? Probably not. "So today you came to see me to tell me you're not awkward," I say, my head tilting. "What were you doing up this way the other night?"

"Looking for Molly's house." She shrugs. "I was delivering paint and got completely lost."

"Then I'm glad I found you." The words come from nowhere, making her withdraw a little. "I mean—" *What the actual fuck, Ryan?*

"I'm glad, too," she says on a mere wisp of air. "Or else I could've been eaten by a bear or something," she adds cheekily, as if she's regretting what she's said.

"There are no bears around these parts." Silly female.

"Wolves?"

I shake my head. "You're in the Peak District, not Alaska."

"Wild dogs?"

"Nope. No man-eating monsters around here, sweetheart." I pick up my axe from its resting place by the pile of logs, swinging it casually as I kick my foot onto a nearby log and lean forward, resting my elbow on my knee. "Only me."

She rolls her eyes for effect, approaching and claiming my axe. "No offense, but you're not the least bit scary," she says casually.

"I wasn't trying to be."

Her teeth sink into her bottom lip as she regards me carefully. What's she thinking? "It's heavier than it looks." She rips her eyes from mine and inspects my axe. Now I know she wasn't thinking that. "Did you chop all these logs?"

"Yep. I love the springtime. It's warm during the day, but early mornings and nighttime are still cool enough to light a fire." I kick a few logs as Hannah studies the handle, both hands flexing around the wood. "Wanna try?" I ask. Where are these words coming from? And is this wise, given she's so fucking clumsy? She could take my head off.

Hannah looks up at me. "At chopping wood?"

"Sure." Why the hell not. Dancing with danger seems to be in my blood. I take a moment's pause on that thought. Hannah? Dangerous? She looks about as deadly as a baby bunny. I bend and collect a pre-chopped log, placing it upright on the stump. Then something comes to me. "Your shoulder."

"My shoulder's fine." She rolls it, stepping forward and lifting the axe. At least, she tries to. She barely gets it past her waist.

"Want some help?" I ask. Help? That would mean being close to her. Touching? Is that a good idea?

She looks at me, silent for a few moments, before quietly replying, "Sure."

I rub at the nape of my neck, struggling to find a reason *not* to help her. After all, I offered. And she accepted. I can do this. And actually, something inside me is satisfied she wants me to, especially since she couldn't bring herself to even look at me before today. So I close the distance between us yet make sure our bodies don't touch, but of course when I lean past her, my plan goes to shit and my front meets her back. I swallow and take the handle of the axe, just below Hannah's grip. She stills, going quiet.

"You get more power if you hold the handle nearer the end," I say quietly, my voice naturally rough. "But you lose some precision."

"Okay," she whispers. "So hold it here?" Her hands move onto mine.

"Yeah." I find my eyes closing when she shifts position, rubbing into me a little. Jesus Lord above, what is she trying to do to me? "You think we're lined up?" I ask, unable to check myself.

"I think so."

I open my eyes and widen my stance, my nose virtually in her hair. She smells of raspberries. Sweet, juicy, delicious raspberries.

I bring my face forward and rest my chin on her shoulder, and her head turns so we're suddenly eye-to-eye. It's tense, as if she knows of all the thoughts currently running rampant in my head. Is it crazy that I have an urge to kiss her? Now would be the perfect opportunity, and the way she's looking at me tells me she wants me to. Our lips are an inch apart. I can taste her breath.

I scan her face, looking for the sign I need. She blinks slowly, her breath fluttering.

There it is.

I start to lower my mouth, unable to stop myself, desperate for the feel of her lips against mine.

But she quickly turns away, and I feel her suddenly shaking as she releases her hold of the axe and ducks under my arm, moving away stealthily. "I'm sorry," she blurts, sounding panicked, refusing to look at me.

Shit. I swallow down my disappointment and pull myself together. What was I thinking? "It's me who should be sorry. I didn't mean to make you feel uncomfortable."

"You didn't." She shakes her head furiously, and I see immediately that she's mad with herself. *Why?* "It's just...just..."

"Hannah, you don't have to explain yourself." I positively hate that she's apologizing to me. What the fuck is that all about? I set the axe down and approach her, completely caught off guard when she retreats speedily. I stop. Her eyes are wide.

She grasps her hands in front of her, her fingers twiddling wildly. "I'm not very good at"—she flaps a nervous hand in front of me—"this."

"What?" I ask. "Chopping wood?"

She gives me a tired look. "No, flirting."

"Flirting?" I ask, trying so fucking hard to lighten the mood. "Is that what we're doing, because I'm pretty sure we were about to chop some wood?" There's something deep and overwhelming inside me that's determined to make her feel better about whatever it is that's gotten her all nervous. There's also an unstoppable appreciation flowing through me because she's acknowledged the attraction between us. I'm not going mad. She likes me. Good, because I've just this moment admitted to myself that I like her, too. A lot.

"Very funny." She reaches forward and smacks my biceps lightly. "It's just...it's been a long time since..."

"You flirted?"

She sighs on a smile. "Since anyone kissed me."

Oh my God, has there ever lived a sweeter woman? She's like nothing I've met before, but I can't shake off the notion that there are many layers to her, and I'm only just peeling back the top one. "Well, *anyone* clearly has better willpower than I do." Just when I think she couldn't be any more gorgeous, her cheeks flush and lashes flutter as she glances away. I grab the handle of the axe. Let's move things along. "Are we gonna chop this piece of wood or not?"

Her smile is out of this fucking world, and she doesn't think twice about putting her body in front of mine again. Taking the handle and steadying her stance, she focuses on the wood. "Hannah?" I say as I move slightly to the side and raise the axe with her.

"Yeah?"

I put my mouth close to her ear, and she inhales slowly. "I'm a good guy," I whisper.

I can't see her face, but I know her smile just widened. Good, because I like her smile. She brings the axe down with power and precision, and on a shout that is way too loud for her small frame. The wood splits perfectly, and she heaves in front of me, staring at it. "Oh my God, that felt *so* good."

"Sounded it, too." If I didn't know her better, I'd say she just channeled a shitload of anger into that swing. And for the first time since I met this woman, I wonder what her story might be.

I step away from her body, but she's not too willing to release the axe, forcing me to tug it gently but firmly until she shoots her eyes my way. "Easy, sweetheart."

"Sorry." She gives me an impish grin. More adorableness. "I should get going."

I put the axe aside and motion to my truck, batting back my disappointment. "Do you want me to give you a ride into town? I'm going that way anyway."

"No, but thanks," she says, though I detect hesitance. "I could do with the fresh air."

She could? Why? To clear her head? Again, why? Because of me? *Fuck me, the questions.* "It was nice to see you," I say, and hate myself the second I utter the pathetic words. Nice? Fucking *nice*?

"Nice to see you, too."

"Feel free to stop by anytime." What the hell has gotten into me?

Her eyebrows raise. "If I feel like being run over, then I know where to come." Her grin inflates my balls.

And something deep and unfamiliar stirs inside me.

Want.

* * *

After throwing on some jeans and a T-shirt, I grab my keys and head out to my truck. And damn, I'm excited. It's evident in my hasty pace across the lawn. My idyllic haven will be complete with one more addition.

The dirt kicks up behind me as I race down the lane, but I find my foot easing off the accelerator without thought. Then my eyes start to scan. And before I know it, I'm crawling along at a snail's pace, just in case any women decide to throw themselves under my truck.

I emerge from the woodland into the sunshine and pick up speed, heading into town. The turn into the grounds of the Hampton Estate is soon in sight, and the familiar coil of my muscles follows soon after. I drive faster up the cobbled driveway than I should, but . . . fuck them. I make sure I skid to a stop by the over-the-top fountain, and I make sure the Stone Roses' "Resurrection" is blaring from my stereo for a good few seconds before I shut the engine off. As anticipated, Lady Hampton appears at the drawing room window, virtually steaming the glass with her rage. I smile on the inside as I get out, heading for the front door of the west wing. I raise my fist, ready to hammer on the wood like the animal I apparently am, but it swings open before I can reaffirm what these arseholes think of me.

It's all I can do not to bare my teeth when Darcy appears, primped and preened as perfectly as normal—her eye shadow heavy, her lips artfully painted, her black hair harsh against her pale skin. Darcy fucking Hampton. Mega bitch.

Her eyes narrow. "You're early."

"By fifteen minutes."

"You'll have to wait. She's not long home and hasn't finished unpacking." Darcy attempts to shut the door on me. Oh no.

"Get one of your many butlers to do it, Darcy." I kick my booted foot out, and the wood hits my toe.

"Ryan!" she yells. "You'll dirty the paintwork."

I ignore her and the precious paintwork and shout past her. "Hey, Cabbage!"

"Ryan, for God's sake!" Darcy wrestles with the door against my foot, her slick French braid losing a few strands of hair. "And don't call her Cabbage."

"Fuck off, Darcy," I mutter quietly, my eyes lighting up when I hear a scuffle behind her. They're the sounds of my girl fighting off the hands trying to make her perfect, too. And then she appears at the top of the stairs dressed in a frilly floral thing, her long brown hair in a high ponytail. What the fuck have they done to her? I disregard the state of my daughter, my smile rare but natural. "Hey, beautiful."

I see her building up to a squeal, virtually shaking with excitement. "Dad!" Her eyes fall to the banister. And my smile widens. *Go on, my girl. Own that banister.*

"Don't you dare, Alexandra," Darcy warns, marching to the bottom of the stairs. "Don't...you...dare."

My daughter's eyes meet mine. I wink. She grins. And then she throws her leg over the banister and slides down like a pro, landing on her feet at the bottom. Darcy is forced to jump out of her way to avoid being taken off her heeled pumps. "For goodness' sake!" she shrieks, hurrying to straighten herself out.

"Chill out, Mum," Alex chirps as she skips over. I quickly turn, ready, and she dives onto my back. I can still hear Darcy hissing and spitting in the background. "I missed you," Alex mumbles, bringing on an edge of guilt.

"I missed you, too." I pace to the truck with her attached to my back. "What the hell are you wearing?" I drop her to her feet, motioning down the monstrosity of a dress. She's ten, for Christ's sake. And she's not a fucking doll.

"Grandmother bought me it." Her face bunches in disgust as she grabs the skirt of the dress and twirls.

"Lucky you."

"Hey, what happened to your truck?" She points to the bumper. "Did you have an accident?"

I shake my head. "Something ran out in front of me."

"What?"

I stall, knowing that if I tell her the truth, there will only be more questions. And I'm not sure exactly what I'd tell her about Miss Hannah Bright. "A weasel," I say quickly. *A weasel?* Not a graceful deer or a cute bunny rabbit. A weasel?

"Oh my God, did you kill it?" The look of horror on her face is ripe.

"No, I swerved and hit a tree."

Her high shoulders drop in relief. "The poor thing. It must have been stunned."

Stunned? It was me who was stunned. "It seemed to scamper off just fine." I open the door of my truck for her, and she jumps in, immediately grabbing one of my baseball caps and pulling out her ponytail. I take the cap from her hand and slip it on her head, slapping the brim. "Perfect."

As I'm walking around the front of my truck, Darcy comes running across the gravel with a bag. "Alexandra, darling, your things."

Alex lets her window down and rests her forearms on the edge, her chin on her arms. "I have things at Dad's."

"You have rags at your father's shack," Darcy retorts, throwing me a filthy glare.

"It's a cabin, Mum."

"Whatever, you have homework in here that needs doing."

Oh, for fuck's sake, give the kid a break, woman. My girl's been holed up at that snooty boarding school for months being worked to the bone.

"She's just gotten home for the spring holidays, Darcy. She has weeks to do her homework."

"Of course you'd be irresponsible," she snipes as she follows me to the driver's door, going below the belt as always.

But I grit my teeth and force a smile, not prepared to get into an argument in front of Alex. "Her homework will be done, and it'll be done on time. She needs some time to recharge."

Alex pulls herself back in the truck when I get in. "Can we go home and get changed?" she asks me.

"No, we have things to do."

Darcy appears at the window. "*This* is your home."

"Throw her bag in the back." I thumb over my shoulder and relish the look of horror on Alex's mother's face.

"It's filthy."

"Then don't." I pull away fast, making sure I kick up the dust, and I hear Darcy's screeches of displeasure fade as we zoom away. Call me immature, call me mean, but that woman brings out the worst in me. Alex starts chuckling, and despite wanting to laugh with her, I put my daddy head on and give myself a telling-off before scolding my daughter. "Don't laugh at your mother."

"Sorry." She kicks off her pink ballet flats and throws her feet onto the dashboard. "Where are we going?"

"Town. Put your belt on," I order, reaching across her body to grab it.

She puts up a lame fight. "I don't need my belt."

I give her *the* look—the one she knows not to mess with. "Do it." Fearless. That's my girl. Sometimes to a fault.

"Okay, okay." On a dramatic sigh, she reaches for the belt. "What do we need in town?"

"Supplies." I turn off the private road onto the main street. "We need to finish our bridge."

"You mean you haven't finished it?"

"You told me not to touch it until you're home," I remind her. "So I haven't."

"Good boy," she quips, earning a squeeze of her knee that makes her squeal and writhe in her seat. "Dad, stop!"

"You stop with the wisecracks."

"Okay!" she laughs, settling when I release her. "Hey, did you see the new arts-and-crafts store in town? I saw it when Grandmother's driver drove through town earlier."

"No." Why would I say no? And the questions in my brain start whirling again. Where has Hannah come from? Who is she?

"Dad?"

I jump in my seat and look across the truck. Alex is looking at me with a little concern. "Sorry, I was thinking." *Fool.*

"What about?"

"How much I've missed your sassy pants." I grin when she smirks.

"How long before you have to go back to London?"

"I'm not going back."

"Huh?"

"I quit my job." I peek at her out the corner of my eye, seeing astonishment and excitement emblazoned across her face. "I'm gonna build a few houses, I think. Wanna help me?"

"Oh my God!" she shrieks, making me flinch. "Like, for real?"

"For real."

"Can I quit school?"

I chuckle to myself as I pull up in a parking bay outside the town store. "No."

"Well, that's not fair." Alex unclips her belt and dives through the seats into the back. "Do I have any Vans in your truck?"

"Under my seat." I remember seeing the black-checkered sneakers a few weeks ago when I dropped my mobile phone down the side of my seat. I jump out and pull the back door open, finding Alex in a pile on the floor of my truck, her face squished against the back of my seat, her hand reaching underneath. Her mother would have a hernia.

"I think I've got one," she says, presenting me with one Van. My eyes nearly pop out of my head when I see something dangling off the toe and Cabbage frowns as I lunge forward, snatching away the red lacy knickers and stuffing them in my pocket quickly. "What was that?" she questions.

"Nothing." I make myself useful and reach under the seat to find the other shoe.

"Were they knickers?"

I laugh, and it sounds one hundred percent crazy. "Why would I have knickers in my truck?"

"You tell me."

I love how smart my girl is. Ten years old and leaving other students of her age for dust in the grades department, but as well as that, she's life-smart. Observant. Skilled. The private education is thanks to her mother's stuck-up family. The life knowledge and skills are thanks to me. At this moment in time, I'm regretting making her so smart. Nothing gets past her. "They weren't knickers." I have nothing else.

"You lie," she mumbles. "You got a girlfriend?"

I laugh, answering without answering. "There's only one woman I need in my life."

"Really, Dad?" Alex leans her shoulder against the side of the truck while I continue blindly rummaging for her other shoe. "You're getting old."

I cough on nothing. "I'm thirty-nine, for Christ's sake. There's years left in me yet."

"And you'll be spending them all alone at this rate."

I lay my hand on something that feels like a shoe and pray to every god that there's no knickers attached to this one as I pull it free. There's not. "I won't be alone because I have you."

"What happens when I grow up and meet a boy? What if I move away?"

"Whoa, easy, girl." I stare at her in horror. She's thought about that? Because I sure as shit haven't. "You'd leave me?" I untangle my body from the back of the truck and join her on the roadside.

Alex rolls her eyes dramatically. "You need someone to love other than me."

Where the hell is this coming from? "I like being on my own. Besides, I'm too grouchy and set in my ways. Relationships require compromise." I drop her Van to the ground. "They hardly match the fetching dress." Let's redirect the conversation quickly.

She slips her feet in the shoes and rearranges her baseball cap, her long hair splaying over her shoulders, and my mind wanders once again. To how impressed Hannah was with my cabin. To how bright her face was when she smiled, taking it all in. She wasn't appalled. Quite the opposite, in fact. What was she thinking when she left my place? What's she doing for the rest of the day?

"Dad, you look troubled."

I blink and find my daughter frowning at me. "I am." I sling my arm around her shoulder and walk us to the store. "My little Cabbage is growing up way too fast."

She bumps into my side and collects a basket. "What do we need?"

"A chisel."

"We have a chisel."

"A bigger chisel." I head to the hardware aisle and scan the tool section. "You go find something for dinner. Burgers?"

"Yes!" She dances off, and I watch her go in that stupid dress with Vans and a cap. My ten-year-old little girl. How the hell did that happen? I grin and get back to finding supplies.

Half an hour later, I have a basket full of everything we need and I'm wandering up and down the aisles looking for my wayward daughter. "Cabbage," I call.

"Second aisle on the left," Mr. Chaps says from behind the counter, so I head that way. But I don't find my daughter, just a mountain of leafy green vegetables. "I didn't mean cabbages, I meant..." I fade off, shaking my head. "Never mind. Have you seen Alex?"

"Only when you came in," Mr. Chaps tells me, starting to scan the basket of items that's been placed in front of him by Father Fitzroy.

"Alex," I call, making tracks to the hardware aisle. No Alex. The pang of worry is unstoppable, albeit silly. She doesn't talk to strangers. She's streetwise. I've taught her to be, not that there's much call for it in Hampton, nor at that godforsaken boarding school she's held prisoner in. But still... "Where the hell is she?" I mutter, traipsing up and down every aisle until I find myself back at the checkout. Still no Alex. Dumping my basket on the counter, I head out of the store, my worry getting the better of me. "Alex," I yell, looking up and down the high street.

"She went that way." Brianna, the store assistant, points down the street, smiling at me coyly as she shifts firewood onto the cart outside the store.

"Thanks," I say with a frown, following my feet down the street. "Alex?"

"I saw her go into the arts-and-crafts store," Bob calls from outside his pub, rolling a barrel of beer toward the cellar hatch.

My eyes swing toward Hannah's little store.

And some strange shit happens in my chest.

CHAPTER SIX

HANNAH

I'm checking my online store when I hear the door open, and I look up from my place behind the counter, smiling at the sight of a girl who's wearing the most hideous frilly dress teamed with a baseball cap and a pair of checkered Vans. I close my laptop, watching as she walks slowly around my store.

"Hi," I say, standing up from my stool.

She swings around, a paintbrush in her hand, and smiles. "Hi."

"I'm Hannah."

"Alexandra," she practically groans. "But most people call me Alex, except my mother's family who insists on using my full name. My dad calls me Cabbage sometimes." She shrugs. "I think he does it to annoy my mum. She hates it."

I wander over to her. "Why would he want to annoy your mum?"

"They're not together." She slides the brush back into the pot and starts combing the lengths of her hair with her fingers as she wanders to the shelves stacked with paints. "They were incompatible. And I was a beautiful mistake."

I laugh under my breath at her indifference. I guess it's a good thing. "Were you looking for something in particular?"

"Nah." She takes a couple of steps to the side and bends forward, looking closely at one of my paintings. "Did you do this?"

"I did."

"It's really good." She looks back and smiles.

"Thanks."

"I love your head scarf."

I reach up and feel, reminding myself of which one I'm wearing today. Blue with white hearts. "Thanks. Do you like painting?"

She shrugs. "Mum doesn't like me doing stuff that gets me messy and ruins my clothes. But Dad loves me getting messy. We get messy all the time."

I go over and pick up a blank canvas, propping it up on a spare easel. "Then maybe you could paint something for your dad without getting messy so you don't upset your mum." I pluck a brush from a pot and a palette of paints from the shelf, then turn toward her and hold them out.

Her eyes light up. "Cool!" She darts over and claims her tools. "What should I paint?"

"Whatever your heart desires." I grab my own canvas and a brush, swirling it in a pot of water. "Or just go with it." I dunk my brush in red paint and flick it at the canvas. "Sometimes it just...happens."

On a grin, Alex imitates me and starts flicking paint, chuckling as she does. "Oh, look, that looks like a heart."

I take a peek, nodding. "I love accidental art. Some of my best pieces were accidents." I pull over two stools and motion for her to sit, and we both settle in, flicking and humming, seeing what accidents happen on our canvases.

"Oh crap," she curses out of the blue, and I look over to see her wiping her forehead with the back of her hand. "I got paint on Dad's cap."

I place my brush down and reach for her cap, pulling it off. "It'll clean up," I assure her, catching sight of her dress. "Oh God, look at you. How'd you get so messy so quickly?"

Looking down her front, she shrugs. "Dad says it's a talent."

"Well, you're sure good at it." I chuckle. "I thought I was the messiest person alive." I motion down my front where paint is splattered, old and new. "You look like me."

She points at my head. "I don't have a head scarf."

I smile at her hint and pull it from my head, tying it in her hair, making the bow on top big. "Perfect," I declare.

She reaches up and feels. "Mum will say it's untidy."

Wait. Speaking of her mum, she's been sitting in my store for twenty minutes. "Where's your mum and dad?"

A cough sounds from behind me, making me swing around. And I nearly fall arse-first from my stool. "Ryan!" I yelp, finding him leaning comfortably against the doorframe. I drop to my feet, clumsily, of course, and start wiping at my cheeks, where I know I'll be sporting various blobs of paint.

"Hi." His crooked smile holds my eyes for too long, and my whole being becomes more flustered. Alight. Alive. I remember our almost kiss. I remember how good it felt when he was touching me. I remember…every tiny detail of my visit to his home this morning.

"Found a new friend?" he asks, pushing his weight off the door and striding casually into my store. His big body, dressed in dark jeans and a black T-shirt, looks out of place surrounded by all my colorful clutter.

Tearing my eyes away from him, I look over my shoulder to Alex, who has turned to face Ryan, too. She's grinning. Why's she grinning? I look back to Ryan. He's grinning as well. "Love the head scarf." He motions to Alex's head, and she reaches up to tweak the bow.

"Hannah gave it to me."

Gave it to her? I did?

"I was worried," Ryan says gruffly. "And look at the state of you."

I find myself glancing down my front, to all the paint there, my forehead furrowed with lines of confusion.

"Chill out, Dad," Alex chimes, completely unaffected by the wrath in Ryan's tone. "I was with Hannah. She likes painting."

"Hi, Hannah," Ryan says, and I hear his boots hitting the floor, coming closer. It prompts me to look up, my eyes dragging over his jeans and T-shirt.

"Hi," I murmur, stopping at his neck and the messy dark stubble coating it. "Ryan, this is Alex," I say, a little dazed. "Alex, this is—" My brain spasms. "Wait, what?" I crack my neck as I look up at him, now only a few feet away. "Did she call you Dad?"

Ryan's smile is small and awkward. "That's me." He looks to his... daughter? "You're in trouble, Cabbage."

"Yeah, yeah." She jumps down off the stool and strolls casually over to Ryan, craning her neck back to look up at him. "You know Hannah?"

His eyes flick to mine quickly before returning to his daughter. "We've met."

"But when I asked about the new art store in town, you didn't know about it."

Ryan's cheeks flush, his jaw tightens, and he clears his throat. "Like I said, we've met. Not talked." He shifts in his boots, looking anywhere around my store except at me. "We'd better get going. I need to have my truck looked at."

"But I'm painting," Alex whines, taking herself back to the stool and sitting down, collecting her brush. My eyes follow her and watch as she dips the paint and starts flicking again. "You do what you've got to do and collect me on the way back."

"That's not a good idea." He goes to her and lifts her from the stool, setting her gently on her feet.

"Why?"

"Because I need your help."

"To have your truck looked at?"

My eyes travel back and forth between them, listening as they argue about whether Alex is going with Ryan or not. It makes me smile as I take myself to the counter and continue to observe her standing her ground against her six-foot-God-knows-how-tall father.

"You're coming," Ryan grates, clearly losing his patience as I rest my elbows on the countertop and my chin in my hands. "I've not seen you in two months."

"If you hadn't run down a weasel, your truck would be fine."

My chin slips off my hand. "Weasel?" I blurt, glaring at him. His big body stills, and he's suddenly quiet, obviously stuck for any answer for his daughter *and* me. A bloody weasel? The nerve. "Like a rat-like creature?" I ask, joining Alex and sitting down again.

"Don't worry, the poor thing wasn't hurt," Alex pipes in next to me, keeping her attention on the paint she's flicking. "Dad swerved and hit a tree."

"Wasn't hurt?" My foot comes up and rests on the stool, and I hug my bent leg, my chin on my knee, just shy of the bandage. "Poor thing," I say quietly as Ryan's eyes fall to my damaged leg. His big body deflates as his apologetic eyes lift to mine. I look at him expectantly, strangely relishing his clear remorse. "I hope it's recovered from the shock."

His eyes now narrow, and I can't help my small smirk, and it only stretches when I see he's trying very hard to hold back his own smile. "Something tells me it has."

"Don't be so sure," I say quietly.

Ryan's head cocks a fraction, his smile faint. "How much for the canvas and paints?" he asks, digging into his pocket as Alex sings her delight and claps her hands. "She can finish it at home."

"To you?" I ask, getting up and putting myself behind the counter again.

"Yes, to me."

I smile sweetly. "Fifty pounds."

On a poorly concealed balk, Ryan pulls off three twenties from a wedge and walks to me, placing them on the counter and holding them in place. "You're ripping me off," he whispers.

I place my hand on the notes, too, never taking my eyes from his.

"Call it compensation for calling me a weasel," I whisper back, tugging the money from under his fingertips. "I'll keep the change, too." Those eyes, they narrow more, though he's still forcing back his amusement as I fold the twenties neatly and slide them into my top drawer, slamming it shut with a bang. And he just stares at me, and I hold it, until the silence quickly becomes uncomfortable and his gaze too intense. I look away, my skin suddenly burning. "Why are you looking at me like that?" I ask quietly.

"What, like I want to throttle you?"

Crack. His question triggers something inside me, and I close my eyes, withdrawing, feeling two big palms wrapped around my throat. I see myself in darkness struggling, fighting the strength, gasping for breath. I snap my eyes open on an uncontrolled exhale, reaching for my neck and feeling there, pushing back the flashback that's caught me by surprise. I haven't had one for years. Why now? My chest heaves. My skin becomes damp. I see his face, no matter how much I try to blink it away.

"Hannah?"

I step back, my gaze darting around wildly, trying desperately to remind myself of where I am. Who I am. "I'm sorry," I wheeze, shaking my head and the memories away. It takes too long for me to gather myself, but when I do, I paint on a lame smile and find Ryan. His head has retracted on his neck, his eyes searching mine. I can't face the questions in them, so I turn my attention onto Alex to escape. "Let me see when you're finished," I chirp, so over the top with enthusiasm.

"Are you okay?" she asks, my little meltdown not being missed by her, either. She lifts the canvas from the easel.

"Yeah." Hurrying over to the shelves, I snatch down some tubes of oil paint and a brush, tucking them in a paper bag. "Here."

Her face lights up, and though I'm relieved I've diverted her concern, I'm certain I haven't Ryan's. "Thanks." Claiming the bag, Alex looks to her father. I, however, do not, instead tidying the already tidy shelves. "Hey, can Hannah come and help us with the bridge. She can paint it."

I still. *What?* "I'm afraid—"

"I'm sure she's got better things to do," Ryan interrupts me, and I turn to look at him, unreasonably injured. It doesn't matter that I was going to make my excuses. But it does matter that Ryan has. And I don't know why. "Go put those things in the truck." He nods to his daughter's full arms without looking at her. "I'll be out in a minute."

Without question, Alex dances out of my store, leaving me at the mercy of her father's raging curiosity. "See you, Alex," I call as I make my way to the kitchenette out back. I just hear her reply over the sound of me placing a mug on the counter with a thud, and I look to the doorway, waiting for him to come find me.

I flick on the kettle, then fetch milk from the fridge and load my mug with a tea bag and a sugar, all the while getting more and more tense. Ryan's not left the store. So where is he? I look at the doorway again, getting myself worked up, knowing he's out there waiting for me. Waiting to ask if I'm okay. Or maybe waiting to ask what's wrong.

The sound of my fingers tapping the counter keeps me company until the boiling kettle drowns it out. And when it clicks off, I lift it, the damn thing shaking on its way to the mug. "God damn it," I mutter, feeling my emotions getting the better of me.

"Give it here." Ryan appears, taking the kettle from my hand, leaving my hands free to rub down my face. "What happened in there?"

"Nothing." I move away from him, his closeness making me uncomfortable all of a sudden. And I hate that notion. Because, really, Ryan has never made me feel uncomfortable. Only relaxed. And perhaps that's why I've been so tense, because of how easy it is to be with him. I'm not used to that.

"Come on, Hannah." The kettle hits the counter hard, and I startle, quickly chastising myself for it. "Look at you."

"I'm. Fine," I grate. I'm not angry with him, more at myself for letting something so stupid affect me, especially in front of Ryan. "I don't need interrogating." I find the strength I need to look at him. "Alex will be wondering where you've gotten to."

His chest heaves on a deep inhale, a sign of him fighting to retain his patience. "Have it your way." Moving toward the kitchen door, he rolls his shoulders as I watch him go.

"I will," I murmur, not intending for him to hear me. Though he does, and he stops in the doorway abruptly, slowly turning toward me. It's a standoff, him raking his eyes over every inch of my face, me doing the same to him. And I soften. Because I see worry, and that isn't something I'm used to seeing on a man. And I feel things, things that are odd but welcome. I feel drawn to him. His weathered face is harsh, but his persona soft. "You were leaving," I remind him, feeling the atmosphere shift, energy sizzling between us.

He steps forward. And I breathe in. "Where did you come from, Hannah?"

I shake my head, his question dulling the electricity, and I so don't want that. I want all the electricity and none of the questions. "Don't," I warn.

"Don't what?" Another step forward, and this time I step back. He stops, alert to my retreat. "Ask questions?" A forward step from him and a reverse step from me. My arse hits the counter, and I reach back to feel it, my head lifting as he gains on me until his chest is touching mine. He breathes down on me. "Or don't kiss you?"

I breathe in, and our chests press together as a result. Those questions in his stare have faded, and replacing them is...want. It only fuels my own unexpected hunger. The distance between our mouths closes, and I feel the heat of his breath spreading across my face, my body warming with it. I swallow. I flick my gaze to his lips and back to his eyes. Every part of me is preparing to be kissed, an exhilarating current sweeping through me.

"It's definitely not the last thing," he whispers, his lips meeting mine and resting there. Sparks erupt, just from that simple touch of our mouths, and this time I have no intention of pulling away.

"Dad!"

Ryan flies back on a curse, looking as disoriented as I feel. "Shit." Wiping his mouth with the back of his hand, he quickly composes himself before looking to the door when Alex appears. She glances between us a few times, quiet and definitely suspicious.

Oh God. I lunge for the kettle and pour, my shakes no better than before, but now for an entirely different reason. "What are you doing?" she asks, making me cringe.

Ryan finds his voice faster than I do. "I was just getting Hannah's bike."

"Her bike? Why?"

Yes, why? I turn around and cock my head, and Ryan looks away, avoiding me.

"It's broken." He goes to the back door and looks back at me for confirmation that he's heading the right way. I nod. "I figured since we were going to the garage to have my truck looked at, we could take it with us." Taking the handle, he starts pulling at the locked door. "Go wait for me in the truck."

Alex throws me a knowing look, and I throw her a shrug before she pivots and struts away.

"How d'you open this damn door?" Ryan snaps, swinging around violently. I withdraw, and he squeezes his eyes closed. "I'm sorry." His arm lifts toward the wood. "Where's the key?"

"You don't have to fix my bike," I say, but I reach into my pocket for the key anyway.

"I'd like to."

I don't put up a fight and instead move forward, unlocking the door for him as I feel his scrutinizing gaze on me. I move away, the tension unbearably thick. "Thank you," I say, feeling the craving in me fading under his lingering questioning stare. I can't help but resent myself for acting so irrationally over something so silly.

"No problem." Ryan goes outside and I keep myself busy around the kitchen finishing my tea, leaving him to it. As I'm putting the milk back in the fridge, something catches my eye across the room, and I frown as I close the fridge door. My phone? I wander over and collect it off the window ledge. It's been missing for days, and I didn't see it sitting there bold as brass?

"Where is it?" I hear Ryan call.

I shake away my wonder and collect my tea. "You can't miss it, Ryan. Against the fence." It's a twelve-foot-by-twelve-foot courtyard, so it's not like there's much space to search.

He appears at the door, his expression tired. "Hannah, your bike's not out here."

"What?" I frown and step forward, setting my mug of tea to the side as I pass. And when I reach the doorway, no bike. "I put it out here myself," I say to the empty space. "The night you nearly killed me."

He ignores my unintentional dig and edges past me. "You been out here since?"

I shake my head, lifting my hand and pointing. "I dumped it right there."

"You sure?"

I feel anger wrestling past my bewilderment. "Yes, I'm sure," I snap. "I'm not crazy, Ryan." I know what I did.

His hands come up, his face pacifying. "Hey, don't get upset."

"I'm not upset." I'm not sure what I am. Annoyed? Pissed off? Worried? I scan the walls of the courtyard, and then stomp over to the gate and check the bolt. All secure. "It can't have disappeared into thin air."

"Maybe one of the kids in town took it for a joyride," he suggests, and I sigh. It was mangled. Why would any kid want a broken bike?

I slowly turn and rest my back on the gate. "I really loved that bike."

"It looked pretty old to me."

"It was. I got it from a secondhand store in Grange. But it was . . ." I fade off.

"Old," Ryan says, and I roll my eyes.

"I liked it." I traipse back inside, swallowing hard when I brush past Ryan.

I reclaim my tea and stare at the wall as I sip it, my mind racing in circles, my body singing again with just that one minuscule brush of my body against his. "Thank you for the thought, though," I say, turning with a smile. But it falls when I find I'm alone.

CHAPTER SEVEN

RYAN

As I walk back to my truck, I can't help but think that there's something not right with Hannah, and with all the will in the world I can't help wondering what. She was fine, playful even, and then out of the blue she shut down. And shut me out. The latter bothers me more than it should. I look back over my shoulder to her store but make sure I keep my feet moving. *What's your story, Hannah Bright?*

"Don't know her, huh?" Alex says, her question tinged with too much sarcasm. I return my attention forward, finding her casually leaning against the side of my truck with one leg bent, the sole of a Van resting on the paint.

I make it to the door and pull it open. "I didn't say I didn't know her," I point out over the roof of my truck. "I said I didn't know the store."

"You lied," she accuses, and what do I do? I glare at her. It's the only defense I have. What does she care, anyway? "Why would you lie?"

"I didn't lie." I throw myself into my seat and start the engine. "Get in."

She's beside me a second later, scanning the cab. "Where's the shopping?"

I'm confused for a second, searching the cab with her. "Huh?"

"I left you in the store. So where's the shopping?"

"I abandoned it to look for you."

Throwing herself back in the seat dramatically, she kicks her Vans up onto the dash. "Can't leave you to do anything," she sighs. "Hannah must have you really distracted."

"What?" I ask.

"You fancy her."

I put my truck into reverse and pull out. "I do not fancy her." I don't fancy anyone.

"Whatever." She pulls a lollipop from the glove box, unwraps it, and has a few sucks. "Just saying, it makes a change."

"What does?"

"Well, everyone fancies you. You fancying someone is new."

What's all this talk of fancying? I take the turn at the end of the high street and follow the dirt track that leads up to Len's workshop. "Alex, I do not fancy Hannah. I do not fancy anyo—"

"Oh my God, if she fancies you, then you two are totally gonna make out."

I choke on nothing and swerve, hitting an enormous pothole. "Make out?" What is this language she's speaking?

"Yeah, you know." She grins at me and puckers her lips. "Mwah!"

Oh Lord, someone help me. "Enough," I snap, more harshly than I mean to. Though it does the trick. She shrinks into her seat and shuts up. Good. Peace. Enough of this crazy talk.

Does Hannah fancy me?

* * *

After having my truck looked at by the local mechanic, I'm told it needs respraying and the closest garage is in Grange, so I make a call and arrange to take it in on Saturday.

Watching Alex fly up the lawn onto the veranda fills me with a joy like no other. "Don't slam the—"

Bang!

"Door," I sigh, following on behind with my arms full of bags. I shoulder my way into the cabin and find Alex with her head in the freezer. She swings around, armed with our vice, and nudges the door closed with her thigh.

I dump the shopping on the counter and grab two spoons from the drawer. "Share," I demand. She comes over, hops onto the counter, and takes one of the spoons. We both dive in, and there's silence for a few moments as we get our fix. The quiet time has my mind wandering again to . . .

The sound of my phone saves me from the imminent straying thoughts, though I can't help being less than grateful. *Darcy.* I pluck the spoon out of Alex's hand and throw it in the sink with mine. "Go fetch some coal for the barbecue." I lift her down and send her on her way. I don't miss her quick glimpse of my phone screen before she leaves. "Darcy," I answer as soon as Alex is gone, replacing the lid on the Chunky Monkey and taking it back to the freezer.

"My brother is visiting. Mother and Father have arranged a special family supper to welcome him. I need Alexandra home by six tomorrow."

"I only just collected her, Darcy."

"You can have her back Wednesday."

I start to pace the cabin in an attempt to walk off my building aggravation. "No."

"She hasn't seen him in over six months. Her cousin will be here. Stop being selfish, Ryan. It isn't always about you."

This woman isn't for real. "It's never about me, Darcy. It's about Cabbage."

"Will you stop referring to my daughter as a vegetable."

"*Our* daughter. She's *our* daughter. Has always been *our* daughter, despite the fact that you tried to tell the world otherwise when she was born." I'm fucking seething, which is standard when dealing with

Darcy Hampton. "I'll stop calling her Cabbage when you tell that dick you married to stop telling her to call him Dad." My fist clenches, and I push it into the wooden paneling firmly. "He is not her father."

"He's a good influence," she hisses. "A provider."

A provider? Give me a break. I earn and I earn good, but I don't wipe my arse on fifty-pound notes, and that makes me a bad influence. Oh, and the cabin. Apparently that's a good enough reason to try to banish me from my daughter's life, too. "I've always provided for her, Darcy, and not just money."

"Casper is a stable man in her life."

"He's a toffee-nosed prick, that's what he is." The man is an uptight arsehole. How perfect they pretend to be, a happy little family. Casper taking over the horse-racing world and earning a mint, Darcy playing the doting, spoiled wife, and my daughter shipped off to boarding school to learn how to be a proper little lady while they live the high life. I am a thorn in their side. A defect in their flawless world. "And to be clear, Alex is my priority. She has been since I found out you'd lied to me about whose daughter she was."

I'll never forget that day—the day I won the right to a paternity test. Darcy's face said it all. I'd well and truly fucked up her plans to live happily ever after with *my* daughter and Casper Rochester. Alex had just turned one. Casper and Darcy had been married for over a year. He was in. No way out without losing face. I lost the first year of my daughter's life because of that scheming bitch, so forgive me for feeling bitter.

I hear Darcy breathe out her irritation. "Well, if she's your priority, then you should be happy to bring her home so she can see her uncle and cousin. I don't see what the problem is."

"The problem is, I haven't seen her for two months because she's been holed up in that school you ship her off to. This is my time, Darcy. It's precious."

She sighs, and for a moment I think I might be getting through to her reasonable side. But then, this is Darcy Hampton. She doesn't have a reasonable side. "I'm afraid I must insist."

The woman exhausts me. I slump where I stand, my back hitting the wall behind me, and I look up to see Alex standing at the door with a basket of coal in her arms. Her face is pensive, and I hate that she's just listened to me ranting down the phone at her mother. I pull my mobile down from my ear and push it into my chest. "Grandmother and Grandpa are hosting a dinner tomorrow evening for your uncle."

"Will my cousin be there?" she asks quietly. Nervously. Fucking hell, she wants to go. I've heard her talk about her cousin often. She's great fun, apparently. Who am I to stop her having fun without me? So pushing aside my need to keep her all to myself, I nod and give her a small smile to ease her guilt. And she smiles right back. I lift my phone to my ear. "I'll drop her off tomorrow." It irks me when Darcy responds with a satisfied sniff. She thinks she's won. Let her think it. This isn't about winning. It's about Alex.

I hang up and nod at the coal in her arms. "Your mother would have a hernia if she saw the state of you."

Looking down her front to the dollops of paint and the smears of black from the coal, Alex shrugs before returning her eyes to me. "Do you really hate each other that much?" she asks, and I fold with guilt.

"I don't hate your mother." *Lying to your daughter, Ryan. Shame on you.* "I love her because she gave me you." Eventually. After I'd fought tooth and nail in court to prove Alex was mine. I knew what it was like to grow up without a father around. Mine left Mum pregnant and without a penny. I'm the man I am today because of my mother, and making her proud has always been so important to me. Being a good dad would make her proud. I swallow and look to the heavens, mentally hearing her telling me to keep my cool. *Easier said than done, Mum.*

I push my back off the wall and head for the fridge. I need a beer. Standard after dealing with Darcy.

"Can I have one?" Alex asks.

"No." Cracking off the cap, I swig and make my way to Alex. "How about we go check out the bridge?"

"Sure." She steps outside and drops the basket of coal on the veranda, then slides her arm around my waist and hugs into my side as we make our way down the steps. "Love ya, Dad."

I smile and swing my arm over her shoulder. "Love you, too, stinky Cabbage."

She giggles and nudges me, and my smile widens.

* * *

"What are you gonna do?" Alex asks when we pull up the drive to the estate the next evening. I spot a gleaming Rolls-Royce under the canopied driveway and roll my eyes when the driver appears, polishing down the side of the passenger door.

"Cry," I quip, coming to a stop.

"Very funny." Unclipping her belt, she dives across the cab and lands a wet kiss on my cheek. "Be good."

"Yeah, yeah." I shove her away halfheartedly. "Clear off."

I look up when I hear someone squeal my daughter's name, seeing a young girl dancing out of the grand entrance. "Hazel!" Cabbage shrieks in my ear, making me flinch, before scrambling out of the truck. She flies across the driveway and into the arms of her cousin, and they proceed to dance around in circles together.

"Goodness gracious, look at the state of you." Darcy throws a glare my way and marches over to the truck, getting up close to make sure her words aren't heard by the girls. "She looks like a homeless stray."

"She looks like a kid who's had fun," I retort quietly. "There's more to life than appearances."

She looks me up and down on a curled lip. "Obviously."

"Oh, come on, Darcy," I coo, reaching out of my truck and cupping her check. She stills, and I know it's because she's remembering the last time I touched her. I bet amid this perfect life full of luxury there are a few things missing. "You hunted me down like a wolf eleven years ago." And she caught me. Okay, so I was under the influence of alcohol and my balls were blue after a particularly long drought, but I can't deny, she's a fine-looking woman on the outside. Even if she's ugly as sin on the inside.

Her eyes narrow, but she doesn't remove herself from my touch. "It was a mistake. I...I..."

"Loved every second," I finish for her confidently, because I'm right. She purred like a pussycat all night long. And then panicked in the morning because God forbid Lord and Lady Hampton found out that their precious daughter had bedded an animal like me. "Bet it's missionary all the way with Casper, right? Does he shower straight after?" I let a little gasp escape. "Does he make you shower before?"

"Fuck you, Ryan."

"That's really no way for a lady to speak, Darcy. What would Mummy and Daddy say if they heard such vulgar language coming from their precious daughter's mouth?"

Her pink lips straighten. "You're disgusting."

"And you, dear Darcy, need a good fucking to loosen you up. Good luck with that."

"Fuck y—"

"Mum?"

I quickly remove my hand from Darcy's face, giving her a cheeky wink, and she proceeds to try to compose herself. It's quite amusing. She's flustered. Still affected by me, even though I'm sure she fucking hates me. Good. The feeling's mutual. Damn my blue balls. But then Alex appears, looking rather concerned, and I retract my previous thought. I can't damn my blue balls. They're the reason I now have my Cabbage.

"Hey, precious," Darcy sings, her voice shaky. On a swallow and a flick of her eyes to mine, she turns toward our daughter. "I was just talking to Ryan."

"You mean Dad," Alex corrects, and I smile. "He's my dad, Mum."

"Yes, your dad." She may as well have spat it out.

"What about?"

"Oh, just this and that." Claiming Alex, she walks her up the gravel drive. "Let's get you cleaned up and ready for dinner." Looking over her shoulder, Darcy shoots me down with another glare, trying to win back some dignity. It's hilarious. I sound my horn and pull away.

So . . . what am I going to do with myself now? Once again I feel like my right arm is missing. I get to the end of the driveway and sit idle for a few minutes. I could turn left and go home. Tomorrow will come quicker if I hit the sack. Or I can turn right and head to the pub for a beer.

I indicate right and pull out.

CHAPTER EIGHT

HANNAH

Karaoke. What was I thinking? But when Molly showed up and asked me if I fancied a drink, I really did. Or needed one. She neglected to mention that tonight is karaoke night, one of the most popular nights at the pub. It's packed, and the noise is cutting as Hampton's finest take to the stage. Mrs. Hatt is currently hogging the mike, delivering her version of "What's New Pussycat." She actually sounds like a cat, too. One that's being strangled.

I cringe and take refuge in my wine. "She's been spending too much time with her pussies," I mumble around the rim of my glass. "Good Lord, kill me now."

Molly starts chuckling as she cracks open our second bottle. "Well, you know what they say."

"What do they say?"

"If you can't beat them—"

"Don't join them," I hold out my glass for her to top up. "There is not a chance in hell you'll get me on that stage." I inspect the makeshift platform that looks like something Bob threw together in an emergency. "And not only because I don't want to sing. That stage looks like it could collapse any second." Mrs. Hatt isn't helping, flinging her old body around it with gusto.

"Safe as houses," Molly says. "Has been for years." Turning toward me, she moves in closer so I can hear her speak at a normal volume over the painful sounds of Mrs. Hatt. Her eyes are dancing. "A little birdie told me that a certain local was in your store," she says.

Oh. Now, it should be easy to guess which certain local Molly is speaking of, since he is one of the only people in town who has ventured into my store, but I still find myself playing dumb. And who is this little birdie? I stare at Molly as she stares at me, waiting for my counter. I don't have one, or I'm not prepared to feed her curiosity, since there's nothing to be curious about.

"Oh, come on, Hannah."

I sigh and take more wine, feeling a lovely numb fuzz taking hold. "You must be talking about Ryan."

"No, no, no." Molly shakes her head and raises her finger, and my eyes fall to it, following it from side to side like a pendulum. "I'm talking about Ryan all-hot-and-outdoorsy-and-without-doubt-an-incredible-lay Willis."

"Oh, that's his full name? I did wonder." I roll my eyes and break out in laughter when Molly snorts and wine sprays from her nostrils. "Oh God," I choke, slamming my glass down to snatch a tissue from my pocket.

"Don't be all blasé with me," she says as she pats at her face. "What was he doing in there?"

"Collecting his daughter," I say casually. "She'd wandered in and we got sidetracked with some accidental painting." The frown that pops up onto Molly's head prompts me to go on. "Accidental painting. It's when—"

"Sod accidental painting. Tell me more."

"There's nothing to tell." No friction. No playful banter. No meltdown when the poor man said something quite innocent. "Really, nothing to tell," I reiterate when Molly gives me a dubious look. "Really."

"Fine."

"What's the deal with him, anyway?" God damn my motor mouth. I scowl to myself and sip.

"Ryan Willis." She sighs. "I think he was a spy or something."

"MI5," I say without thought. And scowl again, this time at Molly when she points high, interested eyebrows my way. I shrug.

"Nothing to tell," she muses. "Except you've clearly had a nice little get-to-know-you chat with him."

"It was brief," I say quietly, turning away from her as Mrs. Hatt takes a bow. I can feel my new friend's eyes drilling holes into me, and such a huge part of me wants to indulge her curiosity. Like girls do. Like I would have with Pippa. On that thought... "We had an...encounter."

Molly's instantly intrigued, moving closer still, even though the dulcet tones of Mrs. Hatt have ceased. "Hannah, please, put a woman out of her misery."

"It's your fault, anyway," I mumble, finishing off another glass and immediately topping it up.

"I take full responsibility. Now tell me how it's my fault."

Staring at my glass, I think for a few moments. And think. This is what my sister would have done. Prodded and prodded me until I gave in and fed her need for information. Maybe it's the drink, or maybe it's just the natural need of a woman wanting to share. After all, having a true girlfriend is alien to me. I should utilize the only one I have. Lucky Molly. Or maybe it's because I miss my sister and our never-ending chats and banter.

I face Molly and shuffle in closer. "I met him a few nights ago when he ran me off my bike on the lane that leads to his cabin."

"What were you doing on that lane? Wait, he ran you over?" Her eyes drop to my legs. "Is that how you got—"

"Yes. And I was on that road looking for your cottage to deliver the paint. Which ended up spilled all over me. That's why I was late delivering it. I had to make it all over again." Oh my God, it feels so good to talk. To share. To blurt all this out and feel the weight lifting from my shoulders.

"Shit," Molly says. "It really is all my fault. But, God, what a dick for running you over."

"He didn't mean to. And actually, he was very sorry." I take a deep breath and jump in feetfirst. "He almost kissed me."

"Oh my God!"

"I know."

"But *almost*?"

"I stopped it."

Her outrage is obvious, and probably warranted. "Seriously, why?"

That I can't share. "I don't know. I was caught off guard. Surprised. Anyway, that was that, and then his daughter came in the store. We talked a bit more, and we almost kissed again."

"Oh my God!"

"I know."

"But almost, *again*?"

"His daughter interrupted us."

"Oh, for fuck's sake."

I nod my agreement, and wonder for the first time if I would have bailed on him again had his daughter not gotten in first. I want to say no. I was adamant at the time that I wouldn't. I want to think I would have kissed the daylights out of him, would have been the best kiss he'd ever had. I also want to think it would have been the best kiss *I'd* ever had. One that would have wiped away all previous kisses. One that would have consumed me so much, there would be no room left for anything other than that feeling. "More wine?" I hold up the bottle on a lazy grin.

Molly presents her glass to me. "This is the juiciest gossip I've ever heard in Hampton. No, wait. Darcy Hampton and what she did to Ryan can't be beaten. Not by two *almost* kisses, anyway."

Oh? "What happened?"

"Now, that was a scandal like no other." Our faces are so close, we both have to pull back to take our drinks. "Long story short, Ryan had a drunken one-night stand with the daughter of Lord and Lady Hampton, he went his way and she went hers, she met some rich older man, found out she was pregnant, and told the world it was his."

I flinch. "Ouch."

"Yes, can you believe that? The witch was never going to tell Ryan he had a kid."

"So how did he find out?"

"He hadn't been in town for months. I think he was working overseas or something, I don't know. Anyway, he saw Darcy Hampton in the store." Molly blows her cheeks out. "Heavily pregnant. Did the math, I guess."

"Wow. Many men would've run a mile."

"Ryan's not like that. His mother was a wonderful human. She would have made sure he did the right thing, even if he didn't want to."

"His mother lives here?"

Molly's face drops, and I sit back, wary of her sadness. "She did live here. She died the day Ryan found out the baby was his after a yearlong court battle. A stroke."

"Oh my God, so she never got to meet Alex?"

Molly shakes her head. "It's so sad. He lost his mum the day he won his daughter."

My heart sinks for him. "That's terrible."

"I know. So you can understand why Ryan hates Darcy Hampton with a vengeance. First she deceived him, then she fought him over the paternity test, obviously because she knew what the result would be. And by doing that, Ryan lost out on the first year of his daughter's life. His mum would have been an amazing grandmother."

"What a bitch." I don't know the woman, but I hate her already.

"Yeah, but to be fair, she's bound by her parents. If Darcy doesn't play ball, she gets cut off by the lord and lady. She's too materialistic to say goodbye to that kind of money and status."

I scoff. What kind of human being is she? Who does that? I pause for thought. Why the hell am I asking myself such questions? I know what people are capable of. "Still a bitch," I murmur meekly. "No one should be kept away from their child." And no daughter should be kept away from her father. Jesus, I feel my nice hazy tipsiness being replaced with something far less appealing. Pain. No daughter should be kept from her mother, either. "More wine?" I ask, jumping up clumsily and smacking my knee on the table. "Shit!"

"Careful," Molly cries, hissing when she sees I've knocked my healing wound. More blood. Great. "Bob!" she yells. "We have an injury!" And the whole pub freezes and looks my way.

I smile, small and awkward, and start hobbling past the crowd to the ladies'. "Some tissue will be fine," I assure them all. "Back in a flick." I fall through the doors and blink back the sudden onset of wooziness. "Oh boy," I mumble, heading for the sink. I have to close one eye to focus on myself, and when I do, I look as drunk as I suddenly feel. A quiet drink, she said. "You're a bad influence, Molly." And I love her for it.

"It didn't look like you needed much arm twisting from where I was sitting."

I whirl around and make a sharp grab for the sink to steady myself. "You're in the ladies'," I shriek in shock. "Wait, from where you were sitting? Where were you sitting?"

"At the end of the bar." Ryan looks me up and down, a rather disapproving look on his face. "You chug down wine quicker than any woman I've known."

Well, maybe because it's a novelty to drink at my own pace, when I like, and without worrying I might get myself into trouble. "How many women have you known?" I say instead, startling at the sound of my own question. "I didn't mean to say that."

"No?" he asks, his head tilting. "Then what did you mean to say?"

I cringe all over the ladies' bathroom. "Got a bandage?"

He smiles that crooked smile and comes over. "Let me see."

"Still feeling guilty?" I ask lightly.

"Something like that." Without warning, he takes me under my armpits and lifts me onto the nearby old table where Bob has an expansive display of female cosmetics set out, as well as lollipops and chewing gum. I try so hard not to stiffen, but when a man like Ryan lifts you from your feet like you're nothing, I would challenge any woman not to come over a bit...tense. Without thought, I reach over and snag a piece of gum, popping it in and chewing. Ryan looks up at me. My chewing slows. And he smiles a very small smile as he slowly casts his eyes down to my knee. "You knocked the scab off."

"Damn it. I like picking scabs."

He looks up at me from his bent position. "You're gross, you know that?"

"I've been called worse." *Like whore. Tart. Bitch. An embarrassment. Useless. Stupid.* And I laugh, for what reason, I do not know. Maybe because now I can. Though my life is anything but funny. My *life* is a poor excuse for a life. But at least it's still a life. And at least I'm safe.

Aware that Ryan is studying me, I wriggle my way off the table, avoiding his gaze. He doesn't make it easy, not moving back to give me space. Which means a brush of contact between us that has us both inhaling audibly. "Tissue will be fine," I murmur.

"Tissue will stick to it."

I ignore him, even though I know he's right, and pull some off the roll in the nearest cubicle. Anything to put space between us. Things just get weird when he's around. My mind isn't my own. My thoughts are out of control. My body behaves as it pleases. Never once during the planning of my time in Hampton did I consider a man being part of it. Frankly, Mr. Ryan all-hot-and-outdoorsy-and-without-doubt-an-incredible-lay Willis has knocked me off balance. He should have left me to crawl home after he ran me down, not be all attentive and nice and concerned. It doesn't suit him. Or...is it me who doesn't suit that kind of devotion? Do I repel it because it's unfamiliar? Because I've forgotten what genuine caring feels like?

I huff to myself. Is it any wonder? I turn and walk smack bang into the door. "Oh!" My hands fly up automatically, and it's only when they come to rest that I realize it's not a door, but a chest. And then the heat hits me, and I virtually melt where I stand.

I don't jump back.

I don't stiffen.

I don't gasp.

Instead, I soften. Every part of me softens. I have no apprehension plaguing me whatsoever. I watch my fingers as they flex against his T-shirt, slowly exploring the feel of him. And he feels good. Strange but good. Unfamiliar but good.

Ryan remains silent and still except for the steady rise and fall of his chest. I stare at the collar of his T-shirt, studying the direction of the thread and the slight fade of the navy color at the edge. And then I'm examining the dense covering of scruffy but even stubble on his neck. Perfect stubble. A perfect neck. He swallows, prompting me to look up farther. His lips. Right now, they're straight and pressed tightly together, the scar on the top right corner faint.

"A few more inches and you'll be looking me in the eye," he whispers, his mouth moving slowly. Then his hands on my lower back shift a fraction, applying a light pressure that gently pushes me closer to him. "Do you think you can handle that, Hannah? Do you think you can deal with what you might read there? Or will you run again?"

I squeeze my eyes closed. "I won't run."

"Then look at me." He moves one hand to between us and settles the pad of his finger under my chin. But he does no more than that. He just places it there, and I lift my face of my own free will. It's as if he senses I need that. To take my time. To be in control.

I open my eyes, and the second I find his lazy gaze, I feel like I'm sucked into a vortex of craving. The rush of desire makes me dizzy, my body rolling with the most incredible feelings. "I'm not who you think I am." My mind's scrambled, words coming that I don't mean to say.

"I don't care who you are."

"Then kiss me."

I expect him to follow my order without hesitation. I can feel his want thrumming against me, yet he holds back, the weight of his scrutinizing stare becoming too much. I'm a heartbeat away from surrendering to the force trying to close the space between our mouths, but Ryan surrenders first, leisurely dropping his face, searching my eyes for... what?

The heat of his breath warms my face, my heart is beating a mile a minute, and my fingers claw into the material of his T-shirt and cling on.

So close.

I can almost taste him.

Nearly there.

And that first tiny brush of our lips hits me like a lightning bolt. I jerk in his arms, my hands flying up to his head as he tugs me into him.

Bang!

"Hannah, are you okay?" Molly's loud slur cuts through the atmosphere like a knife, and I shoot back into the stall in a daze as Ryan steps out, making his presence known to Molly. "Oh," she says abruptly. "Where's Hannah?"

He clears his throat and looks at me, and a few seconds later Molly's bumped him out of the way to find me.

"I was just helping clean up her knee," Ryan says, moving to the sink and grabbing a washcloth.

I know I look like I've seen a ghost, and I know it hasn't escaped

Molly's notice, though she appears more concerned than intrigued. *You okay?* she mouths, and I nod.

"I'll be out in a moment." I somehow walk out of the stall steadily, despite being a hot mess—trembling, struggling for breath.

"Take your time," Molly replies coyly, and I dip to inspect my knee to avoid the increasing questions in her eyes. I stay there until I hear the door close behind her.

I feel the atmosphere thicken the second we're alone again. "I'm so clumsy," I blather to fill the difficult silence. "I can sort it myself. I don't want to keep you."

Ryan's kneeling in front of me a second later, dabbing around my wound with the cloth. "You're not keeping me from anything." He sounds sharp now, almost pissed off, and the wretched quiet descends once more.

It's uncomfortable, and I'm suddenly itching to remove myself from the awkward vibes bouncing around the small space. "I can do it—"

"What did you mean when you said you're not who I think you are?" He looks up at me, and I stiffen from top to toe, immobilized by the raging wonder looking back at me. How could I have been so stupid? To give him a scrap of a clue like that and not expect him to press me? Or maybe I wanted him to press me in that moment, when my mind wasn't my own. Maybe a desperation I didn't know I had was unearthed by his tenderness. Maybe I wanted to spill all my secrets to him and let him wrap me up and tell me he'll keep me safe. How stupid of me.

I need to avoid him in the future. Ignore the pull, because it'll only get me in too deep. I must have lost my mind. I'll be moving on from Hampton soon. I'm already getting attached to the quaint little town. Best not get attached to its residents as well.

I look away and skirt past him, leaving him kneeling behind me. I wash my hands, dry them, and make my escape, just catching him in the mirror as I turn. He's slowly rising from his knees. Still watching me. I hate to think what he is thinking. I need to get away.

I tug the door open, but his hand appears over my shoulder, quickly slamming it shut again. I stare at the wood. "Let me go," I order, my voice shaking terribly.

Ryan removes his hold in an instant, and I rush out, hearing him curse as I go. Molly is looking for me when I round the corner into the bar, and I brace myself for the interrogation I'm about to be hit with. I don't know what I'm going to say, so I lose myself in my wine, stalling. I shouldn't have shared anything with her. I should have kept my stupid mouth shut. Because now I'm seeing sense, and getting involved with a man is completely impossible. It would also be selfish. And irresponsible. And cruel. I look at Molly. My new friend. I shouldn't get attached to her, either. My new, safe life away from London doesn't seem so freeing in this moment. It suddenly feels very lonely. I can't get attached to anyone. I can't ever share my secrets and my woes with anyone. All I can do is pretend to be Hannah Bright.

"Are you really just going to sit there and say nothing?" Molly finally says.

My mind is a tangled mess, but before I can unravel my thoughts, something catches my attention out the corner of my eye, and I glance past her to see Ryan walking through the pub. He doesn't look this way, and I don't know why that bothers me. I peer down into my wineglass. The still, calm liquid is a stark contrast with the swirling, chaotic feelings inside me. "There's something odd that pulls me toward him, and I can't stop it." I peek out the corner of my eye and find Molly rapt. "But I kind of *want* to stop it." I *must* stop it.

"Why?"

I've said too much. I can't very well tell Molly that I don't plan on staying in town forever. That this is just a temporary home for me until I have to leave. "I came here to get away." A lie. I came here to get closer to someone. My mum.

"After your breakup?" Molly lays her hand over mine.

I nod and drink to drown my guilt. "It's too soon for me to move on from that. I have a lot more work to do on myself first." I smile, though I know it's sad, and Molly mirrors it. That wasn't a lie at all. "I can't depend on someone else to fix me." The wobble in my voice isn't avoidable, and I really hate not being able to talk about my history, albeit vaguely, without emotion controlling my words. I shouldn't be so hard on myself, yet I can't help feeling resentful that I'm still held prisoner by my past. Because it's just hit me hard that the mental scars will prevent me from ever being happy and relaxed in a relationship with a good man. I'm ruined. It's ironic, really. I'm free, but far from it.

"Time is an amazing healer." Molly takes my hand and pushes my glass to my lips. "And so is wine. Drink."

I laugh—it's genuine—and it's just what's needed in this moment in time. And once again I think of my sister. She was an expert at distracting me from anything that ever made me glum, not that there was much to make me glum back then. And when there was something—many things—to make me sad, Pippa wasn't there. Because I left her behind.

"To new beginnings and new friendships." Molly toasts us and immediately tops us up once we've both finished our drinks. "Right. Up you get."

My eyes rise with Molly, my face blank. "What?"

"We are going to show this pub how it's done." She grabs my spare hand and wrestles against my instant resistance.

"Oh no." I laugh, glancing around the bar where dozens of people are drinking and chatting. They look like they're having a great time. Best not ruin it. "Molly, I can't sing for shit."

"Neither can I." She winks. "Support your sista, sister."

Sister. I blink, seeing Pippa's face. Her smile. Her tears from laughing at me. I so wish I could make her laugh again.

Molly stops struggling with me and starts walking back toward the makeshift stage. "What would the old Hannah do?" she asks, and I frown around my smile. That's easy. The old Hannah would never have been in a place that hosted karaoke in the first place—oh no. But what about the Hannah before the old Hannah? The old-old Hannah? The girl who whiled her days away painting and laughing. The girl who was so messy, Mum gave up on tidying up after her. The girl who would have danced up onto that stage with her sister and showed the world just how creative she was. *What would the old-old Hannah do?*

I grab the bottle of wine and take it with me, having a swig from the bottle before planting it on a nearby speaker. I join Molly on the stage and take a mike from her hand. "Let's do this." I clear my throat and flex my neck. Old-old Hannah would own this moment. And then the intro begins and I throw a stunned glare Molly's way. She just shrugs.

And the first words to Destiny's Child's "Survivor" spring up onto the screen in front of me. All attention is pointed this way.

"Fuck it," I say, grabbing the bottle and chugging down more wine. And I sing. Molly sings. We sing like our lives depend on it, and I'm guessing it's a damn good job they don't. But I keep telling myself that nothing could top the ear-piercing shrieks of Mrs. Hatt and her appalling rendition of "What's New Pussycat." The closest I've come to expressing myself creatively since I arrived in town is in my painting. Quietly but messily. And privately. There's nothing private about this.

Hi, Hampton. I'm Hannah Bright. I'm about to make your ears bleed, and I don't give a flying fuck. Cheers.

As Molly and I inject some zest into our performance, practically the whole town is watching. But in this moment, now I'm in my stride, I'm oblivious to them all, my energy and focus set solely on the words I'm yelling at the screen with Molly and the odd twirl in between our lines.

We. Are. On. Fire.

At least, in our warped imaginations we are. I'm not sure the rest of the town thinks so—those who are here and those who aren't, because I'm sure as hell everyone who stayed home tonight can hear us, too. I turn my attention to Molly and sing at her, bending at the waist as she laughs. And then her movements slow, and I find her face morphs into Pippa's, and I'm thrown back fifteen years to the time she visited me at the university and we spent the night downing shots and hogging the karaoke in the local bar. We danced on that stage. She was Elton John, I was Kiki Dee. She was Gary Barlow, I was Lulu. She was Michael Jackson, I was Janet. We cleared the bar. We laughed until our bellies hurt. We wobbled home together, holding each other up. Neither of us could talk the next day. But we could still laugh, even with our killer hangovers, when we both woke up in my single bed with the microphones still in our grasps. Pippa mailed them back to the bar. I never went there again.

Soon after, I graduated. Then soon after that, I moved to London. And soon after that, it was the beginning of the end of my life.

I blink and find Molly, realizing I'm still singing as she holds my hand, facing me.

And then the applause begins, and I laugh. I place the mike down and throw my arms around my friend, silently thanking her for talking me into doing this. Yes, it brought back memories, but they're happy memories. And they're one of the only things I have left. "I needed that," I say, pulling away.

"Me too, but I don't think the rest of the town did."

I giggle as I carefully follow Molly to the edge of the stage, my gaze naturally following the line of the bar to the end. Ryan's there, but unlike everyone else in the pub, he's still seated and he's not smiling. But he is looking at me, and I sense annoyance. Or is it disapproval?

He doesn't like that I've made a show of myself. Well, I guess that's probably best. Screw him. This is who I am.

"That was epic!" Molly falls to her seat and wipes her brow, and I join her, slightly out of breath.

"I don't know about epic." I reach up to clench my head. I need to go before I pass the point of tipsiness and fall into the realms of full-on drunkenness. Pushing my hands into the table, I get myself up. "All that singing has gone to my head." Along with the alcohol, and it's mixing with my emotions.

Ryan looked at me in disapproval. No one has that right. I'm a second away from marching over there and telling him where to stick his disapproval.

"I'm going to stay and have one more with Mrs. Hatt," Molly says. "We'll wobble home together."

"Don't walk on your own."

"I won't," Molly singsongs, linking my arm with hers. "I'll walk you across the road."

"You can literally see my front door from the window. Just watch me." I unlink us and point, and Molly takes up position on an agreeable nod. I make my way through the pub saying my goodbyes and eventually make it outside into the fresh air. There's a chill, and I fold my arms tightly across my chest as I hurry across the road.

I slip my key into the lock, then pause before turning it, looking over my shoulder to the window of the pub. I see Molly there, watching me, and she waves before disappearing from view.

"Hannah?"

I startle on a fast inhale but quickly see Ryan by his truck across the street. "Jesus, Ryan, you scared me."

"I never want you to be scared of me."

I straighten my lips as he hovers by the driver's door, pulling his keys from his jean pocket. "I'm not," I retort softly, turning back to my door and turning the key. "Good night."

"Good night, Hannah," he says quietly, and a few seconds later I hear his truck door open and close. I push my way into my store, looking across the road.

But Ryan's not in his truck. He's pacing toward me with purpose, and the streetlights illuminate his face, his expression as determined as his stride. I hold my breath, waiting ... for what?

I step back as he gets closer, my focus glued to him. His pace doesn't falter, and he enters the store, leaving the door open behind him. He grabs me with a gentle but possessive force, one hand on my nape, the other on my hip. And he looks me straight in the eye, breathes deeply.

Then he drops his mouth to mine and gives me the tenderest of kisses. No tongue. No moans. No movement anywhere, except for his lips gently traveling across mine. My useless hands remain by my sides. I forget my name, who I am. The world as I know it ceases to exist, and it is so welcomed. So...unlike anything I've ever experienced. It's the smallest of gestures, yet it's also colossal. Does Ryan know that? Does he realize what he's doing? He's making no attempt to deepen the kiss; his hands aren't moving or exploring. He's just dotting my lips with his, over and over, lazily and softly. It's dizzying. And despite his apparent lack of desire to push it to the next level, there is passion pouring from him, the air surrounding us electric.

My mind blanks and I remain still in his hold, my eyes closed, my senses hijacked, as I savor the light pressure moving across my mouth. I can only ever remember my heart racing with fear and apprehension, yet since I've met Ryan it's pounded with life and anticipation. Every near kiss we've had. Every moment of silence when we're looking into each other's eyes and the sexual tension between us ramps up another level.

Every time we're in physical contact.

Every reason to avoid him is suddenly negated by my hunger for him. And then he breaks our kiss, breathing shallowly, as he keeps me in his hold. I stare at him, lost for words, and he drops one final, lingering peck on the corner of my mouth before he moves back. I quickly feel so very lost. His fingertip draws a delicate line down the bridge of my nose, slowing when he passes over the small bump. Then he turns on an inhale and leaves, pulling the door closed behind him.

And I stare forward at nothing for a long time. I've been kissed into a trance. I move across my store to sit in the wicker chair in the corner, the pads of my fingers resting on my lips as I stare at the door. I hear his truck start. I hear it pull away. And then...silence.

He just kissed me, and then he just left. Seriously, what the fucking hell?

He said nothing.

But everything I needed to hear.

And now I'm left alone with just my screaming thoughts. Stay away from him. Run to him. I know what I want to do, but should I? Can I? I stand up and start to pace my shop, wringing my hands. I stop, feeling my lips, and then my nose. I look at the door. I hear his words.

I don't ever want to scare you. I'm not scared of him, not like that. I'm scared because he leaves me completely breathless.

CHAPTER NINE

FIVE YEARS AGO

Katrina could hear him showering in the adjoining bathroom from where she was curled up on the bed. She knew he'd be finished soon. She knew he'd return any moment, wondering why she wasn't up. And she knew he'd be disappointed. Yet her energy was depleted completely after their day traveling to the Bahamas, where their yacht was anchored offshore. She felt sick, and she was certain the seafood they'd eaten for lunch was responsible. With every slight move she made, her tummy twisted, threatening to spill the contents far and wide. She was sweating, too. Bottom line, she felt like death warmed up.

When the sound of the shower spray stopped, she tried in vain to push herself up on the bed, to at least show *some* willingness to get herself ready for their sunset dinner on deck with friends. But after a few seconds struggling against her uncooperative body, she gave up and flopped back to the mattress on a groan.

"Why aren't you ready?"

Katrina looked up to the bathroom door where her husband stood, rubbing at his wet black hair with a towel. His well-honed body seemed to shimmer under the moody lighting of the bedroom on their yacht. "I feel terrible." Her words were meek, quiet, and loaded with a plea that she knew he could hear.

Jarrad pouted in sympathy and wandered over to the bed, lowering to the edge and reaching for his wife's forehead. One brush of his palm across her damp flesh confirmed that her body was a furnace. "Oh, darling," he murmured, reaching for the bottle of Evian on the bedside table. "Some water will help." Unscrewing the cap, he handed it to her. "Here, drink up."

Forcing herself to sit up with his help, she accepted the bottle with a small smile and brought it to her lips. And the second she swallowed just the tiniest drop, her stomach revolted, and she flew up off the bed, darting to the bathroom. She made it just in time to throw up, emptying her stomach of all the seafood she'd indulged in. "Oh God," she breathed, feeling blindly for some toilet paper as she dropped to her arse in front of the toilet.

"Katrina, darling," Jarrad whispered with concern as he crouched beside her and rubbed at her back. "Get it all up."

"I think I need a doctor." Drops of sweat poured from her forehead as Jarrad took her arm and pulled her to her feet. He walked her to the mirror and stood behind her, studying her in the reflection as he flipped the tap on and wetted a washcloth. "You don't need a doctor." Patting her face with the cool material, he held her firmly in place as he watched himself tend to her. "You just need me." Dropping a gentle kiss on her shoulder, he smiled across her flesh as he raised his eyes to her in the mirror.

Her lips curved naturally in response. "Just you, Jarrad."

This pleased him. His mouth stretched wider, his happiness genuine. She knew how happy she made her husband. "Feel better?"

"Much, thank you." She rested her palm on his forearm where it was wrapped around her stomach. "I should get ready. I don't want to keep our guests waiting." The show must go on, no matter how sick she felt, and she felt as sick as a damn dog. But it was all about image. They were the perfect couple.

Jarrad grinned and reached for the hairbrush on the vanity unit, taking it to Katrina's hair and brushing meticulously through her long, dark waves. She let him do his thing in peace for a few minutes, the silence comfortable. He only stopped when her scalp started to numb with the constant strokes. "Perfect," he murmured, setting the brush down. "I don't know why you wanted to cut it all off."

It didn't matter what she wanted. She rarely got what she wanted, but she'd long ago learned that if her husband was happy, then so was she. "I'll be twenty minutes," she said quietly.

"Good girl." Reaching for her hand, he lifted her arm to his mouth and kissed the fading bruise just past her elbow. She could see the despair in his eyes, as well as the anger. She'd been reckless with her well-being, and he still wasn't happy about it. "I wish you'd stop being so damn clumsy, Katrina. You know how it upsets me. I hate seeing you injured like this."

She dropped her eyes, ashamed. "I know. It was impulsive and stupid, I'm sorry." She certainly wouldn't be pulling a stunt like that again. What was she thinking?

Jarrad gripped her jaw gently but firmly and directed her face up again so she faced him in the mirror. "You know how precious you are to me," he said softly, and she nodded, prompting a smile from him before his eyes dropped to her wrist again. He frowned. "Where's your watch?"

His question had her feeling at her wrist. The diamond-encrusted platinum piece he'd bought her for their fifth wedding anniversary hadn't been on her wrist since they'd left their home in Belgrade. She panicked. "I think I left it at home." She bit her lip nervously. "On the vanity unit in the en suite."

"You think?"

"I'm certain." She corrected herself quickly.

"We should call the housekeeper and have her check." He made to turn toward the bedroom to get his phone, and Katrina was quick to stop him. Jarrad stilled, and she smiled, small and apologetically. "I'm sure it's there. Let's not keep our guests waiting, darling."

Jarrad relented easily, his wife's soft smile melting him as it always did. "You're right," he murmured, taking her in a hug. "It would be rude, forgive me."

"Nothing to forgive."

"Ever so thoughtful." Resting his lips in her hair, he breathed her in on a contented sigh. "You should wear long sleeves tonight," he said, stroking down her arm. "It's chilly. And black, yes?" Turning her back toward the mirror without waiting for her confirmation, Jarrad left Katrina to get ready for their sunset dinner.

CHAPTER TEN

RYAN

I drive slowly up the high street away from her store, completely lost in my thoughts. Unusually of late, though, my mind isn't swirling with questions about Hannah, it's spinning with questions I'm asking *myself.* Why did I do that? And how the hell did I keep myself from taking it further? I never knew I had it in me. Maybe it was because I know she's had a lot to drink tonight. I hate the thought of her waking up feeling regretful or thinking I took advantage. Or maybe it's because I've sensed she needs handling with care. Or maybe it's a bit of both.

"Fucking hell," I breathe, shifting in my seat, my head beginning to ache from the weight of my questions. "What have you gotten yourself into, Ryan?" I indicate right when I approach the road that leads to my cabin. "And now you're talking to yourself." Laughing under my breath, I take the turn, but something by the roadside catches my eye, and I pull to a stop. "What the hell?"

I leave the engine running and hop out, pacing a few yards into the overgrowth that's lit by my headlights. I stare down at the wheel of a bike. A bike I recognize. On a frown, I pull the mangled thing from the bushes and look it over, before scanning the darkness around me. These woods are familiar to me. The sounds, the trees, every species of animal that lives here. The owl currently calling and the bats currently flapping through the air above me never usually cost me a thought. Yet tonight, they cause an odd lick of uneasiness to work its way down my spine.

Picking up Hannah's bike by the crossbar, I back away, instinctively scanning the darkness as I head to my truck and load the bike in the back. When I slam the tailgate shut, the noise echoes, bouncing off the trees around me. "Kids," I say, getting back in my truck and continuing on my way to the cabin, my eyes watchful the rest of the way.

When I pull up outside, the detector lights spring on, basking my place in bright light. I jump out and put Hannah's bike by the shed before making my way inside. The emptiness that hits me is palpable. No Cabbage.

I grab a beer from the fridge, kick off my boots, and flick on the lamp before I light the open fire and slump down in the armchair. My bottle rests on the chair's arm, and I study the flames dancing before me. A woman has never had me in such a tangle. I want her. I can't explain it, but it's troubling, because I have a horrible feeling that Hannah isn't available. Not just to me, but to any man. Though I would bet my life on the fact that no man wants her more than I do.

I groan to myself and slurp my beer, uncomfortable with my train of thought. I've never met a woman so fascinating. She's determined, but that resolve is edged with a vulnerability that makes her even more attractive. She's kind. Sweet. Funny in her own witty little way. "Jesus." I rub at my forehead with the tips of my fingers and rest my head back. I'm fucking exhausted.

My eyes become heavy.

The flames of the fire start to blur and blend together.

My tired brain begins to shut down.

I doze off with visions of Hannah Bright filling my mind. She's dancing close to the fire. She's dancing with danger.

* * *

I'm jerked from sleep by a cold, wet sensation on my chest and the smell of beer. *Shit.* I jump up from the chair, sending the now-empty bottle crashing to the wooden floor, and pull my soaked T-shirt away from my chest. The sound of rain pelting the windows soon registers in my drowsiness.

Yawning, I scoop up the bottle and set it on the hearth, then pull off my wet T-shirt and toss it in the wash basket as I head to my bedroom. But I don't make it to my glorious bed. A noise outside stops me on the threshold, and I look toward the front door as I take a few backward steps, my movements cautious, my muscles now *very* awake and *very* tense.

My focus is trained on the front door as I walk on light feet down the corridor back into the open space of my cabin. It's way too late for visitors, not that I get many.

I blindly feel for the axe tucked by the side of the freezer and take a firm grasp of the handle. My pace falters when I hear something again. Something loud enough to be heard over the storm. What the fuck is that?

Edging toward the window, I pull back the curtain a fraction and scan outside. Sheets of rain hamper my ability to see past the veranda, the trees swaying violently under the force of the howling wind whipping through the branches. Lightning zigzags through the sky, making the edges of the black clouds glow. "God damn you, Mother Nature," I say quietly as a wicked crack of thunder pierces the air. Someone could have turned on a megawatt lightbulb, as everything outside is suddenly basked in a blinding light.

It's then I see her, surrounded by empty gas canisters that she's knocked over near the barbecue. "Hannah?" I drop the axe and rush to the front door, yanking it open and running out onto the veranda. Wearing only what she had on at the pub—a flimsy little red dress— she jogs across the lawn toward me, drenched through, her hair heavy and stuck to her face, the fabric of her dress sticking to her body.

When she reaches the foot of the steps to the veranda, she looks up and sees me and comes to an abrupt halt, still exposed to the elements. The rain continues to attack her, not that she looks aware of it. Her unbelievably big blue eyes widen, as if she's surprised to see me. Something tells me to keep back, so I hover at the top of the steps looking at her being beaten by the downpour.

She eventually drags the back of her hand across her face, roughly wiping away the wet, for what it's worth. "Why did you kiss me?" she calls over the deafening storm.

Her question has me automatically taking the first step down to her, though her hand quickly shooting up warns me to stop. So I do, because it feels only natural to obey. I see her swallow when she registers I'm listening to her, and she follows that up with a small nod to herself. "Come inside, Hannah," I plead. "You're soaked."

"Tell me why, Ryan," she calls, ignoring me. She's going to catch a death, for God's sake. Not to mention myself. I'm standing here in my jeans, nothing on my chest, my feet bare.

"I . . ." I fade off when something comes to me. "Wait, how did you get here?"

"I walked. Now tell me."

She walked? In the dark and rain? The knowledge irks me no end, my urge to scold her overwhelming. Too overwhelming to hold back. "That pisses me off, Hannah."

She smiles. She fucking smiles. It's beyond me why, and I find myself laughing in disbelief. "Tell me why you kissed me," she shouts.

I stare at her, my smile unsure. Where's she going with this? And actually, why did I kiss her? It's a silly question with a simple answer. Because I couldn't stop myself. Because I want her.

"The constant near misses were getting ridiculous," I call back. "The interruptions for one reason or another." I pause for a beat, studying her gorgeously bedraggled form. "And," I go on, this time not as loud, "more important," I take one more step down toward her, knowing she won't stop me this time. "I wanted you to see how good it felt."

The weight of the rain on her lashes makes her blink of surprise slow. "How'd you know it would be good?" she whispers.

I smile. "There aren't many things in life I'm certain of. I'm certain I love my daughter with everything I have. I'm certain I'll live my life, and I'm certain I'll eventually die. And after I met you, Hannah, I was certain you'd turn my world upside down when I kissed you." One more step. "And you did." Her gaze follows me down the remaining steps until I'm before her, now being drenched by the rain, too. "And now I'm certain I want to kiss you again." One last step, and we're on even ground.

"I'm certain I want you to." She walks into me, her head tilted back in invitation. Then she places her hands on my bare, wet chest. "And I'm certain it'll be as incredible as our first."

My head dips, catching her lips, unwilling and unable to delay myself. I taste rain. I taste acceptance. I taste *Hannah*. It's mind bending, and like nothing I've experienced in my thirty-nine years. I hold my mouth still on hers but slowly slide my hands onto her lower back and pull her closer. And then she tilts her head a fraction, her lips parting, and I groan quietly, following her lead. The second our tongues touch, my upside-down world starts to spin, the rain pelting down on us, the thunder rumbling, and the lightning cracking, all drowned out by the sweet feeling of acquiescence.

My God. By a million miles, this is unquestionably the most consumed I have ever felt. There's no motive behind my kiss. I have no urge to rip her clothes off. My only wish in this moment, when I'm being swallowed whole by this sweet, unexpected woman, is to make sure she feels comfortable in my arms. And she does. All my senses are screaming at me that she does.

The loudest rumble of thunder shakes the ground beneath our feet, but Hannah doesn't react, too lost in me, and that's beyond satisfying. It surpasses bliss.

Through my utter drunkenness on her, I manage to convince my legs to move and get us inside. But I don't stop kissing her. Nothing would make me stop kissing her, and if her firm hold of my head is a measure, she doesn't want me to. Our lips continue to slip, and our tongues continue to softly tussle as I move my hold and lift her, opening my eyes to find the first step and take them without any hurry. I'm quickly lost in the vision of her so clearly lost herself.

I kick the door closed behind us and set her gently down. Her eyes remain closed. Her mouth stays sealed against mine. She's soaked to the bone, and now that we're in the warmth, I can feel how cold she is. She'll get ill.

It's without doubt one of the hardest things I have ever had to do, but I break our kiss, and her eyes flip open. She smiles a smile that can only be defined as serene as she looks down at her hands that are back on my chest.

"You're cold," I say quietly. "Let me get you something dry and warm." Reluctantly, she surrenders her hold. I immediately miss it. "The fire's still warm." I turn her by her shoulders and walk her over. "You want a hot chocolate or something?" I have never in my life offered a woman a hot chocolate. My hospitality has only ever stretched to a beer, a screw, and an offer of a ride home in the morning. I'm not an arsehole, but I'm certainly no gentleman. Women have only ever been a form of company on lonely nights away from home to kill time until I can pick up my life with Alex.

"I'm good, thanks." Hannah gingerly lowers to the chair by the fire, her hands going straight between her knees. She looks small and awkward all of a sudden, and she's peering around my cabin, chewing her lip. I don't like it. I shouldn't have stopped our kiss. Is she wondering why she came? Does she like my home?

I turn and stride to my bedroom before the questions fall out of my mouth. I grab a towel and rub it over my chest, then tug off my jeans and boxers, replacing them with some gray sweats. I fetch a fresh towel for Hannah and stare at the contents of my wardrobe. What can I give her to wear? On a shrug, I snatch down one of my button-front shirts for work because isn't a white shirt what every woman wants to prance around a man's place in?

When I make it back to her, she's moved from the chair and is sitting on the rug by the fire, her hands held out in front of her to warm. I can see the goose bumps on her skin from here. "I got you something dry to change into."

She looks over her bare shoulder to the shirt in my hand, and I immediately see something in her expression change before she quickly corrects it. What was that? "I'm fine in this."

Is she for real? My arm drops to my side. "Hannah, you're freezing and wet."

"No, honestly, I'm fine."

I don't like the thought of being firm with her, but I can't let this slide. If she doesn't want to wear the white shirt, that's fine, and I don't care why, but she's not staying in that saturated dress. "You'll catch a chill." I move across to the couch and pull a throw off the back. "How about this?"

She nods, agreeing to the blanket easily, no fuss at all, and now I suddenly do care why the shirt is such a problem. Then it dawns on me. Does she think other women have worn it? Shit, have they? I look down at the shirt in my hand and cringe. Yes, they have.

"Thanks," she says as she unfolds herself from the floor and comes to me. Her smile is perturbed, and I don't like it at all. A few minutes ago, we were completely at ease. Now it's difficult. Horrible.

She reaches for the blanket, but she doesn't take it, just holds it, and I don't release it. She looks up at me, her teeth sinking into her bottom lip. And the atmosphere shifts again.

I understand her unspoken demand.

I drop the shirt and release my hold on the blanket, then take my hands to the hem of her dress and pull it up her thighs and over her waist. The blanket falls to the floor, her arms lifting, her eyes never straying from mine. I don't look down. I don't surrender to the part of me that's desperate to take in the rest of her. Because there's a bigger part of me that's content with my current view of her face. And then she's only in her underwear, and the tides change. I have to squeeze my eyes shut to stop them from straying, and for the first time I acknowledge the demand pounding behind my sweatpants. The blood flowing there is fierce. Hot. I try to shake off my wandering thoughts, try to tamp down my growing need. My jaw tenses along with my muscles, and I dip, blindly feeling the floor for the blanket. Cover her. Just cover her up. I find the throw and rise. And stupidly open my eyes before I'm back to standing, coming face-to-face with her tummy. I freeze. Get hotter. The need in me intensifies.

No.

I blink away my temptation and stand, taking the blanket over her shoulders and wrapping her up. But as soon as I step back, she rolls her shoulders and it falls back to the floor, my eyes following it down. And while I stare at the pile of fabric, something else lands on top of it. My stomach flips. Her bra. God help me. I breathe in, just as her leg flicks out and her knickers join the heap. "Hannah," I warn on a swallow, daring to look at her.

"Don't you want me?" she asks timidly, definite uncertainty threaded through her words.

Her question is ridiculous, but it also prompts me to take in every piece of her body for the first time. Shapely legs, a seamless, smooth curve from her hip to the small of her waist. Boobs the perfect size. Flawless skin, elegant collarbones. A long, slender neck. Do I want her? Jesus, I've never wanted anything more.

A rush of blood zooms south, and a low, broken moan vibrates at the back of my throat. For a second, I wonder why I'm punishing myself, why I'm fighting this, why I'm reluctant to take what Hannah's making clear she's willing to give. The revelation is daunting: I don't want sex with her to be like all the other women I've slept with. Rushed. Meaningless. I need Hannah to know how much I want her, beyond the physical signs my body is radiating. My sole purpose isn't to get her off and then myself. I actually just want to be as close to her as I can. Not just physically, either. *Fucking hell.*

But what will happen after, because I'm sure as shit this woman doesn't sleep with just anyone? What will she expect from me? A future? A relationship? Of course she will. Am I capable? It's always just been me and Alex. My priority since my daughter was born was to be a father. To bring her up as best I can. Women have only ever been a pastime. A bit of fun.

Alex's words from the other day stampede through my mind: *You need someone to love other than me.*

Could Hannah be that someone? My game changer? And what would Alex *really* say? Does she appreciate the meaning of another woman in my life? She's used to having me to herself.

Pain sears my head, and I reach up to push the ball of my hand into my temple.

How did this happen?

Hannah quickly crouches and collects the blanket, throwing it around herself. She says nothing and makes a mad dash for the door, slamming it behind her, leaving me a little lost and confused by the fire. My mind takes too long to catch up. My muscles take too long to engage. What just happened?

"Hannah." I run after her, nearly taking the door off its hinges when I haul it open. "Hannah!" I dart down the steps and across the lawn, wondering how the fuck she got so far away in the few seconds I was a zombie. She's made it to the lane already, the blanket billowing behind her. Rain is still hammering down, the storm still raging. "Hannah, for fuck's sake!" I yell over the wind and rain. "Hannah, will you stop running?" I'm sure she actually speeds up. "Jesus Christ," I pant, blowing out of my fucking arse as I build up to a sprint. I gain on her quickly, and the moment she's in reach I grab her arm, desperation getting the better of me. "Hannah, please."

She jolts to a stop, heaving from her exertion. "Let go of me, Ryan."

Something in the tone of her voice refuses to let me ignore her, so I release her, giving her space. "Where are you going?"

"Home."

"No, you're not. It's dark, it's raining. Come back inside." I motion back to the cabin. "You're all wet again." I look down the drenched blanket to her bare feet. This is ridiculous. "God damn it, Hannah, I should just pick you up and carry you inside."

Her perfect jawline pulses. She's angry. Frustrated. *Good.* Me fucking too.

"Why did you do that?" she asks, tugging the throw tighter, like it's a shield between us. Right now, it is, which makes me hate the fucking thing. "You walked in my shop tonight, kissed me like you did, and then walked away. Do you know how much courage it took me to come here? To acknowledge that you've woken up my heart? To admit to myself that I'm madly attracted to you, and actually, yes, I really like you." She throws her hand out toward my cabin while I stand like a lifeless fool before her. "And then that kiss. I offered myself to you, Ryan. Laid myself bare, and you couldn't even look at me."

"Hannah, it wasn't that—"

"I'm so stupid," she rants on, her wet cheeks shining red with her growing anger. Is it bad of me to think how much more attracted to her I am when she's got fire in her? "I should never have come." Pivoting fast, she marches away. "Don't ever try to kiss me again."

Whoa. I recoil, everything she's shouted at me sinking in. I've woken up her heart? And now she's running away. Again. "Fuck's sake," I mumble, jogging after her, rounding her huddled form and blocking her. "Will you shut the hell up for a second?"

It's Hannah's turn to recoil, and God love her cuteness, her little nostrils flare dangerously at me. "No, I won't shut—"

I lunge forward and attack her mouth before she can attack *me* with her acid tongue again, this time my claiming of her anything but gentle and careful. I don't have time to tread carefully. Or the patience, for that matter. And I can't risk her trying to run again. I'm knackered.

My fingers weave through her hair, getting caught in the tangled wet tresses as I kiss her hard and with purpose. If this kiss doesn't say it all, then I'll happily tell her. But the sound of her whimper and the equal force of her tongue dueling with mine tells me she understands. She gets it. She's letting me in, and as I languidly roll my tongue through her mouth and feel her hands move to my hair, I get the first taste of her secrets. She's completely relaxed in my arms, and I just know she's not used to surrendering to a man like this. Willingly. Uninhibitedly. Comfortably.

I heave as I break away, pushing my forehead to hers. "Clear enough?" I ask as she blinks herself back to life. I wait until I have her full attention before I go on. "I wasn't torn about taking you to bed, Hannah. I was wondering how I would meet your expectations." And that wonder has only increased with her admission. She's wary. Of me? Or of men in general? I'm dealing with something fragile. She's revealed a piece of herself now. A weakness. It's suddenly so obvious that everything she is, all her wonderful, attractive traits, is driven by something ugly. Fear. Or her fierce determination not to let that fear hold her back. My instinct to protect is as powerful as my ability to sense fear. I've seen it in too many eyes just before I've pulled the trigger. And now I see it in Hannah.

"What?" she asks quietly, confused.

I close my eyes and take a breath. "You're not the kind of woman a man fucks, Hannah." I look at her so she sees my struggle. My shame. "And all I've ever done is screw women."

Her eyes go unfathomably wide. I can't be sure if she's shocked or thrilled. Both? "Wow," she breathes, and I conclude it's the former.

"Yeah," I say, a little shyly. "It's very unlike me." Good God, I'm saying plenty, but all the wrong words. I inhale and search for some way to untangle my thoughts before they fall past my lips and she's running again. I look up to the sky, welcoming the fat drops of rain hitting my face. "From the moment I watched you crawl out of the bushes covered in paint, I've had the unrelenting urge to kiss you every time I've seen you."

"And you've tried to kiss me," she counters softly.

I drop my gaze but not my head. "Are you expecting an apology?"

She shakes her head.

"Good." A flash of lightning illuminates the sky, and suddenly the beauty of her face is crystal clear. It's disarming, and my thoughts are suddenly pouring from my mouth. "God, Hannah, I think you're the most stunning woman I've ever met."

A small, embarrassed smile tweaks the corner of her mouth, her arms pulling the blanket in as she looks away from me. "Beauty is a curse."

I don't like her counter, and I especially hate the idea that that's all she thinks I care about. But actually, I wasn't referring to her looks, though she really is beautiful. Naturally so.

"I was talking about your soul," I say, ready to put it all out there. "Your quirkiness. Your carefree nature. Your passion for all things paint and messy, and your absolute indifference for anything materialistic. Your simplistic lifestyle. Your fucking dungarees and those scarves you tie in your hair. Your makeup-free face and natural raspberry scent." Hannah Bright defies the composition of a woman in every way. She's unique. Beautiful without trying. Sexy without trying. Tempting without trying. I can't shake off the notion that she's not only not trying, but doing everything in her power not to be those things at all. To be a wallflower. To blend into the crowd. To live her life under the radar. She's failed. She's on *my* radar—a huge, bright, flashing blip. But as if her wildness isn't enough of a draw to me, the secrets I sense she's keeping are only amplifying my curiosity.

She looks at me, and I see with perfect clarity that she loves what I love about her. I reach forward and slip my hand into hers, squeezing. "So what do you like about me?"

Her lips twist, a smile threatening as her gaze drags over my face. "Your smile is crooked."

"Hazard of my past job."

"And your nose is crooked." Her own nose wrinkles as she speaks.

"I had a fight with an axe." I shrug, remembering teaching Alex how to swing. I didn't anticipate her strength. Or the speed at which she would bring the blade down, cracking me on the nose with the handle as I was moving out of her way. My eyes fall onto the bridge of Hannah's nose and the small bump there. "And you're hardly Miss Straight Nose yourself," I say gently.

Her finger immediately goes to it, feeling. "I was going to have it fixed."

"Don't. It's perfect." I shift the hold of my hand in hers and lace our fingers together. "We're really wet."

She looks up to the sky, closes her eyes, and smiles. "I hadn't noticed."

Good. She's as oblivious to the world happening as I am when we're together. "Come to bed with me?" I ask gently, and her head drops fast. I stare at her deeply, mentally begging for her to agree. The tiniest of nods is all I need, and I get it. So I walk us back to the cabin and into the warmth, and I lead her all the way to my bedroom. I pull the heavy blanket from her shoulders and let it drop to the floor in a wet heap, then wait for her to face me again before I push my sweatpants down my thighs. She keeps her gaze on my eyes.

I have her. And it's a revelation to me, but I'm silently wondering how I can keep her. I don't like the pang of pain that stabs at my heart.

Because once again, something deep and unshakable is telling me she isn't available.

CHAPTER ELEVEN

HANNAH

Ryan won't make the first move, I know that, so I look at him, taking in the scar on his lip before reaching up and tracing the length of it. I feel his hand slip onto my lower back and apply a light pressure, just enough to tug me in. I breathe out, the feeling of our skin touching taking my breath away. He feels so warm. So firm. So strong. I look into his eyes. They're lazy. Shining with want.

There's nothing left to do. I push my mouth to his and swallow his broken groan, linking my arms around his neck and pulling us close together. And I'm lost in him.

All our resistance in recent days pings like an overstretched elastic band, and suddenly we're mad and clumsy, rushed and frenzied. He kisses me with a hard passion, our heads tilting, our hands fumbling in each other's hair, our feet clumsy as we stumble toward his bed. We crash down in a heap, and he's quickly rolling us so he's beneath me, giving me full control. Not that I know what to do with it.

Reaching for my legs, he guides them over his waist so I'm straddling him, and I get the first dash of contact from his erection on the inside of my thigh. I whimper into his mouth, lifting my hips and lowering my upper body onto his chest. My arms frame his head. My boobs squish into his pecs. My wet hair falls onto the pillow. His hands on my back. The feel of his arousal resting between my thighs.

It's sensation overload. I rip my mouth from his, leaving him panting, and find myself frantically kissing every part of his face—his chin, his cheeks, his nose, his brow. This hunger in me is new. It's out of control.

It's him.

"Hannah," Ryan wheezes, taking his hands into my hair and trying to pull me back. My hair is pulled as a result, but the sharp pain doesn't stop me, my crazed appetite for Ryan getting the better of me. "Hey."

I'm suddenly flipped to my back and pinned to the mattress by his body blanketing mine, and I blink, getting him in focus. The vision of him breathing down at me, his wide shoulders and thick biceps caging me in, doesn't help my cause. He's built well, muscled and tall, yet he's gentle. He's rough but soft. He's just wonderful, and now he's gazing down at me knowingly with that small crooked smile. I force my hands over my head, scared to touch him again, scared to lose my mind.

"Let's slow this down, shall we?" He drops his lips to the corner of my mouth and kisses me tenderly. "There's no rush."

My starvation disagrees. I don't want these feelings to end. "You shouldn't be so irresistible."

Ryan laughs lightly as he shifts his legs and uses them to spread mine. "I love how frank you're being with me this evening." Settling between my thighs, he lays his arms over mine above my head and pecks the end of my nose. My *perfect* nose. "I don't want our first time together to be a desperate rush. Though, to be clear, I'm pretty fucking desperate for you." He's in better control of himself than me. I don't know why that stings a little. It's not because I'm easier to resist for him than he is for me. I know that's not the case. Is it because he's used to these feelings of ecstasy? Does he have them frequently, whereas I have never had them? I flinch, hating where my thoughts are taking me. "What's wrong?" he asks, not missing my inner unrest.

"Nothing." I force a smile.

It doesn't wash, and his eyebrows are suddenly high. "Hannah, you can tell me anything."

He's wrong, but rather than refute him, I give him just a tiny scrap of me to appease him. And to get him off my case. "It's been a long time for me," I admit, cringing at the sound of my confession. God, how pathetic does he think I am? "Five years and two months, to be precise."

"That's pretty precise."

I look away, utterly embarrassed. What if he thinks I'm terrible in bed? What if this is the one and only time I get to have all these feelings? What the hell am I thinking? Urghhh, I'm no good at this. "I'm just sayin—"

His lips are suddenly on mine, effectively silencing me with another kiss. "Just take a breath. Can't you tell already that this is going to be amazing?" Biting my lip, he tugs playfully. "Do we need protection?"

I shake my head.

"And I'm assuming since it's been a while, you're—"

"Clean, yes."

"Me too." He smiles at my urgency and immediately shifts his hips, falling to my entrance. I breathe in quickly, tensing. "I said, take a breath, Hannah. Relax."

Relax, relax, relax. Take a breath? Then he should stop stealing it. I use everything I have to talk myself down, and my body softens as his mouth opens and invites me in again. I go with ease, humming around the swirl of our tongues as Ryan inches forward a tiny bit, pushing into me. I flex my hands, and he moves his, lacing our fingers together and squeezing until they're fists. I know his plan, and it's fine by me. He's bombarding my senses again, making it impossible to focus on just one thing. Like the fact that he's pushing forward again.

His kiss becomes firmer, his hands tighter around mine. I can feel every single pulse on his shaft as he slips deeper. My back bows when he thrusts that final bit, my face falling into his neck as I cry out.

And he stills, allowing us both to settle into the feeling. "Are you okay?" he asks quietly, and I nod, unable to speak through my pleasure.

Pulling away so I lose my hiding place in his neck, he looks down at my sweaty cheeks. His stubble is glistening, his top lip wet. He's a vision, his wet hair dark and messy. God, he's so handsome, ruggedly so.

Slowly, he withdraws, sliding free, and then he carefully and precisely rocks back in. His breathing is instantly ragged, his eyelids heavy. "Amazing, right?"

Oh my goodness, yes, completely. But I want to feel him, so I flex my hands, and he releases, allowing me to bring them to his shoulders. "Kiss me and it'll be even better." I fist his hair and tug him down to my mouth, and my pleasure goes off the charts. I'm teetering back on the edge of lost control, my movements becoming a little crazed again, though hampered by his body on me.

I throw my legs up, circling his back tightly. His momentum doesn't falter, his drives smooth and exact, each plunge better than the last. My blood starts to burn, my hearing starts to buzz, and the pressure in my lower belly builds and builds. My swallow is lumpy, a ball of emotion lodging in my throat. I'm overwhelmed. Amazed by how incredible this feels. How wonderful *he* is.

He's watching me with fascination as he drives me wild with his measured lovemaking. Then his fists sink into the mattress and he pushes his torso up, never once faltering in his pace. Now he's splitting his attention between my breasts and my face, and the sweat is beginning to pour from his brow as he rolls his hips carefully. He has more leverage, more room to send me even crazier, and he does, the expression on his face cut with pleasure.

I throw my arms back and grab the wooden headboard as I watch him, his face twisting, and he falls to a forearm, taking his spare hand to one of my breasts and covering it, massaging. I brace myself for the feel of his mouth there, seeing the intention in his eyes as he dips slowly and latches onto my nipple, sucking firmly on a moan of bliss. I close my eyes and I'm gone, a slave to Ryan, his mouth, and his hips thrusting at a mind-bending pace.

The pressure continues to build until I'm panting to keep myself from exploding. He must sense my waning control, because he moves back to my face and cages me in again, nudging my cheek with his nose in silent demand. I open my eyes, and the vision of him pushes me past the point of return. My muscles lock, claiming the pleasure, and I get sucked into a vortex of peace as I'm captured by my orgasm.

Ryan never takes his gaze away, and though desperate to close my eyes, I don't. I do, however, have to brace my arms into his shoulders to deal with the onslaught of pleasure, going to unthinkable heights.

He jerks on a grunt, and his drives become grinds that accompany a long, drawn-out moan, his jaw tight as he comes. And he blinks, appearing dazed, before he falls onto me on an exhausted puff of air, crowding me, still rolling those gorgeous hips, milking every last drop of pleasure from me.

I'm wiped out.

Yet bursting at the seams with a new kind of energy as we lie in a sweaty, breathless tangle.

In my daze, I notice that the storm has died. At least, it has outside. Inside me, it's very much alive, and I'm worried it could be damaging. My dormant heartache has gone as if it was never there. Could Ryan be my cure? It's a tempting thought—for so long I've had to be unrelentingly strong—but it's also dangerous. This distraction, as lovely as it is, could make me weak again.

I wrap my arms around Ryan's broad back, my nose buried in his clammy shoulder. He smells as good as he looks and tastes. Manly and tough. I inhale through my nose and let out the breath on a broken sigh, storing every second of the last half hour to memory. I wait for regret to creep up on me as our breathing gradually evens out. It's peaceful, but that storm inside rages on.

Eventually, Ryan finds the energy to peel himself away from me, shuffling down the bed and laying his arms across my stomach, his chin resting on top. He looks up at me with that crooked smile, and I find myself reaching down and drawing a line across the scar at the corner. "How did you get this?" I ask.

"If I tell you, I'll have to kill you."

I grin at him, half expecting him to start laughing and tell me he's kidding. A few moments pass before I realize he's not joking at all. I bring the pad of my finger to my lips and kiss it, then place it back on his scar. He turns his head, eyes on me, and kisses my finger, too. I smile and drag my touch to his nose, circling the bridge where it bends slightly. He crosses his eyes to watch my finger, and I laugh beneath him, jerking him on my tummy. "And this?"

"My daughter cracked me with the handle of an axe when I was teaching her to chop wood."

My finger pauses. "Ouch."

"Blood everywhere. Cabbage thought I was going to die."

I smile, wide and amused. "Why'd you call her Cabbage?"

"Because her mother hates it," he says easily, and with no remorse. "And because she stank when she was a baby."

A small laugh escapes me, and I lie here, naked, with a naked man sprawled across me, imagining Ryan with a baby girl. There's something very endearing about it. And very sexy. He's a good father. That's a great measure of any man. I remember everything Molly told me about Ryan and how Cabbage came into his life. "You're a good man," I say, and he smiles, his eyes falling to my boobs, a wolfish smirk forming before he takes a cheeky bite.

I yelp on a laugh as he crawls off me and tugs me onto my side to mirror him, his hand on my hip holding me in place. "She wasn't planned, but everything happens for a reason."

"I hate that saying," I blurt before I can think twice. But I do hate it. It's bollocks. Anger rises in me, hot and unstoppable. "What's the reason for the bump on my nose?" I ask Ryan quietly, my mouth running away with me. "What's the reason for me living a life under the ra—" I cut myself short, withdrawing a fraction.

"Radar," Ryan finishes for me, and I look away, kicking myself. "Hey." He grabs my face and tugs me back to where he wants me. "The reason for the bump on your nose is because I love it." Leaning in, he kisses it, and I press my lips together, my hand coming to my face to cover my crazy smile. Ryan soon pulls it away. "And the reason for you living life under the radar is because you were destined to be found by me."

I'm not smiling now, and I don't think I'm breathing, either. "Ryan..." Ryan, what?

"Simple as that." Grabbing me, he rolls to his back and arranges me on his front, pushing me up to sit astride him. "Now, what are you cooking me for breakfast?"

My smile is back, brighter than before. That's it. End of discussion. He could press me. Ask questions. Demand answers. Yet he won't. He'll never know how thankful I am. "So I'm staying?" I ask, wanting nothing more than to spend the entire night with him, cuddled up close.

"Yes." Taking my hands, he threads our fingers. "Because I need breakfast."

I gasp, though Ryan, miraculously, keeps a deadpan expression. "You should make *me* breakfast. Whatever happened to chivalry?"

"Whatever happened to looking after your man?" he counters cheekily, his face still poker-straight.

"My man?" I ask, interested, though loving the sound of it.

"Well, I don't belong to anyone else." His big shoulders shrug against the pillow. "Just putting that out there."

If electricity was run on smiles, the world would be short-circuiting right about now, because mine is epic. "I don't belong to anyone, either." I bite my lip, my finger circling his belly button. "Just putting that out there."

He nods agreeably on a little pout. "Then I'd better stake my claim before someone else does."

"Me too." Our grins collide, and Ryan shoots up, tackling me to the other end of the bed. I yelp, disoriented when I come to rest. I don't get the chance to gather my bearings. His lips are on mine, staking his claim.

Chapter Twelve

RYAN

My bed. God, I love my bed. I know the smell, where to find the cool patches, every dip and lump and how many times I can roll before I reach the edge. Three. That's from the middle. I sleep in the middle. Two pillows—goose feather, of course. One leg out of the covers, too.

I feel myself coming around, slowly waking, and I quickly register the absence of everything familiar about my bed. It smells different. I inhale the scent of raspberries as I shift my leg. No cool patch. I slide my hand out from beneath the pillow, feeling that the edge of the bed is close. No way I'm rolling three times this morning. My neck is sore because I only have one pillow. And there are no covers on me at all.

Opening my eyes, I turn my head on my *one* pillow and forget the absence of everything familiar. She's on her back, the duvet entwined around her legs and finishing at her waist, one arm over her head, her face turned in to it. She looks dreamy. Gorgeous. So fucking peaceful.

I gingerly turn my body onto my side to face her, propping myself up on a bent arm. Her chest rises and falls steadily, calmly, her lips parted a fraction. Naturally, I make the most of my opportunity, studying her, every tiny piece, from the hair on her head all the way down to the tips of her toes. Every inch of her, inside and out, is beautiful.

I reach forward and kiss her tummy, and she stirs immediately. I feel her hand rest on the back of my head and stroke sleepily, and I smile against her skin. She probably has no idea what she's doing right now, which makes her gesture even more touching.

I wait for her feeling fingers to stop before I break away, happy she's fallen back into a deep sleep again. Then I gently peel myself away and throw on some sweats, leaving Hannah to her dreams. I hope they're happy dreams. I hope I'm the starring role.

I turn at the door when I make it there, looking back at the unusual sight of a woman in my bed. Except it doesn't feel unusual. It feels perfectly normal.

Kind of...right.

I smile to myself as I head for the kitchen to make some breakfast, checking the time as I drag the pan out. Eight o'clock. Shit, I never sleep in this late. I feel energized. Content. I look down the corridor to my bedroom as I set the pan on the stove, unable to stop my smile growing. There's a woman in my bed, and I have absolutely no desire to remove her.

Being sure not to make too much noise, I set about preparing breakfast, my absolute favorite, whistling happily while I go. When the stove throws up a bit of smoke, I rush to open the door to get a bit of ventilation. The scattering of twigs and branches reminds me of last night's storm, as well as the heavy damp smell of kicked-up dirt. But it doesn't overpower the smell of Hannah that's lingering on my skin. I lift my arm to my nose and inhale. I never want to shower again.

Leaving the door wide open, I head back to the kitchen and pull down two plates before collecting the pan.

"Morning."

I look up and find Hannah across the room, her eyes sleepy but bright, her body covered in one of my old lumberjack shirts. "Wow," I breathe, unable to hold back my awe as the pan hangs in my limp hand.

She looks down her front on a demure smile. "Hope you don't mind." She tugs at the hem on her thigh as I rest the pan on the counter, moving in closer to conceal the twitching happening behind my sweats. It takes everything in me not to abandon breakfast, seize her, and take her straight back to bed.

"Not at all." I realign my focus and serve up breakfast before I succumb to that temptation. "Hungry?" I head for the freezer.

"Starving." She moves across to one of the stools on the opposite side of the counter, settling as she watches me.

I spoon out two huge dollops of my vice onto the pancakes and push her plate across to her. She looks at it with a grin but doesn't say a word, collecting her fork and tucking in. I'm starving, too, but watching Hannah eat is unexpectedly enjoyable. I lean down and rest my forearms on the counter, getting comfortable. "Good?" I ask, despite her little moan of pleasure telling me what she thinks of my favorite breakfast. Alex's too.

With her mouth full, Hannah nods, pointing her fork at my plate. She quickly chews and swallows. "Aren't you hungry?"

"Starving."

"Then eat," she says on a little laugh, popping another helping in her mouth, watching me as she chews. I continue to observe her until her eating slows and she sets down her knife and fork. "What?" she asks, half smiling.

"How did you sleep?"

"Very well."

I nod, knowing this already. I just wanted to hear it. "Any regrets?"

Her lips press together tightly, her gaze moving away from me. Is she thinking about it? I push my folded body upright, not liking the small pang of pain in my gut, and I wait with bated breath for her answer. When she looks back to me, I see a steely confidence in her eyes. I'm not sure I like that, either. Wasn't last night amazing for her? Our connection was palpable.

"Hannah?" I say, my voice evidently broken.

"I don't regret a thing," she virtually whispers. "It was the best night

I've ever had in my life." Do I see tears in her eyes? "You?" she asks, and then inhales. She's bracing herself.

Keen to put her mind at rest, I lean over the counter and take her hand in both of mine. "Last night was the best thing that's happened to me since Alex came into my life." Bringing her hand to my mouth, I kiss her knuckles, and she deflates. Last night was earth moving, and I suspect it might be life changing for me, too. I want to see her again. But I already knew that before I took her to bed. Before I kissed her. Before I made love to her. Not once in my thirty-nine years have I ever thought that about a woman. There was always something missing. There were no game changers. No...eruptions in my chest. I inwardly smile. I want more of this feeling of sweet contentment.

Dropping Hannah's hand, I round the counter, and she turns on her stool to face me. I put myself between her thighs and take her arms, directing them around my waist. She looks up at me as I slide my fingers into her hair, bringing my nose down to hers.

"Stake your claim," I whisper. Her smile blinds me, and she uses the footrest to launch herself up my body, wrapping all her limbs around me and slamming her mouth against mine. Stake her claim she does, kissing me with a hardness and passion that I've never experienced before. I shift us so my arse rests against the counter, steadying me, as Hannah eats me alive and I try to keep up.

"That'll fucking do," I mumble, holding her close, and she giggles, the sound so damn sweet. I'm forced to take her hair and gently pull to get her attention. Withdrawing a little, she finds my eyes, and we spend the next few minutes just looking at each other, her hands slowly moving across my bare shoulders, mine through her hair.

This exquisite, sweet woman in my arms, no matter how happy she looks in this moment, is carrying pain. I saw it last night. Heard it in her words. She's been hurt. I hope she lets me ease that pain. Maybe I already am.

"I think nearly killing you could turn out to be one of the best things that ever happened to me." Fucking hell, what has she done to me? A few encounters and one night with this woman have derailed everything. And I couldn't care less, because here now, with her in my arms and a million memories from last night, I've never felt so sure about anything in my life. I have to see how this grows.

She nibbles on the end of my nose. "It's definitely the best thing that's happened to me."

I'm glad we're clear. "Your ice cream is melting." I tap her bottom to release her legs from around my waist, and I lower her to the stool, reaching to my neck to pry her hands away. Pulling my own plate over, I drag another stool across and sit beside her. "Eat," I order gently, spearing a piece of pancake and swirling it through some ice cream before holding it out to her. She opens her mouth and takes it, then mimics me, feeding me some of her breakfast. And that's how we go until both of our plates are clean.

"Your breakfast was very good," I say as I gather the crockery and load it into the dishwasher.

"So was yours." She slips down off the stool and wanders to the open door, looking outside. "Is there much damage?"

"Only a few fallen branches." I pass her and take the steps down to the lawn, collecting a few and throwing them onto the woodpile. When I look up, Hannah has found her way to the outside shower and is peeking over the top. She's on her tippy-toes. My shirt has ridden up her arse. "Oh boy," I more or less groan, reaching for the front of my sweats to restrain my wayward dick. My eyes are glued to the cheeks of her bottom, my mind off on a tangent. She clearly wants to try the shower, and I really want to try *her* again.

Two birds, one stone, Ryan.

I slip my thumbs into the waistband of my sweats and push them down my legs, kicking them off. And then I'm moving toward her, eyeing that arse like it's my prey. She stills when I reach her, lowering from her toes. The shirt drops. Her arse is gone. "Arms up," I order, and they immediately rise. I take the hem of my shirt and pull it up and off, discarding it on the floor. She turns around before I can command it. Hooking one arm around her waist, I lift her and walk us into the shower, flicking it on as I do. The water is freezing when it hits us, and she gasps, huddling closer. "Give it a few seconds and it'll be hot," I say, nudging her face from my neck. I push her back into the wooden paneling and hold her in place with my front, pushing her arms up. "Until then, I get to keep you warm."

I take her mouth softly and decide here and now that this morning is the best wake-up I've ever had. She's on a mission again, and not for the first time I question my approach. *Handle with care*, that's what I thought. Still do. I instinctively want to be gentle, though it's fucking hard when she's attacking me with such desperation and force. I don't know what her secrets are, and until I do, I'll stick to the plan. Build her trust. Earn her confidence. But now, just like last night, she's swiftly losing control, getting carried away. It's as if she's been given something new and exciting, and she wants to make the most of it before it's taken from her. My thought doesn't only hurt. It angers me, and I feel my kiss hardening to follow Hannah's lead. I hiss when I feel her short nails sink into my shoulders. I moan when I feel her teeth sink into my lip, and while it's all fucking amazing, I hate the potential motives behind her eagerness.

I rip my lips away, panting, and turn my face when she goes for my mouth again. It doesn't deter her from trying to pull me back. I remain where I am, and eventually losing her patience, she grabs my jaw and pulls me to where she wants me, holding me there as she tries to kiss me again. I withdraw, and Hannah frowns. "What's wrong?" she asks quietly, her worry clear.

"I don't know, what's wrong?" I throw it back at her, my simmering annoyance leading me. God damn, I'm condemning her lack of control and trying to analyze it, and here I am losing control, too. Should I analyze that? I laugh. *You already have, Ryan. You're smitten. You care. It's old news. Move it along.*

"Nothing." Her voice is small, and I see with perfect clarity that she's starting to shut down. Fucking hell. I'm pushing her away. I'm desperate for her to share her sorrows. I'm desperate to ease her pain. I look at this impassioned woman and imagine things that I thought were beyond my capability to imagine. Like sharing my life.

I wrestle myself back into line and place a soft kiss to her mouth. "You're always in such a rush," I say around her lips. "There's no need to be." The water is warm now, hot meeting the cold morning air, steam billowing up, shrouding us.

"Sorry," she replies, and fuck me, I quickly feel like shit. I shouldn't condemn her for being so eager and desperate. I should be chuffed. If only I could shake the notion that there's more to her rush than simple hunger for me. Could it be that simple? "You're irresistible," she confesses unapologetically.

"I can live with that." I reach between us and take hold of my dick, guiding myself to her, and she tenses against me, bringing her forehead to mine. As I slip into her with ease, both of us cry out, my fist hitting the wood behind her. Fuck me, the feel of her around me is arresting. "I need a second," I admit, ready to shoot my load at any moment. My eyes cross behind my lids, my teeth gritting. I can feel her warmth pulsing against my shaft. It's not fucking helping. "Don't move."

"I'm not moving."

"Oh Jesus, Hannah." I flex my hips, sliding out a fraction. "You feel out of this world."

She moans when I hit home on a grunt, my teeth locking onto her neck and biting gently.

I find my stride quickly, easing in and out of her on semi-controlled drives. I feel our wet bodies sliding and have to jack her up a little when she slips down my torso a bit. The result is an unplanned pound into her, and she yelps, her eyes flying open, her hands fisting my hair painfully, as if to return the favor. Her viciousness only spurs me on, and I lock stares with her, my face tight. I'm rapidly losing my control.

She pulls my head forward and plunges her tongue deep, and I swallow down every sound of pleasure she makes as I'm claimed by a craving that's way out of my control. The friction is debilitating, my nerve endings on fire.

I grab her thigh and squeeze, our tongues clashing. My body is burning up, my thrusts automatically gaining momentum. Fuck, is she with me? I open my eyes and find her staring at me, and I pull back to get a better view, seeing all too clearly that she is. Then I feel it, too. She stiffens against me, pulling in a deep breath, tightens her thighs, and her eyes glimmer madly. Fuck me. The sight alone pushes me over the edge, and I detonate, my whole body going into spasm as I'm torn in half by the power of my climax. I hear Hannah scream, the sound broken and jagged, but distorted through the rush of blood swirling in my head.

My knees give out, forcing me down to the cold tile floor in a heap. At the mercy of her own exhaustion, Hannah has no choice but to fall with me, landing on my front, and my arms fall above my head, unable to keep holding her.

I close my eyes, drained.

Yet more alive than ever.

She hums and rolls to her back next to me, sucking in air when her skin meets the stone tiles. "Shit," she gasps, and I drop my head to the side, finding just enough energy to smile. But I can't talk. Can't even find the will to think of anything to say. So I just reach for her hand and hold it while we lie side by side and recover, both of us staring up to the sky.

"I like your shower," she says after a while, tugging my hand to her face and nuzzling it.

"I've always liked it. Now I fucking love it." I shift onto my side to face her. "You'll have to be here every morning to shower with me, because I don't want to just *like* it ever again."

Her response is to simply smile at the sky. "I really love it here," she says wistfully. "It's so quiet and peaceful. Hidden from the world."

Hidden. She's hiding from something. All the scraps of information Hannah's unintentionally throwing my way are slowly building a picture. But the picture is fuzzy still. Will it ever be clear? I don't know, but what I do know is she's here, hidden, and whatever she's hiding from can't find her. And if it does . . . I quickly shake off those dangerous thoughts. It's obvious now that Hannah's scared to trust, and everything tells me she's scared to feel. Now I just need to find out why. Or do I?

"Is that a car?" Hannah breaks into my thoughts, and I still, listening.

"Sounds like it." I quickly jump to my feet and look over the top of the shower stall. My eyes widen. "Shit."

"What?"

I fly around in a panic and collect a startled Hannah from the floor, putting her on her feet and ushering her out of the shower. Hurrying us across the lawn, I look back over my shoulder, seeing Darcy's Jaguar emerging from the darkness of the trees canopying the road. What the hell is she doing here? "It's Alex's mother."

I direct Hannah into the bedroom and throw a shirt at her. "She can't see you." I scramble for some more sweats and yank them on, quickly peeking out of my bedroom window. "Oh no," I mumble, seeing Alex in the passenger seat.

"What, Ryan?" Hannah sounds reasonably annoyed.

"It's Alex, too, and she *definitely* can't see you." I hurry over to Hannah and help her into the shirt, tugging the sides in and buttoning it up, albeit wonky, leaving one tail longer than the other. Then I run into the kitchen and snatch up my keys from the counter. "Get in my truck," I say when I make it back into the bedroom, finding Hannah has abandoned my shirt in favor of her dress from last night. It must be wet. But then again, so are we. Whatever, I don't have time to waste on what she's wearing and why.

I shove the keys in her hand and take her shoulders, turning her and leading her to the back door. "If you go around the back of the shed they won't see you. Wait for me." I turn her quickly, smack a huge kiss on her lips, and then send her on her way. I slam the door and turn, running to the living room. *Fuck, fuck, fuck.* I fly to the door, take a moment to compose myself, and then pull it open with a stupid smile.

Alex skids to an abrupt halt halfway up the steps to the veranda, taking me in, and I shift and squirm guiltily under her scrutinizing glare. "What are you doing here?" I ask.

She narrows her eyes. "What's up?"

"Nothing." I laugh like a twat, looking past her to Darcy. "Morning," I chirp.

Just like our daughter, Darcy stops in her tracks, assessing me suspiciously. My smile widens. Darcy cocks her head. "You were supposed to collect Alexandra at eight."

Shit. I was? I look to my girl, who now has her arms folded over her chest. I give her sorry eyes. "I'm sorry, Cabbage. I just woke up." That's bullshit, and she must know it. I'm out running by six every morning, no matter what day, no matter the weather.

"Then why is your hair wet?" she asks.

I reach up and feel, cringing. "Because I just showered."

"You said you just woke up."

"Like ten minutes ago."

Silence falls, and I stand like a plum being studied by two sets of beady eyes. Fuck me, won't they just stop? Eventually, Alex passes me, though her eyes remain glued to my guilty form the whole way, until she's in the cabin and it's just me and her mother.

"Good night?" I ask, taking the steps and collecting a few more stray sticks and twigs.

"What do you care?" Darcy retorts, and I pause, half bent over, asking myself that very question. I couldn't give a shit about her night. Alex's, on the other hand . . .

I straighten. "I don't."

"Then why ask?"

I roll my eyes and make my way to the compost heap, tossing the debris on top and collecting some more sticks from nearby. "Is that all, Darcy?" I turn and find her standing motionless, lost in a bit of a trance. At first, I'm confused, but then I note the direction of her stare. I look down at my bare chest. It's been years since she's seen this torso. Back then, it was cut from a very active job and youth. Now it's still cut, sure, but I have to work a lot damn harder to keep myself in physical shape.

I break the stick in my hand, the crack snapping Darcy right out of her daydream. "All right over there?" I ask on a wicked smirk.

She startles, coming over all flustered. "Yes, fine." She sniffs and looks around with obvious disdain. Hannah didn't look at my haven like that. She loves it here. And I loved having her here. Darcy, however, I can't wait to get rid of.

She treads her way back to her shiny Jaguar carefully on her heels, the disgust never leaving her. "Alexandra is in the beauty pageant at the town fete a week from Sunday." She opens her door and looks back at me. "I'll want her back that Saturday evening to prepare her."

Prepare her? For fuck's sake. She makes our daughter sound like a turkey that needs stuffing. The fucking pageant. Every damn year my daughter is put in some frilly crap, has makeup plastered all over her face and a tiara set on a pile of huge curls. I hate it. And come to think of it... "She hates it, Darcy. Why d'you make her do it?"

"I don't make her," she retorts indignantly. "She holds the town record, has won every year she's entered."

"Nothing to do with the fact that she's Lord and Lady Hampton's granddaughter," I mutter.

"Are you saying the only reason my daughter wins is because of her lineage?" Darcy balks at me. "Some supportive father *you* are."

"Don't push me, Darcy." Typical of this woman, taking my words and twisting them. "She'd win if she'd rolled out of bed and turned up in her pajamas." My girl's a stunner. She certainly doesn't win the pageant each and every year because of her fucking clown outfits. "And she's *our* fucking daughter." I throw the broken sticks down with force, my anger palpable. God, does this woman love pushing my buttons.

Without another word, Darcy slips into her car and pulls away, and I snarl as her sparkling Jag disappears. "Urghhh." I stamp my way back into the cabin and go straight to the fridge but slam it shut again when I register the time. Too early for a beer. "Fuck's sake."

"Oh, Daddy," Alex says from the sink. "What's got you all weird this morning?" Her little head tilts, and I'm unable to stop myself from scowling at her. What's got me all weird? *My morning was perfect. I was happily lost in Hannah. Then your mother showed up and doused my good mood in a healthy helping of Darcy Fucking Hampton.* "Nothing," I grunt, going to the sink to wash my hands, nudging her out of my way with my hip. "What the hell have you got on? You look like you've been attacked by a crazed glitter fairy."

Alex chuckles as she passes me a hand towel, and I accept, drying my hands as she watches.

"I need you to explain something," she says, all too casually for my liking.

"What?"

Pulling open the dishwasher door, she points inside. "Why are there two dirty plates and two sets of used cutleries?"

Fuck.

My mind shuts down on me completely. "Well..." I clear my throat, shifting from bare foot to bare foot. "There was a..." *Fuck, fuck, fuck.*

"What?" she presses, pouting in that way she does when she knows she has my number.

"I forgot you weren't here," I blurt, my bullshit coming from nowhere. "So I made you breakfast."

"Our favorite?"

"Of course."

"And you threw it away?"

I shrug.

"What a waste, Dad." She marches to the bin and stamps on the pedal, making the lid flip up. She's searching for the evidence. The rascal. I laugh like a fool, and she looks back at me.

"Actually, I ate it." Fucking hell, she's like a super sleuth. I pat my stomach on a ridiculous grin. "Go get changed, Cabbage. We have a bridge to finish." I turn away from her and start faffing with nothing on the counter, moving shit here and there, anything to avoid the suspicious eyes that are now nailed to my back. It feels like a lifetime, but I eventually hear her bedroom door shut, and I look over my shoulder to see the coast is clear. I sag against the counter, exhausted.

And then I think. Hard. When do I tell Alex about Hannah? What will she say? How will she react? I look out the window, falling into deeper thought. When Hannah and I are going steady? Is that what you call it these days? Shit, I'm so out of touch with the protocols of relationships. Have I ever been *in* touch? Am I in a relationship? I frown to myself. Surely I must be... right? I quickly replay every detail from last night, from the moment I stepped into the ladies' room at the pub. I work my way through every word we said to each other and every kiss, every moan, every smile. Fuck, yes, I think I *am* in a relationship. Should I clarify that with Hannah?

Hannah.

"Fucking hell," I curse, running outside to my truck to check on her. But I come to a screaming stop when I find no Hannah. The keys, however, are on the hood. She didn't want to wait?

I return to the cabin and grab my phone to call her and make sure she got home okay. And maybe ask my dumb question. Yeah, I should do that. *Hi, Hannah, it's the guy who took you to bed last night. Should I call you my girlfriend?* I drop my phone and take my hands to my face, dragging them down slowly. I'm all nervous. Nerves never get me. Ever. I don't know how to tell Alex, I don't know how to clarify with Hannah exactly what we are, and, come to think of it, I have not the faintest idea how to be a... boyfriend? I laugh. I'm thirty-nine years old. A boyfriend? A girlfriend? "No," I say to myself. Partner? No, Jake's my partner. Lover? I nod to myself. Then frown. No, she's more than that. "Oh fuck."

Bracing my hands against the edge of the counter, I breathe through my growing panic and wait until I've gathered myself before I retrieve my mobile again to make the call. Maybe I won't ask Hannah over the phone what my relationship status is, but I do need to check she got home okay. "Shit." I don't have her number. How can I be in a relationship with a woman and not even have her number?

I need to rectify that pronto. So I might not have Hannah's number *yet*, but I do have someone's. I scroll down and dial, walking out onto the veranda to make sure I'm out of earshot from Alex.

Jake's voice is familiar, and I can't lie, it's welcomed. It's something I know in a world I don't know. "Ryan," he says, sounding gruff and sleepy.

"You in bed?"

"Bad night with Caleb."

Shit. In all my madness, I forgot about the new addition. "Sorry, mate. I'll call you later."

"No, I'm up now. What's up?"

"You at your country place now?" I ask, walking around the cabin.

"Yeah, why?"

"It's not too far from here, right?"

"An hour. What's with all the questions?"

"Fancy coming to see me? I'll put the barbecue on. We'll have a beer." I can hear myself. I sound very unlike me.

The small pause before Jake talks again tells me he's noted I'm behaving out of character. "Right. A barbecue and a beer. I'd love to, but we've kind of got our hands full. I can't leave Cami to deal with them both so soon. She's knackered."

My heart warms. "I meant for them to come, too."

"Huh?"

"All of you. Here. It'll be nice."

"What's going on?" Jake asks, full of suspicion. It's warranted. In the years I've known Jake, not once have I suggested a family get-together. Only a drink in the pub. Man time. That's us.

I exhale and take the plunge. All in. Confession time. I need a mate's ear. "I think I've gone and got myself a girlfriend."

Silence.

"Jake? Are you there?" I pull my phone from my ear to check my signal. Four bars. "Jake?"

"You?" he finally says. That's it. Nothing more.

"That's what I fucking said, didn't I?"

"I don't know. I thought you did, but then I thought it must have been a mistake. You? Ryan Willis? The eternal bachelor?"

I find a post and let my forehead fall against it. His reaction is only cementing what we all know. This is way out of my comfort zone. "Help a man out, won't you? I'm having a bit of a melt-down here."

"Okay, take a breath."

"Took loads. Still having a meltdown."

"Who is she?"

"Her name's Hannah. She's moved into town. Opened a little store."

"What makes you think she's your girlfriend?"

"Well, she spent the night last night." I show the heavens my palm, as if it's as simple as that.

Jake starts laughing hysterically, then he quickly zips it, and I hear him apologize. Then two seconds later, a baby starts squawking. "Damn," he mutters. "You woke the baby."

"Me?"

"God damn it, Ryan, I only just got him off to sleep."

"Sorry," I say with a shrug.

"Spending the night with someone doesn't make her your girlfriend." Jake says, bringing us back to the trouble at hand.

"I know that," I retort indignantly. "But I'm not just talking about that. There's the things she said, the things *I* said. Fucking hell, Jake, I said some serious shit. *Thought* some serious shit."

"How long have you known her?"

"A week."

"And last night was the first time you slept with her?"

"Yeah."

"Fuck, you're slacking, boy."

I sag where I'm standing, my teeth grinding with frustration. "She's not that kind of woman. I had absolutely no desire to screw her blind. It was meaningful. Inevitable. Fucking amazing, and I can't stop thinking about her."

He huffs a small shot of laughter, and I know beyond a doubt that he's starting to relate. I know his story. I know he understands. "Does she know about Alex?"

"Yes."

"Does she know about her snaky mother?"

"Yes."

"Then what's the problem?"

"I don't know. I get the feeling something isn't right with her." I walk away from my truck and start pacing the lawn, kicking some twigs as I go. "I think she's been screwed over or something. By a man."

"Okay, so she might have an issue with trust. Maybe she just needs time before she spills it all to you. I of all people understand that."

I stop in my tracks, hearing him but struggling to accept what he's saying. "It's not just that." I hope she'll eventually tell me why she's a little wary and cagey, but how this progresses isn't resting on it. "I'm worried about Alex. She's had me to herself for as long as she can remember. She says she wants me to have a girlfriend, but I'm not sure she understands the implications."

"What implications?"

"Sharing her Chunky Monkey, for a start."

Jake laughs. "Oh, Ryan. You kill me sometimes. Tell me, how would you feel if you never saw this woman again?"

"That would be hard. Do you know how small Hampton is?"

"Answer the fucking question."

"Horrible," I spit, forced into imagining it. "Empty. Angry. Hard done by." *Whoa.* But it's all true. I had the most incredible evening that stretched into this morning. It was perfect. Until Darcy showed up.

"Stop being such a fucking pussy and go with it. What's the worst that could happen?"

What's the worst that could happen? Oh, I don't know. Breaking my heart? Breaking Alex's heart? "So you think I should tell Alex?"

"Yes, if you like this woman that much, tell her."

"Okay." I will as soon as I've spoken to Hannah. She should know I'm telling my daughter about her, I guess. "About that barbecue. I want you guys to meet her."

"Let me speak to Cami. When were you thinking?"

"Next weekend?"

"I'll get back to you. Got to go before the baby brings down the fucking house." Jake hangs up, and I look back at the cabin.

Alex will be fine, I know that deep down in my heart. She's always going on about me meeting someone, and really, I know my fear isn't anything to do with how *I* might handle this. Or Alex, for that matter, though telling my daughter about a woman is a huge deal, a massive step, and I would never do it lightly. It would have to be serious, and now, when I seem to have leveled out my thoughts and gotten over my stupid panic, I realize that my trepidation is actually a result of how little I know about Hannah. I have a lot to learn about her. And my biggest fear is that Alex will start falling for her like I am, and Hannah will leave us both.

Chapter Thirteen

HANNAH

I'm shivering by the time I make it home. Shivering and mad. Ryan couldn't have gotten me out of his cabin faster if he'd shoved a supersonic engine up my arse.

"Arsehole," I mutter, pushing my way into my store and slamming the door. I'm wounded. I understand that meeting his daughter is a big step and her finding us soaked and all cozy in the shower wouldn't be ideal, but the way Ryan carried on, his urgency and panic, made me feel like he was embarrassed. Of me? And what's the deal with Alex's mother? Why can't she know about me? What's it to her if Ryan sees a woman? That's bad enough, but his statement about his daughter is what really stung.

She definitely *can't see you.*

What, ever? Am I going to be a secret fling, a fuck to call upon whenever he's not playing dad? I thought I meant more than that. I thought Ryan *wanted* more than that. Everything he said suggested it. I feel like I've been hoodwinked. Reeled in and then tossed away.

I stamp up to my apartment and head for the shower, dead set on scrubbing myself clean of Ryan Willis. I'm furious for letting myself get carried away. But above all, I'm angry because the sharp jab of reality has made me remember something important: I shouldn't get attached. I shouldn't get too swept up in the feelings of something lovely. Because it'll be too hard to walk away when I need to. And I *will* need to. Eventually, I will have to leave Hampton. And that's not Ryan's fault at all.

Last night taught me something important, though. It taught me that I'm not completely broken. That I could be fixed. But what's the point in being fixed if you know you'll always end up broken again?

* * *

It's another quiet day in the store. I try to create something, tossing paint at the canvas haphazardly, but not even anything accidental happens. I sit back after an hour of trying and notice for the first time since I planted myself on this stool that every color I've used is dull. Gloomy. It's indicative of how I'm feeling. I give up and clear away, pulling my laptop out and loading my online store.

I nearly come out of my skin when I find I've made a sale on one of my paintings. "Oh my God," I whisper, looking across to the landscape oil that's currently hanging on my shop wall. I smile, returning my attention to the details of the buyer. "Scotland," I say to myself, noting that the address is a castle. Excitement tickles my tummy as I print off shipping labels and set them aside, ready for when I've wrapped the painting to post. And then I find myself pulling up Facebook.

When I type in my sister's name, my heart sinks and my excitement vanishes. She's changed her profile picture again. My throat clogs with emotion as I stare at my mother in her bed, her eyes empty as she looks back at me. She's gripping the blanket over her legs hard, her arthritis-plagued fingers deformed. My sister is sitting on the bed next to her, smiling, though it's a sad smile. I feel a teardrop roll down my cheek, and I look down when it falls, seeing it splash when it hits the counter. This picture was taken on a bad day. Mum looked perky on Saturday. It was a good day. Has it been bad days since? Another tear falls.

"Hey."

I jump and look up, finding Molly approaching. I quickly snap my laptop shut and brush at my cheeks. "Hey."

"Are you okay?" She places her handbag on the counter, assessing me worriedly.

I sniff and pluck a tissue from the box nearby, flapping it casually before taking it to my nose. "Hay fever." I blow my nose hard. "It's got me good this year."

Molly's nose scrunches in sympathy as she pulls up a stool and parks herself opposite me. "Come on, then."

"Come on what?"

I notice that her usually neat ponytail is askew, and her rosy cheeks are rosier than normal. "I ran here from school on my lunch break, Hannah."

"Why?" I rub at my running nose.

"I saw you with Ryan last night."

The tissue stills as I bring it away, my mouth forming a straight—guilty—line. How much did she see? "He was making sure I got home okay."

"And that involves a snog, too, huh?"

I'm up from the stool quickly, heading into the kitchenette out back, stalling having to spill. But when I do spill, it's definitely a conversation that requires tea. I flick the kettle on and grab two mugs as Molly arrives in the room sounding a little wheezy. "Tell me everything."

I find myself throwing the tea bags in the mugs with a bit more force than necessary. "He kissed me."

"Yes, I saw. And?"

"And that was it."

"Oh, come on. This is Hampton. Nothing exciting happens. Don't spoil my fun." Molly's beside me in a second, resting against the counter as I pour the water and stir. Her eyes are excited. I laugh on the inside. I'm about to piss on her bonfire.

"And I went to his place and we had sex and then I left this morning."

"Oh my God!"

"It was a mistake." I grab the milk from the fridge and slam the door, leaning against it. "It shouldn't have happened, and I'm kicking myself that it did."

Her face drops. "Why? He's gorgeous. Not to mention single."

And he kicked me out this morning like I expect he boots out every other woman he seduces. God, why am I even letting that bother me? I've already convinced myself it was for the best. I was very close to falling in too deep, and that would be stupid. I should be thanking him for snapping me back to reality. I told Molly last night that I didn't need a man to make me strong again. I should remember that, and I should definitely disregard all those feelings of liberation and freedom that I felt during the best sex ever. With the loveliest man I've ever met. No, not lovely. He's an arsehole.

I push my back from the fridge and finish the tea, handing one to Molly. "I was drunk. Stupid. I'm really in no position to get involved with a man."

Molly gives me a small, understanding smile, probably remembering our conversation in the pub last night. She reaches for my hand and squeezes. "But a great rebound screw, yeah?"

I laugh a little. I suppose I could see it like that. A rebound screw that's come years too late. "Yeah."

"I better get back." Molly takes a few sips of her tea before swilling her mug and setting it on the drainer.

"Sorry it was a wasted sprint," I quip lightly, and she laughs, going back through to the store and collecting her bag.

She looks back at me, her grin poorly hidden. "I have a feeling this isn't the end of you and Ryan."

"Trust me, it's the end."

"If you say so." She waltzes out and I follow, standing on the street, pondering what to do with the rest of my day. I see Mrs. Hatt head into the store and Father Fitzroy wandering down the high street. I smile as I watch him, now familiar with his daily routine. It's one thirty. Time for his lunchtime pint of ale.

"Mind your feet." A broom hits my ankles, and I jump out of the way of Cyrus as he sweeps past me.

"Afternoon," I say, dipping and collecting a candy wrapper that he's missed. I drop it in the bin on his cart and dust my hands off. "Ever thought about getting into painting, Cyrus?"

"And why would I do that?"

"Something different."

"I like what I like. Have done for years. Not much call for change around these parts." He slips his broom into the cart and pushes it into the road. "Good day to you, miss."

"Good day, Cy—" My goodbye is cut short when I see a truck at the top of the high street. Ryan's truck. Heading this way. "Shit." I dive into my store and slam the door, quickly locking it and running out the back. It's only when I'm on my way up the stairs to my apartment that I wonder what on earth I'm doing. Avoiding him? That's assuming I was his intended destination, and why would I be? Surely *he's* avoiding *me*.

I go to the window and look past the curtain, seeing him pull into one of the bays outside the store. Alex jumps out first and runs into Mrs. Heaven's café, and then Ryan appears. My face bunches in disgust. Just look at him, all outdoorsy and hot as sin in his ripped jeans and shirt. Wait, I recognize that shirt. It's the one he wrestled me into this morning and buttoned up all wrong. Why's he wearing that shirt in particular?

He wanders around the front of his truck, heading in the direction of the café, following his daughter. Then he stops and looks down the street toward my store. My heart begins to pound, getting faster every second he remains a statue, staring this way, until he continues on to the café and I start breathing again. But then he slows to a stop, reverses his steps, and turns, stalking down the street. I can't see his expression, but his pace tells me he's determined. Determined to do what?

He reaches the shop door and tugs on the handle a few times before stepping back and looking up, and I quickly dive away from the window, my stupid heart back to pounding, my stomach performing cartwheels. I hear him trying the door again.

"I'm closed," I mumble, inching forward a little and craning my neck to see him. He's just standing there, staring at the shop front. "Go away," I order quietly, and as if he has heard me, he starts up the street again, looking back a few times as he goes.

I deflate and take a seat on the couch. And now what will I do with myself?

Chapter Fourteen

RYAN

She's avoiding me. It's now Saturday, and it's been nearly three days since I saw her. I've been to her store every day twice a day and each time it's been closed. I asked Molly when I saw her in the café yesterday if she'd seen Hannah, and all I got was a shake of her head before she scuttled off with her blueberry muffin. I didn't believe her. Everything about her behavior was shifty.

What's going on?

Has Hannah had a change of heart? Has she decided a man with a kid isn't for her? Or is she truly going to let her trust issues get in the way? I don't know, but I can't stop thinking about her. Every second of every damn day, she's on my mind.

Alex and I have been busy; I've made sure of it, but it hasn't helped. We've nearly finished the bridge; all that's left to be done is paint it, and we've also fixed Hannah's bike. I listened to Alex rattle on the whole time about Hannah and how cool she is, and all I could do was offer the odd hum or one-word answer. Hearing my girl sing Hannah's praises at every opportunity only cemented my previous worry. It isn't just my heart on the line here, and given Hannah's apparent flightiness, it's probably a good thing it ended when it did, not that I knew it had ended. I'm a big boy. I can take rejection. But I can't expose Alex to it.

My girl smacks the hammer on the head of the final nail in our bridge and stands back, admiring our work. "We should go to Hannah's to get the paint."

"What?" I look up from my toolbox.

"The paint," she says again. "For our bridge." She tosses the hammer into the toolbox before me. "We should go to Hannah's to get it."

I slam the toolbox shut and stand. "Mr. Chaps sells paint."

"Only boring white. I want it to be colorful and bright." Alex follows me as I trek back through the woods to the cabin. "We'll get the paint from Hannah."

I throw my toolbox on the back of my truck and wipe my hands down with an old rag. Alex has found her way to Hannah's bike by the shed and is inspecting our handiwork. It's as good as new. I'm sure Hannah will be pleased, not that I plan on finding out. I'll let Alex deliver it back to her just as soon as I've attached that silly bell that Alex insisted we buy.

"I'll get the base-coat paint from Mr. Chaps, you can get the colorful paint from Hannah." If her store is even open. "Come on, we've got to get to Grange to have my truck sorted."

I jump in and start the engine as Alex skips over, her jeans dragging the floor. They're all frayed, they have oil stains everywhere, and you can't see her Vans they're so baggy. "You should wear those to the beauty pageant," I say when she's hopped in. "Guaranteed winner."

She snorts and drags her belt on. "Are you going to laugh at me?" she asks, pulling off her baseball cap and putting it back on back-to-front.

"Of course."

"Thanks." Winding down the window, she rests her elbow out and kicks her Vans up onto the dashboard. "Can you bring a paper bag for my head?"

"You being in the pageant makes your mother happy."

"Nothing makes Mother happy," she muses quietly, gazing into the woods as we roll down the track.

Where did that come from? I glance across to her, flicking my elbow out to nudge her. "Cabbage?"

"She's crying a lot lately." She shrugs. "Grandmother said it's because she's depressed or something."

"What's your mother got to be depressed about?"

My daughter's mouth twists, and she looks away, avoiding my eyes.

"Hey." I pull the truck to a stop and turn in to her. "Talk to me."

"Promise you won't say anything," she orders.

I give her my little finger and she hooks it with hers. "Pinkie promise," I say, squeezing. "Now what's up?"

"Casper wants a divorce. I heard them arguing."

Whoa. I wasn't expecting *that.* "Why?" That's the stupidest question a man's ever asked. Darcy Hampton is insufferable—a self-important, spoiled brat of a woman. She's scheming, manipulative, sly. And Casper's not my favorite person in the world, granted, but he's always treated Alex like his own, and past my irritation and annoyance, I know that's something I should be grateful for. But he's still not her dad.

"Something about growing apart," Cabbage says, waving a hand in feigned indifference. "That's what Casper said, anyway. I guess that's life. You love someone, they love you back, and then one of you decides that, actually, you don't love the other person. And one person leaves. You know, you're better off single, Dad. I'm never having a boyfriend or a husband." She looks across to me. "I'm glad it's just me and you."

Baseball bat, say hello to my stomach.

I return forward and stare at the steering wheel, my cheeks blowing out. "I'm glad, too," I reply quietly, putting my truck into gear and pulling off.

Fuck me.

* * *

Whitesnake's "Here I Go Again" blares from the speakers on our way to Grange, Alex and I jigging in our seats. She sings at the top of her voice, slapping the side of the truck out the window as we speed through the countryside. Her head starts jerking in time to the beats—my little headbanger—and I laugh, her hair whipping around her face as the breeze gushes through the cab. "Dun-dun-dun!"

I join in, cranking up the volume even more as I smack the steering wheel.

"Woohooo!" Alex laughs, stamping her feet repeatedly on the dashboard.

"This was one of my mum's favorites," I tell her. "Every Sunday morning on repeat while she vacuumed."

She chuckles, reaching forward and turning the volume down. "I wish I could have met her. She sounds so cool."

I smile sadly. I lost my mum just ten minutes after I won shared custody of Alex. She didn't even get to meet my daughter, and that is something I will *never* forgive Darcy for. My mum would have loved my girl. And my girl was the only reason I survived my mother's death. Had I not had Alex to take care of, I don't know what I would've done. "I wish that, too," I say, smiling across at her.

"It's been a while since we visited. We should get some flowers for her grave when we get home."

"Good plan." I pull up to a roundabout, indicating left for the main street in Grange. Something catches my eye across the street, and I squint, trying to zoom in. What the...?

"Dad!"

I jump and slam my foot on the brake, just stopping in time for the red light. "Shit," I breathe, immediately scanning the other side of the road again. I thought I saw...

"God, Dad, you scared the shit out of me."

"Hey!" I scorn her, reaching across and slapping her leg. "Don't let me hear you talk like that."

"Hey, is that Hannah?"

I follow Alex's pointed finger, finding Hannah up ahead getting in a taxi. "Looks like it," I muse quietly.

"What's she doing in Grange?"

I pull away when the light turns green, forcing nonchalance. "Beats me." I peek up at my rearview mirror, seeing the cab pull out and take a right. But really, what is she doing in Grange? And why do I care?

* * *

I don't know what it is with Alex lately, disappearing on me constantly. She was supposed to be getting flowers from Mr. Chaps's store, while I got something for dinner. I stalk up and down the aisles with my basket full of stuff, scanning the space, and with each aisle that turns up no results, my dread multiplies. I have a horrible feeling I know exactly where she is.

I grab a few bunches of white roses—Mum's favorite—and slam my basket on the counter at the checkout, ignoring Brianna's starry eyes as she scans my things. "Did you see Alex leave?" I ask her.

"Yes, she went toward the post office."

The post office, which is just past Hannah's store. "Great," I say to myself, tossing a few notes on the counter and claiming my bags. "Keep the change."

I stomp out and dump the shopping in the back of my freshly repaired truck, then throw myself in the driver's seat, my eyes laser beams trained on the front of Hannah's store. Ten minutes pass. No Alex. My muscles become more tense by the minute, until I'm forced to remove myself from my truck before a cramp sets in. I walk up and down, constantly looking up to Hannah's store. "For fuck's sake," I snap at no one, striding down the street. What's the problem, anyway? Hannah's the one who's been avoiding me. Maybe now I can get the explanation I deserve. Or perhaps an apology. Not that any of it will make a difference. I'm over it, and Alex's words earlier have only confirmed that it's a good thing.

My heart does some weird galloping shit the closer I get to the cute little arts-and-crafts store. Stupid heart. I reach the door and butterflies join my thumping heartbeats. Stupid butterflies. I open the door and smell her immediately. Stupid raspberries. Then I see her and my whole damn world turns inside out and upside down. Stupid fucking world.

She's sitting at an easel, swishing a brush loaded with paint from side to side. And she's wearing the dungarees she had on the night I met her. Her hair is piled high, wisps falling here, there, and everywhere around the huge red scarf tied in a bow on her head. The legs of her dungarees are rolled up messily, she's in a sleeveless T-shirt, revealing her shoulders, and her feet are adorned in a pair of red Birkenstocks.

She is perfectly Hannah.

"One second," she says, the sound muffled. I register the brush in her mouth as she gets up close to the canvas and dots the brush that's in her hand from one side to the other. Then she leans back. Inspects her work. Nods to herself. Looks at me.

And life as I know it ends here. Her eyes widen in surprise, and definitely panic, and she quickly shoves her palette of paints to the side, taking the spare brush from between her teeth. "Hi," she says, pushing up off the stool.

"Hi," I reply, lifting a pathetic hand. And then we stare at each other, the silence unbearably difficult. I've slept with this woman. Had the most amazing night with this woman. And now . . .

Hannah decides to break the awkward silence, which is a good job as I have no idea what to say now that I'm here. "Did you want something?"

Yes, take your clothes off and let me go to paradise again. "No, nothing." I stuff my hands in my pockets. "Actually yes, I came to get my daughter."

A few creases stretch across Hannah's forehead, and I notice a blob of paint above her eyebrow. I should wipe it off. And the bit on her arm. And the splash on her neck.

"Your daughter isn't here," she says tiredly.

"Oh." Great. So not only do I look like I've made an excuse to venture in here, I also look like a terrible father. Where the hell is she, the little sod?

And as if by magic, Alex prances into the store, all smiley. "There you are," she sings. "What have I told you about wandering off?"

I hear Hannah start chuckling, and although the sound is orgasm inducing, I still growl at my wayward daughter. "We've got to go." I pace to her, turning her straight around and directing her out of the store, letting the door slam behind me.

"Hey, I need to get the paint for the bridge." She struggles in my hold as I march her down the street, but I don't let her win, pushing her onward, having a mental row with myself.

I could have handled that so much better. And what was with that god-awful atmosphere? I had Hannah in my bed only a few days ago. Said things I've never said to anyone in my life. Thought things I didn't know I would ever think.

"Fuck it," I spit, releasing Alex and turning back toward the store. "Get in the truck," I shout over my shoulder, just catching her stunned expression. Good. Let her think I'm mad at her. It'll keep her away while I say what I've got to say to Hannah.

I push my way into the shop and slam the door harder than I mean to. "Just for the record, the other night was amazing." I point a finger at Hannah, and she recoils, her already stunned face stunned further. "I don't know why you've been avoiding me, but I think it fucking sucks."

"Are you for real?" she asks, her delicate jaw ticking wildly. "You shoved me out of your cabin so fast, I'm lucky I don't have fucking bruises!"

My hand drops limply, and I retreat, pointing to the door behind me. "Alex," is all I manage to splutter, as if that's a perfectly reasonable explanation. But apparently it's not, judging by the fire that springs into Hannah's glare.

"Oh, I know. She can't *ever* see me." Turning away, she starts to tidy things up, slamming things here, tossing things there. "That's fine, but you'll have to find someone else to busy yourself with when your daughter's not around. I'm checking out." She swings around. "Now get out."

Fuck me. She really does turn me on when she's mad. "No," I spit back petulantly.

"Yes!"

"No!"

"Fucking yes!"

"Fucking no!" I roar, making the shop shake. "I didn't fucking say *ever*, Hannah. Just not that morning when we were bollock naked and had just orgasmed in my damn shower."

Her mouth snaps shut and she moves back, breathless from her outburst. "What?"

Oh my God, has she completely misread everything? I take my palm to my head and rub, squeezing my eyes closed. Has this just been one huge misunderstanding? "Listen," I breathe. "I know I didn't handle it particularly well, but amid my panic, I did conclude one thing."

"What?"

"I do want my daughter to *meet* you, but not like that."

"You mean naked?"

"Yes, that, and still flushed from the amazing sex we just had." And the flush appears, her hands joining and fiddling in front of her. "Is that why you've been avoiding me?" I ask. "You thought I kicked you out because that night didn't mean anything to me?" I step forward, frustrated not only with Hannah for even thinking I would do that to her, but with myself for giving her reason to. I've been in fucking turmoil the past few days, second-guessing everything, talking myself around in circles.

"Well, yeah." She looks away from me. I don't like it.

"Hannah?"

"But maybe it was for the best, anyway," she says, refusing to look at me.

My stomach turns. "What?"

She swallows, and something tells me it's because she's trying to force words past the lump there. "It couldn't work between us." She turns to walk away.

Oh no she fucking doesn't. I catch her by the wrist, pulling her around and forward, not giving her a moment to protest or fight me. And I show her why her reasons are pathetic, kissing her with all the delicacy she needs, but with all the passion to remind her.

And. It. Is. Fucking. Heaven.

I don't know what her game is, but I just ended it. "It wasn't for the best," I say, nipping the end of her tongue and kissing the edge of her mouth. "So don't you dare say that again." Having her in my arms settles the storm inside me. "Look at me," I demand, and she does. "Do you really think it's not for the best?" I will not let her lie to me. "Or are you telling yourself that?" She looks so very guilty all of a sudden, telling me all I need to know. "No more, okay?"

Hannah brushes under each eye, nodding. "And Alex?"

I think about what Alex said this morning. How resolute she sounded. "I'll talk to her. I just need to find the right time." But when will that be?

Hannah's eyes widen, and she spins away, marching back to the checkout. "Hey, I promise I'll—"

"Dad?"

Nooooooooo!

I stare at Hannah, who has her back to us, frantically searching for words. Why am I here? What am I doing? *Paint!* "Hannah was just getting what we need."

"Yeah, about that," Alex says, casually strolling past me and scanning the shelves. "I didn't tell you what we need." She turns a sickly sweet smile onto me, and I shrink where I stand. Does she know? Is she purposely making me sweat? And does this mean her words from this morning don't stand? Or is she just continuing her silly little teasing game because she's cottoned on to the fact that I fancy someone? Is she getting a kick out of this?

I cough my throat clear. "I used my initiative."

"So what do we need, then?"

Returning Alex's fake smile, I wander over to the shelf, pulling down random tubes of paint. Who the hell knows if they're right, or even suitable for what we need, but I have to keep my hands busy or risk strangling my daughter. "We'll take these." I keep my glare fixed on the little shit as I wander to Hannah and slam them down one by one on the counter, making Hannah jerk each time.

"Thanks, Hannah," Cabbage sings, skipping over, all smiles. If she wasn't okay with me dating, then why's she all chipper? Did she say what she said this morning on the spur of the moment? "We're finishing our bridge."

"You want these to paint a bridge?" Hannah asks.

"Yes."

She reaches for a tube of oil. "You'll need about a hundred of these to paint one of the posts."

"Really?" Alex says, holding back her smile. She knew that. Of course she knew that. Why didn't I think of it? "Oh, well." She sighs. "We'll have to go to Grange, Dad."

I close my eyes and gather patience, not being able to help thinking that Alex has set me up. But then, isn't that a good thing?

"Hannah," Alex says, resting her elbows on the counter.

Poor Hannah's eyes dart briefly to mine, nervous. "Yes?"

"How do you feel about Chunky Monkey?"

"Never tried it," she says, way too fast, her cheeks filling with blood. "Why do you ask?"

I cringe, seeing Hannah cringing, too, regretting her follow-up question. "You should definitely try it," Alex declares. "It'll change your life." She twirls on the spot, throwing a knowing smile at each of us before sashaying out of the shop. "I'll meet you at the truck."

Both Hannah and I watch her go until she disappears around the corner. And then I laugh lightly to myself, shaking my head.

"Oh my God, she knows." Hannah descends into a full-blown panic, pacing to the window to look out.

"She doesn't know." She so fucking knows. But the question is, what does she *think* she knows? That we fancy each other? That we've kissed? Spent the night? *How do you feel about Chunky Monkey?* She really does know.

Hannah shuffles around from the window, her head low, her chin on her chest. I don't like despondency on her. "I'm sorry."

Whoa. Sorry? "What for?"

"I could have played that better. Been more convincing."

"How exactly?" I laugh, now quite amused by the whole situation. I underestimated my daughter, but right now I don't care. She hasn't flown off the handle. She hasn't given me a hard time or made me feel guilty. All my fears have been blown out of the water, because I know my girl, and I saw happiness past her need to play with me.

"I don't know." Hannah sighs, her hand coming to her forehead and rubbing. "This is strange ground for me, Ryan. You, your daughter, my feelings."

I miss everything except the *feelings* bit. "What feelings?" I ask, and she looks up, stunned, like she can't believe she said that. I cock my head in prompt, and I see with perfect clarity what's standing before me. A woman in just as much turmoil as me. Our reasons might be different, but for now I'll take comfort in the fact that this is new territory for us both. I know what'll make me feel better, and I hope it serves the same purpose for Hannah. I go to her, cup the side of her face, and kiss her.

Everything is right in an instant. The sounds she's making, the feel of her, my thoughts leveling out.

And then the door to the store flies open, and Hannah is suddenly out of my arms. I startle, my head still dropped to accommodate our height difference. *What the . . . ?*

I look to my left and find Alex.

Oh God.

I die a thousand deaths when her eyes pass between Hannah and me, her lips pressed together. I straighten. Roll my shoulders. Cough my throat clear. And poor Hannah stands frozen on the spot, looking as guilty as she is.

"You two are fools." Alex sighs, turning and looking out the door again. "Mum's heading this way."

That quickly snaps me back to life. "What?"

"Mum." Alex points down the street and quickly shuts the door. "She's heading this way." She guides Hannah to a stool, helping her down. "Just look busy." Then she turns to me. "Go hide!" she snaps, and I dash out the back quickly as ordered. It's only when I come to a stop in Hannah's kitchen that I wonder why the fuck I'm here. I don't have time to go ask.

The door opens, and I hear Darcy. "Alexandra, darling!"

"Mother!" My girl's way of talking changes in an instant. "What are you doing here?"

"I was passing on my way to the post office and saw you come in."

"I'm just chewing the fat with Hannah."

"You're what?"

"Chatting."

"Oh, I see. Nice to meet you, Hannah."

"And you!" Hannah practically shrieks. I sag against the wall, done for the day. Why the hell did Alex want me to hide? What's my life got to do with Darcy, anyway? It's none of her business who I date. Date? I smile, wide and satisfied, as I stand like a fool listening to my daughter make small talk with her mother. And the whole time, I'm wondering what the hell Hannah must be making of this. My crafty daughter. Her unbearable mother. The poor thing didn't bargain for this.

When I hear Darcy say her goodbyes, I peek around the door, and the look on Hannah's face says it all. She's wondering where the world went wrong. I give her a nervous smile, and she rolls her eyes going to the checkout.

"Seriously, you guys," Alex mutters, jumping down from her stool. And she leaves. With that statement in the air, she just leaves, and I'm suddenly worried that, actually, she doesn't approve.

"You slept with *her*?" Hannah asks, throwing her arm out toward the door once Alex has gone.

I should have expected it, I suppose. "You mean, she's all well turned out and perfect, and I'm not, right? The princess with the pauper. The lady with the tramp."

Hannah withdraws, horrified. "No, I didn't mean that," she says quietly. I take no pleasure from her apparent remorse. "She's awful, Ryan. And I feel terrible for saying that because she's Alex's mother, but, seriously, who does she think she is, looking at me like I'm dirt on her Manolo Blahniks? Who wears Manolos around here, anyway?"

"What the hell are Milano Blankets?" The look that fires my way is a mixture between surprise and . . . something I can't quite read. She waves a dismissive hand at me, and I shrug, because I have nothing else.

"That was Darcy Hampton," I say, exasperated. But back to more important matters . . . "When can I see you again?" I know this really rides on me. I need to have *the* conversation with Alex. Get it all out in the open. Move forward. I'm actually excited for that. Or am I? I glance back at the door, remembering Alex's final words.

"You tell me," Hannah retorts on a pout. Those lips. Magnets. I'm pulled closer, first slowly, but the nearer I get, the more powerful the pull, and I'm soon breathing down on her. Slipping my hand around her back, I haul her close and steal a kiss, making it deep and hard.

She's immediately mine, soft in my hold, a puppet to the passion. God, she's like a drop of heaven.

I release her, though it's a task. "I will." I walk away, pulling the door open. "Just as soon as I've broken the surprise news to Alex."

"I don't think she's going to be shocked." Hannah's out of breath, her words ragged. She's dazed.

I smile and leave her to gather herself, feeling the lightest I've felt in years. The past few days have been completely wasted, our wires getting all crossed. Now that they're untangled and we're both clear, it's time to move this thing along. Maybe I'll cook Hannah dinner. Maybe we'll have a date in the bath. Yes, with candles and all that mushy stuff. Hannah deserves that. I frown to myself. Ryan the romantic? Well, that's one I haven't been called before. I can do romance.

Alex is leaning against the truck when I make it there, her eyebrows high. "We need to talk," I say, getting in the driver's seat, starting as I mean to go on. Positive. Determined. Confident.

"No shit, Sherlock," she replies, hopping in the other side.

I growl at her. "I'll wash your mouth out with soap if I hear another curse word from you."

Kicking her feet up on the dash, she straightens her cap and turns to face me as I start the truck. "How long have you been dating her?"

Dating. I'm not sure what Hannah and I did the other night qualifies as *dating*. But for the sake of my daughter's innocence and setting a good example... "I don't know. Like, a week or something."

"Are you gonna marry her?"

I pull out of the parking bay with a laugh. "Jesus, Cabbage, calm down, will you?"

"Do you love her?"

"What?"

"Is she gonna move into the cabin?"

"Cabbage—"

"Are you going to have babies?"

"No!"

"Have you kissed her?"

That's it. I slam my foot on the brake and turn to face her. Good grief, let's pull this back a bit. "We're dating. That's it. Just dating."

Her face twists, unsatisfied. "That doesn't answer my questions."

"Your questions are all too premature."

"Even the kiss one?"

I nearly choke on my tongue. "*Especially* the kiss one," I clarify, not in the least bit sorry for lying. The last thing I need is Alex thinking kissing on a first date is acceptable. Or even in the first year.

"You're a bad liar." She laughs, quite hysterical. "Two plates in the dishwasher, Dad. She stayed over that night I was at Mum's."

Snookered. What am I supposed to do with this? "We played Monopoly," I mumble like a fool, increasing her hysterics.

"Dad," she sighs once she's got herself under control. "Did you forget I grew up?"

She's something else. "You're ten." I pull off up the high street. "Last time I checked, that doesn't make you the fountain of life knowledge."

"Last time I checked, thirty-nine doesn't make you clueless when it comes to women."

"I'm not clueless." The cheek. "What's gotten into you?" I ask as we approach the bridge. I wave to Mrs. Hatt, but she's unable to wave back, her hands full of cats.

"I just don't want you to screw it up."

I look across the truck, a little surprised. "You don't?"

"No." Alex shrugs, like it's nothing. It's not nothing at all. "I like her," she admits, not telling me anything I don't already know, but it still warms me to the bone.

I grin from ear to ear, reaching over to take her hand. "Me too, Cabbage." Now for something that's been bothering me ... "Tell me why you told me to hide from your mum."

She's quiet for a few moments, as if figuring out how to word it. "It wouldn't be fair." Her head resting back against the seat, she looks across to me. "Her life is falling apart. Yours is falling into place." She squeezes her small hand around mine. "I'm happy for you, Dad. I hope it works out."

I don't think my daughter has ever said anything that's meant so much to me, and I love her so much for it.

I smile, the sun breaking through the clouds right on cue.

My life is falling into place. And it *will* work out.

CHAPTER FIFTEEN

HANNAH

I'm aware of my fixed smile for the rest of the day. It only grows as I'm wrapping the framed painting that I've sold in bubble wrap. The sale won't make me rich, it's just one painting after all—hopefully more soon—but I'm rich on more important things these days. Like peace. And happiness.

I think about Ryan's daughter as I tape the edges of the parcel paper. She's a smart girl. I bet nothing gets past her. And she's so like Ryan, which I conclude is a good thing after meeting her delightful mother. But though Darcy Hampton rubbed me the wrong way, I can't help but feel sorry for her. I've abided women like her before—women who hide behind layers of makeup and designer clothes. Women who exude happiness and confidence, but are empty and lost. I can spot women like that a mile off. After all, I used to be one.

But no matter how deep my internal traumas, I was never mean. I didn't raise myself up by lowering others. I never wanted to hurt anyone, even though I had very good reasons to hurt. Instead, I ended up hurting people who didn't deserve to be hurt. The good people suffered. But it was the only way.

Since Ryan left earlier, my smile has been fixed, but it wavers and it angers me. I have something genuine and real to smile about for the first time in many years. Something to build hope on. Is it possible I could build a life here? Could I stay in Hampton?

I ignore the sting in my eyes and the pang of hurt in my gut as I attach the shipping label. Then I close my shop and wander to the post office to send the painting. But before going back home, I head to the store, deciding I need to celebrate my first sale.

"Hey, Mr. Chaps," I say as I reach up to grab a bottle of wine.

He doesn't look away from stacking one of the freezers, looking at a tub in his hand. "Phish Food," he mutters, placing a tub on top of another on the shelf. "Never heard of fish eating ice cream." He takes another tub, and I make my way over, smiling to myself. "Chunky Monkey? What is it, monkey-flavored?"

When I reach him, I pluck the tub from his hand. Wine and ice cream. That's my night sorted. "It's delicious. You should try it."

He snorts and goes back to stacking the shelf. "Karamel Sutra? My, my, what is the world coming to?"

"You more of a vanilla kind of guy?" I ask with a poorly concealed grin that seems to go way over Mr. Chaps's head, along with my question.

"Nothing wrong with vanilla." He creaks up to standing with the help of his walking stick. "It's my favorite." He wobbles past me on his way to the checkout, and I turn to follow, but come to an abrupt halt when I find someone blocking my path.

Alex's eyes are on my hands, and I look down, quickly remembering what I'm holding. "Delicious, huh?" she asks, making me shrink on the spot.

I don't try to talk my way out of it. Alex is intelligent, and I shouldn't treat her otherwise. I look past her, searching for Ryan, my tummy fluttering with the onset of butterflies.

"He's not here," she says, opening the freezer door. She then proceeds to load her basket with all the tubs of Chunky Monkey.

"Stocking up?"

"Well..." The door swings shut and Alex swings around. "Someone ate my last tub." She lifts the full basket with both hands, her smile sweet.

I feel my cheeks burning furiously. What do I say? Did Ryan talk to her yet? And if so, what did he tell her? Does she approve? Does she hate me? Have Ryan and I come to an end before we've really begun?

She nods at the tub I'm holding. "I'll let you have that one."

"Thanks," I mumble meekly as Alex slinks past me, her face unreadable. "Does your dad know you're here on your own?" I ask like an idiot, for what reason I couldn't tell you. Maybe to remind her that she's a kid and I am not.

"Seriously, Hannah? I'm ten. I can go to the store without a babysitter." She dumps her basket on the counter. "How was Monopoly?"

"Sorry, what?"

"Monopoly. Dad said you played Monopoly the other night, right before you ate my Chunky Monkey in the morning. Did you win?"

I'm in actual physical pain. "Yes." I cough, and she chuckles, the little minx. I straighten my back, just catching Mr. Chaps wiping the grin from his face.

"Cool it, Hannah," Alex says on a sigh. "I'm a woman of the world."

Oh, the dear thing. I join her at the counter and place my wine and ice cream down as she loads her shopping bag. "A woman of the world, eh?"

"Yep."

"Good for you."

She pays for her lifetime supply of ice cream with a credit card, and Mr. Chaps doesn't bat an eyelid.

"Your dad's?" I ask as Alex pulls the card from the machine and slips it into the pocket of her dungarees.

She tugs the bag off the counter. "Considering I'm too young for a credit card, that would be a yes."

"Oh, you woman of the world, you," I tease on a smirk that's returned by her.

"I'm glad I ran into you." She drops her shopping to the floor and hops up onto the counter, kicking her legs. Once again, Mr. Chaps doesn't bat an eyelid, just gets on with ringing my buys through the till.

"Why, so you can get a sick thrill out of making me blush?"

Her grin turns impish. "I'm sorry. I think it's hilarious watching you and Dad pretending you don't fancy each other."

This kid. "Was it that obvious?" I ask, deciding not to beat around the bush any longer. Besides, I'm curious as to what she's making of her dad fancying the pants off me.

"It's a good job you're into painting and not acting, because you're rubbish at it."

She's wrong. I was an amazing actress for years. I even fooled myself for a time. I blink hard, fighting to keep the impending flashback at bay.

"Hannah, are you okay?"

Alex is looking at me with concern, and I scan my surroundings, reminding myself that I'm not in that world anymore. That woman is dead. "Yes, sorry, I'm fine." I swallow and force a smile as I pay and collect my things, picking up Alex's bag and handing it over. "You'd better be going before your dad starts to worry."

Slipping down, she takes her ice cream and we walk out of the store together. "I'll walk you to the end of the street," I tell her, leading the way. I need some fresh air, anyway, something to clear my mind. I slip the bottle of wine under my arm and take off the lid of my Chunky Monkey, diving in as we stroll. "I was thinking . . ." I offer Alex the tub and plastic scoop, and she takes it, helping herself. I owe her, I suppose. "You know the town fete?"

Her eyes roll. "Yeah, I know the town fete."

Of course she does. I forgot; she's a direct descendant of the Hamptons. "So there's this painting competition I'm organizing and I think you should enter."

She stuffs the tub back in my hand. "Really? Do you think I'm good enough?"

God bless her. "Of course you're good enough." I smile around the scoop. "But it won't be anything accidental. You have to paint the high street."

She slows to a stop and turns back, looking down the street, and I join her, my head tilted as I continue to spoon ice cream into my mouth. It really is a lovely high street.

"I'm in," Alex declares, taking the container from my hand. "It'll be nice for me to paint something rather than something painting me." She feeds a huge blob into her mouth and goes on her way.

"What?" I say, following on behind.

"The beauty pageant." She gives me an exasperated roll of her eyes. "I've won it every year since Mum started putting me in disgusting dresses, putting loads of stupid makeup on me, and making me stand on the stage in front of everyone."

"You?" I laugh but quickly rein it in when Alex stops walking and throws me a miffed look. "Sorry, it's just..." I let my eyes travel the length of her body, from her back-to-front baseball cap, past the oversize dungarees, to the beat-up old Vans on her feet.

We get on our way again. "Don't laugh." Alex surrenders the ice cream.

Guilt grabs me. "I'm sorry. Why'd you do it if you hate it so much?"

"Because it makes my mother happy."

"Arh, Alex. You're not responsible for your mother's happiness. She's a grown woman."

"Yeah, I know. She's a real pain in the butt, but she's having a hard time at the moment so I'm trying not to be difficult." We pass the churchyard on the right and the school on the left. I'm desperate to ask what this hard time is all about, but I refrain, not wanting to be nosy. It's really none of my business. "Look at that," Alex says, pointing into the graveyard. "Me and Dad put down those flowers."

I see a spray of white roses. "Is that your dad's mum's grave?"

She nods. "I never got to meet her. Nanna died when I was a baby. I don't remember, but Dad said she thought I was a little angel."

My heart squeezes. "I'm sure she'd be very proud of the lovely young lady you've become."

"Dad says I've inherited her sass and beauty." She gives me a grin, and I smile softly, looking back to the high street.

"I suppose I should be heading back." Handing over the last of the ice cream, I start to wander away, looking back over my shoulder. "My debt is paid."

"Why don't you come back to Dad's with me?"

My getaway is halted by her question, and I turn, wondering if the hope I see in her eyes is my imagination. "Oh, I don't think so," I say, backing away.

"Why?"

I'm stopped again, and I ask myself that very question. Why? "You went to the store for ice cream. If you turn up with me, too, your dad might not be happy." Would he be happy?

"Oh, he'll be *very* happy."

He will be? "How d'you know that?" Listen to me, trying to get reassurance from the ten-year-old daughter of the man I'm crushing on. I can't even bring myself to be ashamed of myself, because, ultimately, her approval means a lot to me. Because it means a lot to Ryan.

Alex drops her bag of ice cream to the ground on an almighty huff. "Because he fed you my Chunky Monkey. Dad's never given away our Chunky Monkey before, and he's definitely never had a woman stay the night."

My back straightens, and while I know this is an obvious sign with how pleased I am, I can't help it. Neither do I want to. I'm *very* pleased. I'm also a little bit surprised. "Oh," is all my brain gives me.

"And, you know, we talked. About you guys playing Monopoly

and all." This kid has the driest sense of humor. "Hannah," she says, stepping toward me. "I don't want Dad to be worried that I might not like him having a girlfriend. So if you come with me now, then that will show him that I'm cool with it. Because I am. Because you're really cool. And I'd love for you to be the lady who Dad lives happily ever after with."

Good God, where did that come from? "That's the nicest thing anyone's ever said to me," I say, feeling a huge lump forming in my throat. She wants her dad to live happily ever after. With me? But suddenly, the gravity of my situation hits me hard in the stomach. If I have to leave Hampton, it won't just be *my* heart that breaks. It'll be Ryan's and Alex's, too. God, am I doing the right thing? I honestly don't know, but I hope I can work it out.

I discreetly sniffle and cock my arm out for her to link. Her smile is huge as she accepts, and we start toward the track that will lead me to Ryan. And Alex doesn't shut up the entire way, talking about anything and everything.

I'm so engrossed by our easy chatter, I neglect to notice that we've arrived at the cabin. Until a sharp *thwack* steals my attention. I look away from Alex and find Ryan by the shed chopping wood.

Holy fuck.

The axe rises. His muscles undulate. His face twists as he puts his full weight behind his swing. And two pieces of wood fly in opposite directions, along with my dignity. Mother always taught me not to stare. She surely didn't mean when faced with Ryan Willis.

"Dad!" Alex yells, and he swings around, giving me an eyeful of that lovely, rough chest. I have to close my eyes and work hard to grab ahold of my scattered senses.

The head of the axe hits the ground, forcing my gaze back up, and Ryan leans on it, wiping his sweaty brow. His relaxed position only accentuates every muscle on his torso. "You picking up strays in the woods again, Cabbage?"

"Oh, you're too damn adorable," I quip, forcing my eyes to my feet so not to ogle Alex's father in front of her.

"I saw Hannah at the store," she declares, releasing my arm and taking my wine from my hand. "I'll put this in the fridge for you." She skips off, leaving me all alone to hold myself up.

The conniving sod. She knows what she's doing. I stand, still as can be, waiting for…I don't know what. A sign that he's pleased to see me? Is he? I glance up and shrug. "I only went to the store for wine and ice cream. She's very persuasive."

"Oh, I know." He wiggles the handle of the axe, drilling it into the dirt so it stands up.

"Hope you don't mind." I motion around his lovely retreat. "Me invading your sanctuary."

His lip quirks at the corner. Ryan Willis has one of those memorable smiles. Not because it's crooked from his scar, but more because it has such an impact on me. It's genuine. Sexy. And not only that, it seems to always trigger one from me. That alone makes it the best smile I've ever encountered. Not to mention the blaze of desire that tears through me each and every time he flashes me one. I have never in my life been so out of control of myself. It's exhilarating. Stimulating. And on that thought, my thighs tighten, and I take a long, stabilizing inhale. It doesn't work. And really, I don't care that my attempts to compose myself fail. I don't care that he sees how flustered he gets me.

He steps forward, his boots crunching through the debris. "I don't mind at all." His full-blown smile breaks as he paces over to me, that chest shimmering with sweat. His jeans are hanging low, the waistband of his boxers peeking out of the top, the hems caught in the tops of his boots. God save me from this torture. My eyes flick to the cabin where Alex just disappeared, worried, and I step back, though my attempt to escape is pathetic. I'm captured by him, his big hands virtually circling my waist.

"Trying to run again?" he asks, lifting me from my feet, leaving me no choice but to grab his naked shoulders.

"Ryan," I wheeze, wanting to check for Alex again, but being unable to tear my attention from him.

He says nothing, just maintains his disarming smile and eases up his hold so I slide slowly down his front until our mouths meet, Ryan dipping to keep us connected when I come to rest on my feet. Every concern escapes me. Every woe I've ever had is forgotten. Every tiny piece of my lost soul is found. He kisses me without a care in the world, so deeply, so meaningfully, and with a pressure that screams devotion.

Lost completely, I slip my hands over his shoulders to his neck, curling around him, squeezing him tightly. And the deadly storm that possesses me becomes damaging for different reasons. Peace has never been so tumultuous. My arms around his neck, his palms firm on my waist. My tongue aches, my lips feel swollen, I'm out of breath. None of it matters. The world melts away, and I melt with it, right in the arms of this breathtaking, mesmerizing man.

"Ryan, what?" he whispers across my lips, pecking the corner lightly before pulling back a few inches to get me in his sights.

I shake my head mildly, telling him I've forgotten what, and drag my palms back down onto his front, unapologetically feeling his chest as I watch.

"You okay?" he asks, and I nod, a while away yet from finding my tongue. "Alex and I were going to head down to the lake. Up for that?"

I nod again, looking up into his eyes. I feel like a million things I want to say are stuck in my mouth, waiting to fall out, but my thick tongue is holding them back. And maybe a little apprehension. It's too soon for my imagination to be running away with me, wondering what could be. Whether Ryan could be the reason I need to stop running. All I know is that I feel like I belong. But...do I? Can I be with a man who is so in the dark? Is that fair? Can I deceive him to that extent?

Sliding his hand to the side of my head into my hair, he closes his eyes and pulls me forward, placing a kiss above my eyebrow. "I'm glad you're here, Hannah," he says against my skin. "And I hope you stay awhile."

I nod once more, and in this tender moment I reluctantly admit to myself that Ryan doesn't deserve my lies. Not when he's been so open with me. Can I tell him everything there is to tell? And what would happen if I did?

"Ahem!"

I don't dive out of Ryan's space, don't panic or dread what's to come. It doesn't appear Ryan's worried, either, his body still, his heartbeats level and calm under my palm. I peek up at him, finding he has a little ironic-smirk thing going on as he turns his head a fraction to the left, remaining close to me. "Ready?" he asks Alex, so casually.

"I've been ready for like five minutes," she counters, and I chance a look her way, finding her taking the steps down from the veranda. She picks up an axe from beside the pile of logs—a smaller axe—and raises it over her head, watching us. "It was you two who were busy." Down it comes, splitting the piece of wood accurately. "Are you done?"

I should be blushing, but instead I'm looking at the axe she's now swinging casually as she regards us with interest. "That's a nice small axe," I say, moving in front of Ryan and pointing at the rather tidy, manageable tool in her hand.

She looks down, clearly confused by my interest. "Don't let the size fool you. It's lethal."

I hear Ryan laughing behind me. "That's the axe I taught Alex to chop with when she was little," he says, sounding wistful. "She's become rather attached to it."

I turn to face him. "So why, when you tried to teach *me*, did you not let me use that one?" It looks far lighter, far more controllable for a first-timer.

"Because"—he dips and gets his face close to mine—"you wouldn't have needed any help." He waggles his eyebrows.

"Crafty," I mutter.

"Or clever." He seizes me and hauls me up over his shoulder, and I squeal like a girl. Collecting his big, manly axe, he marches across the lawn. With me draped over his shoulder.

"Seriously, Dad!" Alex calls after us. "Put her down."

"Yes, put me down."

Ryan stops, tosses the axe aside, and turns, marching back to his daughter. "There's room for you, too, Cabbage." He bends and claims her, tossing her up over his other shoulder, and I laugh, seeing her flop over his muscled back like a sack of spuds, her cap falling from her head. Alex's squeal is far less girlie than mine, but it's still shocked.

"Oh my God, Dad!" She wedges her palms into his lower back as Ryan paces off with us each draped over a shoulder, like he could be carrying nothing, heading to a nearby opening through some trees. Once Alex has successfully flicked her hair off her face, she looks across to me, our faces only a few inches apart, as we bounce up and down in time to Ryan's stride. I can't stop smiling, and, thank goodness, Alex is beaming, too.

"How are you two back there?" he calls, and I freeze when I feel his hand slip onto my arse and squeeze, my eyes widening unstoppably. *What's he doing?*

"Fine," I squeak, giving Alex an awkward smile and a pathetic, nervous laugh when she frowns at me.

Craning her head, she tries to look up and immediately rolls her eyes. She flops back down and grins across at me. "So, has my dad kissed you yet?" She feigns throwing up down Ryan's back while I stare at her in utter astonishment. I mean, it's great that she's being so accepting, but does that mean constant bouts of embarrassment on my part? I'm a thirty-three-year-old woman. She's ten.

"Never give a boy your kisses until he's earned them." *Back at ya, Cabbage.* I need to get this on an even keel before I disintegrate under the constant blushes.

I feel Ryan's palm squeeze my leg. "Hannah's right."

"Well," Alex says casually. "I've kissed a boy before."

Ryan stops in his tracks, and we both jolt as a result. "What was that?"

I give Alex wide eyes before wriggling for Ryan to let me down. He does, although he keeps Alex where she is, helpless and at the mercy of what's to come. Silly girl. "Hey, how come Hannah gets free and I don't?" She has a futile shuffle around. "Dad!"

"*I've kissed a boy before*," Ryan mimics, scowling. "When? Where? Who?"

"All right, I lied!" She huffs and goes floppy on his shoulder. "But my friend has."

"What have I told you about lying?"

"That every lie I tell you, a little piece of you dies."

I can't help my little swoon. Ryan lowers Alex to the ground and she does everything she can to avoid facing him. "Hey." He squeezes her cheeks in one hand, forcing her to look him in the eye. "Stop acting all big britches. It's not funny and it's not clever."

"Stop acting all Romeo, then," she mumbles back through her puckered lips before smacking his hand away. "It's not cool and it's not . . . cool."

"Who says?" I move in and cuddle into Ryan's side, nestling my face under his neck. "I like him acting all Romeo." His arms come around me, and Alex's face twists terribly, disgust creasing it, but I can see clear as day the twinkle in her eye.

Lifting her chin, she pivots and wanders off. "No petting by the lake," she calls over her shoulder.

"Lake?" I question, looking up at Ryan. He just nods the way, and I release him, following Alex through the overgrowth, so intrigued. When I break through the clearing into the open, what I find takes my breath away.

"Welcome to Coca-Cola Lake," Alex calls from a nearby tree, looking up into the branches. "I think this could work, Dad." She points at something—I don't know what—and Ryan wanders over to her and inspects whatever it is she's found.

I turn and make toward the lake and kick off my shoes, walking down to the small shore. I'm completely blown away. The water is so still, no ripples anywhere, and as I gaze around I see a small jetty with a boat. The whole lake is concealed by trees, massive trees, all towering up into the sky, guarding this little gem.

"Hidden enough for you?" Ryan whispers in my ear, coming in behind me.

"Yeah," is all I say, reaching behind me to clasp his head, bringing him closer. I look to my side to find him, and something in his eyes speaks to me. Except I don't know what he's saying. "Why's it called Coca-Cola Lake?" I ask.

"When Alex was little, I taught her to swim here. She thought the bubbles underwater looked like the fizz in cola."

I smile. So cute. "Do you still swim?"

"All the time." Ryan looks across to the tree where Alex is, and I follow his stare, finding her shimmying up the trunk. "She's growing up. I don't like it much."

"But she's such a well-rounded girl. Funny, smart, full of personality. You should be proud."

"She's my biggest achievement in life." Nuzzling into my neck, Ryan bites me with a low growl, and I squirm in his hold. "I'm going to need someone else to focus all my attention on when Alex doesn't need me anymore."

"Oh yeah?" I ask, quite liking the sound of that and ignoring the small pang of guilt for encouraging him.

He chuckles into my skin, planting a chaste kiss there, and tingles roll through me. We both get distracted from our moment when the crack of a branch kills the silence. Alex curses, watching from her position a few yards up the trunk as an arm of the tree plummets. "I'd better go help her before she pulls the whole damn tree down." Ryan releases me and makes his way over.

"I think it's dead," Alex says, starting to shuffle down the trunk. "We can't put it on this one."

Joining Ryan at the foot of the tree, I look up into the branches. "Put what on this one?"

"Her swing." Ryan inspects the ragged end of the branch, frowning when he pokes at the middle. "Diseased," he mutters, brushing off his hands. "You go get the tools, I'll find another tree."

Alex jumps the last few feet from the trunk and dashes off to collect the equipment while Ryan wanders from tree to tree, inspecting each.

I take myself back down to the shore and wade in, wriggling my toes in the dirt, breathing in the clean air and absorbing the stunning scenery. I could get used to it here. It's almost ethereal, so still and silent. Beautifully eerie. "Is this private property?" I call back.

"Depends who's asking."

I peek over my shoulder, seeing Ryan smiling up at some branches. I narrow my eyes a little. "*I'm* asking."

He casts his smile my way. "It's all yours," he says, knowing what I'm thinking. I'll be back as soon as I can with my paints and a blank canvas.

Alex appears loaded down with wood, ropes, and a toolbox. "I'm back!"

"You measure the rope. We're using that branch." Ryan points up and Alex nods her confirmation. "I'll drill the holes in the seat."

"Can't I do the drilling?" she asks, totally put out.

"Does it look like I'll shimmy up that tree, Cabbage?"

I laugh and wander the few paces to dry land, lowering to my backside and settling in. Watching them together is beyond joyous, their banter, their playfulness, their obvious adoration for each other. Ryan's way with his daughter is so endearing, how he guides and instructs her, always patient. He never tries to take over a task, even though it would probably be done in half the time if he did. He's got all the time in the world for her. And she him. I don't think she'll ever not need him; he doesn't have to worry about that. Their bond is too strong. Unbreakable. And studying them here, lost in something they love doing together, I wonder for the first time with any kind of positivity if I'll ever get the chance to be a mum and have this kind of incredible relationship. Or has my chance passed me by?

"It's not level," Alex yells from her position, hanging like a sloth from the branch they're fixing the swing to.

"It is." Ryan places a metal spirit level on the seat of the swing. "Perfectly level. Now get down from there."

Instead of shimmying her way down, Alex releases her legs and dangles, and I hold my breath as she lets go and falls, landing precisely and steadily on her feet. Fearless. I'm in awe of her. I can't imagine living my life so unafraid of anything. I'd love to try, and as I look across to Ryan, I wonder again if this is my chance. My chance to be who I really am, without the mental baggage, and, most important, be that person fearlessly. Am I capable of that?

"Hannah," Ryan calls, snapping me out of my silent pondering. He jerks his head as he holds on to one of the ropes, sweeping an arm out to the wooden seat. "You can be the first to test it."

Me? I haven't been on a swing since I was a teenager. It was with Pippa. She was seventeen, I was fifteen. She sneaked a bottle of Dad's whiskey out of his drinks cabinet and we went to the park and had a few sips. It was only a few sips, but it was enough to make us woozy. And Pippa thought it would be funny to push me on the swing until I threw up. I smile at the memory. Dad went loopy when we got home. Mum shook her head in dismay. And Pippa and I struggled to hold back our drunken laughs while Dad gave us a royal telling-off. Pippa and I couldn't touch whiskey after that. The mere smell made us heave. Still does.

Eager, I push myself up from my backside and make my way over to them. "Is it safe?"

Giving the rope a good yank, Ryan demonstrates its sturdiness. Then he lifts me from my feet and places me on the seat neatly. "Comfy?" he asks, guiding my hands to the ropes on either side of me. I nod, smiling like crazy as Ryan take my ankles and starts walking back.

"Hold tight!" Alex yells, running around the back of me. "Real high, Dad."

Ryan grins, and I hold my breath as he continues back as far as he can go with my ankles in his warm grasp. "Ready?" He stops, holding me in position.

"For anything," I reply on instinct, our gazes locked, my eyes telling him that I trust him. I'm sure he reads my hidden meaning, because his smile fades and he nods the tiniest bit. Then he pulls me back even more and puts weight behind his push, launching me into the air on a shout.

I hold my breath and close my eyes as I sail into the air, relishing a new sense of total abandon as I swing back and forth. The wind is loud, speeding past me, my hair and clothes flailing wildly. It feels purifying, like the web of deceit that has been spun around me over the years and kept me contained is being ripped away by something more powerful than the secrets and lies that have controlled me. It's not the wind that's the force behind my cleansing. It's happiness. It's here, it's now.

It's Ryan.

I throw my head back and open my eyes, looking up into the dusky sky. The clouds are rolling, the sky now darkening. I want this sense of overwhelming freedom to be with me forever, to feel this wild, this fearless, and this happy.

"Hannah!" Ryan yells, and I seek him out, my body naturally leaning back to maintain momentum as I sail toward him. "Higher?" he calls, jumping to claim my feet and using them as anchors to push me.

"Higher!" I yell on a laugh, his face coming close before he's fading away again, sending me up into the clouds. I'm exposed to the elements, but I've never felt so shielded from the world. Hidden. Safe.

I could do this all day, lose myself in this incredible feeling of uninhibitedness, but I start to lose momentum, and Ryan steps back, letting me swing freely until I eventually slow to a stop. My face must say it all. I'm slightly breathless, yet completely invigorated. Windswept and disheveled, and completely unbothered by it.

I let Ryan unclaw my hands from the ropes and pull me up to my bare feet, walking me away from the swing. He's quiet as he pushes some strands of hair from my face, carefully and meticulously fixing me. His expression is thoughtful, his task executed as if he has all the time in the world. "How was it?" he eventually says, kissing my cheek gently.

There is only one word that comes to mind. *Healing.* It seems a little outlandish to say it. So I don't. "Wonderful," I murmur, and his thoughtfulness transforms into satisfaction as his hands still in my hair. The space between us shrinks to nothing, our lips brush…and a cough.

I drop my head so Ryan's mouth slides onto my cheekbone, and he laughs lightly into my skin. "Your turn, Alex."

I look back over my shoulder and see she's planted herself on the seat of the swing, hanging freely as she watches us, a small smile on her face. "I have to go," she says, jumping up. She turns, saying no more, and strides off toward the pathway back to the cabin.

I feel Ryan tense, and I look up at him as he releases me, going after her. My heart drops a little, feeling so guilty for making her feel like she has to leave. "Cabbage, wait," Ryan calls, picking up his pace.

"I'll be late." She waves a hand flippantly in the air without turning back, carrying on her way. Oh God, is she crying? "Have fun, you two."

Oh no. I can't be an obstacle in between her and her father, and that's exactly what I am right now. I feel terrible, and as I glance over to Ryan, I can see he does, too. We shouldn't have been so openly affectionate—shouldn't have pushed this in her face. We should have been more considerate. I need to fix this. "Alex," I call, making chase. I pass Ryan and catch up with her, bracing myself for the worst, but when she turns to face me, there are no tears. In fact, she's smiling, and the sight has me withdrawing, taken aback.

"What?" she asks. "I'm fine."

I stare at her, stuck for words. Is this a typical case of *I'm fine but I'm not fine?* On the outside she's all sunshine and smiles, but on the inside is she thunder and sadness? Crap, I don't know. "I feel like I've invaded your territory," I admit, wondering if I should be speaking so frankly to her. She has to me, so I guess I should adopt the same approach. "I'd rather you didn't leave, Alex. I'll go."

She shakes her head, and I find myself mirroring her, my head moving slowly from side to side, too. "But I want you to stay."

"Then you stay, too. I'll feel better if you stay, too."

"I'm hanging out with my cousin tonight before she goes back to Singapore."

Oh? I look back to find Ryan, and I see he's relaxed now. "I forgot," he says, holding up his phone. "Her mum's here to pick her up." He backs off, leaving me and Alex alone.

"Hannah." Alex tugs on my hand, and I face her again.

"You fixed this up," I say, realizing in this moment what's happening.

She dips and collects her baseball cap from where she lost it earlier, putting it on back-to-front. "I don't like it when he's on his own." She gives me an impish grin. "So look after him."

"What?" I blurt, recoiling. "Look after your six-foot-three-inch ex-MI5 dad?"

"MI5?" she parrots. "What's that?"

"Shit." I slap my hand over my big mouth and kick myself to the other side of the lake and back again.

Alex starts laughing. "Cool it, Hannah. I know what he did."

"You do?"

"Sure. He protected people." Pivoting, she dances off through the overgrowth, all happy, leaving me standing like a loose part alone.

Ryan protects people. That's his job. Or *was* his job. Is it instinct, too? "Alex!" I shout, pulling her escape to a halt. I wait until she's facing me before I speak, if only so she can see the sincerity in me. "Thank you." She knows I don't mean for this. For now. I mean for her acceptance.

She trots back and throws her arms around me, giving me a fierce hug. "Thank *you*." Tears come from nowhere and fill my eyes as Ryan's daughter clings to me like she never plans on letting go. I quickly sniffle back my emotion when I feel her hug ease up, and she pulls away. "Do you know how cool it is watching my dad fall in love?"

My recoil isn't preventable. "What?" I all but whisper, feeling the ground disappear from under my feet. "Alex, that's crazy talk."

"No, it isn't." She doesn't say another word. She disappears, and I stand on the spot, motionless, staring at the empty, darkening pathway.

My palms come to my cheeks, holding my face, as the magnitude of Alex's words rains down on me. Love? It's too soon. But . . . never would be too soon. I look over my shoulder and slowly turn, feeling the pull of something magnetic commanding me. I take careful steps, one by one, measured and tentative, as if going back this way could be the end of me. The question is, will it be a happy end? Or a tragic one? Can I live with myself not knowing?

My walk back to the lake feels like a walk of redemption. Like for the first time since Ryan Willis ran me off the road, I know what I'm doing. I've been shocked into reality, brought around from my dreams by his daughter with the delivery of one sentence. Snapped from a beautiful place of escapism, where I'm not a lost, vulnerable woman living in the shadows of this world but a vivacious, wild, courageous woman with the bravery to take a leap of faith. Ryan found that woman. Doesn't he deserve to keep her?

When I breach the overgrowth into the clearing on the lake's shore, I come to a stop, my situation slamming into me from every direction when I see him. I have to fight to maintain my ability to breathe, appreciation and devastation at war inside me. Ryan deserves everything a woman can give, but this woman only has secrets and lies.

The moonlight hits the still water, ripples of light traveling across the surface. It's beautiful. But more beautiful than that is Ryan standing in the lake, the water up to his waist, the moon casting reflections across his naked back, making it sparkle like he's some kind of magical creature. He's motionless, staring out to the glimmering darkness.

Oh God.

Letting my instinct guide me, I reach for the bottom of my dress and pull it up over my head. I drop it to the ground at my feet before slipping out of my bra and knickers, then walk into the water quietly, my breath hitching when the cold hits my skin. Ryan's head moves, just a fraction, now alert to my presence. But he doesn't turn to find me. He wants me to find him.

I wade through the calm water, and by the time I make it to Ryan, the water is halfway up my back. I move in close behind him, my attention dancing across the beads of water on his skin that are sparkling like crystals when the fading light hits them. And still, he remains motionless, waiting for me, patient. Quiet. He calls to me without a word. And I admit to myself for the first time, I'm desperate to stay here. With him. Forever.

I lift one hand from the water and rest my palm on his shoulder gently as I drop a kiss to the middle of his back. His skin is fire, and so is the blood in my veins. Pure, uncontrollable fire. Ryan started the inferno that's been blazing within me since meeting him, and not even he can put it out.

I drag my mouth across his skin to the edge of his back, and he hisses, his head dropping, the water disturbed by his twitching hands.

I like seeing his fight for control. I like the idea that I can do this to him, send him to the edge of insanity. I want to keep him there.

Taking my hand from his shoulder, I replace it on his hip, flexing my fingers a little, holding on to him, and then I kiss my way down the side of his back until the water stops me from kissing farther. So I work my way across his lower back, and then up the other side, all the time slow, all the time soft, and all the time feeling how tense he is.

The sounds he makes are a mixture of pain and indulgence as he endures me worshipping every inch of his broad back with my mouth, sliding my hands across his skin, feeling every piece of him. I have to reach on my tippy-toes when I get to his nape, using his shoulders to help lift me a little, my boobs pushing into his back as a result. And there I bite at his neck gently, working my way around to his throat. His chin lifts to give me space, but that is his only movement. That and his out-of-control pumping chest.

I can feel his resistance stretching, and now I just have to wait for the moment he breaks. The moment he can no longer remain still. But he's making me wait. He's making me work for that moment when my already tilting universe spins into bedlam. I flatten my tongue and drag it up the column of his throat, forcing his head back farther, the taste of his skin intoxicating. His restrained moan vibrates against my mouth, and then I'm at his ear, breathing against it, and his body solidifies. He's about to break. I bite down on his lobe and drag it through my teeth, then press a kiss in the hollow below his ear. It tips him.

Reaching back, he takes my upper arm and pulls me around his body, and I come to rest on his front, arms locked over his shoulders, legs wrapped around his waist. The tips of our noses touch, his big hands cupping my bottom. Half of his face is shadowed, the other half vividly clear. I wonder for a moment if the moon is casting the same shadows on me. It would be appropriate. Symbolic, even. He can only know half of me. Ryan doesn't know me as well as he believes, and that pains me so much. For him, I want to be just this girl. This Hannah.

The woman he's letting me be. I couldn't face his disappointment if he knew of the woman I once was.

I glance away from him, hiding, and rest my chin on his shoulder, looking out across the still water, my unbearable thoughts getting the better of me. The burden of my past will never leave me. I can pretend to be free of it, but a sadness so deep doesn't ever fade.

Ryan pushes his face into me, encouraging me out, and when he has my eyes again, he still doesn't speak. He doesn't ask questions, even though I know he's sensed my sudden despondency. Instead, he separates our chests a little, giving him just enough room to slide his hand between us.

I breathe in and hold it, bracing my hands into his shoulders. The first feel of him guiding himself to me has me biting my lip. The feel of him nudging at my entrance has my jaw tightening. The feel of him sliding into me has my eyes closing, my forehead falling onto his. And when he hits me deep and stills, I cry out, the sound of my pleasure echoing in the evening air all around us. He releases a strangled gasp, and I roll my head across his, forcing myself to look at him when he flexes his hips and withdraws. His eyes tell a thousand stories. His silence speaks a thousand words. I've never experienced a connection to someone like this, not just physically. This closeness could crush the bleakness in me. With Ryan, there could be only sunshiny days.

I frame his face with my hands, trying to express my gratitude without saying it. He's comfort. He's happiness. He's strength. He's everything a man should be to a woman. The idea that he could be mine forever is too good to be true. The possibility of him giving me this crazy sense of wild uninhibitedness for the rest of my life is hard to let go of. What would he get in return, except my lies and secrets? I blink, and an unexpected tear rolls down my cheek, because realization has just ambushed me.

I'm falling in love with him.

Part of me is desperate to stop myself. I mustn't love someone.

Mustn't let anyone close enough to find the old me. Another part of me wants to let myself go and free-fall into the unknown. Except it won't be the unknown. And that's one of the things I admire most about Ryan Willis. He is who he is, no apologies. He has nothing to prove, no one to impress. Take him or leave him, this is who he is. Can I take him? Can I truly have him and all his wonderfulness?

Ryan must sense my further turmoil, because he's suddenly moving, albeit lazily, driving in and out of me with an almost cruel flow. My woes are forgotten—a tactical move on his part, I'm sure—and I loosen my legs a little, giving him space to indulge me. I wrap one hand around his neck, using it as an anchor to follow his drives, and hold his biceps with the other, feeling his muscles roll. His face is a foot away, but his breathing still warms my cheeks, and I get the perfect view of his handsome ruggedness, every bit of his pleasure there for me to see. His expression is strained, his stare concentrated with dizzying intensity.

The water splashes up our bodies, our pace becomes a little more hectic, and his hands move to my hips, lifting me and bringing me back down onto him. The build of my climax comes fast, and I fight with it, trying to push it back, not ready for this to be finished just yet. "No," I grate, hauling myself forward. Our fronts collide, and I grab his hair at the temples, holding tightly. "Slowly," I order, giving him a purposely soft kiss. He accepts easily, panting around it. "I don't want this to end yet."

Pulling away abruptly, Ryan slides one of his hands up my back to my nape and grips hard. Possessively. "This never ends, Hannah," he whispers, driving forward with purpose.

Does that say everything I need to hear? Or everything I don't need to hear? "Everything ends," I counter softly, my mouth working before my brain. His response to that is another hard pound, and I whimper, trying to fall forward onto him for support. He doesn't let me, tightening his grip of my neck to keep me where he wants me.

"This," he grates, gliding out slowly, ensuring I feel the throb of blood in his veins, "never"—he pauses, his lovely face twisting as he drives forward with power—"ends." He chokes, and I scream, our bodies crashing together. I get no more breathing space, no time between each drive to control my pleasure. Now Ryan owns it, I'm his to control, and I let go, surrendering to the formidable power. Surrendering to him.

Though commanding, his strikes are controlled; he knows exactly what he's doing, and with each pound into me, I lose myself more and more until I'm certain I've passed into another world—a world where only he and I exist.

"Let me kiss you," I gasp, desperate to touch him everywhere possible, hauling myself forward.

"Let me see you," he counters, forcing me back and hitting me with an unforgivingly mind-bending grind. As we maintain our deep connection, flowing in and out of each other, releasing moan after moan, our lovemaking precise and exact, I comprehend that Ryan doesn't want to actually *see* me. He's telling me something. I slowly move in and kiss him, and this time he doesn't stop me. With our mouths working each other's slowly, our tongues twisting carefully, our hands in each other's hair, we climb together to the point we're both shaking violently, the water rippling and swishing around us.

The pressure becomes unbearable, the sizzling heat in my blood out of control. "Ryan," I wheeze, and he nods, telling me he's with me. Our kiss deepens. Our bodies tighten. Ryan loses all control first, his fingers in my damp hair constricting, his open mouth moving to my cheek and resting there as he fights for breath, his body jerking madly. All these effects in him shove me over the edge, and I lock up against him, trying to stem the intensity. My mind is spinning, the pleasure dizzying, my orgasm raging on and on and on. My lungs feel like they've been squeezed dry, my body drained. It's like a chemical reaction inside me, two volatile elements being mixed together and reacting fiercely to each other.

I sag against Ryan's wet chest, replete and dazed, clinging to him with what little strength I have left. My eyes close, and I feel him move through the water slowly, his breathing still labored, and when he reaches the shore, he drops to his knees and lays me on my back, coming down on top of me. He gently kisses my cheek. His arms cage my head. His face falls into my neck.

Ryan wants me. Just the way I am.

He's filling the empty spaces inside me. And I can't help letting him. I can't help admiring him more every day. This is the man I was always supposed to be with.

And now I fear I've found him too late.

Chapter Sixteen

RYAN

Raspberries.

It's new on my list of favorite smells. The woods, the water, the fresh air. And now raspberries, too. She smells so good. *Feels* so good. I'm sure she looks good, too, but I'll be damned if I can raise my depleted body to look at her. So I concentrate on feeling and smelling, my skin on her skin, breathing her into me like she's life.

Her presence has woken something in me that I never knew was sleeping. It's something exhilarating yet fear provoking. Because despite seeing the merciless wildness in her eyes, I can now see something else, too.

A lingering emptiness she's trying to mask.

She's hiding something from me. Keeping me close but distant. But will I push Hannah away if I demand answers? Can I risk that? This exquisite, sweet woman in my arms, no matter how peaceful she is in this moment, is carrying too much pain. I hope she finds it in herself to share her secrets with me. And I hope she lets me ease that pain. Maybe I already am.

I feel Hannah move beneath me, and I shift to give her space, grudgingly giving up my place in her neck to peek down at her. The moment our skin separates, I feel the cold.

"We should get back to the cabin." I want her in my bed and cuddled into my side. I want her warm and safe.

"Are you going to throw me out in the morning?" she asks as I help her up, her face a picture of innocence.

"Depends if you hog the entire bed again," I reply, my gaze dragging down her naked front. I smile at her hard nipples, and she tuts, taking her palms to cover them. What's she doing? I smack down her hands and turn her away from me, reaching under her armpits and cupping her boobs. "Walk," I say into her shoulder, nudging her onward.

"My dress."

"We don't need your dress." We only need skin.

Hannah's arms reach back and hold my waist as we make our way through the overgrowth back to the cabin. It's pitch black now, but the lack of light doesn't hamper me. I know these woods too well.

I only release Hannah once we're inside. I throw a few logs into the fireplace, light them, and pull a blanket off the couch. "Cozy enough?" I ask when I've finished wrapping her up in it.

With a demure smile, she opens the blanket and steps into me, wrapping me up with her. "Yes." Her cheek hits my chest and she sighs.

"So we're just going to stand here all night?"

She nods, and I laugh, detaching her arms from around my back. "Go sit by the fire and warm up." I turn her by her shoulders and send her on her way, and she traipses to the fire and lowers to the rug before it.

I head across to the kitchen and pull the fridge open, grabbing two beers and cracking the caps off, swigging mine as I head back to Hannah. Lowering to the rug, I pass Hannah hers and knock her bottle with mine. I get comfortable, leaning back against the sofa and lifting my arm. She crawls into me with a satisfactory easiness, snuggling close. But not close enough. So I haul her in, squeezing her to my side.

"I could get used to this," she says quietly, taking some beer and resting the bottle on my exposed thigh.

"I'd love it if you did," I answer, prompting her to look up at me a little surprised.

"You mean that?" she asks.

"I don't say things I don't mean," I tell her. "I hope you don't, either."

She's quickly buried back into my side, avoiding my eyes, and that's the worst thing she could have done. Hide. Something tells me she's good at hiding. I stare down at the back of her head, my mind whirling. *Gently does it, Ryan.* I lift my beer to my lips, sipping some back and swallowing as I return my eyes to the crackling flames in the fire.

"That's not very reassuring," I muse quietly, immediately feeling her body harden against me. And neither is that. I see her in my peripheral vision take a sip of her own beer. If I didn't know better, I'd say she's occupying her mouth so she doesn't have to speak. Or filling it to stop from saying something she might regret. I'm a big boy. Whatever it is, I can take it.

My inhale is deep, meant to be heard, a clue that I'm about to speak. I set my bottle down by my thigh and reach for Hannah's, having to tug it from her grasp when she puts up some resistance. I place it next to mine and move in on her, pulling the blanket away, exposing her nakedness to me, but I disregard the endless expanse of creamy, inviting flesh and arrange her body as I hover over her. I lay her down, place her arms by her sides one after the other, and push her thighs apart before lifting myself onto her, gritting my teeth when my dick settles on her lower stomach. I take a much-needed moment to fight the compulsion to have her again. Then I lift my head and look at her. Lust is what greets me. Pure, penetrating lust. *Fuck.*

I'm helpless when Hannah lunges upward, attacking me with hungry lips, and for a brief moment of weakness I succumb to her demand.

No.

I wrench myself away, my breathing shot, and close my eyes as I work hard to talk some sense and resistance into myself. "No," I say calmly, and she moves, rubbing into me, taking that calm back to unbalanced.

God damn her. Opening my eyes, I nail a warning stare on her. It doesn't have the desired effect. She lunges for me again, but this time I move back, escaping her, and she drops to her back on an exasperated gasp. *She's* exasperated?

I tilt my head.

Hannah narrows her eyes.

I quirk an eyebrow.

Hannah's lip curls.

And we stare. I won't break. Something tells me she won't, either. I'd best get comfortable. So I snuggle on down, taking her wrists and pinning them to either side of her head. She growls. It's fucking bliss. Her head jerks up again, trying to catch my lips, but she's not fast enough. I keep my face straight as she settles again, eventually closing her eyes and relaxing. I reward her with a gentle peck on her neck. "Hannah," I whisper across her skin, feeling her pulse quicken under my lips.

"What?" she replies throatily.

"If you ever wanted to share something with me, I would listen." I kiss my way to her jaw, and she closes her eyes, her body trying to arch. "I wouldn't judge." I make it to her nose, kissing the tiny bump. "And it would make no difference to how I feel about you." I reach her eyes and kiss each closed lid before pecking my way to her cheek.

She moans, the sound so sweet, and turns her face into me, finding my mouth without needing to open her eyes. I let her at me, giving a little, hoping to take more. "I'll remember that," she says, her voice rough. "If I ever want to share something with you."

For fuck's sake. I breathe out my impatience, letting my head fall limply back into her neck. I'm surprised when I feel her hand cup the back of my head, holding me to her. It's as if she's trying to comfort me while I deal with defeat. I love the gesture but hate the possible trigger. She's a closed book. Will she ever let me in?

"What's the matter?" Hannah asks, sounding sincerely muddled by my frustration. I'm astounded. Is she being ignorant? Or is she being strategic? Or am *I* being paranoid? Reading too much into this? God damn, is my sixth sense failing me? Do I have this all wrong? Propping myself up on my forearms, I rest my chin on her tummy. "I saw you in Grange this morning," I say, watching to gauge her reaction. Her face remains straight and her body remains soft.

"And?" she asks.

"And . . . what were you doing there?"

"Buying flowers for my mother."

A breakthrough. She has a mother. "Why from Grange? The town store sells flowers."

"Have you seen them?" Hannah laughs. I can't argue with that. The selection isn't exactly wide, and unless you buy them on the day of the weekly delivery, they're not going to last very long.

Moving on. "Where's your mother?"

"She died."

I wince and kick my sorry arse all over the cabin. "I'm sorry."

Her smile is small, but not without emotion. "Why? It's not your fault."

I suddenly feel like a prize chump. I'm not only sorry for her loss, I'm sorry for prying, too. For pressing. For being like a dog with a bone. "You want some Chunky Monkey?"

Her hands land on my arse, her fingernails digging in. "If you've finished wringing me for information, then I'd love some."

"Mockery won't get you anything except—"

"What?"

I look down at her exposed breasts. Smirk. Lick my lips. And dip quickly, taking a bite.

"Ouch!" she shrieks, kicking out her legs and smacking at my back. "Bloody hell!"

I suck her nipple hard, swirl my tongue a few times, have another nibble, and eventually release it with a satisfactory pop. She immediately gives me a good whack on the arm. I chuckle like an idiot and jump to my feet, leaving Hannah to rub some life back into her breast.

"Ryan," she calls, stalling me at the freezer. I look back as I pull open the door. She's on her front now, and that arse is looking mighty tasty, too.

"Yeah?" I say, blindly reaching for the ice cream, my stare glued to her peachy bottom.

"This is me," she replies, rising to her feet, taking the vision of her arse from me. Not that it matters. Now I have her face. And those words. Motioning down her naked form, prompting my eyes to follow, as if I need a reminder of her perfection, Hannah repeats herself, this time clearer, louder, and with a firmness in her voice that I've never heard before. "This is me, Ryan. There is nothing else for me to give you, just this. Isn't it enough?"

I find myself smiling almost immediately, her message received loud and clear. It is *more* than enough. I stalk forward, determined not to waste any more of our night playing silly mind games. I seize her with one arm, hauling her body close to mine. "This is enough. *You* are more than enough. And for the record, I wouldn't change one tiny thing about you."

Her smile blows my world in two.

God, this woman. Whatever's hurt her in the past is gone. I'm here. In her present. Right now, it's me and her and an empty cabin. I need to make the most of it. "How d'you feel about ice stimulation?" I ask.

"I have no idea what you're talking about. What is it?"

"I made it up." I grin wickedly and rest the tub of ice cream on her back, firming up my hold of her, ready for it.

Her eyes widen, her boobs thrusting forward as she bends her back to try to escape the cold. "Oh my God," she says on an inhale. "Ryan!"

I laugh, thoroughly amused with myself, and pace to the bedroom, keeping the tub exactly where it is. She bucks and yells the whole way, thumping my shoulders with deranged fists. "You arse!"

"Behave," I order, tossing her onto the bed and quickly following her down, trapping her before she has the chance to gather her bearings and escape. Sitting on her upper thighs, I pin her arms under my knees and hold up the tub of ice cream, smiling down at her persistent wiggling. "Well, well, well," I muse, and she stills, panting hard. "Seems you're at my mercy." I sit the tub just shy of her chest, watching as it dips when she sucks in air.

"Ryan."

"Ryan, what?" I ask, taking a spoonful and slipping it into my mouth, rolling it around. "Stop?" I slowly bend, lowering toward her breast. "Don't stop?" She surprises me when she wrenches an arm free, but I quickly seize it and slam it down to the bed, continuing my descent, wrapping my mouth around her nipple and letting the ice cream coat it.

"You bastard," she breathes, but that breath quickly turns into a moan when I slather her boob with my hot mouth, dousing down the cold. "Ohhhhh."

That's more like it. Surrender. I release her hand when she fights with me, knowing she's past wanting to inflict pain. She needs something to hold on to, and I happily volunteer my hair, leading her hand there. I wince with her first yank and return the favor by clamping down on her nipple, tugging threateningly, pulling a long, drawn-out hiss from her. "Stop?" I ask, taking more ice cream and moving to her other boob. "Don't stop?"

She forces my face onto her chest, and I feast on her, wondering if Chunky Monkey has ever tasted so good. She writhes, arches, throws her head back, and each lap of my tongue seems to send her crazier and crazier, her hands yanking at my hair viciously. Tell me this isn't fucking heaven. Tell me there's a place I'd rather be.

"You. Taste. Incredible," I mumble, dipping my hand in for more ice cream and scooping out a huge blob. I slap it on her other boob and massage it in while I devour the other. I'm in my element. Then suddenly...not.

"Ryan!" Hannah yelps. "Ryan, stop!" Her panicked voice snaps me from my euphoria in a split second, and I scramble up, knocking the tub of ice cream onto the bed.

"Shit, what?" I ask, my frantic eyes scanning her, searching for what the problem is. She winces, pain invading her face, and doesn't that just rocket my worry. "Fucking hell, Hannah, tell me what's wrong." I faff at her with my hands, not sure what to do, where to touch, how to help.

"Just give me a moment," she wheezes, trying to sit up. I rush to help, easing her up carefully, searching for more signs of discomfort. This horrible pain inside me—it's fear, I think. I've never felt anything like it. I feel helpless. Useless. All I can do is wait for her to enlighten me as to what's wrong. So I sit and wait, seeming patient, but feeling anything but.

"Hannah?" I say softly, unable to stand the torment any longer.

Slowly, she looks up at me. I feel my head pulling back on my neck, my uncertainty crippling. Her face is a blank canvas. There's no clue there for me to read, nothing to tell me what on earth is going on.

"I'm sorry," she barely whispers, holding her hand out to me. I stare at it for a second before I gingerly reach out, taking a hold.

"For what?" Whatever it is, it can be fixed. I know it can be fixed.

She inhales, as if building strength to say what needs to be said. I fear the worst. "Ryan." Her eyes zero in on mine. I hate the resoluteness I see there. I find myself moving back, as if my instinct is trying to pull me away from the danger.

"What?" I reply quietly. Fuck me, have I ever been so nervous?

She's suddenly moving, so fast I don't have time to even blink my vision clear. *What the fuck?* She crashes into me, her palms meeting my shoulders and launching me back onto the mattress. I land with a thud, blinking, looking around, confused. My wrists are grabbed. They're thrust above my head. My waist is straddled. And a face appears, floating above me, the grin splashed across it smug.

"Your turn." She blows the words across my skin.

And I get mad. I can't help it. "For Christ's sake, Hannah. I was worried!"

"Good." She wrestles my arm down to my side and secures it with her knee before repeating on the other side. My eyebrow cocks as I watch her. This is ridiculous. We both know I'd break free with one flex of a muscle. But I let her have her moment. She deserves it, the sneaky little fucker. My heart feels like it's been through the wringer a million times. But now it's lowering to a more stable beat that's not likely to kill me on the spot, I relax, happy to watch her *think* she has control. It's endearing.

She bends over, her face coming closer until her lips are virtually touching my chin. She plants a light kiss on my bristle.

"I thought this was supposed to be torture?" I say, humming my contentment and sinking farther into the softness of my bed. This is more like heaven. "Carry on." I close my eyes on a smile, but they flip open immediately when I feel her teeth sink into my nipple. I inwardly curse to high heaven, but outwardly I won't give her that satisfaction. "Oh yeah, baby," I mumble through my teeth, rolling my hips up and catching her exactly where I intended. Her little gulp makes me smile, and it only widens when I feel her shift to escape my tactical move. *Don't mess with me, gorgeous.* "More," I urge her, flexing my chest up, pushing it closer to her mouth.

I'm annoying her. It's evident in the restrained huff of breath as she snatches up the tub of ice cream from the mattress. I open one eye and find her digging out the remnants, the melted cream trickling down her arm. "Damn, are we out?"

Her scowl is worthy of instant death, and I recoil, feigning fear. "You're going to regret you ever met me, Ryan Willis." She tosses the tub aside and slaps her palms into my pecs, but her attempt to spread the ice cream is really quite pathetic.

I peek down at her hands working circles into my muscles. "You know, Hannah," I say, returning my eyes to hers. She stills. My smile slowly falls away. All of a sudden, the mood is serious. "I don't think I am," I murmur, and she visibly softens above me, every part of her loosening.

I gently pull one arm free from under her knee, and then the other. She doesn't fight me on it. I sit up, slide my arm around her back, and turn her, taking her down to her back. Leveling up our mouths so she'll feel my words as well as hear them, I scan her eyes for a while, examining every fleck of blue. "I'll never regret anything where you're concerned."

Her lip wobbles. "Promise me," she orders, taking her hands to my head and pulling me onto her mouth.

"I promise you." I whisper my vow into her mouth and pray it reaches her heart, her soul, and deep into her mind.

Because never before have I said something and meant it so much.

CHAPTER SEVENTEEN

HANNAH

They say the way to a man's heart is through his stomach. As I stand at the freezer eyeing the endless tubs of Ben & Jerry's, I conclude that the way to Ryan Willis's heart is through his Chunky Monkey, which, I guess, is ultimately through his stomach. Depending on whether he chooses to spread it on my boobs first. There's not much left to land in his stomach after it's melted all over me.

I smile as I reach forward and take a tub, digging my spoon in as soon as I've removed the lid.

"Boo!" Ryan grabs me from behind, and I jump out of my frigging skin, being spun around a few dizzying times before I'm set back on my feet. "Morning." He slams a hard kiss on my forehead and swipes the ice cream from my grasp before getting a spoon and strolling casually to the front door.

I look down at my own spoon, surprised to see the ice cream still there. I shrug as I slip it into my mouth and watch him go, my lips pouting around my spoon. His boxer shorts are tight. His thighs are . . . I cock my head in silent contemplation, the spoon sliding slowly out of my mouth. Edible. I roll the ice cream around, licking my lips when a small piece dribbles out. His hair is tugged to death. I swallow slowly, grin lazily, and go after him.

"What's for breakfast?" he asks as he takes the stairs and wedges his spoon into the tub.

"You're eating it." I rush down and join him. "Don't you get sick of it?" I ask as I shove another spoonful in my mouth.

Reaching for my nape, he tugs me forward onto his lips and forces my mouth open with his tongue, stealing the ice cream I've just put there. He swallows. Smiles at my surprise. And lands a smacker of a kiss on my lips. "I'm finding new ways to enjoy it these days." Slowly turning, he wanders casually over to the outside shower and flips it on. Lord, he looks so good moseying around the wilderness in his boxers. I look down my front, to the shirt I snatched off his floor and threw on this morning. Navy-and-gray plaid. It's perfectly Ryan, therefore perfectly me.

Catching my breath, I pad over to his hammock by the tree and climb in, getting comfortable and swinging in the light morning breeze as I stare up at the cloud-dotted sky. I don't know what time it is. I don't *care* what time it is. I'm not ready to leave this heaven just yet. I bring the spoon to my bottom lip and tap lightly, thinking. *This never ends.* What a wonderful notion.

Ryan Willis is the epitome of peace and freedom. To me, he is the cure, and I love the idea that the cause can't touch me so long as I'm with him. Can this be my new life forever? I smile and close my eyes, the gentle swing of the hammock hypnotizing. He is an unexpected gift after living amid so much ugly for so long. I'm safe here in Hampton. And I'm safe here with Ryan. So I should stay . . . right?

The hammock suddenly jerks, and my eyes flip open as Ryan dives in to join me. "Whoa!" I cry, tossing the spoon aside and grabbing the fabric on both sides. He laughs as he settles at the other end, his feet by either side of my head. I shift my own legs to mirror him. "You've ruined my peace," I grumble playfully, placing my hands on his thighs and stroking in wide circles.

"I am your peace," he replies without hesitation, grinning know-ingly around his spoon. My hands pause in their strokes, one eye narrowing on him. This only encourages a bigger, more satisfied smile from Ryan. Maybe I should be concerned that he's so very right. Yet I'm not. It doesn't mean he has to know the gory details as to why I feel that way. Last night, he pressed me too hard. The way he looks at me, the way he is with me. I don't want that to change. If he knows my story, he will treat me differently. I don't want to be some kind of victim to him.

"I want to paint your lake," I declare, poking at his cheek with my big toe.

"I know," he replies simply, turning his face into my foot and gnashing his teeth playfully. "Like I said, it's all yours." Our smiles collide. "Just let me know when, and I'll pick you up. You can put all your equipment on the back of my truck."

"Maybe I'll close the store early one day, if that's okay with you."

"I'd have you here every minute of the day if I could," he says, the statement breezing out effortlessly and naturally. I study him, searching for any clue that his declaration has surprised him as much as it has me. I find nothing; he just flashes me a half smile, as if he's aware of what I'm doing and he's further reinforcing his declaration. I'm about to yell, *You can!* because I'd love nothing more than passing the days away here with him—painting, cuddling, eating his ice cream, making swings, showering outside, and painting bridges. But this isn't just about him and me.

"Have you spoken to Alex this morning?" Ryan's daughter is his priority. Not me. She's been so accepting and encouraging, but I don't want to overstep the mark. First and foremost, Ryan belongs to her. I respect that.

"I'm picking her up from her mother's later this morning." He digs deep into the tub and licks the spoon before tossing them aside. "Until then"—he struggles up from his back, making the hammock swing precariously—"you're all mine."

I yelp as we're rocked, my hands clinging tightly to the sides. "What about the shower?" I say on a laugh, steam now billowing up from the concrete tiles in the stall.

"The shower can wait." The sight of his big, strong, manly frame negotiating the hammock as he crawls toward me is really quite amusing. He moves forward a few inches gingerly, gasps and stills when we wobble dangerously, waits for us to stabilize, and then moves forward again. And repeat. More than once, I'm certain we're going to be flipped and tossed to the ground, my whole body tense.

When he's halfway to me, he obviously decides he's going about it all wrong and launches himself the rest of the way, landing on me with a grunt. I laugh hard, grabbing at his shoulders to stop him toppling out. It doesn't work. The sky flips up on me, and my laugh turns into a squeal as the sense of falling takes over, the speed and gravity making my stomach cartwheel. "Ryan!" I close my eyes and wait for impact, our tangled bodies seeming to take forever to reach the ground.

"I got you," he says calmly, performing some kind of stealth shoulder turn that has him landing on his back and me splatting onto his chest. He grunts on impact. "That didn't quite go as I planned," he chuckles, helping me to untangle my limbs from his.

"You clumsy oaf." I wedge my palms into his chest and push myself up. "I was quite happy relaxing in the hammock."

"But I wanted a cuddle," he whines, seizing my shoulders and hauling me down again. I'm engulfed in his arms, to the point I can't breathe. But still it's heaven.

"Happy now?" I ask quietly, turning a kiss onto his pec.

"You'll never know," he sighs, returning my gesture and pushing his lips into my hair. "Let's go back to bed."

Wouldn't that be wonderful? But I have a store to open, a fete to prepare for, and he has a daughter to collect. "I need to shower and get all this sticky ice cream off." I sit up, straddling him, and point to various parts of my body where the evidence of his little game last night remains.

"I think you'll find I cleaned you up pretty well with my tongue."

Quickly he sits up and unbuttons my shirt. "See?" He smiles at my chest and reclines, using his arms as a rest, all relaxed.

"You're incorrigible."

"I love your boobs." He shrugs, like it's nothing. Like it's a given. Eyeing him as I slowly rise, standing over him, one foot on either side of his hips, I wonder if he realizes that to me, it's everything. To Ryan, I am perfect, and I've never been perfect to anyone. Not even myself.

I step over him. "You can play with them again tomorrow." I jerk to a stop when his palm wraps around my ankle, and I look down to find he's rolled onto his side to stretch and reach me as I walk away. His face is a picture of cuteness.

"Come back."

"I have to get showered. And you need to pick up Alex. I don't want you to be late." I try to shake off his hold with no success. "Ryan, come on." I can't lie, I'd love nothing more than to disappear in his bed for all eternity, but it's both unrealistic and unfair. If he doesn't take those puppy-dog eyes off me now, I can't promise I won't test how unrealistic and unfair I can be. "Let go," I say, shaking my leg.

"You won't regret it." His voice is low and rough and entirely meant to be.

He's set for a win. I put up some resistance when I feel him pulling against my ankle, and I try to avoid his lazy gaze. I'll be doomed. Alex will hate me. My store will be closed all day.

"No." I kick out my leg more aggressively than I mean to, and as a result a plume of dirt and leaves wafts up into his face, making him cough and splutter. Oops. I use his distraction, while he's brushing at his nose and mouth, coughing, to claim back my leg. "Sorry," I say meekly, smiling nervously when he slowly casts his eyes my way, his chest pulsing as a result of his deep, patience-gathering breaths. "Well, you should have let go," I argue and take a step back when he slowly starts to rise to his feet. Oh boy. He looks mad, but I know otherwise. I'm in for it. I'm thrilled.

Nothing Ryan Willis does or says scares me. I don't second-guess his motives. I know where I stand. And I know he'd never, ever intentionally hurt me.

He straightens, rolls his shoulders threateningly, and even flexes his head from side to side, cricking his neck. I flash him a knowing smile, and he fights his natural instinct to return it. Then I pivot and make a mad dash for it, circling around the back of his cabin. I hear his feet thumping the ground, and I laugh uncontrollably, my adrenaline thundering through my veins. Looking over my shoulder, I see him gaining on me, his smile rampant. I zoom around the back of his truck and skid to a stop, panting. Ryan stops on the other side, his eyes narrowed, his attempt to look ominous absolutely wasted on me.

"You know I'll catch you," he says, not even a little bit out of breath.

Me, on the other hand...I'm already bloody knackered. It's the anticipation. Must be, since I've barely run fifty yards. "Probably," I admit. "You're ex-MI5, after all."

"Then why are you running?" He circles one way, and I circle the other.

"Because I like you chasing me," I say coyly, reversing my direction when Ryan does. He stops. I stop.

"I already caught you, though."

Oh, he did. Fair and square. "Have you ever caught anyone else before?"

His head cocks. "Are you talking about my job or my personal life?"

"Personal life." I press my lips together, holding back my grin as he watches me with playful narrow eyes.

"No, because I've never chased anyone."

My grin breaks, my satisfaction clear. I believe him. "And for work?"

"I've chased loads of people for work."

"And caught them?"

"Yes."

"And killed them?"

"No."

"I don't believe you," I whisper. He's lying. I don't know how I know, yet I know. Maybe it was his instant answer or his suddenly straight face. Or the warning look in his icy stare. He has killed people.

"You should believe me," he says quietly.

I bite my bottom lip, assessing him. Everything is telling me not to push further—his expression, his body language. "Okay," I say, an understanding seeming to pass between us.

"But it doesn't mean to say that I wouldn't."

"Kill someone?"

He nods. "If I had to, yes."

My inhale is quick, my eyes nailed to his. Is he trying to tell me something? "Okay," I say again, and he nods, satisfied.

"Let's stop with the fun and games." His voice is pure gravel. "Come to me."

I shake my head, and he breathes in. "Hannah," he warns.

"Ryan," I counter sweetly.

He chuckles, looking down his bare chest and taking the waistband of his boxers, fixing them. Naturally, my eyes follow his hands. His stomach. An artist couldn't paint a more perfect stomach. His muscles, his physique. He's a warrior. *My* warrior.

He's suddenly moving, and I yelp, bombing off around the cabin. I don't make it very far, feeling his big arm hook around my waist and lift me from my feet, stopping my escape dead in its tracks. I laugh wildly as he mauls at my neck, walking back around to the front of his cabin with my back pinned to his front, my legs flailing, my hands wrestling with his arm across my stomach. "Accept your fate," he mumbles into my flesh. The vibrations of him talking against my throat create a heaviness between my thighs, and I immediately quit fighting him, letting my head roll back, giving him better access.

"What's my fate?" I ask, reaching back to his hair and combing through the strands with my fingers. He detaches his mouth from my neck and turns me in his hold.

"Me," he says, cupping my head with both big hands and kissing me into oblivion. I'm instantly short of breath, instantly consumed, instantly all his again. I'm completely and utterly wrapped up in him, in more ways than one. I hum around his mouth, wanting him to hear just how content I am with his conclusion. If Ryan's my fate, then I wouldn't dream of challenging it. And if he's my fate, then surely I am his.

So his fate is to be fooled into falling for someone who isn't the woman he thinks she is?

His fate is to be deceived and lied to?

I squeeze my eyes closed. I can't think like that. His fate is me as I am now. I sigh into his mouth despondently and break our kiss, going in for a hug, clinging to him like he's life. If he senses my sudden melancholy, he doesn't acknowledge it, but instead picks me up in that easy way he does, just lifting me from my feet with a flex of one arm around my back, and carries me back toward the cabin.

"Wait," I say abruptly, pulling him to a stop. I zero in by the shed and slowly break away from him, rounding his body and wandering over to what's caught my eye. I approach, if cautiously, and rest my hand on the seat. "My bike," I murmur, looking up at him.

"Alex wanted to give it to you," Ryan says, completely unperturbed as he joins me, assessing it himself. "I found it dumped in the bushes down the road. Alex and I fixed it up for you."

I just stare at him, and for reasons I'll probably never know—or maybe I do—I become tearful. I quickly look away from Ryan when he diverts his attention from my bicycle, swallowing down my emotion. It's sparkling like new. Actually, it wasn't this sparkly when I bought it from a secondhand shop. It's positively gleaming.

"What did you do?" I ask, circling it, taking in the transformation. New wheels, with fancy little colorful beads on the spindles, a complete paint job in a vibrant, fire-engine red, a new padded floral seat cover, rainbow tassels hanging from the handlebars.

"We Hannah'd it," he says simply, and I dart my eyes to his. He shrugs. "Alex's words, not mine."

The emotion I managed to beat down comes steaming back to the surface. They Hannah'd it. They made it pretty and bright and colorful. They injected life into my worn-out bicycle.

"Hey, why the tears?" Ryan asks, moving in as I cover my face to hide the rivers running down my cheeks. "Shit, don't you like it?" He takes me in a cuddle, trapping my arms between our chests. "If not, that's cool. I'll buy you a new one, but can you pretend to like this one? Alex has been so excited to show you it."

"No, I love it." I shake some sense into myself, forcing our bodies apart and taking another peek at my born-again bike. Now I notice the new basket, too, which is extra deep. There are even lights on the front and back, and I see my name on the cross frame.

"And this is to transport your arty stuff to wherever you want to paint." Ryan pulls forward a mini trailer and hooks it to the back.

Oh my God. He's thought of everything. "No one's ever done anything so nice for me." I look at Ryan, now unbothered about the state of my face and him seeing it. I want him to know how much this means to me, and it means the absolute world. This simple, thoughtful thing. Ryan didn't just go and buy me a new bike. He knew how much I loved this one, so he repaired it. He and Alex spent hours doing this.

"Not even last night?" Ryan says, and I laugh, nudging him in the side with my shoulder. He wraps an arm around me and pulls me in. "I'm glad you love it."

"I more than love it. Can I take it with me?"

"Afraid not." He kisses my head and walks me back to the cabin. "Alex wants all the glory. And she's still got to fix your new bell on."

I look back, smiling at my fancy new bike. "So I should look surprised?"

"Yes, very surprised." He motions to the bedroom. "Surely your new bike deserves some kind of reward."

How can I refuse? Not that I would, bike or no bike. I swivel on my bare feet and sashay into his room. "Will Chunky Monkey be joining us?"

"No, you're all mine." He stalks after me and tackles me down to the bed. "And I, Hannah Bright, am all yours." And he kisses me.

* * *

As Ryan pulls up outside my store, he cranes his neck, leaning forward in his seat to look up at my shop front. His position gives me the perfect view of his stretched throat. He's in black running shorts and a T-shirt, his hair still damp from our shower, and his scruff a bit scruffier from a missed shave. Because we ran out of time. I grin to myself as I admire him. His voice is rough. His hands large. His jaw sharp. His voice deep. So unassuming and gentle.

I don't realize I'm more or less gawking at him until he turns toward me in his seat. I blink and take the handle of the door. "Thank you for bringing me home."

"You're welcome."

"And thank you for making my bike pretty."

"Welcome."

"And for last night."

"Welcome again."

"And—"

"Hannah." He laughs lightly. "I get it. You're thankful." Rolling his eyes, he hands me his mobile phone. "Put your number in."

I grin as I do, calling myself so I have his, too, before handing it back to him. He jumps out and rounds the truck, collecting me by my hand. I stare down at our woven fingers as he leads me to the door, just so overcome by the rightness of his touch. How he handles me. It's sometimes rough, but I don't ever feel angry vibes. I don't lose my breath with fear. I lose it with something else. For the first time in my life, I like the feel of a man's hands on me. Ryan's hands.

When we reach the door, he motions to the lock, and I quickly slip my hand into the pocket of my dress to retrieve my keys. But they're not there. I pause, thinking. I remember slipping them in my pocket on the way to the store last night. So where...

Oh no. I look up at him, my eyes full of apologies. I've already way-laid him this morning, not that it's my fault, of course. He was the one who couldn't keep his hands off me. Now he's going to have to drive all the way back to his cabin so I can find my keys.

I see the thought click in his mind, and he closes his eyes. But he smiles. "Where are they?"

"They *were* in my pocket." I could kick myself. I seriously need to get myself a handbag. But I don't like handbags. Any accessories, in fact. To me, they symbolize restraint. Control. They symbolize apologies.

"*Were?*" Ryan questions.

"Well, they were until you came over all caveman and threw me over your shoulder last night. Now..." I shrug.

"So basically, they could be anywhere in the woods?" he says, looking up at the windows of my apartment. Basically, yes. Which means they're probably gone forever.

"Is there a locksmith nearby?" I ask in vain, knowing it's a stupid question.

"Yeah."

"There is?" My high-pitched voice is a little surprised, a lot relieved.

He takes hold of the drainpipe to the right of my door and gives it a little tug. "Me." His feet leave the ground, and he hauls himself up the pipe a good three feet, taking the metal with both hands. And I watch in utter astonishment, and maybe awe, as he shimmies up the drainpipe, his trainers wedged into the wall, his arms at full length as he leans back. This explains Alex's fondness for climbing things. It also brings on an onslaught of mental images. They're of Ryan. Armed. Stalking the enemy. My suspicions are only increasing the more I get to know him. He was definitely a spy or something equally thrilling. He might not ever admit it to me—he's probably had to sign a secrecy act or something—but I know. I just...know.

"What are you doing?" I call up to him.

He stops and looks down at me, letting go with one hand and pointing up to my bedroom window. "It's open."

I frown and follow his pointed hand. It is? How could I be so silly? "But I . . ." I fade off and refocus on Ryan. "Just be careful."

He smiles, and the vision is nothing short of gorgeous. His smiles are wicked, in the best possible way, his eyes sparkly each time. "You worried about me?"

I snort. "Not likely," I reply, taking hold of the pipe like I might be of some kind of assistance. "Because you were a spy in MI5, right?"

The sparkle in his eyes grows. "If you say so."

He's off again, moving far too nimbly and efficiently for a guy of his build, pulling himself up with his big arms with ease. And from here, I have the perfect view of his backside. And his thick thighs. And his . . . I shake myself out of my untimely ogling session. "I do say so," I whisper to myself.

He reaches across to the window. Oh, bloody hell. I wince, squinting, as he virtually flings himself across and catches the edge. My breath hitches in my throat. "Be careful!" I yell as he dangles from the ledge.

He looks down at me. He's still smiling, the lunatic. On a cheeky wink, he does some crazy acrobatic move, his legs coming up the bricks, his hand grasping the top of the window. He's literally hanging off the side of my shop, has performed some serious gymnastic-type moves to get there, and the man hasn't even broken out in a sweat. He's a living breathing James Bond. I release the drainpipe I'm still clinging to and step back, watching as he throws his legs through the window, his body following smoothly behind. "I bet he landed on his feet, too," I say to myself just as his head pops out.

He's grinning, and it's wolfish, his head cocking to the side. "Your bedroom?"

I scowl at him. "Yesssss," I say on a drawn-out warning. "Don't get any ideas."

"Like what? Rummaging through your knicker drawer?" He waggles an eyebrow, and I laugh out loud. But mainly because if he's hoping to find anything resembling sexy underwear, he will be sorely disappointed. Plain, simple, white cotton all the way for me. These days, anyway.

"Come open the door," I order as sternly as I can through my laughter. He's gone quickly, though the aftermath of his playfulness remains with me as I smile all the way to the doorstep and take a seat. What an enlightening morning it's been.

Ryan. Even his name makes me smile. He's so easy to be around, and I never expected to feel like that after . . .

I let my thoughts stop there.

"Hey." He appears behind me, and I look up, unable to keep my smile at bay. I take his offered hand, and he helps me to my feet. "Do you have spare keys?" he asks. "If not, I can arrange for a locksmith to come from Grange."

"I have spare keys," I assure him, unexpectedly liking the sound of him taking charge like that. I go to him and reach up, kissing him lightly on the lips. "See you later?"

"You absolutely will." He returns my kiss, though it's only chaste, probably because we both know what will happen if tongues are introduced. Then he leaves, and I wrap my arms around myself, as if to contain the warmth radiating through me. Wandering to the window, I lean on the frame and look out onto the street. This incredible feeling of lightness and serenity is lifting me higher than I thought possible.

I hate the tiny part of my brain for screaming at me that what goes up must come down.

I see Ryan break into a jog before I lose sight of him, and, reluctantly backing away, I go to check that all the windows are locked, trying to recall when I opened the one in my bedroom. I didn't . . . did I?

CHAPTER EIGHTEEN

RYAN

By the time I've finished my run around the town and I'm back at my truck, I feel like I could do it all over again, ten times over. I'm light on my feet. Constantly smiling on the inside.

As I pull the driver's door open, I peek across to Hannah's store. She's sitting on a stool, a paintbrush wedged between her teeth as she stares at a blank canvas. The urge to go in there and give her the inspiration she's looking for nearly gets the better of me. But...

Don't crowd her too much. Give her space. Especially when she's locked and loaded with paints. But what if she doesn't want space? What if I make her day by going in there and smothering her?

What if I don't?

I bully myself into my truck and pull off quickly before I can argue with myself anymore. I can see her later.

As I drive up the high street, I spot Molly on a stepladder reaching up a lamppost. For a moment, I wonder what the hell she's doing. Then I register the small army of children on the playing field, and I remember...

"The town fete," I mutter under my breath, my mood taking a nosedive. I think of Alex, of every year she's been paraded around the stage like a show pig in drag. I should put my foot down and end that madness. She's ten, for crying out loud. Enough is enough.

I nod to myself as I take the turn up to the Hampton Estate, my attention diverted from the upcoming annual fete when I see a Rolls-Royce idling outside the main house. I know that car. I slow to a stop as Darcy's husband, Casper, marches out of the house, dragging a suitcase across the even gravel. He's leaving tracks in his wake that are sure to send Lady Hampton into meltdown. Darcy's mother will have the groundsman out here with a click of her fingers to rake everything back into perfect place.

As I get out of my truck, Casper clocks me, and I raise my hand in a civilized hello. He nods sharply, as brusque as ever with me, and carries on his way, hauling his case into the trunk of his car without waiting for one of the household staff to help. He looks like he's in a hurry. Then I hear her. The delightful mother of my child.

"Casper!" Darcy flies out of the house, looking as frantic as she sounds. "Casper, wait!" She's in a satin robe that's wafting behind her as she scuttles along in the most ridiculous slippers I've ever seen, though they're perfectly Darcy. They're fucking heeled, with baby-pink pom-poms on the toes and a huge sparkling diamantés nestled in the fluffy bobbles. I sigh in disbelief, though I don't know why. This is Darcy Hampton, after all. The woman has been staggering me with her stiff upper lip and bejeweled body for too many years.

She doesn't notice me and my big truck as she hobbles precariously across the gravel in those ankle-breakers, wailing like a banshee. "Casper, you can't go!"

"I'm leaving, Darcy," he grunts as he slams his trunk shut and makes his way to the driver's door. I don't know how, it's really quite a miracle, but Darcy makes it in time to stop Casper closing the door. "Darcy, get out of my way!"

"No, I won't let you leave. I can't be without you, Casper. What will people say? I'll be a laughingstock!"

I shake my head in disappointment. A laughingstock. I take the tips of my fingers to my temples and rub firmly, listening to her squawk on about the family name, the scandal, the embarrassment she'll have to face.

"Casper, be reasonable." She grips his arm with her perfectly manicured fingers. "I'll try harder. Spend less."

"I've met someone else, Darcy," Casper grates, and I snap my head up, shocked. He's leaving her for another woman? "I'm in love with her."

I wince on Darcy's behalf.

"It doesn't matter," she says, her desperation growing. "We'll figure it out. There has to be a way." She reaches in to cuddle him, but he pushes her away. "Casper, please. Don't do this to me. I can't face the humiliation."

"Get away, woman!" he yells, shoving her aggressively. Darcy staggers back, those heels doing her no favors to help keep her upright, and she falls to her posh arse with a surprised cry, her palms hitting the gravel with a slap.

What the hell? I run across the driveway in a blind rage, my blood boiling, and yank Casper out of his fine car, thrusting him up against it by the scruff of his fine shirt. "Seriously?" I growl. "Where do you get off, you string of piss?" His eyes are wide and alarmed, his head rearing back.

"She wouldn't give up. She wouldn't let me leave."

"I don't care if she held a fucking gun to your head. You do *not* raise your hand to a woman, do you fucking hear me?"

He nods, looking away, and though I'm fucking raging, I can see through my anger that he's ashamed. Good. I release him with a shove and turn to Darcy. She's staring up at me, a messy tangle of glamour splayed on the gravel driveway. Yes, I despise the woman, constantly mentally threaten to strangle her, but it's all in jest. Kind of.

I offer her my hand, and her lip wobbles as she takes it, letting me help her up. "Okay?" I ask, and she quickly releases me, setting about fixing her hair and robe. I take no pleasure from her mortification, though why she's mortified is up for debate. Because I've witnessed this little domestic, or because I've seen Darcy with a strand of hair out of place?

"Fine," she spits in that lovely Darcy way before stomping off across the gravel and quickly disappearing into the house.

"Ryan, I've never laid a finger on her before," Casper says, setting about fixing himself, too. "I snapped. The frustration. The stress."

"The circumstances have nothing to do with me. I couldn't give a flying fuck. Just don't ever touch her like that again." I head back to my truck, but something catches my attention out of the corner of my eye. "Alex?" I call, stepping closer to the pillar outside the canopied driveway as she ducks back behind it. I sigh and pace over, my trainers crunching across the gravel, and round the tall stone column. "You'd make a crap spy." Clearly she hasn't inherited my stealth moves. I steer her by the shoulders back to my truck. "How much of that did you catch?" I ask, opening the passenger door and motioning for her to get inside. I bend and brace my hands on the edge of her seat, leaning in.

She pouts as she pulls off the black patent-leather ballet pumps and tosses them into the footwell. "All of it."

Shit. "Sorry you had to see that."

"Don't sweat it." She shrugs. "Shit happens."

I don't admonish her, not this time, just tug the band from her ponytail and toss the ruffled scrunchie thing on the dashboard. "Want to talk about it?"

"Nah."

I give her one last long look before I shut the door, then head around to the driver's side. This conversation isn't over by a long shot, but I'll give her some breathing room for now. I start the engine and pull away as Alex rummages around on the floor for some suitable foot-wear. She finds some beaten-up old red Converses and wrestles them onto her feet.

"How's Hannah?" she asks.

I look across to her, my expression wary. "Fine."

"That's what adults say when they're not fine. Mum's always *fine*." She waves her arm back, indicating the mess we just left behind. "Clearly, she's not fine."

I can't argue with that. "Hannah's good," I tell her instead. *Very* good. That's as much as she's getting. I take the bottle of water from the holder between us and twist off the cap with my teeth. I spit it off in Alex's direction, smiling when she catches it.

"How good?"

I swallow and wipe my mouth with the back of my hand. How did we get onto Hannah, anyway? "I thought we were going to talk about your mother and Casper."

"No, *you* were going to talk about my mother and Casper. I want to talk about Hannah." She helps herself to the water in my hand and swigs. "So talk."

"You're nosy, you know that?" Fuck me, I've faced some uncomfortable situations in my time. Have maintained my expert poker face when on a job, have kept my cool. Yet when my daughter interrogates me about my love life, it all goes to shit.

"We're dating," I mumble.

"Dating, my arse," she says.

"I didn't raise you to talk like that." I toss her a displeased look. I know it'll have zero impact, but still. Who's the parent around here? "Now, back to your mother."

She looks away, staring out of the window. "I just want everyone to be happy."

My heart drops like a stone in my chest. "Cabbage, you can't control other people and what they do. Life will throw you curveballs all the time. It's how you deal with them that shapes who you are." She scuffs her Converse on the dashboard, her face sulky, and I reach across to squeeze her leg. "Mum will be fine."

"If you hate her so much, why'd you rough up Casper?"

I don't know how many times I have to tell her. "I don't hate your mother. I just find her...challenging." Good choice of word. "I might not love her, but I care about her."

"Because she's my mum?"

"Exactly, and without her, there would be no you."

I park up outside the cabin and Alex skips across to the shed where Hannah's bike is. "I think we should give it to her later. I'm gonna put the bell on today. And polish it up."

"Anything you want." I hope Hannah is a good actor. I head inside, toss my keys on the counter, and grab a bottle of water from the fridge. "Wanna go chop some wood for the fire?" I call back as I stride to my bedroom.

"Yes! Dibs on riding shotgun in the wheelbarrow!"

"You don't ride shotgun in a wheelbarrow, Cabbage. I've told you before." I swap my shorts for some combat trousers and shove my feet into some boots, pulling on a fresh T-shirt as I head back out.

"Yeah, but it sounds real cool," she says as I pass, making me laugh my way out of the cabin. She's in quick pursuit, racing past me to make it to the barrow. She falls in, her legs dangling over the edge, and collects one of the axes from beside her, pointing it forward. "Charge," she yells.

"Dressed for the occasion, I see." I take the handles of the barrow and lift, pushing on into the woods.

Alex looks down at the sequins on her puffy floral skirt where her axe now lies across her lap. "You don't like it?" Her tone is full of sarcasm as she strokes across the fabric. "How about the top?"

I look down at the frilled satin monstrosity. Then to the baseball cap on her head. And the Converses on her feet that look about ready for the bin. "Gorgeous."

She relaxes back, looking up at me as I push on. "This is what I'm wearing when you and Hannah get married."

My eyes drop. "Quit it."

She chuckles and jumps out the barrow while it's still moving, running across the clearing we've reached. "This one looks like it's ready to come down." She kicks the trunk of the dead birch, looking up into the branches. "What d'ya think?"

"I think you're right." I set the barrow down and take my axe, swinging it as I make my way over. "But it's too big for you." I look around, hearing Alex snort her displeasure. I spot a small conifer a few yards away. "You take that one, I'll take this one."

"That's tiny!"

"So are you." I pull my T-shirt off and toss it aside, raising my axe and bringing it down with a roar.

* * *

We spent four hours in the woods and collected enough firewood to last us a year. My muscles ache deliciously as we drive back into town to pick up some dinner, but my ears are bleeding as Alex belts out the lyrics to "Wild Thing" by the Troggs, using the dashboard as a drum kit.

I reach forward and turn the stereo down. "Anyone ever tell you that you have really odd taste in music?"

"Yeah. You. All the time." She reaches forward and cranks up the volume again, going back to hitting and smacking at the dashboard. My daughter's a nutter. And I love her all the more for it—unashamed, uninhibited, wild. At least, she is when she's with me. I glance across to her, smiling, just as her arm flies toward the windshield. "Dad, watch out!"

I startle and take both hands to the wheel, seeing a truck coming at us head-on. "Fuck!" My mind takes way too long to register that it's on the wrong side of the road. Our side. And it's not shifting out of the way.

"Dad!" Alex yells, smacking me on the arm and pointing at the road again, as if I could have missed it coming closer and closer. It's going way over the speed limit for around these parts.

I smack at my horn repeatedly, torn whether to swerve or not. If I swerve and then this twat swerves, we're going to hit head-on.

"Fucking hell," I breathe. Adrenaline powers through me, and I yank the wheel hard at the last second, wincing as the sound of screeching tires pierces the air. The other truck clips mine, jolting it violently as I hit the dirt on the side of the road, slamming on the brakes to avoid hitting a huge oak tree.

We skid to an abrupt stop. "Good Lord Christ," Alex breathes from beside me, her hands clawed into her seat on either side of her waist.

"You okay?" I ask as I undo my belt, registering her nod through her shock as I jump out and run around the back of my truck to try to catch the license plate of the asshole who ran us off the road.

"Fuck." I kick the pile of leaves at my feet, just seeing the tail end of the Mitsubishi disappear around a bend. Everything in me wants to chase the stupid fucker down and kick ten tons of shit out of him, but...

I inhale, trying to calm my rage, and go to Alex, opening the door and noting her stiff body. She turns her wide eyes onto me. "What a twat!" she screeches, unclipping her belt and hopping out. She runs to the roadside, her arms flailing. "Learn how to drive, moron!"

"I don't think he can hear you," I mutter, checking the damage. "Motherfucker." A tidy gouge stretches from the bumper to the door.

I hear Alex stomp her way back to me, her hands on her hips. "It's good MI5 taught you how to drive properly when you were a copper, or we might be dead."

I laugh under my breath as I straighten, staring down the road to the bend. "Yeah," I reply quietly.

* * *

We make it into town with no further incidents, and I park outside Mr. Chaps's store, my gaze naturally drifting to the shop a few buildings down, wondering what kind of day Hannah's had and if she found inspiration for that blank canvas. I inwardly smile, thinking I'll pop in and find out, just as soon as I've gotten what we need from the store.

"Hey, Dad, can I go get one of Mrs. Heaven's blueberry muffins?"

"Sure." I dip in my pocket and pull out a pound, flicking it to Alex. She catches it and skips off. "What do you want for dinner?" I call.

"You choose." She pushes her way into the café, and I grab a basket from the entrance to Mr. Chaps's, mentally running through my shopping list as I wander up and down the aisles, deciding on burgers. I make small talk with Brianna at the checkout as she scans and I pack, and flash her a smile as I leave, seeming to surprise her.

What can I say? I'm in a good mood, imbecilic drivers aside. But my mood crashes when I nearly collide with Darcy as I'm leaving. "Oh!" she yelps, jumping back.

I sidestep her, being sure not to catch her with my bags, which is unlikely when she's cleared my path for me, pushing herself up against the crate of potatoes nearby. She's put herself back together since I saw her this morning, her pencil dress absent a single crease, her hair and makeup flawless. "I'm not contagious, Darcy."

"I never said you were," she replies as she pulls off her leather driving gloves.

"You don't have to." I pass her, making sure I keep my distance.

"Ryan, wait." There's urgency in her voice, and a certain softness I'm not used to. Therefore, I'm wary of it. Really wary.

I slow and turn. "What?"

She shifts on her heels, her eyes darting a little. "About this morning."

"You don't have to explain." I saw what I saw, heard what I heard, did what I did. That's it. I start to carry on my way.

"I don't want to explain. I wanted to thank you."

Say what? I slow to a stop again. "You don't have to thank me. Any man would have done the same."

"Maybe, but it was *you* who defended me."

Since when has Darcy Hampton ever thanked me for anything? Mind you, have I ever done anything for her to justify a thanks? Yes, I have. I didn't strangle her when she tried to pass my daughter off as another man's. That deserves a thank-you.

"So, thank you."

"Welcome." I continue to my truck, surprised when Darcy follows me out. "Was there something else?" I ask, not curtly, but not particularly friendly.

She moves in a little closer, which in itself is odd. She's usually very set on putting as much distance between us as possible. "Would you mind if I borrowed Alexandra this evening?"

She never asks me anything, just tells me. Who is this woman? "Why? You had her last night."

"I know, but last night I . . ." She pulls herself back and takes a deep breath. "Last night I wasn't myself. I just want some mother-daughter time with her. You know, makeup, dress-up, a few nibbles."

Nibbles. Like caviar on cute little flatbreads? I look at the bags in my hands, full of ingredients to make some big, fat, juicy burgers. And makeup and dress-up? An image of Alex chopping wood in her frills and Converse sneakers this morning flits through my mind. "Darcy, I don't—" I quickly stop myself from condemning her for inflicting her prissiness on our daughter. Her husband walked out on her this morning. *And* for another woman. Whom he apparently loves. Darcy's lonely. Sad. Wants company. "Sure," I agree, without much more thought, surprising me *and* Darcy. Maybe I should've run it by Alex first.

She smiles brightly at me. I don't think Darcy Hampton has smiled at me since that fateful night over eleven years ago when she batted her lashes and my dick rose to attention. "Thank you, Ryan."

Another thank-you. What's the world coming to? "No problem." I put my shopping on the back of my truck and slam the tailgate up, looking across to the café for Alex, seeing no sign of her. "You want to take her now, or should I drop her off later?"

"Where is she?"

I point my keys to the café just as my girl comes dancing out with a muffin shoved in her gob. "There."

Darcy whirls around and throws her arms up. "Darling!"

"Mum?" Alex waffles, spiking a chuckle from me. She quickly chews and swallows, wiping her face with the cuff of her blouse. I wait for the backlash, bracing myself for the gasp of horror, not just at Alex's manners, but at the state she's in. Unlike me, Alex didn't shower and change after our time in the woods. Instead, she polished Hannah's bike and attached the bell. A flash of guilt comes over me. She wanted to give Hannah the bike this evening over burgers and beer. I'll talk to her. We can give Hannah her new bike any day of the week.

As I lean back against the side of my truck, I watch as Darcy hustles over to Alex, but there's no meltdown over her attire. "Sweetheart," she coos, not even faffing with her clothes or wiping the stray crumbs from her chops. "Dad's agreed to you staying with me tonight."

"He has?" She flashes me a curious look.

"Yes." Darcy links arms with Alex and starts walking them to the store. "We'll have a girlie night. Me and you. How exciting!"

I stifle my laugh when Alex's face morphs into something close to incredulity. I give her a look. *Go with it*, I mouth, and she rolls her eyes.

"Exciting!" she squeals, tossing the paper from her muffin in the bin. "Can't wait."

"Me either, darling. Now we need supplies." Darcy swings around to me, bringing a staggering Alex with her. "Oh my, I just had the most terrific idea. Why doesn't your father join us?"

My back slips against my truck, and I stagger a few paces to the right. *What the actual fuck?*

"Yes!" Alex sings. "That's a terrific idea."

It's the worst idea I've ever heard. What's going on? I rough up her absconding husband, show a bit of respect, and now I'm a part of the family? I don't think so. "That's kind of you, Darcy"—weird of you, actually—"but makeup and dress-up isn't really my thing." I motion down my front to my ripped jeans, battered shirt, and scuffed boots, as if she could have forgotten that I'm the barbarian she always claims I am.

"Oh." Darcy titters all over the pavement, laughing hysterically. "I didn't mean the girlie part. But you could join us for supper."

What weird dimension am I in?

"Come on, Dad," Alex pleads, coming forward with praying hands. Is she kidding me? I'm civil toward her mother, but my girl knows Darcy and I are so far apart on the human spectrum, I may as well be another species. Mixing us together for any longer than needed to exchange our daughter is a risk I'm not willing to take. Darcy's malignant. I'm benign. She's caustic. I'm mild. She's conceited. I'm humble. I inhale, ready to deliver my resounding *fuck no*, but Alex's pleading face sinks my intended refusal and I find myself saying, "Sure," before I can stop myself.

Alex's grin isn't smug or satisfied. It's truly happy. God damn me, what have I done?

"We'll go home and prepare," Darcy says, thoroughly delighted. "We'll cook your dad his favorite."

I only just stop myself from pointing out that she has no idea what my favorite is. In fact, Darcy knows fuck-all about me. Except, of course, the size of my dick. And the fact I'm her daughter's father, albeit proven in court. And obviously, that I live in a cabin—one that's apparently as appealing as a mass grave.

"You don't know what dad's favorite is." Alex speaks up where I won't, pulling her excited mother to a stop at the door of the store.

"Well, you can tell me," she says.

"Burgers," Alex declares proudly, and like I knew she would, Darcy recoils in revulsion, though she quickly composes herself. "Then we will make burgers."

"Great!" Alex claps her hands, and I shake my head, utterly flabbergasted by what's transpiring today. Darcy Hampton is cooking me dinner. The world really has gone mad. "We need to get beers, too," Alex declares. "And gherkins."

I save Darcy the trauma of shopping for all the vile things she needs to make me burgers, heading for the back of my truck and pulling the tailgate down. "You may as well take this." I pull the bags out and make my way to Darcy's car. "Everything you need is in here. Pop the trunk."

She does as I ask, probably for the first time in her life, and I dump the bags in the back. "I have a few things to do, so I'll catch up with you soon."

I look back to Hannah's store, feeling the disappointment starting to set in. I really wanted to see her tonight. *Really* wanted to. Instead of Chunky Monkey, beer, laughs, loose and carefree Hannah, and lots of amazing sex, I've got silver service, champagne in crystal glasses, false smiles, uptight and prissy Darcy Hampton, and no sex. Great.

I drop a kiss on Alex's forehead before she gets in her mother's car, reminding myself that this is for her and no one else. "Say hi to Hannah for me," she whispers.

"I will."

They drive off together, and I even get a cheerful honk of Darcy's horn as she goes. Lord almighty, I'm not sure which Darcy is more insufferable.

I quickly shoot back into the store, deciding I'd better show some hospitality and turn up at Darcy's with some kind of offering, and snag a bottle of wine.

I feel my stomach tickle inside as I pay for it. Butterflies. It's ridiculous yet...amazing.

I walk out of the store with a certain urgency to my pace, my mind telling me that I can snatch half an hour with Hannah before I join Alex and Darcy, but I slow when I see Hannah outside. My smile is instant, and I find myself coming to a gradual stop and standing at a distance, just looking at her. Admiring her. Wondering, again, where on earth she came from. I don't think I care. Somehow, she's here. And somehow, I'm the lucky guy who found her.

She's lost in thought, staring down at something—I don't know what—and her hair is pinned up haphazardly on top of her head, today's scarf lemon with green stars splattered all over it. Does she purposely make the bow on top bigger than her head? Probably. Just like she ensures every piece of clothing she wears is a few sizes too big. Her shirt today is knotted by the tails, and the sleeves rolled up to her elbows. Her jeans are ripped and covered in numerous shades of paint, and her Birkenstocks are worn out but, I'm guessing, dead comfortable. She is simply a stunning disarray.

My heart flutters in my chest and I swallow down some restraint before I tackle her to the pavement. I quietly approach, still watching her, still admiring her, and come to a stop a few feet away, expecting her to notice me and look up. She doesn't.

"Hey."

She jumps nearly a yard in the air, making me jump, too. My hand settles on my chest, but before I can find the will to laugh, I catch sight of her eyes. They're not full of the sparkle I love. Nor the fun and wildness. In fact, they're empty. Haunted. I withdraw, taken aback. She looks like a shell. A hollow vessel. Even her clothes seem gray all of a sudden.

The temperature of my blood drops a few too many degrees, instigating prickles across my skin. "Hannah?" I say quietly, my apprehension clear. She stares at me for a few moments, seeming to be in a trance.

Then, as if something has stabbed her out of her daydream, she jerks, shakes her head, smiles, and blinks a few times. "Hi," she croaks, her gaze dropping to the pavement. "Sorry, I'm in a bit of a rush."

She turns and walks away, her pace not urgent, but I can see the resistance it's taking her not to break out in a run. She makes it to her store, unlocks the door, and is inside before I've had a chance to let the past few minutes sink in.

So I stand and stare down the street, now in my own daze, my head instantly pounding with the effort it's taking to figure out what the fuck just happened. Did she really just sack me off like that? *"I'm in a bit of a rush?"* I say to myself, getting frowned at by Father Fitzroy when he dips past me to take a newspaper from the stand.

"Sorry, son?" he asks, folding it and slipping it under his arm.

"Nothing." I talk my muscles back to life, walking over to the truck and throwing the bottle of wine on the passenger seat. She doesn't seriously think I'm going to smile my way back to my cabin, no questions asked? Oh no. She can forget that.

I slam the door of my truck with brute force and stalk down the street to her door. I'm about to hammer on it, my fist raised and ready, but something pulls me back, my hand lowering, my breathing starting to level out. Awareness trickles into my system, and I stand back, battling against my instinct to bulldoze in and demand answers. She was spooked. Something had frightened her. I close my eyes for a few seconds and talk reason into myself. Handle her gently. For some reason, I've told myself that frequently recently. What the fuck is going on with her?

I knock on the door with an element of control that I'm really not feeling. And wait. Probably not for long, but it feels like eons. So I knock again, ensuring it's calm and controlled. And wait again, counting to twenty to distract myself from charging down the door. Nothing. I get up close to the glass, looking inside. No Hannah. Taking a few steps back on the pavement, I look up at the windows to her apartment. All the curtains are drawn. I frown, looking around me, as if to check it's daylight. The sun's not even close to going down. Why the blackout on her apartment? My bones tingle. It's a feeling I haven't had in a very long time. Apprehension.

I approach the door again, shielding my face as I look through the glass for any signs of life. I find no sign, but I do find something on the floor. Broken glass. The chills that come over me are unstoppable, and I pull my phone out, dialing her. The whole time it rings, I'm itching to burst through the door, and when it finally goes to an automated voice mail, I curse, stuff my phone back in my pocket, and pull out my wallet. I get a credit card from inside and get up close, sliding it down to the point where the door meets the frame by the lock. I hear the catch flip, but when I push into the wood, the door doesn't shift. Bolts.

I stand back, breathing in, starting to shake. It's not anger that has me this way. It's fear. I move in, shoving my body against the door on a grunt as I hold the handle, not wanting to create too much noise. I hear the sound of metal hitting the floor on the other side and push my way in, my eyes immediately falling to the broken glass. I gently close the door behind me and stand still for a moment, listening.

Silence.

Agonizing silence.

My years in the job warn me not to call out. Instead, I walk on quiet feet through her store to the back kitchen, ever watchful, ever alert. I make it to the kitchenette, looking toward the door to the stairs of her apartment. I take the handle. Turn it as softly as I can. Pull it open a fraction, tensing when the wood creaks. And when the gap is big enough for me to peek through, I freeze.

Because I'm staring down the barrel of a gun.

I inhale, taking one calm step back, and slowly follow the length of the arm to the body of the person holding it. "Put the gun down, Hannah," I say coolly, watching her closely, her whole form quaking. "It's me. Ryan. Put the gun down."

It's a staring deadlock for a few, nerve-racking seconds. Me calm. Her completely spooked. I say nothing more, just stand there, motionless, waiting for consciousness to break through her barrier of terror. Her shakes get worse, and her grip on the gun tightens. *It's me, Hannah. It's me.*

She whimpers, her arm drops, and she staggers back, falling to the stairs behind her.

Jesus.

I move in, gently taking the gun from her limp hand. Naturally, I release the magazine and check if it's loaded. I don't know why my heart sinks when I see the bullets. Maybe because it tells me she's prepared to use deadly force. She's afraid for her life. The question is: Who is she afraid of and prepared to kill? But it's a question for later. For now, I have a terrified woman to take care of.

Slipping the magazine in my pocket and the gun in the waistband of my jeans, I move in, taking her hand gently, letting her feel me for a few moments, her fingers weaving through mine as she watches. When I'm sure she's comfortable, her shakes calming, I crouch before her, taking the other hand. She looks up at me. And in this moment, the only thing I can think to do that doesn't involve demanding answers is make her feel as at ease as possible. So I drop to my knees and walk forward on them, getting as close as I can and slipping my hand into her hair at her temple. She leans into it, closing her eyes and breathing deeply but now steady.

"I'm going to kiss you," I say softly, applying a light force to her head and encouraging her toward me. When our lips touch, I taste her fear. It's potent.

My kiss is soft, and meant to be. It's something familiar to her. Something comforting. No tongues. Just lips. Just the feel of me close to bring her around. I only peel my mouth from hers when her body softens. It takes a lot longer than I'd like.

"Come." I help her up and turn her, holding her waist as she climbs the stairs in front of me. I take her to the couch and sit her down, then head for the kitchen on the other side of the room, putting the kettle on, though Lord knows I could do with something stronger. I navigate around the small kitchen, constantly looking across to Hannah as I make us tea. She seems vacant, her body heavy, like there's too much on her mind to deal with. I have to lighten the load. Take the weight off her shoulders. Seeing her like this physically hurts me.

I go to her with the mugs of tea, settling on the other end of the couch, not wanting to invade her space too much. *Handle with care.* "Here." I hold out a cup, and she looks at it for a few seconds, seeming confused, before lifting her gaze to mine. She smiles meekly and wraps both hands around the mug, but she doesn't drink any, just rests it in her hands on her knee.

Then, quiet.

I really don't want to be the one to lead this conversation; I want her to willingly open up. So I wait, resting back, silently willing her to reach deep and find the strength she needs. Long moments pass, and with each second, I slowly lose any hope I had of her confiding in me. She's not going to talk. Does she really think she can nearly shoot my head off and we sweep it under the carpet like it never happened?

No.

"Hannah, we need to talk about this." I lean forward and place my mug on the table, moving to the edge of the couch and turning in to her, my elbows on my knees, my hands clasped.

She looks at me out the corner of her eye, avoiding facing me. "I'm sorry," she whispers on a swallow, finally taking a sip of her tea.

I pinch the bridge of my nose, trying so hard not to show my frustration. She's shutting down. I can't let that happen. "You're sorry for what?"

She shrugs a little. It's the most insulting thing ever.

"Hannah, why do you have a gun?" I feel its cool metal resting against my back. What the fuck do I do with it? Throw it? Reload it? Put it under her fucking pillow? Jesus Christ, where did she even get it?

"I'm a single female. It's just for my own peace of mind." She pushes herself up and wanders to the kitchen, tipping the contents of her mug down the sink.

She's putting too much space between us. Distancing herself. I want to go to her, to shake her secrets out of her, but I force myself to remain where I am. I ignore the *single* part of her pathetic statement. She most definitely is *not* single. Not now. "Right," I say slowly, my frustration growing. Does she take me for a fool? I breathe in some patience before I lose my head. I've lost her in this moment. She's not going to talk, and I know her well enough to realize that the more I push, the more withdrawn she'll become. And that might mean I lose her forever. I can't risk that. I need to think outside the box, figure out what the fuck is going on. And I need to keep her close while I do it.

Resigning myself to my defeat this evening, I stand up from the couch and join her by the sink. She's staring down at the plug, but she looks to her side when she hears me. I haven't touched her, but I know she feels me. "Hannah," I say, and she peeks up at me, all doe-eyed. Her look alone tells me a million things I want to hear. She doesn't want to piss me off. She doesn't want to keep me in the dark. She wants to trust me. But something is stopping her.

I pick her up and sit her on the counter, putting myself between her thighs and taking one arm at a time, placing them around my shoulders, wanting her to feel me. To feel my strength. Resting my fingertip under her chin so she can't dip her head and hide, I put my face as close to hers as I can. "You are not single," I whisper, and she instantly goes soft, her chin wobbling a little. "Can we at least be clear on that little detail?"

Her nod is jerky, and a tiny broken sob escapes before she hauls me into her and hugs me with a force that defies her petite frame. This hug tells me a million things, too. It tells me of her relief. It tells me of her comfort in my hold. It tells me she needs me.

I sigh and cuddle her like she needs to be cuddled—firmly, to lay emphasis on how safe she is. And I settle my face into her neck, getting a hit of my favorite smell. Raspberries and Hannah. I ignore the lingering stench of fear on her and vengeance on me.

With her wrapped around me, I slide her from the counter and walk her to her bedroom, physically having to pry her limbs from around me to free myself. "Get changed," I tell her, resting her on her bed and going to the chair. I scoop up a T-shirt and pass it to her to change into. "I need to call Alex."

"Where is she?" she asks.

"With her mother." I don't go into details. Hannah doesn't need to know about my dinner arrangements with Darcy. I make my way to the door, planning how I'm going to explain myself to my daughter.

"Where are you going?" Hannah blurts, and I stop, looking back.

I have to think on my feet. Why wouldn't I just make the call here? "That glass needs clearing up. And I need to repair your door." She settles immediately, and I ignore the pang of guilt for lying, telling myself that I have no other option. "Where did the glass come from?" I ask.

"A jar. I knocked it when I passed the shelf."

I nod, pulling my phone from my pocket as I head back downstairs. She knocked it off in her haste. In her panic.

Alex answers quickly. "Where are you?" she asks impatiently. "Mum's acting weird. I need reinforcements."

I find a broom propped up in the corner of the store and start sweeping the glass into a pile. "Weird how?"

"In every way! She's not asked me to change out of my Cons and cap. She's not even told me to wash my hands before entering the kitchen. She keeps playing with my hair, but she hasn't tried to tie it up all neat. And don't get me started on the girl talk."

I laugh lightly, grateful for the alleviation of stress for a while, courtesy of my Cabbage. "Girl talk?" Should I have asked?

"Boys. Love. That kind of thing."

Definitely shouldn't have asked. "Where's your mother?" She's talking far too openly and loudly for Darcy to be in the vicinity.

"Gone to change into some slobby clothes."

Yikes. This is serious. "Does she have slobby clothes?"

"No! She has silk robes. When will you be here?"

"That's the thing," I say, guilt consuming me already. "I'm with Hannah. She's not feeling very well."

"Oh, what's up with her?"

I set the broom aside and go to the door, collecting up the broken bolt and inspecting it. I'll need my tools to sort this. "Just a bug, I think. Nothing serious. But would you mind if I stay and take care of her?" I find my shoulders rising, nervous for her reaction as I make sure the latch is secure on the door.

"You'll probably catch it, if you haven't already with all that snogging you two have been doing." She pitters off to a whisper toward the end, which means Darcy is back in her slobby clothes.

"Ta-dah!" I hear her sing in the background. "Perfect, don't you think?"

"Fabulous, Mum." I can hear the exasperation in Alex's voice. "Dad, seriously, I'm confused," she hisses down the line. "What am I supposed to do with her?"

"Embrace it, Cabbage. She's making an effort."

"Fine."

"Don't say fine."

"Super!" she yells, making me wince. "What am I going to tell her?"

Good point. I need to find a way to break my relationship with Hannah to Darcy. I wouldn't have thought she'd care before I learned how concerned Alex is. "Tell her someone drove into my truck." It's not a lie. "Say I had to take it back to the cabin."

"She's going to be devastated. You should see these burgers. They're like magical or something."

"They can't be better than mine."

She snorts. "Never. Say hi to Hannah for me." She hangs up and I go in search of a dustpan, wondering, like Alex, what the hell has gotten into Darcy. She's a mystery.

I stop in the kitchen and look up at the ceiling. Not as big a mystery as what's upstairs, though. I rest back on the counter and spin my phone in my hand, thinking about...

Don't think, Ryan. Do it.

I dial Lucinda and quickly go to the door that leads up to Hannah's apartment, checking that the coast is clear before gently closing it.

"Tell me you're coming back to London," Lucinda blurts in greeting. "Tell me you hate Hampton. Tell me I can put you on the next job."

"Hampton is great."

"Fuck Hampton," she spits. "So to what do I owe the pleasure?"

"I need a favor." I cut to the chase. I know Lucinda will appreciate it. She's not a woman to mince her words; I learned that many years ago.

"And what do I get in return?"

Case in point.

"Fucking hell, Lucinda, what's a man got to do?"

"Well," she purrs. "Since you've asked..."

I recoil. "It was rhetorical."

She cackles wickedly. "What do you want?"

"I need you to look into someone for me."

"Name?"

"Hannah Bright."

"Reason?"

My head drops heavily. Of course it wouldn't be that easy. "Please, Luce."

She's silent for a second, and I imagine her at her desk, a glass of wine set to the side, already typing in Hannah's name on the keyboard. "What else can you give me?"

I quickly check past the door to her apartment again before I speak. "Early-thirties, blond, mother dead, owns an art store in Hampton."

I hear the tapping. "Cute. I'll see what I can turn up."

"Thanks."

She doesn't acknowledge my gratitude, just hangs up. It's probably a good thing, because a second later Hannah appears. I slip my phone back into my pocket and smile. "Okay?"

"I thought you'd gotten lost."

I claim her and steer her back up the stairs. "I'll need to fix the bolt tomorrow when I have my tools."

"Is the door secure?" she asks, looking back over her shoulder.

"Perfectly," I say, if only to settle her. Anyone who knows what they're doing would break in easily. I did, even with the bolts. "And I'm not going anywhere."

I take us to her room and pull back the sheets, motioning with a nod of my head for her to get in as I take the gun from the back of my jeans and smack the magazine back into place. She watches me closely as I open the top drawer of her nightstand and put it inside. What the fuck am I doing? I honestly have no clue. Take it? Leave it? She has it for a reason, and until I find out what that reason is, I'm just gonna have to go with my gut. My gut says the gun stays.

I unbutton the fly of my jeans as I watch her crawl in and plump her pillow before resting back and watching me strip down. I love the sudden loss of bleakness in her eyes. Now they're shimmering. Much better. I slip in and roll onto my side, seizing her and arranging her back to my front, wrapping myself completely around her.

She's safe. And it's my mission to keep her that way.

Chapter Nineteen

FIVE YEARS AGO

Their guests, Curtis and Hayley, were smiling brightly as Katrina made it up onto the deck. The nighttime air was heavy, a faint breeze teasing her loose hair as she made her way to the table. Jarrad stood, ever the gentleman, and pulled out his wife's chair, kissing her cheek when she offered it in her usual way.

"You look stunning, darling." His eyes shone with pride as she lowered to the chair and he took in her choice of dress—a black satin Versace piece with sleeves just past her elbows. Perfect. "Still chilly?" he asked.

"A little," Katrina confirmed, prompting Jarrad to hold out his hand. A moment later, his wife's shawl was in his grasp, courtesy of their onboard butler. Flapping it out, he lay it across her shoulders.

"Thank you." Katrina took the glass of water at her place and downed it all. "Apologies for keeping you waiting."

Hayley reached across the table and patted Katrina's hand, her bright-red hair falling over her shoulder. Katrina had liked her from the moment they were introduced seven years ago at a charity gala. It was Katrina's third date with Jarrad. The first two were at the gallery she worked at, where Jarrad, tall and distinguished, had wandered in one day to buy a piece of art. He walked out with Katrina's number, and though he was a little older than her, she was bowled over by his apparent love of art. She smiled at the memory of how Jarrad had swooped her off her feet with endless romantic gestures and extravagant gifts. How on their fourth date, he whisked her off to Paris because he knew she'd love to see the Banksy exhibition that was on for one weekend only. How he showered her with all the things she loved, and how he seemed to embrace her quirkiness. He was so easy to fall in love with.

Katrina's secret smile faded as she glanced around their yacht. There was no time anymore for spur-of-the-moment trips to Paris. There was no time for her to paint and explore her own passions. There was only time to be Jarrad's wife. When did it all change? She looked at her husband who was lowering himself to his chair, his bespoke suit pristine, every strand of his hair in place, and not a wrinkle on his forehead. A few months ago, Jarrad took her along to one of his appointments with his private doctor. Botox. Apparently, Jarrad decided Katrina was ready for it, too. She was too shocked at the time to say no. Her husband's obsession with perfection was climbing as high as his bank balance.

"No need to apologize," Hayley said, nudging Katrina from her thoughts.

"None at all," Curtis chipped in, rolling his wine around his glass, coating the sides before taking a sip and moaning his approval. Of course the wine was good. Everything was good when you moved in the same circle as Jarrad Knight, and Curtis, being Jarrad's long-serving, loyal right-hand man, certainly moved in Jarrad's circle. "Chapoutier Ermitage l'Ermite Blanc," Curtis said on a sigh. "Damn, that's divine." He toasted the air and grinned at Jarrad.

"The year?" Jarrad asked his friend, wanting specifics.

"Twenty thirteen."

"Correct." He took a sip himself and rolled it around his mouth as Katrina watched, his eyes closing in bliss. She didn't understand it; the wine that set her husband back four hundred pounds a bottle was terribly acidic, gave her rotten heartburn. Jarrad insisted on having the luxury wine with most meals. If it wasn't available wherever they were going, he'd have it shipped. It was just another status symbol. Their wine cellar was jam-packed with the stuff.

"I take it fish is on the menu." Just as Curtis uttered the words, a beautifully dressed lobster was placed in the center of their table, and it was all Katrina could do not to decorate it with vomit. She urgently reached for her water again and chugged down another glass before taking her cloth napkin and patting at her dampening forehead.

"Are you okay?" Hayley asked, a worried frown marring her lovely face.

"Katrina's had a little too much sun, I think," Jarrad piped in. "She'll be fine with a little wine." He looked at the butler and nodded, and a glass was immediately poured for his wife.

"Thank you." Katrina took a discreet breath before she managed a tiny sip as her husband watched, forcing her lips not to twist as she swallowed. "Stunning." She smiled and set her glass down.

"Tomorrow we're exploring the caves." Jarrad diverted the conversation swiftly away from his wife's queasiness. "There are some beautiful waterfalls and rock pools on the island."

Curtis nodded agreeably. "The Taynee?"

"Yes, it's been on my bucket list for years," Jarrad said with a smile, fixing his tie. Katrina hated that tie. It was blood red. Jarrad's favorite. "Since we're here for a week and our meetings don't start until Wednesday, I thought we'd take the girls out for the day."

Katrina was looking forward to tomorrow. She knew of Jarrad's plan because she'd heard him on the phone in his office back home arranging a helicopter to get them to the other side of the island. But she didn't want to spoil his surprise. So she widened her eyes and feigned shock. "Oh my God, Jarrad! I can't wait. What time are we heading out?" She also knew that part after searching his desk for the itinerary.

His smile was fond and proud. "After breakfast." He motioned for their guests to help themselves to the lobster while he relaxed back in his chair. He turned his eyes onto his wife, looking down at the sleeves of her dress. She saw that flash of displeasure, but he was quick to blink it back.

"How's Tilly?" Katrina asked Hayley, redirecting the attention from her husband.

"Oh, a typical six-year-old girl. Knows it all." She laughed, at the same time rolling her eyes. "It's nice to have a little break from being Mum, to be honest, and you two know how to show people a good time. So cheers to the Knights."

"Hear, hear." Curtis chinked glasses with his wife. "God, they're hard work at that age."

"How would you know?" Hayley gave her husband an expectant look. "You're working sixteen-hour days with Jarrad taking over the tech world."

"And we're doing a damn fine job of that, right, Jarrad?" Curtis tucked into his lobster as Jarrad laughed softly. If Jarrad Knight was anything, it was driven, focused, and power-hungry.

"What about you?" Hayley asked Katrina. "When are you two going to take the plunge and have children?"

Katrina laughed under her breath, flicking her nervous eyes to her husband. His smile was wicked. "My gorgeous wife knows I'd have a baby tomorrow." He topped up her wine, giving her a roguish wink. "I don't know why she won't indulge me."

"Because I like having you to myself." Katrina couldn't very well tell him that she was scared to become a mother. She didn't want to upset him or give him reason to doubt her ability. Because to him, she was supposed to be perfect, and that would make her quite imperfect. "For now, anyway."

"Greedy girl," Jarrad quipped, and they all laughed.

* * *

The evening passed by quickly, the chatter and laughs constant. Jarrad and Curtis talked tactics for an upcoming merger, but the women checked out of that conversation rather speedily, leaving the men to talk business as they strolled across the deck to the bow of the yacht to watch the sun drop into the ocean. The main sail cracked in the wind, the breeze increasing, forcing Katrina to wrap an arm around herself.

"So beautiful," Hayley mused as they stood with their wine in hand. "I don't know how I came to be so lucky, but I'll never take it for granted."

Katrina hummed on a small smile, sipping some more wine. She didn't know if her slight alcohol buzz was masking her earlier sickness, but she felt a little better. The outlandishly expensive wine was good for something, after all. "To be blessed with money, happiness, and good men."

Hayley chuckled and nudged her friend in the arm lightly. "To good men."

"Cheers to that." Katrina raised her glass to the sunset, and as she did, her wedding rings sparkled blindingly.

"Jesus, let me fetch my shades," Hayley teased, not missing the flashes of light from the diamonds decorating Katrina's ring finger. Jarrad had bought Katrina an eternity ring for their recent six-year anniversary, and the new addition to her wedding band and engagement ring took that one single finger from insanely expensive to priceless. All three rings were commissioned, the stones rare and precious. The heart-shaped yellow diamond of Katrina's engagement ring was complemented by two diamond-encrusted bands, made specifically to frame the huge showpiece. They never left her finger. The thought of taking them off gave her cold sweats. She never asked Jarrad their value, wouldn't dream of it, but she had seen the insurance paperwork on his desk in his home office. The rings on her finger would buy a substantial family house on the outskirts of London. Her husband loved nothing more than lavishing her in expensive jewelry. He didn't need excuses to buy her nice pieces, but he always seemed to have one. He took the greatest satisfaction in flaunting his wealth, to make sure everyone knew he had pots of cash, whereas Katrina was far more humble. She didn't see their wealth as something to be proud of. In fact, she would go as far as to say she hated their money.

"He has exceptional taste, your husband," Hayley said.

"He does." Katrina cocked a sideways grin. "He married me, after all."

The friends laughed together and returned to watching the sun go down. The amber rays were almost fluorescent, the ocean sparkling madly.

It was beautiful.

Perfect.

Just like their lives.

Chapter Twenty

HANNAH

Just when I thought I could finally relax, all it took was one little thing, one little reminder, and that familiar spiraling sense of fear from years gone by took me prisoner. I was at its mercy. I couldn't control my fear. Couldn't think clearly. So I hid. And I listened. My mind spun off endless scenarios. I convinced myself he'd found me again. That he was in my store. That my life would be over.

And I would do anything to protect myself.

Then I saw Ryan's face. Heard his voice. Felt safety engulf me. Suddenly everything was going to be okay. But what if I had pulled the trigger?

As I lie next to Ryan, watching him sleeping, my hand resting on his bristly cheek, I make myself a promise to be more in control in the future. To not let my fear beat me. A simple picture of a face from my past brought my new world crashing down, almost beyond repair. I can't let that happen again. I can't ruin this new, beautiful thing I have with Ryan.

Leaning in, I kiss the corner of his mouth softly, smiling when he hums sleepily. Then I carefully edge off the bed and go to make coffee. I'm not single. That's what he said amid the madness. The man who's made me *not single* is in my bed. Sleeping. After staying the night with me. "Don't fuck this up, Hannah," I say to myself. Ryan's a good man. He deserves my all. But one thing I have to accept is that he can't have one piece of me. My secrets. No one can ever know that part of me. That alone could ruin everything.

Once I've made Ryan's coffee, I set it by the bed, then throw on my red dress and head downstairs as I knot my hair. It's only now I notice the time. "Shit," I blurt at the clock, blinking my sleepy eyes and checking again. Nine o'clock. How did that happen? I walk to the door and check out on the street, seeing the usual suspects all out in force, going about their daily business. I'd better wake up Ryan.

I pivot and hurry back through the store, but a rap at the door stalls me by the checkout. I look back and laugh when I see Alex's face squished up against the glass. She spots me, and her eyes light up as she waves somewhat frantically.

I rush over and open the door for her, and she bursts through in a whirlwind. "Where's Dad? I need to speak to Dad." She flies around in a panic, to every corner of my store, like she might find him tucked away in a nook. Does she remember how big her dad is?

"What's up?" I ask, closing the door.

"It's my mum."

"Oh my God, is she okay?"

Alex quits the urgent march and levels me with a serious look. "No, she's not okay."

"Why, what's wrong with her?"

"I think she's in love with my dad."

I cough on nothing, not sure what I'm supposed to say to that. From what I know, Darcy and Ryan share a mutual hatred. "What makes you think that?" I ask, and instantly wonder if I should have kept my stupid mouth shut. It's nothing to do with me. But then again...I look back to the stairway to my apartment. He's in my bed. I'm not single. God, am I going to find myself with competition? Should I be worried? *Am* I worried?

"She spoke about him more last night than she's spoken about him in my entire life. And all nice stuff." Alex stamps her foot and starts pacing again, throwing her arms up and down. "God damn him, he should never have pulled that knight-in-shining-armor stunt and saved her. She's gone all mushy."

Now I'm definitely worried. "What knight-in-shining-armor stunt?"

Alex freezes, turned away from me. I wait for her to answer me, hating the swirl of anxiety in my gut. Darcy Hampton is a woman who gets what she wants. I knew that after spending two seconds in her company. Am I capable of fighting for a man? Do I want to? Do I have the strength? God, I knew all this was too good to be true. Finding Ryan, his daughter accepting me. Coming to terms with what I need to do in order to move forward. And now his ex is going to swoop in on her Manolo Blahniks and take my happy place away.

Alex eventually turns to face me, a stupidly fake smile on her face. "You feeling better?"

"What?"

"Dad said you were ill."

I *am* ill. I feel sick to my stomach. But my brain quickly engages, telling me Ryan must've made up the excuse on the phone last night to save telling the truth, which, of course, he can't do. Because he doesn't know the damn truth. "Much better." I take myself behind the counter and open my laptop, just for something to do. She hasn't answered my question, and I hate that I need her to. But I refuse to ask again. So I tap at the keys aimlessly, the silence stretching.

I look up at her and she gives me straight lips, and I go back to tapping. I look at her again. More straight lips. God damn it. I slam the lid down. "What knight-in-shining-armor act, Alex?"

"Urghhhhhh." She sags, her head dropping. "So there was this thing that happ—"

She's interrupted when the door flings open and Darcy Hampton appears. "There you are!" She breezes in, smiley, looking all casual in jeans, riding boots, and a Barbour jacket.

I cock my head, eyeing her suspiciously. She looks rather *outdoorsy*, actually. *Oh my.* The stops have been well and truly pulled out. Whatever knight-in-shining-armor act Ryan has performed for Alex's mother, she's running with it.

"Hi!" she sings, pulling off her leather gloves and picking up a pot of paint from the shelf, inspecting it. "Alexandra tells me you're running a painting competition at my parents' town fete on Sunday."

I shoot Alex a look, and she shrugs. "Yes," I say, because it's all I have.

"How exciting!" Darcy proceeds to collect up a few more pots and brings them to the counter. "My girl had better get practicing, then." Giving me a delighted grin, she pulls out her Mulberry wallet from her Mulberry handbag and hands me her black Amex. This is a very different reception from the last time I saw Darcy Hampton. She seems...bouncy. Nice. Polite. Alex is right to be worried. And so am I.

"I'm sorry, I don't take American Express," I say, smiling in apology.

She recoils, looking rather indignant. "Whyever not?"

"The transaction fee is so high. I simply can't sustain it."

"Oh." She tucks it back in. "I'm afraid I don't carry cash."

"It's fine." I push the paints across the counter, keen to get her out of here. I hope Ryan is still asleep. I can tell Alex is concerned, too. She keeps flicking nervous looks up to the ceiling. "You can pop in and settle up with me when you have some."

"Oh." Darcy beams at me. "How very lovely of you."

"No problem." I quickly load the pots into a carrier bag and walk around the counter, taking the bag to the door with me and opening it for her. "Let me know if you need any help, Alex," I say as I hold up the bag on a smile and Darcy takes it, returning my friendliness.

"Come on, Mum," Alex says urgently, claiming Darcy's hand and pulling her onward. "Lots to do, so little time to do it."

"What's the rush?" Darcy laughs, pulling her hand from Alex's and rearranging her bag in the crook of her arm. "Oh, wait, where did I leave my gloves?" She turns and scans the store. "Ah, there they are," she says as she makes her way back to the counter.

Darcy only takes a few strides in her fancy riding boots before coming to an abrupt halt, just as Ryan comes breezing in from the back, his head down as he rubs at his hair with a towel. His chest is bare. His jeans are undone.

"I would have liked a cuddle in bed when I woke up," he says, and I cringe. "And a shower together."

Darcy gasps, and Ryan looks up. His smile drops, as does the towel to the floor. "Darcy," he breathes, his blue eyes all big and round and *What the fuck?* "What a surprise."

"Shit," Alex hisses, her back flopping against the door. I'm with her. What a shitter.

"Oh my," Darcy all but murmurs, standing stock-still in the middle of my store. "I didn't . . . I wasn't aware . . ." She flies around, and I take no pleasure from the embarrassment on her face. She marches forward, not even looking at me as she passes. "Come along, Alexandra." She's gone like lightning, and Alex sighs, giving Ryan a look of pure exasperation.

"What?" he asks, showing the ceiling his palms. "I didn't know she was here."

"Yeah, well, she certainly knows *you're* here. Half naked. God, Dad!"

"What are *you* doing here, anyway?" he asks.

"I left Mum in the store to come find you."

"Oh, so it's *your* fault." Ryan dips and collects the towel.

"I was dealing with something urgent," she cries. "I needed to tell you."

Ryan's instantly alert. "What?"

I move to the table in the middle of the store and start faffing with the display of art tools, feeling like an intruder. I still don't know what this knight-in-shining-armor stunt is. Am I going to find out?

"I think Mum is in love with you."

Ryan bursts into hysterical laughter, having to hold the counter to prop himself up. Glad he finds it funny. I roll my eyes, and he must notice that no one's laughing with him, but rather scowling, and shuts up immediately, his laughter gone, worry replacing it. "You're joking. Aren't you?"

"No!" Alex yells. "Since you beat up Casper on the driveway, she won't shut up talking about you."

"Beat up Casper?" I ask. "Who's Casper?"

"Her husband," they say in unison.

"And I didn't beat him up. I simply had a word," Ryan says quickly, as if that explains everything. It doesn't. Alex snorts, obviously agreeing with me.

"Why'd you beat him up?" I fire back, unable to stop myself.

"Because he got physical with her when she tried to stop him leaving her. I stepped in. That's all."

"Oh." So he saved her. Now she's fallen in love with him. I can relate. "I'm sorry, Alex," I say sincerely, wishing there was something I could do.

"It was inevitable, I suppose." She pushes her back off the door and wanders out after her mother. "Bloody parents," she mutters as she goes.

The door closes, and I peek across to Ryan. He still looks a little shell-shocked. "It's gone nine o'clock," I say like a fool, at a loss. I want to know how he feels about this breaking news. I realize he's stunned, but is he feeling anything else? Is he considering the potential of playing happy families? Is he wondering if that would be good for Alex? My face screws up. I should be happy for them, I guess. Why wouldn't he choose a glamour-puss like Darcy Hampton over a messy, broken woman who nearly blew his head off last night?

"Hannah?" Ryan calls, and I look at him, quickly wiping away my disappointment. "No," he says simply. I deflate and don't bother trying to hide it. That's all he needs to say. "Not even if I didn't have you."

"I feel bad," I admit, pointing to the door. "She's gone all outdoorsy."

He laughs and comes to me, taking me in his arms. "She's gone crazy, that's what she's done. She doesn't love me. She's just looking for a rebound."

"Really? How do you know that?"

"Because that's exactly what she was looking for eleven years ago when she hunted me down in the pub."

"Oh," I breathe, and he hums and dips, sweeping me off my feet on a squeal. I grab onto his shoulders. "What are you doing?" I laugh as he stalks through the store to the stairs.

"You owe me a shower and a cuddle in bed."

"But I have to open the store!"

"The store's open." He takes the stairs with me draped over his arms, unperturbed by my concern.

"What if anyone comes in?"

"Who comes in the store besides me and Alex?"

"Darcy a few times," I joke, making him snort a burst of laughter. I grin and kiss his cheek. He chose me.

"Baby, I don't think Darcy will be coming back to your store anytime soon."

"She better. She owes me cash."

He looks at me when we reach the top of the stairs. "What for?"

"I gave her some advice."

His eyebrow quirks. "You did, huh?"

"Yep." I raise my nose in the air, and Ryan takes the corner at the top into my apartment. "I told her to stay away from my man."

"Good advice." He launches me into the air and I land with a yelp on the bed. He's on me a second later, blanketing me with his huge body. And he releases a long, deep, satisfied sigh. "Heaven."

Curling myself around him, I silently agree. This has to be heaven, here in his arms. He doesn't try to rip my clothes off. He doesn't flex his groin into me. He doesn't even try to kiss me. He just holds me, and it's out-of-this-world blissful.

"I have some friends visiting on Friday for the night," he says quietly. Friends? How strange I've never thought about Ryan's friends. "We're having a barbecue," he goes on. "A few drinks. That kind of thing. Will you come?"

He wants me to meet his friends? "Yes." One hundred percent, yes. I get an extra-tight squeeze and another contented sigh. I'm meeting his friends. His daughter knows about me. His daughter's mother knows about me. Is all this too fast, though? "If you want me to," I add, searching for the reassurance I suddenly need.

Ryan lifts a little, looks at me, and rolls his eyes. "Shut up." He falls back down and chews at my neck, and I laugh, letting him roll us on the bed until I'm on top. He pushes me up until I'm straddling him, then takes my hands, lacing our fingers, and plays for a few moments. What's he thinking? Or is that a monumentally stupid question? "I want you to know that I'm not going anywhere." He sets my palms down on his chest and pushes them into his pecs. I smile, unsure where he's going with this. "When you're ever scared in the future, I want you to think of me."

I don't mean to, but my body naturally hardens, my hands lifting from his muscled torso. He pushes them back down. "That's all I'm saying," he continues. "If you get scared, think of me."

"I won't get scared," I retort adamantly. I made a promise to myself earlier. I won't let my past get in the way of my future.

"You might." He reaches for my neck and pulls me down until my nose is touching his. "I know I will get scared. And if I do, I'll think of you. How much you make me smile. How complete you make me feel."

I melt on him. "Why would you be scared?"

"Because being in a relationship is scary."

He doesn't mean that, but I appreciate his sentiment. "So we're in a relationship?"

"I hope so," he whispers around a grin, rolling his forehead against mine before kissing me softly as his hand skates under my dress and tugs at the waist of my knickers. He rolls us again, and a second later my underwear is gone, his jeans are around his thighs, my dress around my waist, and he rears back and pushes into me on a strangled groan.

And once again, I'm breathless.

CHAPTER TWENTY-ONE

RYAN

Fuck, fuck, fuck!" I toss the overflowing pan into the sink and dance around the kitchen, cursing my head off as I shake my hand. After three laps, I finally locate enough sense through the pain to get it under the tap. I flip on the cold and shove my hand into the flow, hissing as steam billows up from the burning pan. I groan and lean against the counter, the relief instant on my throbbing hand. That'll teach me for daydreaming.

I take a peek at the damage, seeing a red welt forming on top of my wrist. Great. I snatch a clean towel from the shelf, then go to the freezer for some ice and wrap it in the cloth, holding it on my wrist as I glance at the clock. Five P.M. Jake and Camille should be here soon.

I hear the sound of rustling leaves and look out the window, smiling before I see her appear around the corner on her bike. I hurry to the door and wedge myself up against the frame, all pain forgotten, and watch her. Just look at her. She's pulling her little trailer, having to stand to pedal and get it up the small incline. Since Alex and I presented Hannah with her new, improved bike on Tuesday, she's refused any rides in my truck. That's the downside. The upside is this—watching her face as she does what Hannah does best. Smile. Be Hannah.

When she spots me, she waves like a loon, sitting back in the saddle.

"Hey, look," she calls. "No hands!" Her arms fly up into the air, and my heart flies up into my throat.

"Be careful!" I yell, and she laughs, taking them back to the handles and squeezing the brakes. She rolls to a stop but remains in the seat, her legs stretched to full length so her feet reach the ground. "Evening," I say, my eyes running up and down her legs. The denim shorts she's wearing are my favorite, and today they're matched with a cute little cropped gingham blouse.

"Evening," she replies around a grin.

"Good day?"

"I sold another painting." Her excitement is palpable.

"That's great." I'm chuffed for her. "Who to this time?" This is the third piece of art she's sold, the first two being to a new fan in Scotland.

"The guy in Scotland."

"Wow. Sounds like he's developing a bit of a fixation. Should I be worried?"

"He really loves my work." She swings her leg over the crossbar and kicks the stand down, letting the bike rest. "I just posted it to him. I imagine his castle full of my work in the not-too-distant future." Reaching up to her hair, she tightens the bow on her cream head scarf. "Where's Alex?"

"Darcy's dropping her off soon." I give her a pained look, and she reads it well. It's Friday, and Darcy has avoided me since the incident at Hannah's store on Monday, which is cool with me. I've spent the last few days smiling, because I've been with Hannah and Cabbage for most of them. I am a man in his element. I'm also a man dreading having to deal with his daughter's mother. A woman I slept with one time and have had to endure for the last decade. I've dropped off Alex and picked her up numerous times in the past three days, and each time Darcy has avoided me. Alex says she's quiet. Unusually so. I need to sort this out.

"Well, at least she's not boiling rabbits in your kitchen." Hannah remains by her bike, and I remain at the door. "What time are your friends due to arrive?"

"Anytime." I frown when she still makes no attempt to come to me. "Are you gonna stay there all night, or come here and give me a kiss?"

Her eyes radiate vivacity as she twiddles her fingers. "I don't know. Maybe I'll stay here."

"Get that cute little colorful arse over here now."

"Why don't you get that cute big muscled arse over *here* now?"

Fine by me. I have no problem letting her believe she has the control. Because she absolutely does. I push my shoulder off the frame and mosey on over, but I only take a few paces before she starts to move, too. Ah, the magnetism at play. The energy pulling her toward me. I stop, but Hannah doesn't, her pace quickening until she's running with a stupid big smile on her face. I brace myself for her attack and catch her when she launches her body at me, the force sending me in a spin. Literally. She's head and shoulders above me, she jumped *that* high, her arse resting just right on my forearms, my face level with her boobs. I can't help myself. I sink my face into her cleavage and breathe in. Her laughter sends blood straight to where it shouldn't be right now. I growl and tear myself away, looking up at her. I swear, the face beaming down at me could blow my fucking dick off. "Stop smiling," I order, walking us back to the cabin.

"Why?" she chuckles, messing up my hair by rubbing her hands through it a few times.

"Your smile does things to me." Every part of Hannah does things to me. "And we don't have time." Just as I say that, I hear the sound of tires, and Hannah looks up over my head. I don't need to turn to see who it is. Hannah tensing tells me. "Darcy?" I ask anyway.

She starts to wriggle in my hold, trying to break away. It annoys me more than it should, and I find myself clinging to her harder. "Ryan."

"What?" I grunt, performing a 180 and releasing my arms so Hannah slips down, just a bit, and I can see. Though I still keep hold of her, even if she's pretty much dangling from my front. Darcy remains at the wheel, but Alex dives out and declares her arrival with a cartwheel across the lawn. She's top-to-toe in Darcy's style once again. It doesn't bode well. Is her mother going to go back to being a mega bitch?

"Go talk to her," Hannah whispers in my ear, reaching behind her and taking my arms, pulling them apart. "Like a brave boy."

I throw her a tired look, despite knowing she's right. We have to put this to bed. "Fine," I mutter as Alex lands next to us.

She grabs my hand and holds it up. "What did you do?"

"Yeah, what did you do?" Hannah joins in the concern party, taking my hand from Alex and unwrapping the tea towel. She hisses at what she finds. I'd forgotten about it, to be honest. Now it hurts again.

"It's just a steam burn." I reclaim my limb and wave off their fussing. "Why don't you two go finish off in the kitchen." I claim them both and push them inside before they can protest, closing the door on them. If this gets ugly, I want them out of the firing line of insults that I'm expecting to be tossed my way. I hear the sound of Darcy's engine revving. She's making her escape. No, no. Let's get this sorted out.

Jogging down to the car, I put up my hand, a kind of *I come in peace* gesture. She looks like a petulant child as she lets the window drop, still looking forward when I make it to her side. "Hey," I say lamely.

"Hello," she sniffs curtly. Oh, welcome back, Darcy Hampton. "Is there something you wanted?"

No, but I hear there's something you *wanted.* I quickly shake off that wild thought and brace my hands on the edge of her window, leaning in. *Be a grown-up, Ryan.* She moves away, looking at me out the corner of her eye. "So, you might have guessed," I begin, feeling awkward as shit. "I'm seeing someone." How the fuck is this conversation supposed to go, anyway? How does a father tell his daughter's mother that he has a girlfriend? Is he supposed to? Especially since said mother didn't want him to be a father to their daughter. Really, I don't even owe her this time. But again, for the sake of Alex and peace, I push back my resentment.

"How lovely." She turns a tight smile my way. "I'm happy for you."

"You are?" I say, cocking my head. "Because, fuck me, Darcy, you actually look like you want to stab me right now."

Her nostrils flare. "You're such an ape."

Now I'm an ape? Earlier this week, according to my daughter, she was in love with me. Okay, so that might be Alex being dramatic, but I do know what I witnessed myself. And that was Darcy Hampton being nice to this ape. Darcy Hampton wanted to cook *supper* for this ape. Darcy Hampton went all outdoorsy for this ape. For fuck's sake. The woman is impossible. "Unlucky for you, Darcy," I say, pushing myself off the side of her car and standing up straight. "That means our daughter is half ape, too." I smile sweetly, and she throws me a look that puts all other filthy looks to shame.

"You disgust me." Ramming her car into gear, she slams her foot down and speeds off, kicking up dirt and leaves in my face. Well, that's karma, if ever there was some. She owed me that, I guess.

I look to the heavens and groan, dragging my hands down my face. That didn't go exactly how I planned, but I don't know what I expected. A hug? Her blessing? Tears of happiness that after all these years I've found my person? *Fat chance, Ryan.*

"How'd it go?" Hannah calls from the door, drying her hands on a tea towel as Alex muscles in at her side.

I smile and give a stupid thumbs-up. "Perfect." And they both disperse happily. "Shit."

My phone rings, and I quickly pull it out, hissing when I scrape my burn on my pocket. "About fucking time," I mutter to myself as I answer Lucinda's call. "I've been calling, texting."

"Busy, busy," she replies. "I had a shitstorm in the PR department to deal with."

"And I'm not the cause? Fucking hell."

"I know. We're celebrating later. Shame you're not here."

"Have one for me. Now what do you have?" I walk away from the cabin, checking over my shoulder as I go. I can see them through the window, faffing around the kitchen, laughing and chatting. My girls.

"Hannah Bright didn't exist before 2014."

"What?" I freeze, my hand tightening around my phone at my ear.

"I've gone back as far as I can. The trail ends in June 2014. She lived in Tenerife for a few years, rented a room above a bar. She rented the store a few months back and moved in five weeks ago when she returned to the UK. The store's on a six-month lease."

"Six months?" I ask, my mind in spasm. "If she rented it a few months ago, that means she only has a few months left."

"Correct."

"Why would she only rent for six months?"

"Because she doesn't plan on staying, would be my guess."

My body turns toward the cabin, my heart turning to stone in my chest. She doesn't plan on staying here? "If the trail ends in 2014, how the hell did she rent the store?"

"Oh, she's got a sparkling credit history that goes back twenty years. But Hannah Bright the woman only goes back five."

My fucking brain hurts. "What does that mean, Lucinda?"

"I don't know. That's all I have."

Not good enough. I need more. "Lucinda, you've got to do better than that. Please."

"Who is this woman, anyway?"

"She's a friend of a friend."

"Oh, so you're asking for a friend?" The sarcasm in her tone is potent.

"Yes, and if you find out a bit more for my friend, he will be most grateful."

"Ryan," she sighs. "I don't have time for this."

I'm not beyond begging. She didn't exist before 2014? What the hell is going on? "I'm asking you, as a friend, please just dig a little further."

"Fine!" She slams the phone down, and I turn, looking through the window again. My girls are both dancing around the kitchen, belting out the lyrics to Jon Bon Jovi's "Livin' on a Prayer." I reach up to massage my chest, trying to rub away the ache, and Hannah spots me, waving a wooden spoon, her smile blindingly bright.

I return it as best I can. Fuck me, I feel like I've had my heart cut out of my chest. Who are you, Hannah?

The honk of a horn from behind sounds, and I force a smile to welcome our guests. Jake pulls up next to my truck and hops out, and I can't lie, I'm alarmed by how tired he looks. "Shit, mate, you look ready for the morgue." I go to him and get a smack on the shoulder before he hauls me in for a manly hug. "Is Caleb still not sleeping well?"

"I've had a better night's sleep in my car on a stakeout in the depths of winter."

"Ouch."

Releasing me, he gives me the once-over. "You're not looking too rosy yourself. You have no newborn, so what gives?"

I shake my head when I see Cami on her way over, giving Jake a look to suggest we should discuss later. He takes the hint quickly and moves aside so I can welcome his wife. "Did someone say you had a baby a few weeks ago?" I ask, looking her up and down. She looks as terrific as always.

"Oh stop." Cami takes me in a hug. "Who's this new woman, then, Ryan?"

"She's in the kitchen."

"Cracking the whip already?"

I'm cracking something, but it isn't a whip. "Charlotte!" I sing when she dives out the back of Jake's Range Rover. "When did you get so grown up?"

"I'm eight in two weeks." She holds up eight fingers, and my eyebrows jump up with feigned surprise.

"She's a big sister now." Cami smiles down at her stepdaughter before directing her attention to Jake. "You want to get the baby out of the car?"

"No, I might wake him."

I laugh as Jake goes to fetch his son and take Charlotte's hand, throwing an arm around Cami's shoulder. "So now you get to meet my little girl, Charlotte. Her name's Alex. And she has something to show you down by the lake."

Her eyes light up. "What?"

"You'll see." I push the door of the cabin open and stand aside, letting the ladies through before looking back to check for Jake. I nearly split my side when I see the big dude creeping across the lawn with a baby seat suspended from his outstretched arms, keeping him at arm's length. "Shhh," I say, earning myself the death stare. I let Jake in and he settles the baby seat on the couch, padding it out with cushions. Obviously he thinks the seat might come to life and jump off the sofa.

"Guys," I say, finding my girls by the sink. "This is Hannah and my daughter, Alex. Hannah, Alex, this is Jake, Cami, Charlotte, and that over there is—"

"Lucifer," Jake interrupts, getting smacked on the arm by Cami. His joke breaks the ice somewhat, and I see Hannah relax as she laughs.

"Hi," Hannah says, her hand coming up and then down, as if she's not sure whether this is a hug or a handshake kind of situation. I smile when Cami moves in and embraces her. Of course it's a hug situation.

"Lovely to finally meet the woman who's tamed him," Cami says, throwing me the eye. I ignore her. I didn't need taming.

"How do you look this good after giving birth?" Hannah asks, motioning up and down Cami's svelte frame.

"She's a model," Alex pipes in. "Dad told me. A super-famous one."

"Oh," Hannah more or less breathes, her smile faltering. I cock my head, wondering what's wrong.

"*Was* a model," Cami corrects Alex. "Now I'm more of a designer. Well, part-time."

"She doesn't have to get naked to design," Jake says, moving in on Hannah. "And that suits her husband just fine." He holds out his hand to her. "Jake."

"Hannah. Lovely to meet you," she says as she accepts, her smile still a bit awkward.

"Come on, Charlotte." Alex takes her hand and leads her to the door. "Let's leave the grown-ups to be grown-ups."

"Are you okay with her going with Alex?" I ask Jake.

"Sure." Jake pulls his keys from his pocket. "Charlotte, listen to Alex, okay?"

"Okay!"

They disappear and Jake heads back out. "I'll just get the bags," he calls quietly over his shoulder, flicking his wary eyes to Caleb on the couch.

"No problem, mate." I turn and move in on Hannah. "Are you okay?" I ask, and she nods, the movement quick and jerky. She's nervous. "Hey, they're lovely people."

"I know," she says, brushing me off and moving across to the fridge. "Would you like a drink, Cami?" she calls.

"Just water, thanks, Hannah. I'm still breastfeeding."

Hannah pours herself a wine and downs half. Wow. She's *really* nervous. I open the fridge and pull out two beers as I watch her fill a glass with water, and she looks across to me, giving me a strained smile. I try to return it, but I'm back to wondering who the hell she is.

"What's on the menu, then, Ryan?" Cami asks, eyeing all the food on the counter.

I collect the tray of homemade patties. "My famous burgers, of course." Then I take the dish of king prawns on skewers and shove them under Hannah's nose. "And a bit of shrimp."

She retreats like I could have just thrust a bowl of dog shit at her, her hand flying up to her mouth as she retches. "Sorry." She moves away, obviously offended by the food, giving the giant prawns a filthy look. "I really hate seafood."

"That's some hate," I quip, withdrawing the bowl before she throws up in it. I'm not imagining it. She's green. "You all right?"

"Yeah." She gives me another strained smile and busies herself refilling her wineglass. "So how did you and Jake meet?" she asks Cami, and I leave them to have their girl talk, taking the shrimp far away from Hannah, frowning as I go.

* * *

A few hours later, we're all sitting around the table on the lawn after stuffing our faces with barbecue food and a few tubs of ice cream. The girls came back to the cabin for just enough time to demolish a burger before retreating to the lake where all the magic happens. Caleb has woken up and is currently being rocked in one of Jake's big arms while he sips a beer with his other, and Cami and Hannah are chatting, both of them sitting forward in their chairs to get closer to each other as they natter. I swear, they haven't shut the hell up all night. It's nice to see that Hannah has relaxed a bit now, too.

"You two going to ignore us forever?" Jake says, settling his beer on the table and swapping Caleb to his other arm, but not before he lifts him for a quick kiss to his forehead. I smile. The tiny bundle isn't much bigger than Jake's hand.

Cami rests back in her chair, and Hannah follows suit. "Sorry, boys. Girl talk."

I turn an interested look onto Hannah, who just shrugs, looking a little too coy for my liking. "Cami was telling me all about how she met Jake."

"It's a long story," Cami adds.

Jake snorts, though his expression is soft on his wife. "Ever wondered what it's like to be in heaven and hell at the same time?"

"Is that even possible?" I ask as Jake claims his beer.

"Trust me." He raises his bottle to his wife, and she grins. "It's possible."

"I think it's very romantic," Hannah says wistfully. "The whole bodyguard-and-client thing."

I take a nervous peek at Jake. *Romantic* isn't a word I'd use. I know the story all too well. It sent the agency into meltdown, Lucinda was nearly carted off to the nuthouse, and the world was a media frenzy.

"It had its moments," Jake says quietly, looking down at his baby boy. He seems to fall into thought for a few moments before bringing himself back into the conversation. "What about you, Hannah?" he asks. "Where do you come from?"

I know what he's doing, and I discreetly cast my attention across to my girlfriend as I tip my beer to my lips. Eyes low, she plays with the stem of her glass. "Not much to tell." She smiles. It's forced. "I moved here a few weeks ago, and I don't plan on leaving."

She doesn't? Is she just giving lip service? I don't know, but my heavy heart softens a little. "Good," I jump in, wanting her to know how happy that makes me.

"Family?" Jake pushes, his face perfectly friendly, his tone purposely soft.

"My mother died five years ago. My dad eight years ago."

I'm quickly more alert to the conversation. Her mother died five years ago? Lucinda could only go back five years.

"I'm sorry," Jake says sincerely. "Siblings?"

Hannah shifts in her chair, her lips tight as she smiles through them. "No."

Jake's head cocks, interested. I don't like it. "No family at all?"

Okay, enough. I give him a sharp kick under the table as I slam my beer down to disguise the sound of my boot meeting his shin, and his jaw tenses, a choked cough escaping. That hurt? Good. "Another beer?" I ask, my head tilting, my eyes telling him to get his arse in the kitchen. I need another drink. I've been so busy cooking, eating, and trying not to let my mind wander all evening, I've only had one beer.

"Sure." Jake rids his hand of his bottle and maneuvers Caleb into both hands, standing. "You can show me that scratch on your truck." Rounding the table, he hands the baby over to Cami before dropping a kiss in her hair.

"Scratch?" Hannah asks. "I thought you had it repaired in Grange."

"I did," I confirm. "Then some idiot in a Mitsubishi driving on the wrong side of the road clipped the side of my truck."

"I'm beginning to question your driving ability." Hannah gives me an ironic look as I get up and go to her, hearing Jake chuckle.

"My driving ability is sound. People just keep getting in my way." I give her shoulder a little squeeze and instantly feel the goose bumps. "You cold?"

"A little."

"I'll get you a sweater." I jog back to the cabin and find Alex and Charlotte on their bellies in front of the TV with a bowl of popcorn. "Hey, when did you two get back?" I ask as I go to the bedroom.

"Well, Chunk is about to do the truffle shuffle," Alex calls. "So about twenty minutes ago."

I snatch a gray sweater down and head back out. "*The Goonies?*" I ask, grinning at the TV as I pass.

"Can you believe Charlotte's never watched it?" Alex is horrified. And so she should be. Charlotte breaks out in fits of giggles, laughing and pointing at the television. "See," Alex says, stuffing a handful of popcorn in her gob. "Told ya it was funny."

I have a little chuckle myself and meet Jake at the door. He gives me a frown, and I point back to the girls. "*The Goonies*. Kills me every time."

"Shit, I haven't seen it in years."

I leave Jake to reminisce and take the sweater to Hannah, though I hardly get a second glance from her as she accepts, lost in *girl talk* with Cami again. I'm feeling a bit neglected, to be honest. I'm not used to sharing her, except with Alex, of course, but my daughter and I come as a package. I bend and put my face right in front of Hannah's, blocking Cami out. She retreats in her chair, frowning at me. "What are you doing?"

"Hi, I'm Ryan."

Cami starts laughing from behind me, and Hannah performs a pretty spectacular eye roll. "Hi," she replies drily. "Is that all?"

I curl my lip playfully and steal a quick kiss before going to find Jake. I'm going to kick his arse for interrogating her. Grabbing two beers, I nudge him as I walk past, knocking him from his enthrallment with the TV. I jerk my head to the door. I have things to say, and I have questions to ask, neither of which the girls should hear.

When we get to my truck, Jake takes a beer and kicks the tire. "What was with all the questions?" I ask on a scowl.

"Just getting to know her."

"That was the Spanish Inquisition, Jake, for fuck's sake. How obvious do you wanna be?" He shrugs, showing no remorse, so I push on. "What do you think?" I ask, keen for his thoughts.

"About the damage to your truck?"

"No, for Christ's sake."

"Oh, about Hannah?"

"Yes."

"Definitely hiding something."

I shouldn't be relieved, but at least he's confirmed I'm not losing my mind. Damn it.

Jake runs a palm down the side of my truck. "This will definitely require an expert's work." He stands back, looking up and down the paintwork. "Handle with care and it'll be like there was no damage in the first place."

"I actually have no fucking clue whether you're talking about the truck or my girlfriend."

"I'm talking about the truck, you dick." He points his bottle to Cami and Hannah before swigging back a good few inches. "As for your girlfriend, I'd call Luce."

"Already have."

"And what did she say?"

"Can't trace her before 2014. The trail ends there."

Jake rests back against the truck, humming, and then he's quiet for a little while, obviously lost in thought. "Yo, Jake," I say after a few long moments of silence. He blinks and looks at me. "What are you thinking?"

"I'm thinking how nice it is to be thinking about something other than diapers, milk, and colic."

"Good for you, buddy. Now tell me what you'd do."

"Nothing."

"What?"

"What *can* you do?" he asks, starting to wander around the truck, trying to look interested in the apparent subject at hand. "You've got nothing to go on. If Luce can't find anything, then no one can."

My shoulders sag. "I can't just do nothing."

"Unless you think she's in danger, I'd chill the fuck out. Don't let your imagination run away with you."

Chill the fuck out? Let Cami aim a gun at his head and see how he feels about that. "She's frightened of something," I say, looking across to Hannah. She doesn't look frightened now. She looks happy. Content. Distracted? "She had a gun, Jake. Nearly took my fucking head off with it."

"Whoa. That's an entirely different set of circumstances."

"Yeah."

"Loaded?"

"Fully."

Jake's lips straighten, his nod mild. He's beginning to grasp the gravity of this situation. "And why did she nearly shoot you?" he asks.

"Because I broke into her store."

"Sounds like a perfectly reasonable reason to blow your head off to me."

I stop myself from growling in frustration, resting my beer on the hood of my truck as Jake crouches by the side, inspecting the damage close up. "I broke into her store because moments before I found her on the street looking like a zombie. Completely vacant. Like she'd had a terrible shock or something. She ran, and I went after her. She wouldn't answer the door, and I saw broken glass on the floor. So I slipped the lock and let myself in. I was worried."

Jake looks up at me. "What shocked her?"

"I don't fucking know," I grate. "But whatever it was, it sucker-punched her in the gut."

"Where exactly was she?" he asks, rising to full height.

"Outside the store."

"What's outside the store?"

I think hard as my eyes dart at my feet, pacing through every second of that few minutes. "The fruit and veg stands, the bread cart, the..." I fade off, looking at Jake. "The newspaper stand."

His head cocks, interested. "And did you see the newspaper?"

Fuck. "No. It didn't even occur to me."

"What day was this?" he asks, pulling out his phone.

"Sunday." I join him, looking over his shoulder. "Try the *Sun* first. The *Independent* sells out by lunchtime."

Jake taps and scrolls, and a second later, we're both staring at the front page of the *Sun*, Sunday's edition. And it means absolutely nothing. "Jarrad Knight," Jake muses, and just his tone tells me it means something to him.

"You know him?"

"I know *of* him." He scrolls down, scanning the article. "Multimillionaire business tycoon. Owns a large tech firm. That's all I know."

I frown, feeling my frustration growing, and look back down to the picture when Jake scrolls to the top again. He's with a woman. A beautiful woman who is considerably younger than him. "Anything?"

"Nothing much. They married last year and are expecting their first baby."

"And that's front-page news?" I ask, flummoxed.

Jake shrugs, tucking his phone back in his pocket, looking as lost as I am. "He's a big hitter and a bit of an *it* guy. I don't know much about him."

I slump back against the side of the truck, walking myself back through the moment I found Hannah outside the store. There's absolutely nothing for me to go on, no clues as to why she had that epic meltdown. Was it something that was said to her? A flashback of some sort? A panic attack?

"We'd better get back to the girls," I say, feeling beaten. "I've asked Lucinda to dig a bit deeper. I'll see what she turns up." I trudge across the gravel, sinking the last of my beer.

"And what if she turns up nothing?" Jake calls, pulling me to a stop.

I look back at him. "I'll carry on looking," I admit. Because I will.

"Ryan." Jake takes the few steps needed to join me, dropping his voice. "What if there's nothing to be found?"

"You said yourself something isn't right," I remind him. "I have a hunch. You of all people should understand that." I don't mean to dredge it up; I know that time in his life is off limits, but I'm desperate. I feel like I'm losing my mind, and I need someone or something to reassure me that I'm not.

Jake swallows hard, but he doesn't swing at me, which is what I half expected. He's not all too fond of being reminded of the time he was assigned to protect Cami and quickly unassigned when her father found out about their relationship. He knew something was off. He knew Cami wasn't safe. And he didn't back down until he'd gotten to the bottom of it.

Throwing his arm around my shoulder, Jake starts to walk us back to the women. "I understand," he finally admits. "Keep me in the loop, yeah?"

I hit my empty bottle against his in agreement. "Of course."

"So, are you still planning on building some cabins?" he asks. "Or are you too busy investigating your girlfriend?"

"Very funny," I retort. "And yes, I am."

"Too busy?" Jake asks, and I throw him a tired look, making him chuckle. "Lucinda will be thrilled. So you're really not coming back."

"Nope. I'm done with protection." Done with danger. It's ironic, really. I'm done with security, yet I feel like I need to protect Hannah from something. Problem is, I don't know what.

"Here," Cami whispers when we reach them, negotiating Caleb in her arms and standing. "Pass me his stroller."

I wheel it over and pull back the blankets so she can lay him down, smiling when his little fists rub at his sleepy face. I never got to lay Alex down like this when she was a tiny baby. I didn't even see her until she'd turned one. "You okay?" Hannah asks, moving into my side.

"Yeah." I nod down to Caleb. "Cute, isn't he?"

"Adorable," Hannah agrees wistfully, almost sadly. It gets my brain whirling again. Does she want kids? Is it appropriate for me to ask?

"Would you have any more?" she says, giving me the perfect opportunity to return her question. But it also puts me on the spot. I've never asked myself that question, therefore never answered it. I've never found myself in a situation when I've *had* to.

"I don't know," I say truthfully, buying myself some time. "I've not really thought about it. You?"

"Yes, I want them," she answers without hesitation. She clearly *has* thought about it. I feel like I've just been thrown an ultimatum, because, with that one-word answer, Hannah's laid her cards on the table. Do I want more kids? "I'd better be heading off," she says, breaking away from me and approaching Cami and Jake, giving them each a hug.

She's going? But I assumed she'd stay the night. My heart drops and my mouth is in action before I can stop it. "You're not staying?" It sounds a bit accusing, and I really didn't mean it to.

"Well, you have a house full, with Jake and Cami and the kids staying." She comes to me and gives me a kiss on the cheek. It feels like a token gesture. Shit, have I touched a nerve with all that talk of babies? Did I say the wrong thing?

"My *bed* isn't full," I point out, unable to stop my forehead from creasing with a frown. Why's she so keen to leave all of a sudden? God damn me, I did say the wrong thing, didn't I?

Hannah gives me a soft smile. I don't like that, either. It's almost as if she feels sorry for me. "I've stayed so much. I don't want Alex to think I'm invading."

"She won't think that," I say urgently, considering going inside and dragging Alex from the TV to confirm I'm right. I don't want Hannah to leave, especially now.

"I'll stay tomorrow." She heads inside to say her goodbyes to Alex and Charlotte, leaving me all alone, urgently rummaging through my mind for a plausible reason for her to stay. By the time she's back, I have nothing other than I simply want her to. Is that enough?

Going to her bike, she kicks that stand up. "You're not riding that home," I bark abruptly, and she stills, her hands on the bars ready to get into the saddle. She regards me carefully, and I can tell she's assessing me, seeing if this is a fight she'll win. She won't. I'm digging my boots in.

"Then I'll walk."

I laugh. "You're not walking, Hannah."

"So I can't walk, you won't let me go on my bike." She kicks the stand back down and squares me with a look of challenge that I quite like.

"Can't you just stay?" I ask. It makes sense.

On a dramatic sigh, she takes a beat and a few breaths. "It's not fair to Alex. I already feel like I've bulldozed into her life. She needs her time with you, too. She needs to know I'm not here to steal all your attention."

Though I'm very aware that she's one hundred percent right, I can't help feeling like there's something more to it. Like me and my big foot in my mouth when I took a century to answer a question that obviously meant a lot to her. But damn, she caught me off guard. And now she's leaving.

Reluctantly, I give in. I never want to force anything on her. "I'll drive you," I say, walking backward to the cabin. "Just give me a second."

"You've been drinking."

"I've had two beers since you arrived," I assure her. It's not a lie. "Wait there."

I run inside to find Jake. "I'm just going to run Hannah home. You mind if I leave Alex with you?" At that very moment, I hear rip-roaring laughter, and both Jake and I turn to see the girls rolling around on the rug in front of the television.

"I might go join them," Jake chuckles, slapping me on the shoulder. "See you in a bit."

"Thanks, mate." I snag my keys off the side, stuff my phone in my back pocket, and leave Jake and the girls behind belly laughing at *The Goonies*.

When I make it back outside, Hannah has taken the initiative to get in my truck without the need for me to physically put her in there. I hop in and reverse past Jake's Range Rover as she tugs on her seat belt and settles in. And quiet falls.

It remains silent the whole five-minute drive to her store, and no matter how deep I dig into the corners of my mind, I can't find anything to say. Actually, that's a lie. I have loads to say, I just haven't the fucking courage. A few times, I breathe in, intending to broach the subject we touched on earlier, wanting to clear the air. But each time I go to speak, I hear Hannah either swallow, breathe in, or shift in her seat, and I'm left wondering whether she's sensed my intention to talk and is telling me in her own little way not to. Where does that leave me?

When I pull up outside her store, I'm about ready to declare my insanity, my head set to explode. I can't bear this tension. The past few days have been complete and utter *easy* bliss. Now it's hellish. I have to sort it.

She opens the door. "Hannah." I reach across and grab her arm. "Wait a minute."

Motionless for a moment, her wrist caught in my grasp, she gathers what strength she needs to face me. And the second she does, my words get caught up on my tongue and I find myself just staring at her. My fix-it speech is drowned out by clarity as I take her in, every inch of her. She's still wearing my sweater, and she looks magnificent in it, no matter that it's drowning her. Her clean skin, her haphazard hair, her clear eyes. Every part of Hannah Bright is breathtaking, and my breath is seriously taken right now. She has a good soul. She's a free spirit and so kindhearted. All that matters to her is being happy and doing what she loves. She's a breath of fresh air.

My reality has hit me. Or more like punched me full-force in the face.

I love her. I'm madly in love with her. This delicate, multifaceted woman has stolen my heart. Or taken it, because I haven't once tried to stop her. What I need to know now is, does she realize what she's done to me? And is there any chance she could feel the same?

I gulp down my apprehension. Just the fact that I'm not sure worries me. Each time I feel like I really know her, something happens to remind me that I don't at all. And now I've had this revelation, all I keep thinking is...she doesn't plan on staying in Hampton.

I gently release her arm and pull back. "I'll see you tomorrow," I say over my thick tongue, getting just a mild nod as she gets out, shutting the door and walking the few yards to her store. She lets herself in. Closes the door. And she doesn't look at me once.

"Fuck." I smack the steering wheel with the heel of my hand before pulling off quickly, my truck taking the brunt of my frustration. Do I tell her? Lay my heart at her feet and risk having it stamped on? I don't think I'd feel so unsettled if I wasn't in such a mess over the gun, her meltdown, and everything else that has clued me into the fact that there's something I'm missing. Or something she's not telling me. Because more disturbing is my fear that no matter what I do or how I feel, she's afraid to love me in return. And that she will, in fact, leave me. *And* Alex.

So, what the fuck do I do now?

Chapter Twenty-Two

HANNAH

The darkness is a comfort for once. I hear his truck roar off up the high street, almost angrily, further cementing the fact that something has gone wrong between us somewhere this evening, and I'm really not sure what. Did he see me falter when I realized who Cami was? God, I thought I might have thrown up at her feet. I remember her well; she was a regular on the London scene. And then, naturally, I wondered if she recognized me. It took me a good few minutes to settle down and conclude that she didn't, but it was touch-and-go for a moment. I had to stop myself from running out of the cabin.

Or was Ryan's silence because of my answer to his question about children? I shouldn't have been so honest, but in that moment, for the first time ever, I truly did see myself as a mother one day, and the realization had me forgetting myself for a second and putting it out there. I could see he was taken aback. His own answer should have made me think before spewing mine.

Or was his dip in mood because I refused to stay? There's no denying I wanted to, but my reasoning about Alex, albeit partly true, wasn't why I stuck to my guns. Truth be told, if I didn't have somewhere to be in the morning, Ryan could have easily convinced me to stay. But I *do* have somewhere to be tomorrow. It's Saturday, and if I don't leave Hampton by nine o'clock at the latest, I'll miss seeing Mum and

Pippa. Staying at Ryan's would have increased the risk, not to mention getting past the inevitable task of explaining why I have to leave before breakfast. I couldn't say I need to open the store. He'd undoubtedly see it closed if he made a trip into town in the morning.

Feeling a little despondent, I make my way upstairs. Finding my iPad on the table by the sofa, I load Facebook and click my sister's name in the search bar. When Mum's face comes up on my screen, I lower to the couch, tracing the edges of her cheek. Each week I get to see her from afar, I wonder if it'll be the last time. A tear hits the screen of my iPad when I silently accept that I won't even be able to say goodbye. Besides, I said farewell in my own little way many years ago. I only have to look at Mum's empty eyes to know that she won't even know who I am anymore. That's both painful and comforting.

Making the picture as big as it can be without distorting it too much, I take a screenshot. Then I scroll through the rest of my sister's previous profile pictures and do the same with them all, stopping when I come across one from six years ago when we had Mum moved into the care home. It was miles from London and me, but not so far from my sister. Given my restrained life, it made more sense for Mum to be nearer to Pippa.

In this picture, she's smiling as she points at the fancy floral curtains in her new room, looking more alive and compos mentis. Back then, her good days outweighed her bad days. Now the bad days are taking over. I remember the day I visited and said my private goodbye to her. She was having a good day. To this day, I still don't know whether I'm grateful or saddened by that. I remember holding on to her hand firmly as she talked to me. I remember Pippa looking at me questioningly each time my eyes filled with tears. I remember her laughing lightly when I attacked her with a cuddle so fierce when we left Mum's room. And I remember the last words she said to me.

God, anyone would think we're never going to see each other again. Get off me, you soppy twat.

Then she kissed me and tugged my hair before she danced off across the street.

I turn off my iPad and drag my heavy body up from the couch, suddenly so very tired. When I get to the bathroom, I pull off Ryan's sweater, take off my clothes, and put the sweater back on. After brushing my teeth, I collect my clothes from the floor and dump them in the washing basket.

Then I fall into bed in a heap and roll onto my side, bringing the cuffs of Ryan's sweater to my nose and inhaling his lingering scent, feeling so very lonely again.

*   *   *

My heart sinks when the heavens open and rain starts to pound on the windshield of the cab. There's no way my sister will take Mum out in the rain. She might not take her out if it stops, either, especially if the sky is still dark. She won't risk Mum catching a cold when her immune system isn't good. I rest my head on the window, my despondency painful. Each week between seeing them feels like a century. Two weeks will feel like forever if I miss them today.

As we drive down the main street in Grange, my mobile rings and I answer on an over-the-top chirpy "Hi" to Molly.

"I popped by the store to check you're all set for tomorrow, but you're not here." She sounds a little stressed; the organization and preparing for tomorrow's celebrations are taking their toll.

I feel a little guilt sweep in and sting me. "I'm on my way to Grange to pick up some last-minute bits." My lie is too easy to tell. "I need a few more canvases for the kids' painting competition."

"I thought you said there were enough?"

I did. There *are* enough. Molly was with me in the store earlier this week when we were going through the final schedule and plans for the fete. "I must have been having a brain fart day," I say lamely.

She hums, and it's light. Suspicious. "Or being distracted by a certain outdoorsy type."

"And that," I admit, unabashed. My relationship with Ryan is no secret in town. In fact, it's caused quite a stir. It's something to talk about in a place where there's never anything to talk about. "I'll be back in a few hours to help with the setting up."

"Okay," Molly says. "See you soon."

I notice the windshield wipers have stopped and look up to the sky, seeing the black clouds moving rapidly away. Oh thank you, God.

The driver rolls to a stop and I jump out, paying him when he lets his window down. I turn and scan the entrance of the park and then quickly check the time. I'm early.

I make my way through the open ornate gate and down the path to my usual spot—a bench set back from the lake between two trees. From here I can see my sister push Mum in her chair the whole way around. I take a seat and look up to the sky, smiling when I see that the black clouds are no longer hanging over me, and then set my eyes on the entrance across the lake.

Each minute that passes feels like an hour as I wait for them to appear. I watch as dog walkers and runners pass, and across the plains a guy in army gear barks orders to a group of people in sweats doing push-ups. Where are they? I get up, I sit back down, and my disappointment starts to hurt my heart. I wait some more, because what else can I do? Give up? Leave? What if they're running late? What if I miss them?

I remain on the bench, sadness my only company, my aching heart heavy in my chest. By ten fifty, I've lost the ability to hold back my tears. I feel so empty. As I brush at my cheeks with the back of my hand, my phone rings, and I feel terrible for wanting to reject Ryan's call. After last night combined with how I'm feeling now, I can't talk to him. Can't force any happiness into my voice. My thumb hovers over the red button, and I close my eyes, pushing down. "I'm sorry," I say to my phone, rising to my feet.

I take one more look around the park before forcing my dead muscles to life, walking back to the path, feeling so very heavy. I stop when Ryan calls again, but I let it ring off and find myself rolling my shoulders without thought, feeling the hairs on the back of my neck stand on end. I look back down the pathway, a sense of unease coming over me.

The black clouds are back, rolling through the sky violently, the wind whipping up and sending leaves swirling around my feet. I fold my arms across my chest, looking around the park. It's suddenly quiet, everyone retreating as a result of the threatening storm.

I shake off my apprehension and hurry to the gates as I call for a cab, flinching when a crack of thunder sounds above. I make it to the road and search for a café or something to take shelter in until my taxi arrives. I don't find a café.

I find something else.

My slowing heart kick-starts again, and I move quickly down the pavement, sure I'm not seeing things. I make it to the corner, just catching sight of my sister pushing my mother across the zebra crossing, back toward the care home.

My instinct to run after them nearly gets the better of me, the urge to see Mum's face overwhelming. Pippa is pushing her away from me. I can't see her. I *need* to see her. I quickly check the road and run across when the traffic clears, trying to get ahead of them, albeit at a safe distance. When they reach another road, my sister turns Mum's wheelchair toward me.

And I stagger back in shock. "Oh my God," I whisper, taking in the frail lady in the chair. Layers of blankets cover her legs, and a fleece hat is pulled down low on her head. But no matter how wrapped up she is, protected from the elements, I can see with frightening clearness how gray she looks. How lifeless. How weak and completely hollow. I'm shocked by the obvious drastic deterioration in just a week. The woman before me used to be the epitome of life. She used to sing as she painted. Her eyes used to shine constantly. Her hugs were full of love and her words always full of encouragement.

My sister walks around the wheelchair and pulls in Mum's coat, re-arranging the blankets around her legs. She continues to stare blankly forward, seeming oblivious to everything around her. I bring my hand to my mouth to hold back the quiet, devastated sob, and just then my mum's empty gaze moves, looking across the road in my very direction. Our eyes meet, and the sob that I was containing escapes. "Mum," I murmur, my voice broken and full to the brim with grief. She just stares at me, keeping me frozen on the spot. But her beautiful face remains expressionless. There's nothing in her eyes. She's there. But not there.

My sister's hands still on Mum's fleece hat mid-fix, and she turns, looking across the road to me, too. I quickly move back into a doorway out of sight, my heart in my throat. I'm shaking uncontrollably. Did I move fast enough? Did my sister see me? I step forward and peek around the wall. Pippa is looking down the street, her frown heavy. Then she returns to Mum, who is now back to staring forward, and cups her face, leaning in and kissing her cheek before she gets back behind the chair and pushes on.

I fall against the wall on a strangled gasp, my breathing all over the place. I should go now. I should get in my cab and leave. I've already taken too much of a risk. I feel utterly deplete. Drained of energy and hope. Today I won't be leaving Grange feeling my usual sadness whenever I steal these moments. Today I'll leave with only fear.

Fear that next Saturday when I come, Mum won't be here. And though I know it is plain cruel for her to live like this—the strong, vivacious, bold woman long gone, being replaced with an old lady I don't recognize anymore—I can't help but wish I could have these private times for a little longer.

I step out of the doorway with tears streaming down my cheeks, look-ing back as I go, trying to stop myself from mentally saying goodbye.

Chapter Twenty-Three

RYAN

I study Hannah walking down the street, her anguish palpable. Every minute I've watched her since she left Hampton, I've felt like an impostor. I almost made my presence known a number of times. I wanted to go to her, to cuddle her when she so clearly needed it. Seeing her looking so utterly broken killed me over and over.

From the corner where I'm standing, I look back, seeing the woman pushing the wheelchair has reached the end of the road. I wait to see which way she turns before I return my eyes to Hannah. I have to know who those women are, but I have to make sure Hannah is safely in a taxi first.

A cab pulls up and Hannah gets in, and I wait until she's gone before I jog back to my truck. I follow the road to the end and make a right, my eyes scanning the street. I spot the women up ahead and pull into a parking space, turning the engine off and jumping out to follow them on foot.

I keep my distance, pulling the camera up on my phone ready to take a picture when the opportunity arises. The opportunity doesn't come. The woman turns the wheelchair into a gated complex, and I lose sight of them. "Shit." Picking up my pace, I make it to the gate, just seeing the glass automatic doors close behind them. The sign on one of the pillars says WILD ORCHARD CARE HOME.

The woman stops in the reception area and takes a pen, writing something down in a book on the desk. A visitor log? She sets the pen down and carries on her way, pushing the wheelchair through some double doors that open after she waits a few seconds.

And then they're gone.

I move to the side and think for a few moments, spinning my phone in my grasp. I've got to know who they are. I make a quick assessment of the reception area as people come and go. A woman at the desk, security cameras at every corner. The doors off the reception area are all locked, opened only by a code entered into the keypad or by the receptionist releasing them with a button under the desk.

A nurse wanders out of the building on her phone, a medical case in her other hand. "I'm dropping off the urine samples for Dereck Walters and then I'll be back." She looks up at me and smiles when I open the gate for her before getting back to her call.

I wait for the perfect moment before I make my move. Tucking my phone in my pocket, I walk up the path and through the automatic doors. The woman on reception looks up at me, and I smile my friendliest smile. "Can I help you?' she asks, returning my smile.

"Visiting Dereck Walters," I say coolly, reaching for the visitor log and pulling it close, like I know the drill. I look down at the list of names who have signed in recently. It also details who they're visiting.

"Oh?" she says. "I'm sorry, I don't recognize you."

I have to think on my feet, just buy myself enough time to memorize the names in the visitor log. "I'm sorry, it's a bit of a spur-of-the-moment visit. I don't live locally. Do you need to call someone to authorize?"

"I'm afraid so," she says, reaching for the phone. "Can I take your name, sir?"

I look up when the doors across the room open, and the woman who was pushing the wheelchair appears, her attention focused on her mobile as she taps away at the screen. She approaches, coming to a stop right next to me and looking up for the book. Her eyes meet mine, and she smiles, pulling it closer to her and taking the pen. And I watch as she signs herself out.

"Thanks, Vera," she says, waving at the woman behind the desk before moving past me and leaving. My eyes fall to the book. Philippa Maxwell visiting Dolly Blake.

"Sir?"

I look up blankly.

"Name, please?" She points to the phone in her hand on a smile.

"Don't worry." I turn and leave, pulling by mobile out and calling Lucinda as I walk back to my truck. "Philippa Maxwell and Dolly Blake. The former is mid-thirties, maybe. Must live in or around Grange. The latter, late sixties, early seventies, resident of Wild Orchard Care Home in Grange. See what you can get me on both of them."

"You sound stressed," Lucinda says, rather observantly. "I hear you had a visitor last night."

"You spying on me?"

"No," she laughs. "I spoke to Jake this morning to see when his paternity leave is done. He said they were on their way home from yours. Nice evening?"

Since when has Lucinda given two shits about whether or not I've had a nice evening? "Lovely, thanks." I drift off. "What do you care?"

"I like to know what my boys are up to," she muses. "It's in my interest."

"How's it in your interest?"

"Your well-being is in my interest. And frankly, you're sounding a bit off lately."

"I don't work for you anymore, Lucinda," I remind her, ignoring her huff of displeasure and getting back to the matter at hand. "The names I mentioned . . ." I don't mention them again. I know they'll already be stored in her elephant memory. "See what you can find out."

"When are you going to tell what this is all about?" she asks.

"When I know what the fuck is going on," I answer truthfully. "Did you dig any deeper on Hannah Bright?"

"Yep. And hit a rock. Dead end after dead end."

I reach my truck and let my forehead rest on the door. "Maybe the two names I gave you might shed some light."

I don't know if she hears my despondency, or whether she's just feeling unusually amenable today, but she sighs, and I know Lucinda well enough to know that it's not an exasperated sigh. It's a worried sigh. "Ryan, whatever shit you're getting yourself into, please be careful, okay?"

I smile at the paintwork of my truck. "You worried about me, Luce?"

She snorts, trying to win back some hardness. "I know you, Ryan. If there's trouble around, you can't help getting yourself into it."

"I'll be careful," I assure her. "Call you tomorrow." I click off and realign my focus on Hannah and how I'm going to put right what went wrong last night.

* * *

The high street looks like a party shop has crapped all over it when I get back to Hampton, bunting crisscrossing the street, stalls and stands erected, lining the road. I slow to a crawl, mindful of the kids all out in force to help set up for tomorrow. I'm relieved Hannah is out helping, too, though past her smile I see the torment weighing her down.

She looks up when she hears my truck, and I hate that she looks washed out. The evidence of her tears is apparent in the slight puffiness around her eyes. Did she cry the whole way home from Grange?

I let my window down when I reach her, slowing my truck to a stop. Her hands are full of bunting, the length of her arm lined with pieces of sticky tape. "Hey," I say softly.

"Hey," she parrots, glancing down at her feet briefly before looking back up at me.

"You okay?" I feel like a prize twat for asking such a lame question, especially after seeing what I've seen this morning.

"Yeah." She lifts her hands and presents the tangles of bunting. "Whoever took this down last year made it as difficult as possible for me to put up this year."

All I see is small talk in our imminent future, both of us awkward and unsure. It's not us. "Want some help?" I ask, getting out of my truck before she answers. I look down at the mess of string and colorful fabric triangles piled in her grasp, my brow furrowed deeply.

"I think it's completely broken," she says softly, and I peek up to find a small smile.

"There's nothing I can't fix." There's a deeper meaning to my statement, and Hannah doesn't miss it, blinking slowly as she breathes in deeply.

"Then fix it," she practically whispers, making a point of maintaining our eye contact. The atmosphere shifts, an understanding between us seeming to settle. Problem is, I'm really not sure if I'm understanding. Should I tell her where I've been? What I saw? How I feel?

I lift my hands to hers and start to unravel the string, feeling her regarding me while I pick at knots and pull bits of fabric through loops. I make quick progress, lengths of bunting starting to pool on the ground at our feet, and a few minutes later Hannah's hands are free. I take them both in mine and lace our fingers together. "See," I murmur, searching out her eyes again. "The bunting is fixed." I step in a little until our hands are trapped between her chest and mine. "And now you are free."

She bites on her bottom lip, and I know it's because she's trying to stop me seeing it wobble. I feel helpless right now. Powerless. I'm a man on the edge of doing what comes instinctively to me, but being too afraid to do it for risk of losing her.

Hannah forces our hands down and breaks our hold, bringing her arms around my waist and crushing herself to my chest. And suddenly

I'm not feeling powerless anymore. I wrap her up in my arms and hold her like I know she needs to be held, my chin resting on top of her head. I let her have as long as she needs, happy to hold her up, happy for everyone to stare, happy not to give a fuck.

"How much more is there to be done?" I ask, looking up and down the street, thinking it's looking pretty complete to me. At least, as much as can be done the day before the fete. At the crack of dawn, everyone will be out stocking carts, setting up tables and chairs, cooking, brewing, baking.

She turns her face into my throat and I feel her blinking, her lashes tickling me there. "I just need to get this bunting up." Her words vibrate against my Adam's apple.

"I'll help you." I have to detach her from me before I put her in my truck and head back to the cabin to quench my rapid onslaught of lust. "Tell me what to do."

She smirks to herself, aware of my issue. She probably *felt* it, too. I can't even bring myself to feel remorseful. At this moment, I need her in every way, that way the most. Our connection. Our closeness. Her peace.

She points to the nearby stepladder and bends to collect up the bunting. "You can pass me this and I'll stick it to the sign above the pub." She turns and points across the street to Mr. Chaps's store. "Then we tape the other end over there."

I eye the stepladder suspiciously. "You've been up and down this thing without any help?" I ask, not liking the thought of that at all.

"Well, yeah."

"Hannah," I admonish her, annoyed, carrying the ladder to the pub and setting it down below the sign, giving it a little shake to check it's level and stable. "Pass it here, I'll do it." I take the first step and hold my hand out for the end of the bunting. "Just tell me where to stick it?"

Her eyes expand. "Stick what?"

Naturally, my eyes drop to my groin on a laugh. She needs to stop that nonsense right now. I will not be held accountable if this bunting doesn't make it onto the side of the town pub. I thrust my hand forward. "Give."

On a demure smile, she passes the goods and feeds the length through her hand as I climb the stepladder, having to go to the last but one step in order to reach the sign. I look down. "You stood on the very top of this thing, didn't you?" I ask accusingly. She's nearly a foot shorter than me. Needs at least another step or two.

She doesn't answer, just pouts her guilt, and I shake my head, annoyed, as I fix the end to the edge of the sign. I make my way down and pick up the ladder, claiming Hannah with my spare hand and taking us across the road as she lets the bunting unravel behind us.

"Hey, Ryan," Molly calls from her own ladder outside the post office. Seriously, has no one any care for health and safety around here?

I stop and set the ladder down, making my way over. "Get down," I order, taking hold of both sides to keep it steady. I watch as she throws Hannah a look, like should she listen? Hannah nods, and Molly starts shifting on the ladder to find the right angle to descend. As soon as she's down, I claim the bunting she was struggling to fix and climb the steps, reaching and attaching it easily. "Is that it?" I ask, looking down at her.

"That's it," Molly chirps, making her way over to Hannah and whispering something in her ear. What? I don't know, but Hannah gives Molly a sharp jab with her elbow and Molly laughs. I descend and eye them both suspiciously as I claim the ladder and carry on to Mr. Chaps. "What are you two smirking at?" I ask, slamming the ladder down on the pavement.

"Nothing," Molly sings, walking off to the crowd of kids who are decorating the ice cream stand. "Mr. Ryan all-hot-and-outdoorsy-and-without-doubt-an-incredible-lay," she calls back.

Hannah spins toward her friend. "Molly!"

She turns and starts walking backward, looking all innocent. "What?"

"Yeah, what?" I ask as I climb and fix the final piece, my grin private.

"Nothing," Hannah says, tossing a warning look Molly's way before meeting me at the bottom of the ladder. "Okay, now we have to decorate the stage, then set up the pie stand, and last but not least make the toffee apples."

My mouth falls open. "What?"

"I'm kidding." She takes my arm and lifts it, moving into my side and settling it across her shoulder. She looks up at me. "Thank you for your help."

"I hardly did a thing." I push my mouth into her hair and start walking us back to my truck. "And it was mostly for selfish reasons." I open the passenger door. "I want you to myself tonight so I can put right whatever went wrong last night."

She pushes back a strand of hair, thoughtful while she does. "I'd like that," she says, climbing into my truck. I shut the door and get in the other side, settling my hand straight on her knee and squeezing. I realize now that things didn't really go wrong. Hannah wanted to stay at home because she had somewhere she wanted to be early this morning. But of course, I'm not supposed to know that. And really, I'm not just going to put things right. I'm going to put things straight. I hope she's ready.

* * *

The journey is quiet, but this time it's not uncomfortable. I often wonder what she's thinking, and I know she's wondering the same about me. Is she even close? Has it crossed her mind? I pull to a stop and brace my arms against the wheel for a few moments before breathing in and letting myself out. I feel her eyes follow me around the front of the truck until I'm at her door. I open it and extend my hand.

She leaves me hanging for a few beats before she takes it, slipping down and moving aside for me to close the door. I start walking, and Hannah lets our arms reach full length before she starts to follow. "Where are we going?" she asks, looking back at the cabin.

I say nothing, returning my attention forward and pulling her on through the overgrowth. When Hannah and I reach the lake, I stop and take it in, never failing to be knocked back by its tranquil beauty and calmness. The sun sits just above the treetops, shimmering across the calm water. It's perfect.

I turn and tug Hannah forward, taking the hem of her dress and pulling it up over her head. "What are you doing?" she asks, though she doesn't stop me doing it. I crouch and take her ankle, lifting her foot and removing her Birkenstock, and then repeat on the other side. "Ryan?"

I cast my eyes up the length of her legs until I find her gazing down at me, a look of uncertainty splashed across her face. I take the sides of her knickers, drawing them slowly down, and when I make it to her ankles, she lifts each foot in turn without the need for me to request it. I lean in and kiss her hip bone, and she folds at the waist, reaching forward to take my shoulders. Her touch energizes me. Pushes me forward. Gives me strength and courage.

I rise slowly, reaching behind her to find the clasp of her bra, kissing between her breasts as I slip the catch. "Ryan," she breathes again. She can keep saying my name. I need to hear it. I pull the straps down her arms and move back as she extends them to help.

And then she's naked. An endless expanse of silky-smooth skin stands before me, calling to me, begging me to feel, touch, kiss every inch. I swallow on a gulp and toe my boots off, unbuttoning my fly and pushing my jeans down my thighs as I pretty much rip my T-shirt up over my head. She bites her lip. Fuck me, she bites her lip and it's like rocket fuel to my groin. I need to get her in the lake before my plan goes to shit and I tackle her to the ground here and now.

I extend my hand. She takes it. And I start walking backward toward the shore, relishing the mixture of intrigue and anticipation on her face. She lets our arms reach full length before she moves, taking small steps with me. The water meets my ankles, though I don't feel the chill. But I hope Hannah does. I hope it wakes up every nerve, every muscle, every brain cell. I want her the most alert she's ever been.

"Ryan," she says on a sharp inhale when the water meets her toes. *Keep walking, baby.* I see her chest expanding more and more the higher the water climbs up her body, and when it skims her breasts, I yank her forward and push her legs around my waist, holding the small of her back. Her arms find my neck easily. Everything is so fucking easy with Hannah.

I bend my knees and take us down until the water passes our shoulders and reaches our necks. And when she inhales, I kiss her. I kiss her with all the words I want to say crowding my mouth, waiting to be said. To be heard. And they will be. But for now, I just need to kiss her with all the crazy passion I'm feeling. There are kisses. And there are *kisses.* I've had many of the latter with Hannah, the type of kiss that makes you forget everything except the feel of that person's mouth on yours. Kisses that make all other kisses seem inconsequential. Kisses that make you ache. That rule you. That breathe clarity and purpose into you.

But this kiss has carried me past even that. This kiss has me signing over my life to this woman. "Hannah," I whisper around her exorable tongue, trying to retreat. She pushes herself higher, increasing the pressure of our mouths. I tilt my head back, allowing her to continue this earth-moving kiss. Her unwillingness to pull herself from this exquisite moment only emboldens me to be the one to end it. It's fine. There will be more.

I turn my head and rest my mouth on her shoulder, feeling her lips now at my ear. The whoosh of her breath as she pants against me makes me shiver, and I latch onto the soft flesh of her shoulder, biting down lightly, finding the restraint I need. It takes me a few controlled inhales and a *lot* of inner strength. But then she catches me off guard and pulls herself up, shifting her hips, and like a radar my cock finds her. She sinks down on a whimper, and I choke on all the words I want to say. My feet push against the bed of the lake, my tense legs straightening. I rise with Hannah attached to my front, a rush of water pouring from us. I need to stand. I need an anchor, something solid beneath my feet. Her internal walls are pulsing around me eagerly as I hold her still against me, trying to catch a breath. "You ruined my plan," I say raggedly, my face buried in her wet neck.

"This wasn't your plan when you brought me here?" she asks, nudging me out and kissing her way across my cheek until she's at my mouth.

"Part of it," I admit, catching her lips and indulging her for a second. "How do you feel?"

"Alive." Her answer is somehow flippant, yet it is also somehow what I expected.

"I don't want that to be my only purpose." I fist her wet hair and pull her away from me, using my other hand to reach around my back and unhook her ankles. She slides down my body, both of us wincing when I slip free from her, detaching us completely. The confusion on her face is understandable. I don't know how I managed to tear myself away, either. I take both her hands and kiss each before releasing and reversing, putting a good three feet of water between us. People say things in the heat of the moment, especially when they're blinded by passion. I don't want there to be any opportunity for a misunderstanding here.

"What's the matter?" she asks, wrapping her arms around her naked torso protectively, her look of uncertainty paining me. "Did I do something? Say something?"

I laugh mildly, though it's not in humor. She's done and said many things. "I know how alive you are when we're together," I say, resting my hand over my heart. "I feel it here." Her eyes fix on my chest where I'm touching. "The past that killed your spirit is of no consequence to us, Hannah." She closes her eyes, and I can see all too clearly that she's talking herself down from turning and running. "Whatever it was that broke you can't hurt you anymore," I vow, and she steps back in the water. "You can run," I tell her, though I beg her silently not to. "But you will be running away from a man who loves you with a power that's crippling him."

Impossibly huge, round eyes lift to mine. They're brimming with tears, and her arms cuddle her body a little tighter.

"I just want to love you, Hannah," I murmur. "And more than that, I want you to give me permission to." I reach for my nape and massage, feeling my apprehension reaching there. Will she run? Or will she stay? Right now, I don't know. She's clearly in a muddle, and I honestly have no clue what way this might swing. But I've started now. And I'll finish. "And even more than that," I say quietly. "I want you to accept it." I take one step forward, like *Here I am. Just take me. I'm all yours if you'll only let yourself have me.* "And if I'm really lucky," I add, shrinking the distance between us until I'm before her. "You'll love me back," I whisper, wanting to touch her, to remind her of the unyielding connection we have. Yet I can't influence her with the sexual chemistry. There is more than that between us. *So* much more.

Hannah remains a statue before me, her gaze low. The silence is agony, to the point I can't endure it any longer. She needs space. She needs some time to think about what I've said. It kills me, but I have to let her have that time. And all I can do is hope that she'll accept my love. And she'll stay.

I step to the side and pass her, wading through the water to the shore, scrubbing a palm down my face as I go.

I hear the water splash before I feel her hand grab my wrist, and I stop, but I don't look back. Will this be an *It's not you, it's me* speech? If so, I can't look at her while she gives it. I can't promise I'll contain my temper. I can't promise I won't shout and yell at her for being so impenetrable. I close my eyes and wait. My world is in this woman's hands.

She moves behind me, coming in close to my back and slipping her hands under my arms, hooking them up. Her cheek rests in the middle of my shoulder blades. "Love me," she says, turning a kiss onto my skin.

Fire shoots from that point to every nerve ending I have. That wasn't permission. That was an order. I go to turn—I need to see her—but she locks down her hold, stopping me. "I don't want to look at you when I tell you what I'm about to tell you," she says quietly. "I don't want your sympathy. When I'm finished, you'll face me and you will look at me like I need you to look at me. Not like you want to fix me. I'm working hard to do that myself. I don't need a man for that." I feel her forehead rest into the middle of my back, and I lay my arms over hers, finding her hands and holding them on either side of my neck. "I want you to look at me like I am yours and nothing came before you."

My teeth clench. I was dreading what there was to know before she said that. I can't promise I won't go on a rampage. So she's going to tell me everything, and then I'm expected to pretend I never heard a word?

"Promise me," she orders, jolting me a little, pushing her front harder into my back.

I've never in my fucking life found it so hard to utter three words. "I promise you," I say through the tightness of my jaw, so hoping I've not just made a promise I can't keep.

"I've had one relationship before you," she tells me, her voice shaky. "It was a very unhealthy relationship. I lost my identity. I lost my self-confidence. And I lost many things I loved." She stops, taking a break, and naturally my mind goes into overdrive. *Unhealthy.* I need a definition of what an unhealthy relationship is, because the spectrum is too fucking broad. Though the gun Hannah had aimed at my forehead clues me in a little. "I left," she goes on. "I moved away and started afresh. My life since then has been lonely, but it's been good for me. I've found myself again. And now I've found you, too. You've helped me truly find happiness again, and now I just want to forget everything that came before."

Motherfucker. I drop my head back, looking up to the sky, like the endurance I'm going to need can be found there. Endurance not to track down that man and riddle him with bullets. Her nose that's clearly been broken. Her fights with flashbacks and meltdowns. What the fuck did he do to her? I breathe through the growing rage that her words and my thoughts bring on, and Hannah tightens her hold on me more, so I know she's feeling the heat of my anger.

I have her here with me. She's safe here with me. Nothing can touch her.

"You promised me," she says into my skin. "Let it go."

There's so much more she isn't telling me. Like the women she was watching in Grange this morning. Who are they? *Let it go.* Can I? Should I? Fuck me, do I have a choice?

It takes everything in me to nod and squeeze her hands. "Okay," I say, turning and looking at her like she asked me to. Like she is mine, because she is. And like nothing came before me, because to her it didn't. What Hannah needs should be my priority. So I have to shake off my own need to know every detail of her past. I have to shake off the need for vengeance. Hannah is here with me, and she's telling me to love her. Loving her is the easy part. "There won't be a day that passes without me telling you I love you." I drag my thumb across her bottom lip. "There won't be a night that passes without you *feeling* how much I love you." I cup her face in my palms, desperate for her to understand the depths of my feelings. "I promise you I'll always protect you. I promise you I'll always be strong for you. I promise you I will walk through hell and back again if it means saving you from hurt. There is nothing in this world that could make me happier than simply knowing you are in my life, and I am what you need." I kiss her hard. "So I promise you, I'll let it all go because I love you."

She slings her arms around me and crawls up my body, and my legs give out on me, taking me down to my knees. With Hannah in my lap, I swathe her, absorbing every pound of her thumping heart. My clarity is back. *She* is my clarity. Nothing else matters. I will be the man she wants. I'll surrender my need to know the gory details, because I want to be her peace, not add to her torment. I can't lose her.

I keep us on the ground for as long as my heels digging into my arse will allow, happy to softly trace the skin of her back, smiling to myself each time I feel her flex her front into me, the sensitivity becoming too much. But I don't stop. Each press of her chest to mine, each smile of hers I feel against my shoulder, each light bite of my flesh, just urges me on.

"Can I stay with you tonight?" she asks, pulling herself out and presenting me with sleepy eyes. "If Alex doesn't mind."

"Alex is at Darcy's tonight preparing for the pageant." My backside has finally declared the onset of numbness, so I push my palm into the ground and lift Hannah as I stand. She's exhausted. I have to admit, I'm there myself. All this talk of love and pasts has drained us both.

She shows no willingness to uncurl her wrapped body from around me, leaving me to dip with her secured to my front to collect our clothes. I hold her under her thighs and walk back to the cabin, feeling the cool air settling across our bare skin. She's starting to shiver.

When I get us inside, I drop our clothes in a pile by the door and carry her over to the fire, lighting it and pulling a throw down from the couch. It takes some negotiating and effort, since she's not helping, but I eventually get her on her back, half cover her naked body with mine, and pull the blanket over us. "Pillow?"

She shakes her head and undoes all my effort to get her comfortable, pushing me to my back and resting her head on my chest. I go about rearranging the blanket again, getting us covered as the fire builds and starts to chase away the chills.

"Ryan?"

I peek down at the back of her head, humming my acknowledgment.

"I promise I'll always love you." She moves her head so her chin sinks into my chest and she's looking at me. "I want you to know that."

I comb my fingers through her wet hair as she rests her head back down and her eyes flutter closed. She's breathing lightly soon after, fast asleep. "I already knew," I say quietly. But what I wanted to hear is that she'll never leave me. Because I'm still not certain of that.

* * *

I don't sleep. Get nowhere close. My thoughts haven't stopped spinning.

Being as careful as I can, I lift Hannah's palm from my chest and inch out from under her, settling her on the rug. She stirs but drifts back off once I've tucked the blankets back in around her.

I pull on my jeans, grab my phone, and let myself out, set on calling Lucinda and telling her to abandon her search. I promised Hannah I'd love her. Her past doesn't matter. I need to let it go.

The phone rings once and Lucinda answers, but before I have the chance to give her my instruction, she hits me with a statement that has the potential to change my mind. "You heard that saying opening a can of worms?" she asks, halting me mid-stride down the steps to the lawn.

Say the words, Ryan. Call her off. Oh, fuck. I take hold of a wooden post and search desperately for the reason I found earlier. "Tell me," I demand. Reason is gone. Sense is gone. Or is it found?

"Philippa Maxwell is thirty-five years old, married with a little girl. Lives in Highspeck about sixty miles from Hampton. Dolly Blake is her mother. She lived alone for a few years after the death of her husband but dementia set in and she became progressively worse until she was moved into the care home six years ago by her daughters."

"Luce, what does this have to do with Hannah?"

"Dolly's other daughter, Katrina, died five years ago. Tragic death in the Bahamas. Body never found."

"Five years ago," I whisper, ice creeping into my veins.

"Yes. She was married to tech giant Jarrad Knight."

"Fucking hell," I breathe, putting Lucinda on loudspeaker and walking away from the cabin. I pull up Google and search for the article Jake found the other day, but this time I read it. And there it is. Reference to the tragic loss of his first wife five years ago. "Jesus."

Lucinda hums her agreement to my shock. "I've just texted you a picture of Knight and his first wife."

My phone dings, and I open Lucinda's message. My knees instantly give, and I grab the side of my truck to hold myself up, the ground feeling like it's disappeared from under me. The woman in the picture is beautiful. Long, dark hair. Perfectly flawless skin. Curves any man would kill to stroke. She's expensive, dressed completely in black, jewels dripping from every part of her. She's on a red carpet with Jarrad Knight, their arms linked, both of them smiling for the camera. But it's not a genuine smile. It's a smile for show.

"Do you recognize her?" Lucinda asks.

"You could say that," I murmur, resting against the door of my truck, unable to rip my eyes away from the woman staring back at me. "I'm in love with her."

Chapter Twenty-Four

FIVE YEARS AGO

Oh my God, I've never seen anything like it." Katrina was absolutely mesmerized by the crystal waters before her. The hidden rock pool they'd discovered was beyond the realms of beauty.

"Well, now you have." Jarrad swooped in behind her and circled her waist with his arms. "Isn't your husband the most amazing man alive for bringing you to these places?"

"Truly amazing," she said mindlessly, unable to comprehend the sheer magnificence. "I wish I had my paints with me." She could lose herself for hours bringing this to life in watercolors.

"You and your painting," Jarrad whispered in her ear, making her shiver. "There's only one thing in the world I want you to be passionate about." He nibbled at her lobe, squeezing her back tighter to his front. "And what's that, darling?"

"You." Her answer was automatic as she broke out of his hold, ignoring his disgruntled grumble. She took a few tentative steps down the rocks to the water.

"Be careful," Jarrad called after her, his voice echoing off the stony walls of the cave. "We all know how clumsy you are."

Katrina forced back her eye roll. "Come on, Hayley," she sang, eager to explore the magical place. She knew exactly where she was heading, having researched the area endlessly after accidentally discovering that Jarrad had planned a surprise trip there. But nothing in the pictures she saw or the words she read did this place justice. It was breathtaking.

"Aren't you hot?" Hayley asked as she followed Katrina down.

Katrina brushed off her friend's observation with ease. It was habit to cover her body these days. "The sun's strong today."

"We're in a cave." Hayley laughed as they wadded through the crystal-clear water to the other side of the rock pool and climbed up onto the edge.

"Come on." Katrina didn't take a breath before starting up the rocks to the daylight she could see spilling through an opening up above.

"Shouldn't we wait for the guys?" Hayley's attention was split between their men and Katrina climbing swiftly up the rocks.

"They'll catch up," she called back.

Reluctantly, Hayley followed an eager Katrina, climbing up behind her.

"You two be careful," Jarrad shouted, not far behind.

It only made Katrina smile and power on faster. When she reached the opening, she squinted. The sunlight spilling in was harsh on her eyes after being shrouded in dusky light for so long. "Oh my God, look at that." The small tunnel led to an opening that was curtained by a wall of pouring water. It was perfect. Just as perfect as she'd seen in the pictures.

Katrina looked over her shoulder, mentally willing her friend on. "There's a beautiful waterfall." She took the few steps back and offered her hand to her friend, helping her up the last few steps. "It's incredible." She looked past Hayley to see the guys halfway up the rock face. She couldn't wait for them; she was too desperate to get to the waterfall. So she hurried along the rocky passageway, the sound of rushing water getting louder until it was deafening. She took in every beautiful inch of the cave as she went, assessing the walls, the tunnels, every nook and cranny. Katrina could see the ground fall away a few yards ahead, and she knew Jarrad would be pissed off with her for getting too close to the edge. But...

Taking hold of the wall, she sidled gingerly toward the drop, losing her breath when she could finally see over the side. The fall was frightening, the bottom of the waterfall not even visible.

"Be careful!" Hayley shouted, but Katrina could only just hear her over the roar of the water.

She looked back, seeing her friend halfway down the tunnel. "You have to see this," she yelled.

"Wait for the guys," Hayley ordered, as cautious as ever.

"Where are they?" They were taking so long. Good.

"I'll check." Hayley started taking backward steps, turning and dropping her eyes to the uneven ground beneath her feet. "Curtis! Jarrad!"

Katrina faced the water again, utterly spellbound. She peered around the space, bending to see a small opening at knee level. There were endless tunnels, some disappearing into blackness, some with light glowing at the end. Hearing voices behind her, she straightened and took one more step toward the edge, peeking over, feeling the water spraying her face. Her smile was huge. Probably the biggest it had been since she married Jarrad over six years ago.

She reached forward, stretching her arm to touch the water. She flinched at the coldness. But smiled even more.

A rock shifted beneath her foot, and she lost her footing. "Shit," she breathed, her heart lurching. Katrina made a quick grab for the wall. "Oh my God," she gasped, gingerly trying to steady her legs. She eventually stabilized herself, looking back down the tunnel for her friend and the men. Nothing. Yet she could hear them. They would be here soon. They would see her.

She took a deep breath, filling her lungs. "Jarrad!" she cried, feeling at the wall. It was smooth, polished, and slippery after hundreds of years of water flowing over it. She smiled. If she were to stumble, there would be nothing to grab onto. It would be easy for someone to lose their balance with all the uneven rocks on the ground, especially if someone was as clumsy as Katrina.

"Jarrad!" she cried out again, her body wetter from the spray as she moved closer to the edge, crouching a little to find what she knew was there.

"Katrina!" Jarrad roared, and she looked back as she let go of the wall, screaming, just catching sight of her husband before she disappeared. He lunged forward but was swiftly yanked back by Curtis, and the two men struggled and fought. "Katrina, no!"

Her scream faded to nothing.

And she was gone.

CHAPTER TWENTY-FIVE

RYAN

I'm unable to talk, and Lucinda is silent on the line, obviously letting my shock settle. I can't form a coherent sentence, can't even think one. I'm shaken to the core. I look across to the cabin where Hannah is sleeping. My messy, cute, wild Hannah. She's nothing like the woman I see in this picture. "She faked her own death?" I mumble mindlessly. "What would push a woman to do that?" I can't go on knowing this and say nothing to her.

"I don't have the answer to that, Ryan," Lucinda says softly. "I'm telling you what I found out."

I smack my palm into my forehead a few times, a feeble attempt to knock myself out of my shock. Knight's remarried. He's over the death of Katrina Knight. Should I leave her dead? "Get me everything you can on Knight. If he so much as took a bar of soap from a hotel, I want to know about it."

"I have no info on stolen bars of soap," Lucinda quips drily. "But I'll trump that with a suspicious death."

"What?"

My phone pings again with another text. "That's Quinton Brayfield," she declares as I stare down at the picture of an elderly well-dressed man. "Owner of Brayfield Technologies. He was found dead at his home in Suffolk just over five years ago. Everything points to suicide, except for one thing."

"What's that?"

"Brayfield wasn't suicidal," Lucinda says. "My sources tell me that Knight wanted to buy Brayfield Tech, taking out one of his biggest rivals. Except Quinton Brayfield wouldn't sell. His son and heir, Dale Brayfield, however, would. But he couldn't do a thing so long as his old man was chairman of the board."

"So you think Knight killed Quinton Brayfield?"

"It's rather a large coincidence, don't you think?"

"Was any of this ever investigated?"

"Knight *assisted* the police in their inquiries. He was never a suspect, and he had a very solid alibi on the night of Brayfield's death. Guess who."

My heart sinks. "Hannah," I barely whisper.

"Hannah," Lucinda confirms. "Or Katrina."

I find a tree and slump against the trunk, utterly staggered by the barrage of information. It explains so fucking much. Hannah's jumpiness, for a start. She's worried he'll find her. Is that what she meant by *unhealthy*? Lying for him? But to fake her own death?

"My head hurts," I admit to Luce. I honestly don't know what to do with all this now that I have it. Do I tell Hannah I know? What will she do? I can't answer. But I do know that if I don't say anything, she'll let me love her. It'll just be like before. I accepted I'd let it go. I promised her I'd let it go. I should just take this information and use it to understand Hannah and why she's like she is. Maybe that's the answer. She'll never have to know that I know. If anything, it's stripped the curiosity away and I won't live each day looking at her and wondering. Because I know.

"It's a lot to absorb," Lucinda says more gently than is in her nature. "Let me know if you need anything else."

"Have Knight watched," I blurt, knowing I'm asking for too much. "Just for a while so I know he's out of the picture."

"You really do owe me," she says, and then she hangs up, and it's just me, the dark, the crickets, and a head about to explode. And then there's the sound of my phone again, too. I see Jake's name, and I feel bad for not answering. I just haven't the brain capacity to explain. But he texts me.

I've spoken to Lucinda. Answer your fucking phone.

It rings again instantly, and I answer. "I'm stunned, Jake. How does someone pull off their own death like that?"

"A lot of planning and fake documents," he says, and I could laugh. Hannah? She wouldn't know how to get a fake handbag, let alone fake documents. "I put a few calls in," he goes on. "After our conversation and speaking to Lucinda, I got the bug."

"What bug?"

"The digging bug. It's been a long time since I got to sink my teeth into something like this."

"Glad I'm providing an outlet for your boredom," I retort.

"I'm not bored. I'm restless. Don't tell Cami." He drops his voice to a whisper. "I saw Reggie Pike."

My ears prick up. Now, there's a blast from the past. "He's still alive?" The old crook has been forging new identities for years. If someone wants fake papers, he's the man to get them from. He doesn't ask questions, he works fast, and he's discreet. The latter being key here.

"Oh, he's alive," Jake says. "Albeit underground."

"And?"

"And a little gentle persuading dug me up something."

My eyebrow lifts. Gentle? Jake Sharp? I'm in that place again, the one between desperately needing to know and desperately not wanting to. But... "So what did the old creep say?"

"He never met the woman, so he can't confirm her identity. But he did produce documents and a credit history for a Hannah Bright."

"Fucking hell," I breathe. "How would she know where to go for that kind of shit?" Reggie Pike isn't the kind of man any woman should be friendly with. He's a total slimeball.

"Can't help you there, but I can tell you how she paid for it."

"How?"

"A diamond-encrusted Cartier watch. She gave him the code for a safe-deposit box at a bank just outside London. Reggie took the watch and left the documents."

I need to sit down. I'm not feeling all too stable. I move toward the nearest log and drop to my arse, rubbing my aching head. Where does it end?

"Is she safe?" Jake asks.

My hand stills on my forehead, and I stare at my bare feet.

"Because that's the only question you need to consider, Ryan. You don't need to get swallowed up in that shit. As long as she's out of harm's way, forget about everything else."

Is it that easy? Just disregard all I know and start a life with Hannah? "I don't know if I can do that, Jake."

"What will happen if you don't?" he asks. "Let me tell you." He goes on before I have the chance to even think about it. "You find out every dirty, tiny, graphic detail. You lose your shit, because you will. Trust me, you'll lose your shit. You'll want vengeance. It'll consume you to the point you lose sight of what's standing in front of you. Hannah is standing in front of you. You'll go on some mercy mission to get revenge for the woman you love, and risk everything you have right now. She's Hannah now, not Katrina. She's yours now, not his. Don't do anything to jeopardize that. Right now, he's remarried, over Hannah, and he's moved on. Just keep this information, store it, because it's not needed now and it might never be. Let. It. Be."

Sometimes, all you need is your mate to kick your arse into shape.

He's right. Of course he's right. What good will come of me digging any deeper? I have Hannah. She's here with me and she's safe. "I love you, mate."

"Fuck off and go be happy, Ryan. She's a good woman. Don't force her back to places she doesn't want to go. Trust me, it's not fun reliving your past when it's so bleak." He hangs up, and I smile down at my phone, taking a few minutes to bring myself down from the tailspin of the past half hour.

Let it go. It's for the best.

I spend a good ten minutes mentally repeating it to myself before I eventually find the energy to stand. Pushing myself up from the log, I wander back to the cabin and take off my jeans, leaving them in the pile by the door. As I approach Hannah, every kind of smile she's ever given me flashes through my mind: cheeky, coy, unsure, happy, excited. Each one, I realize now, is so very precious. And I'm the reason for them. I'll be dead before I'm the cause for her not to smile again. I have her. It's enough.

I lower beside her and crawl in under the blankets. Her eyes open and she blinks. "Where have you been?" she croaks, letting me get comfortable before she crawls onto my chest and settles again.

"Nowhere important." This here is important. Just this. "Go to sleep." I kiss her hair and close my eyes.

All the things that still haunt her, I plan on eliminating with the power of my love.

Chapter Twenty-Six

HANNAH

I'm not asleep. I woke up as soon as I felt him moving, though I kept my eyes closed. He gently rolled me off his chest and eased me to my back, and then carefully spread his body all over mine, supporting his torso with his arms on either side of my head. I can feel his breath on my face, he's so close. I keep my eyes closed, wondering what he's going to do. Just watch me?

Ryan gave me so much at the lake last night. His heart. His trust. His love. After such a traumatic day, it was the greatest gift. All I saw in that moment was a man who knows me completely. Ryan accepts who I am. He loves me as I am. It's more than I could ask for and probably more than I deserve when I'm keeping so much from him. But I don't want to tarnish my happiness with misery from my past. I don't want him to see me differently. Ryan made it possible for me to dare dream of something more than freedom.

A light breeze ghosts across my cheek from him blowing softly on my skin, and my lips start to twitch.

"And she smiles," he whispers, kissing the corner of my mouth.

"She can feel you watching her." I open one eye and bring my hands up to his head. "Why are you watching her?"

"Because she's a perfect mess, and she is *my* perfect mess." He wrinkles his nose and kisses the tip of mine, reaching back and taking one of my hands from his head. He pushes it into the floor above me before claiming the other and doing the same, effectively pinning me down. His knees shuffle up until he's straddling me.

"Wait," I blurt, and he closes one eye and pouts. "I need to tell you something."

"What?"

"I love you."

"I already know that." His face plummets to my neck and mauls me, biting and sucking, driving me instantly crazy.

"Ryan!" I laugh, my legs pointlessly wriggling beneath him. "Stop!"

"On one condition."

"Whatever you want." I giggle uncontrollably.

"Oh good. I'll collect your stuff later."

I still. "What?"

Ryan appears in my line of sight, his expression thoughtful. He seems to withdraw a little. "Will you move in with me?" he asks this time, rather than telling me.

Moving in? Like living here? He disappears into my neck again and starts going at my flesh like it's a steak and he's a wolf that hasn't eaten in a year, but I'm not laughing now. Now I'm too stunned. "You want me to live here?"

He doesn't feel it necessary to come up for air or face me during this monumental conversation in our relationship, though his lips stop moving across my neck. "Yes."

"Look at me."

He pops up sporting an adorably shy smile. "I didn't mean to demand it. Guess I got carried away. But you said you'd do anything." He shrugs. "So I'd love it if you did that."

His face, his words, the bloody crazy subject matter. And maybe my unrelenting happiness, too. It all has me bursting out laughing, my knee coming up and colliding with something.

I hear his blood-curdling retch first, followed by a rather high-pitch squeak, before his eyes go round and he falls like a sack of shit to the floor next to me, whimpering. My laughter disappears. Oh shit. He cups his groin and curls onto his side like a baby, whining in pain. "I can't fucking breathe," he gasps.

"Oh my God, I'm sorry!" I dive up and kneel next to him, patting at his naked body as he groans and whimpers. "Are you okay? Should I get ice?" What's the protocol for such situations?

"Just give me a second." He gags, and recoils on a wince. "Just a second."

I wait, useless beside him, as he takes the time he needs, his breathing eventually falling into controlled, deep inhales and exhales. "Is there anything I can do?" I ask.

He rolls to his back and looks up at me, his hands still cupping his groin. "You might have just kissed goodbye to that baby you want."

My back straightens. First I'm moving in and now babies? "This morning is moving pretty fast."

"Yeah, I know. And your knee is moving the fastest."

"Should I kiss it better?"

His eyes light up like diamonds. Of course they do. "Well, you know, it might make it better. And maybe you'll save my baby-making abilities and we can have one someday." He shrugs a little. "Of course, if you want to. When you're ready."

God love this beautiful man. "Are you hanging the possibility of us having a baby on the quality of a blow job?" What is this crazy conversation we're having?

"Absolutely." He winks and props his arms behind his head, getting all comfortable.

Oh, the pressure. But *oh* the sight of his lean body stretched out before me. I rest my palm on one side of his torso and swing my bent leg over, coming to rest on his stomach. He half smirks up at me, rolling his groin up into my bottom. "Someone recovered quickly," I quip, slowly lowering and kissing the middle of his chest.

"You're the cure for everything, Hannah." He growls, the sound rumbling up from his toes, and I smile against his skin, thinking the very same about him. I start kissing and sucking my way down his body, and with every inch I progress, Ryan's body becomes harder, his hands moving to my head and holding me steady. "Gentle," he murmurs as I stroke down his shaft with my flat palm. I leave his arousal resting on his lower stomach and kiss the base, watching as the vein running the length of his cock pulses. His hips rise, his hands firming up on my head.

"Dad!"

I scramble up, straddling his thighs, and Ryan's neck cricks with the speed at which he looks at the door. "No."

"Dad!" Alex's distant yell kills our passion dead in its tracks.

"She sounds panicked," I say, rushing to get up and wrap myself in the blanket, leaving Ryan naked and with nothing to cover himself.

"That's not panicked. That's angry." He sits up, seeming in no rush to remedy his nakedness. "I've never wished you to fuck off, Cabbage, but, please, just this once, fuck off."

I smack his stomach on a sharp burst of laughter. "You can't say that."

"God have mercy on my soul," he grunts, dragging himself to his feet. "Shit, I've got a bellyache." He walks to the door a little gingerly and pulls his jeans on with a few uncomfortable hisses. Then he swings the door open. "Hey, Cab..." He recoils. "What the hell do you look like?"

"I know!" she shrieks, throwing her arms up in the air in complete exasperation.

I don't blame her. She could've had a fight with a psychotic makeup artist and a possessed hairstylist. I have to put my hand over my mouth to stop my laughter from breaking free and undoubtedly pissing her off even more. She's a pile of ringlets, pink frills, and puffy fabric.

"Dad, you have to do something." Alex pushes her bunched fists into his chest. "She's lost it completely, and it's your fault."

"How?" Ryan asks, staring down at his daughter like she just disembarked from the circus train.

"Because she fell in love with you," she cries, her forehead flopping forward, no doubt smearing foundation all over Ryan's chest. "Since she found out about you and Hannah, she's been worse, Dad. Ten times worse!" Nudging Ryan out of the way, Alex storms into the cabin, and my ability to contain my amusement is lost. I snort past the hand on my mouth, quickly looking away, hoping I can pass off my laughter with a cough.

"Stop laughing," Alex mutters. "I'm blaming you, too."

"Me?" I blurt, pulling the blanket in and getting to my feet. "What did I do?"

She huffs and stomps over to the fridge, and a chorus of bangs and clatters ensues as she opens and slams a few doors and drawers until she's scoffing down a tub of Chunky Monkey. "I'm not going like this," she waffles around her spoon. "You'll have to kill me first."

Ryan sighs and shuts the door, joining Alex and claiming the spoon when it's halfway to her mouth again. She battles his intention to steal her goods and lunges forward with her mouth open to take the spoonful before Ryan gets it. "Share," he orders, prizing the tub away.

"It's not so bad," I say, trying to appease her, making another quick assessment of her pageant outfit. God, it's terrible. What is Darcy thinking?

"Really?" Alex asks sarcastically.

"Okay, you look like the Sugar Plum Fairy gone wrong," I admit on a shrug.

Ryan coughs around his mouthful of ice cream, dribbling some down his chin, and of course this just sets me off again. My laughing only encourages Ryan's, until we're both howling and Alex is red in the face. Her head looks like it's about to pop off.

"Right." She throws each of us a filthy glare and marches over to the door, looking back fiercely as she swings it open. "I'll blame you two." Stepping out, she slams the door with brute force.

I frown at Ryan, who's currently staring at the door a bit bewildered. "Blame us for what?" I ask, following him to the kitchen window. We both look out as Alex stamps her way to the compost heap. "What's she doing?"

Ryan wedges the spoon into the tub as Alex comes to a stop. "She's about to dive into that pile of mud."

"What?" I watch in horror as she takes a few steps back, giving herself space to run. "No!" I yell, scrambling for the door. Oh my days, her mother will have heart failure and it'll be all my fault. "Alex, don't do it!"

I trip my way down the veranda steps, the blankets getting all caught up in my legs. I'm not even halfway across the lawn before I realize I'll never make it in time to stop her. I slow and close one eye on a screwed-up nose as she runs and jumps, her arms and legs out like she could be skydiving from a plane twelve thousand feet up.

Splat.

She lands front-forward in the compost pile, but not satisfied with that, she proceeds to roll around, covering every inch of her fancy outfit in mud, at the same time ensuring that her mother's meltdown will go down in history. And probably that she'll hate me forever for ruining her girl.

I sag where I stand. Great. "Alex," I sigh as she sits up, arms and legs akimbo. "What have you done?"

"Me?" she chirps, all happy with herself. "But you pushed me, Hannah."

Ryan snorts from behind me, and I throw a lethal glare his way, making him soon snap that smug grin into shape. I stomp up to the edge of the compost heap. "Out," I order, realizing I sound like a stern adult. But heavens, it'll take me all morning to fix her and save us all from the wrath of her mother. I need to get to town to help Molly.

On a little pout, Alex holds her hand out to me. I shake my head— more adult disapproval—and stretch forward to take it, holding the blankets to me with my spare hand. "Oh my God, Alex, look at you."

She tugs, catching me off guard, and hauls me forward. And I land with a splat in the pile next to her on all fours. "Oh my God," I breathe, my face inches away from the mud. "Alex!"

She flops to her back in fits of laughter, rolling around some more, holding her tummy. I'm going to wring her bloody neck. I lift a hand, the damn thing squelching as I pull it out of the mud, and grab onto the blanket that's now draped over me, holding it close as I stand. The little minx finds it in herself to calm enough to register my irritation.

Then she grins at me. "Sorry."

I slowly turn to find Ryan. He has a hand over his mouth covering his smirk. I tilt my head, my jaw tight. "Are you going to kill her, or am I?"

He bends at the waist and releases all the laughter he's been holding back, bracing his hands on his knees to keep himself up. "I'm sorry," he chuckles, and Alex joins him, both of their bodies vibrating uncontrollably from their hysterics.

"No, you're not." I look down at the blanket around me. "I have to go." I make my way to the outside shower, aware of their sudden silence.

"Wait, what?" Ryan is in hot pursuit, chasing me down, albeit a little slowly, obviously still sore from his encounter with my knee earlier. Good. I hope they're blue. "You have to help me fix her," he says urgently.

I round the edge of the shower out of eyeshot of Alex and turn toward him, throwing off the blanket. He forgets himself for a second, his worried eyes falling into appreciation as they drop the length of my body. "You can fix her yourself." I open the wooden door and flip the shower on, standing to the side while it heats up. "I have to go help Molly." I smile sweetly and step under the spray as Ryan moves close to the edge of the stall, peeking over. I can tell by the umbrage on his face that he wishes he could join me.

"Hannah, come on." He looks back over his shoulder to Alex. "Oh Jesus."

"It's not so funny now, huh?" I wash my hair quickly and grab a towel draped over the top of the stall. As I step out I see that Alex has lost her smugness, too, reality setting in. "Is that your phone?" I ask Ryan, hearing a ring from inside.

"Shit." He makes a mad dash for the house, Alex in quick pursuit.

"If it's Mum, I'm not here," she yells, and I laugh, following them into the cabin. "Don't answer it." She wrestles with Ryan when he picks up his phone.

"She'll be worried." He slaps his palm into Alex's muddy forehead and holds her back as her arms flail and swipe at him. "Darcy," he breathes.

I tuck my towel in and take a seat in the nearby armchair, crossing one leg over the other and settling my hands on the arms. I can spare a few minutes to watch them wriggle their way out of this.

"Stop panicking. She's here." He looks his daughter up and down, still keeping her at a distance with his outstretched arm. "I think we have a winner on our hands."

I don't bother holding back my amusement. They deserve everything that's coming to them. I'm checking out. I was never here.

Alex ducks so Ryan loses his hold on her, diving at his body to try to win the phone. He turns just in time and she lands on his back, hanging there as he starts to pace the cabin.

"She won't be late," he assures Darcy. "We'll meet you there." He hangs up and tosses his phone to the side before reaching back and detaching his daughter from his back. She drops to her feet in a huff and pouts, and Ryan scowls at her.

I stand and collect my clothes from the pile by the door, then head to the bedroom. "Good luck," I sing as I go, shutting the door behind me and shaking out my dress, hearing hushed shouts from beyond as I get dressed.

I pull my wet hair into a knot and when I pull the door open to leave, I'm met with two cheesy smiles. I look from Ryan to Alex, who proceeds to flutter her lashes. "Hannah," she coos.

"No." I edge past them to avoid being caked in mud again, and get on my way.

"See," Ryan hisses. "Look what you've done."

"It's your fault," she retorts. "Mum's gonna bust your balls."

"I already did that," I snicker, taking the steps down to the lawn.

"Dad!" Alex wails. "You have to fix it!"

"What have I told you about actions and consequences?" he asks on a growl.

"I know!" she cries. "I promise I'll listen to you for the rest of my life."

"Shitting hell," Ryan curses, and a second later he lands in front of me, blocking my way. His cheesy grin is back. I raise my eyebrows, waiting, and he eventually slumps on the spot. "I'll do anything."

"Anything," Alex reiterates frantically from behind me.

"Give me one reason why I should help?"

He pouts, his eyes going all puppy-like. "Because you love me."

"I knew it!" Alex screeches, appearing by my side. My gaze is set firmly on Ryan, an unstoppable smile creeping across my mouth.

"And I love you," he says, loud and proud.

"Yes!" Alex starts jigging on the spot, her jerky movements sending blobs of mud flying everywhere.

I laugh, amused, but mainly relieved that she seems so thrilled by this news. I step into Ryan's chest and stuff my hands in his front pockets, looking up at him. "Fine, I'll help."

"Thank God." He plants a chaste kiss on my lips, and I frown, feeling at something in his pocket. I step back and pull my hand free, my frown growing when I see what's between my fingers.

Ryan's eyes widen.

Alex stops with her happy dance.

And me? I stare at the slinky red G-string I just found in my boyfriend's jean pocket. "These aren't mine," I say to them.

"Uh-oh," Alex breathes, and I look up at Ryan, my head cocked in question.

"I can explain." His hands come up in that kind of mollifying way that's telling me not to turn and walk away.

"He can explain," Alex parrots, moving in and swiping the red knickers from my hand.

"Then explain," I order, sounding stern, though I'm not feeling particularly mad, and I don't know why. I should be raging. I should be stomping off. I should be slapping his face. But my gut is telling me not to. It's telling me there's a perfectly reasonable explanation, because I know deep down in my heart that Ryan would never betray me like that. I find myself smiling on the inside. This feeling of faith, even when I'm staring a pair of red knickers in the face that aren't mine, is something special alone.

His face bunches. "They're...I...it isn't what..." He sighs, struggling to find his words.

"I found them in his truck when he got home." Alex flies to her father's defense and drops them to the floor, stamping on them, throwing a dirty look her dad's way. "Stupid."

He just shrugs. It's lame, but it's also quite endearing. I dust my hands off and head back to the cabin, feeling Alex's and Ryan's eyes follow me. "Are we going to get you cleaned up or not?" I call behind me, looking back. They stare at me like I've lost my mind. I haven't. I'm not irrational. I'm sure Ryan had plenty of women before I came along. I grimace at his truck. "Well?"

They look at each other, lost, and then shrug and trudge after me. I direct Alex to the shower and send Ryan to get towels. Let's fix this mess.

*　*　*

Ryan shakes his head in disbelief, putting his foot down to gain some speed and increase the chances of Alex's dress being dry by the time we make it into town. "You're a genius!" she sings as I hold her frock out of the open window, the fabric flapping in the wind.

The high street is buzzing as Ryan pulls up at the top end, unable to get through because of all the stalls and stands. I look back to Alex, checking her over again. She's not perfect, but I did the best I could with what limited tools I had at my disposal. I pull her dress in the window and pass it back.

"Put it on."

She inhales sharply as she wriggles around on the backseat. "It's freezing!"

I spot the stage outside Mr. Chaps's store, where, apparently, Darcy keeps her beauty case for touch-ups throughout the day and pre-presentation, so that is where we're heading. "Can you see your mum?" I ask, scanning the street for her.

"There." Alex appears between the two front seats, pointing down the street. I home in and see Darcy with a well-dressed elderly couple.

"Your grandparents?"

"Yep."

I look at Ryan and smirk, and he slumps in his seat. "You're going to ask me to distract them, aren't you?"

"Good boy," I quip, jumping out and ushering Alex around the back of the truck. "If we can make it to the back of the stage without your mother seeing us, we're home free." I point out our route and as soon as Ryan is with the Hamptons, we hustle down the street, keeping close to the shop fronts. We make it to the stage undetected, and Alex lugs up a huge case from under a table.

I balk, astounded. "I know," she agrees, as I shake away my exasperation and open up the box of tricks. And I stare at it for a few minutes, the endless items of makeup stimulating memories from my past. Lipsticks in every color, primers and fixing sprays, eye shadows and pencils galore. Everything a woman needs to look perfect when her life is anything but. I swiftly push those thoughts away and grab what I need, turning to Alex.

She remains perfectly still as I blot and dab at her, though her eyes watch me carefully as I work. My ability to apply makeup as perfectly as I wore it hasn't left me. I smoke her eyes, draw a perfect line of liquid liner across her lid, adding a tiny flick at each corner, and highlight her cheeks. A bit of contouring, a dash of blush and bronzer, and the perfect shade of nude lipstick to make her blue eyes pop.

I sit back as she rubs her lips together, admiring my work. And as Alex grabs a mirror and inspects herself, I realize that I've just created a version of my old self. "Oh, wow!" she blurts, checking herself out at every angle. "I don't look like a clown."

I smile, though it's strained, and close the box. "Turn around."

She does as she's told quickly and I gather her long hair up, messily pinning it here, there, and everywhere. "How come you're so good at makeup but you never wear it?" she asks, and my working hands falter as I push a grip into her hair.

"I used to wear it," I tell her. "It doesn't interest me anymore." I tap her shoulders and spin her around to face me. "There, you're done." She twirls, and though her face and hair are a major improvement, the dress still sucks. "Perfect," I say anyway. I'm still expecting a freak-out from Darcy, since Alex's face is no longer an inch thick with cosmetics and her hair isn't stiff ringlets.

Ryan appears around the back of the stage. "Tell me you're fin—" He steps back. "Wow."

"I know." Alex curtsies. "I look pretty, right?"

"You always look pretty." Ryan stares at me questioningly, but I brush it off and stand, giving him a quick kiss.

"Now I really must go."

He pouts, disappointed, and I smile as I leave them to go set up the painting competition. I make it to my store and slip the key into the lock.

"There you are!" Molly strides into the store with me and grabs some of the stacked chairs.

"I'm sorry, we had a disaster with Alex's pageant outfit." I follow her out onto the street and set out the chairs.

"A disaster?" We head back inside to get the easels.

"Don't ask. How's everything going?"

"No disasters here." She places a few easels and gives me a quick peck on the cheek. "Can you finish up alone? I've got to go set up the sack race before Lord Hampton declares us open."

"No problem."

She hurries away, claiming a pint of cider from Bob as she passes, and I finish setting up the competition area, giving each place a palette of paints and a blank canvas before rushing up to my apartment and quickly changing out of my dress and into my dungarees.

When I make it back down, I look up the street as I fix my scarf in my hair, seeing every stall and stand swamped with locals. A country dancing pole is next to the stage, a few kids dancing around it, entwining their ribbons, and Mrs. Heaven is outside her café dishing out her famous muffins to anyone who passes. It's bustling, smiles are on the faces of all, and the atmosphere is alive. It's wonderful.

I spot a kid hovering nearby, maybe nine or ten, eyeing up the paints. My first contender? "Hey." I grab an apron off the closest chair and hold it out to him. "Want to enter?"

"What do I have to paint?"

I point up the street. "Paint what you see. Lord Hampton will announce the winner at the end of the day."

"I'm so gonna win." He's in his apron and on his stool a few seconds later, loading his brush up and taking in the street before him. I smile and leave him to it, set on finding kids to fill the other stools.

Half an hour later, my class is full and paintbrushes are swiping furiously at every canvas. I weave through the stools, checking out the works in progress, offering small tips here and there if I feel they need advice. There are some seriously talented kids in Hampton, and Alex is one of the most brilliant. I bend over behind her and put my mouth to her ear. "Please, please, please don't get any paint on your dress."

"Seriously, Hannah." She peeks out the corner of her eye to me. "You've wrapped me up in three aprons and a raincoat. No paint is making it to my clothes."

She may say that, but this girl gives me a run for my money when it comes to getting messy. "Have you seen your mum yet?"

She shakes her head and dabs her brush on the canvas, placing perfect little dots on the bunting. "She's busy escorting Grandma and Grandpa around."

Good. Hopefully I can avoid her all day. But when I look up over Alex's canvas, I see Darcy heading this way with her parents. Oh shit. I slap a smile on my face when she clocks me. "Hi." I round Alex and offer my hand to her grandfather. "Hannah Bright, lovely to meet you."

He looks down at my hand. Another sniff. What wonderful people. Peeking at my hand, too, I roll my eyes to myself and wipe the paint down the front of my dungarees. "Would you like to see some of the entries? They're coming along quite nicely."

"Oh, is that our Alexandra?" Lady Hampton coos, and then pretty much twitches in her posh frock when she registers the paintbrush in her granddaughter's hand.

"Oh, Alexandra!" Darcy rushes to Alex's side. "What in heaven's name are you doing?"

"Painting." She points to the canvas with her brush like her mother could have missed it. I sigh, bracing myself for it.

"And your face!" Darcy stares at Alex in horror, seeming a bit stuck for words.

"Problem?" Ryan asks, appearing from nowhere.

"Yes!" Darcy shrieks. "Just look at her."

"She looks beautiful." Ryan flips Alex a wink, who merrily carries on about her painting business, unperturbed by the current anxiety attack her mother is having.

Darcy tosses Ryan and me a ferocious glare, and I find myself moving into his side, seeking protection from the explosion. "This is all your fault," she hisses, and I flinch. "Her winning record will be broken."

"Maybe she'll win the painting competition instead," I say without thinking, and I hear Ryan snort from beside me. "Or maybe not." I retreat out of the firing line.

"Cool it, Mum." Alex continues dotting her brush across the canvas, peeking past it from time to time to check the subject. "It's in the bag."

I have to purse my lips to keep myself together. "I'm going to get one of Bob's special ciders," I declare, hurrying over to his stand, accepting the pint glass he hands me with a smile. His cheeks are rosy, making me wonder how many he's had already.

"Cheers," he says, pouring himself another.

I raise my glass and have a big swig, coughing after I swallow. That's stronger than I expected. "Share?" Ryan whispers in my ear, reaching past me to take the glass.

I turn in to him, keeping myself shielded from Darcy's daggers. "Has she calmed down?"

"She'll get over it." Ryan has his own little wince after taking a sip, holding the glass up to inspect it. "Jesus, a few of those and I'll be anyone's."

"Just make sure they don't leave their knickers in your truck this time," I tease, taking back my glass on a sweet smile.

He softens before me. "You know my heart is yours."

"I know."

"And my body. And my soul. And my Chunky Monkey."

I laugh as he sweeps me from my feet, draping me across his arms. Half the contents of my cider spills in the process, and he ravages my cheek as he carries me up the street for all to see. "It's time to pie some faces," he declares, setting his focus forward.

I look and see the stall where some stocks are set up. "Is that Father

Fitzroy?" I ask, sipping away at my cider as I'm carted up the high street. The old boy is on his knees, his head and wrists secured in the stocks while kids throw pies at his face. He's laughing, watching as pies splat everywhere around him except on his face.

"He won't be laughing in a minute." Ryan sets me on my feet and claims a pie, encouraging the kids aside as he lines up his target. The old priest soon pipes down. "Hi, Father," Ryan says, spinning the pie on the top of his finger cockily.

"You'll go to hell," he mutters, clenching his eyes shut as Ryan pulls back his arm and fires like a pro pitcher.

It lands with frightening accuracy slap bang in the middle of the priest's face. "Bull's-eye!" Ryan yells, and the kids go wild, all trying to surrender their pies to the champion shooter.

"You really will go to hell." I shake my head at him as he takes me in a headlock and walks us across to Mrs. Heaven's cake stall to claim a muffin.

"You come see me, Ryan Willis," shouts Father Fitzroy as he wipes the cream from his face. "I have an opening next month."

I frown, looking to Ryan for some clue as to what the old man is talking about.

"For the wedding," the priest adds, and I balk.

"What wedding?" I shout back, making him chuckle. I divert my attention to Ryan. "In the past twelve hours, there's been talk of moving in, babies, and now a wedding?"

"You panicking?" he asks, shoving a chunk of muffin in his mouth and chewing as he watches me.

"No." I down the rest of my cider and place the glass on a nearby table. "I have to go check on my budding artists." I walk away but stop, feeling his smirk burning my back. "I'm not marrying you," I declare to the blank space before me.

"We'll see," he muses casually.

This smile on my face is so big, it's reaching both ears. "We will," I retort, lifting my chin and getting on my way. I hear him chuckle as I go, and all I can wonder is what it would be like to be married to Ryan. To be his wife. I wouldn't be a trophy. He wouldn't dictate...everything. He loves me the way I am.

The warm fuzzy feeling inside is squashed when I see Darcy approaching. Oh no. She stares me down as we walk toward each other, and just as she's passing me, she stops briefly. I fear the worst. "Don't try to replace me," she mumbles, and then she carries on her way.

"Darcy, I would never—" I'm cut short when her silencing hand lifts, and she looks back over her shoulder, a filthy glare being fired my way.

Oh boy. I sigh and continue back to my artists to check their progress. "Looking good, guys," I say, nodding my approval. "You have an hour remaining."

"I'm almost finished," Alex yells back at me. "The pageant starts soon." Her tongue comes out and rests on her lip as she leans in, concentrating on the last finer details.

"Alex, this is so great," I say, taking in her effort.

"Thanks. Do you think I'll win?"

"It's going to look a bit dodgy if you win the pageant *and* the painting competition, especially since your granddad is judging both." I reach forward and point to one of the shop fronts. "A little more shading there."

"I knew there was something missing." She dunks her brush in the gray paint and gets to shading quickly.

"And what's this?" I ask, pointing to a black blob in the background.

"Oh, that's a truck."

I peer up, looking for it. "Where?"

"It drove off so I had to use my memory. I mean, didn't he know I was painting it?"

I laugh. "How inconsiderate."

Alex jumps up. "Done. I've gotta go."

"I'll look after it for you!" I call as she dashes off.

"Okay!"

I straighten and take in the busyness around me, unable to stop myself wondering how I got so lucky to choose Hampton. I see Molly blowing her whistle, declaring the start of the egg-and-spoon race, and Mr. Chaps is outside his store dishing out toffee apples. Mrs. Hatt is holding a crocheting class, and then I see Ryan, who's on the stage shifting boxes so Cyrus can sweep it clean, ready for the pageant. No matter where I turn, I see smiles. I see happiness.

Ryan looks up at me as he unbends, a heavy box in his hands, and he flashes me his crooked smile that sends my insides to mush. That makes my heart swell. It's the smile that was the start of something beautiful. I see a million promises in his eyes as he watches me watching him, and I believe every one of them. I nod and he nods in return as he turns and follows the directions being given to him by one of the volunteers. I sigh, utterly content, and slowly peruse the high street.

The cotton candy stall, the apple-bobbing barrel, the face-painting tent, the—

I do a double take, back to the top of the street, seeing it again. A truck. I step forward, squinting, but a few people walk across my path, and I quickly step to the side to get it back in view.

There's no truck. But there was a truck. A black one. A Mitsubishi. Didn't Ryan say it was an idiot in a Mitsubishi who ran him off the road? I find myself reaching to my nape without thought and rubbing there, my feet suddenly welded to the ground. Chills. They glide down my spine like melting ice, and I look around me, a horrible sense of unease rooting itself in my gut.

"Oh my God, Hannah." Molly appears beside me, but I can't see her face because it's concealed behind a huge spray of red roses. "These were delivered to your store this morning before you arrived. I totally forgot and stored them under the toffee apple stall." She thrusts them at me, and my arms automatically come up to take them. "Who knew Ryan Willis could be so romantic?"

As she hustles off, I stare at the flowers, my unease not leaving me. I pluck out the card nestled amid the roses but have to put the arrangement on the ground to free both hands and open the envelope. I pull the card out, and I frown when I see a photograph with it. What? I stare down at the image, confused for a moment, until I realize what I'm looking at. My paintings. The ones I sold. They're hanging on the bare brick wall of a room. I open the card, but there are no words, just one single *x*. A kiss. My head tilts a little, my stomach turning. The man who bought my paintings sent me flowers? Why? I pull the photograph back to the front, gazing down at my art, and the temperature of my blood seems to drop a few too many degrees. I look up and around.

And I see the Mitsubishi again, parked at the end of the street. My heart flies up to my throat as I back away. I make out the silhouette of someone in the driver's seat, and I'm definitely not imagining the feel of their eyes on me. "No," I breathe, blinking away the sudden bombardment of familiar feelings. Fear. Anxiety. Dread.

My feet get caught in something, and I trip and stumble, crashing into the toffee apple stall, sending things flying everywhere. But I can't tear my terrified stare away from that truck. It's just sitting there, almost threateningly. Then the headlights flash a couple of times, as if the driver is acknowledging that I've seen him, and I retch. The happy noise around me fades and all I can hear is every single nasty thing he ever yelled at me. My surroundings start to spin.

"No." I turn and run, staggering and tripping as I go and falling through the door of my store clumsily, locking it behind me. "No," I sob, shaking my head, as if I can shake myself from this nightmare.

He's found me.

Chapter Twenty-Seven

RYAN

I swing the mallet with as much force as I can, smacking the target on a grunt, and the ball shoots up the shaft and smacks the bell, earning me a few cheers. "Piece of cake." I drop the mallet and brush off my hands, ready for the next game.

"Young whippersnapper," Father Fitzroy grumbles, entering my name in chalk at the top of the scoreboard. My chest puffs out. It's childish, I realize, but I'm having fun being champion of everything.

I look back to where all the easels are set up for Hannah, hoping she's seeing me annihilating the competition. I pout to myself when I don't find her, and head to that end of the street to track her down.

"Hey, Dad!" Alex yells, and I look back, seeing her ready to climb the steps to the stage. It's my girl's turn to prance up and down and be assessed by the townspeople. She pulls that ridiculous dress out and twirls for me, rolling her eyes as she does. "You're coming to watch, aren't you?"

I look back toward where the artists are painting, still seeing no Hannah. Where is she? "Of course," I say, reversing my steps, making my way to the foot of the stage just as Darcy's father speaks. "And now, ladies and gentlemen, the ravishing, and incredibly intelligent, might I add, Alexandra Hampton-Willis!"

The crowd cheers, and I join them, clapping my hands as my Cabbage struts across the stage dramatically, like she could be on a cat-walk. I chuckle as her grandfather continues to sell her, detailing her grades, her passions, and her strong lineage. "Crock of shit," I mutter, listening to him harp on about her talent with a violin. She fucking hates the violin. I cast my eyes back again, looking for Hannah. She should be here. She should be seeing this.

"She'll win, of course," Darcy says as she swoops in to my side, smiling proudly at Alex as she claps. "Woohoo for Alexandra!"

Alex gives her mum the death stare, her little nostrils flaring. "You're embarrassing her," I say.

"No, I'm not."

"It's actually a novelty to see her squirm." I raise my hands and clap, too, then belt out an ear-piercing whistle. "Go on, Cabbage!" Her face is a picture of horror, and I grin at her. It's payback for her little stunt this morning.

Darcy giggles, her hand covering her mouth. That's a novelty, too. "All right?" I ask, and she looks at me, all bashful and... flirty? I'm immediately wary. She looked at me like this recently, and the next minute she wanted to cook me supper.

She bats her lashes, toying with a lock of her hair.

Oh no.

"Darcy..." I stretch her name out, taking one step back away from her, worried she's going to pounce at me any minute. She closes the gap, and I hold my hands up, warning her back. "No," I say assertively, aware that I'm about to get either a mouthful of abuse or a face full of her palm. "It's never going to happen."

It must be the tone of my voice, or maybe the resolution on my face, but she backs off, her face falling. "I just thought..." She fades, looking across to Alex on the stage.

"What, that we'd pick up where we left off eleven years ago?" Does she need a reminder of what actually happened that night, because as far as I remember, it consisted of lots of alcohol and a quick wham-bam. There were no fireworks. There was no passion. We were both scratching an itch. Or at least, I was. "Darcy, we have nothing in common."

"Well, we do have *something* in common."

I look at Alex, who is still parading up and down, but her attention is straight on us. Her parents. Talking. She looks worried. She should be. I force a smile onto my face to reassure her, coughing my throat clear. "Darcy, I respect you, I care for you, but only as my daughter's mother. You don't want me." Does she?

She nods a little, reluctant, turning away from me. "I can't stand the thought of being lonely, Ryan. Alexandra is such a daddy's girl. I know she'll always choose you over me. What if she wants to live with you forever? I'll be all alone." She looks at me, and I see the true fear in her. I take no pleasure from it.

I sigh and do what instinct is telling me to do. "Come here, silly." I pull her into me and give her a hug, catching her fleeting look of surprise just before she's tucked in my chest. Darcy Hampton doesn't receive many hugs, if any. She needs one. She molds against me easily, and I sigh into her hair. "You'll never be alone. Alex adores your neurotic bones."

She chuckles and sniffles, wrapping her arms around me. "She's a good kid. Messy but good."

"She is," I muse, looking across at the stage. Our messy but good kid is looking at us like we just stepped off an intergalactic flight from Mars. Her head tilts, her eyes widen, and her hands come up like, *What the hell is going on?* I wave off her concern and gesture for her to get on and win the pageant. "Do me a favor, yeah?" I say to Darcy.

"What?"

"Go take a look at the painting she's done."

"I already did."

"And?" I prompt.

"And she's not just beautiful and intelligent, but creative, too."

I smile. "Make sure she knows that."

"I will," she sighs.

"You heard from Casper?" I break away before she gets too comfortable, and she wipes at her nose.

"No. I know it's for the best. It's been a long time since there was any love in our marriage."

"You'll find your Mr. Perfect," I assure her softly. "There's real love out there waiting for all of us."

"Like you?" she says a little suggestively, prompting me to scan the street for Hannah again. Where'd she go? "She's nice," Darcy adds, and I know it took everything in her to admit it.

"How much did that hurt?" I ask seriously.

"Stop it." She gives my arm a playful slap. "I don't mind admitting when I'm wrong. I shouldn't have stepped on her toes."

"You didn't step, Darcy. You stamped." I'm back to searching for the woman in question as Darcy chuckles. "Have you seen her?"

"Oh, yes." She motions back up the street. "She fell into the toffee apple stall."

"What?"

"Wasn't looking where she was going. Backed right into it." Darcy arranges her bag in the crook of her arm as the crowd erupts again. "She ran into her shop. Embarrassed, probably. She made a right mess, poor thing."

I'm running toward Hannah's shop before I've had a chance to let all the information Darcy just fed me sink in. I don't like the sudden increase of my heart rate. I don't like the whoosh of blood in my ears. And I fucking hate the prickles of apprehension stabbing me all over.

I reach the door and push, but it doesn't budge an inch. I peek through, seeing her store empty. "Hannah," I yell, banging on the glass with my fist. I'm aware of what happened the last time I broke in, namely, nearly having my head shot off, so I'm sure to make myself known, hoping she'll answer before I kick the door in.

"Hannah, it's me. Open up!" I cup my hands around my face and peer through the glass again, cursing under my breath. I pull my phone from my pocket and dial her, pacing up and down outside her door as it rings. It goes to voice mail. I growl and dial again, looking back through the door. "Answer your phone," I order. She doesn't. "Fuck this." I wedge my shoulder up against the wood near the lock to get my aim just right, and then rear back, throwing my body into it. It flies open, hitting the plaster behind with a *thwack*. I still for a moment and listen.

"Hannah!" I yell, stalking through the store, scanning high and low. "Hannah, where are you?" I pass through the kitchen and fly up the stairs, barging into each room like a bulldozer, my heart sprinting faster with each room I find empty.

I push into her bedroom and my eyes fall straight to her bed. The sheets are strewn everywhere, clothes scattered here and there. A nasty, dull ache stirs in my gut, threatening to break out into agony. I cast my eyes across her room to the wardrobe. The doors are open, empty hangers scattered on the carpet before it. The drawers of her chest are all open, too, items of clothing hanging over the edges.

"No," I breathe, shock and devastation immobilizing me. I swallow, spotting her phone on the nightstand. I walk over and slide it off the edge, looking down at the two missed calls from me. I inhale. Take the handle of the drawer on her nightstand. Slowly drag it open. No gun.

"Noooooo!" I roar, turning and stalking out, smashing the door against the wall as I charge through it. I run down the stairs and through the kitchen to the back door onto the courtyard. The gate onto the rear alleyway is swinging back and forth. "God damn you, Hannah." I race into the alleyway, looking up and down. There's no sign of her. "Fucking hell." I take a left and sprint to the end, onto the country road that leads out of town. I nearly cough my heart up when I see her in the distance, running toward a taxi. "Hannah!" I yell, sprinting after her.

She looks back, but doesn't stop, struggling forward with her duffel bag. Her rejection is like a knife through my fucking heart.

"Don't you get in the fucking taxi, Hannah!" I sound possessed, but I'm completely out of control, being fueled by panic, hurt, anger. Something's happened. Something to make her run. Fuck, what?

She reaches the taxi and tosses her bag in, jumping in behind it. "Hannah, I know!" I yell as the door slams shut. The driver pulls away quickly, driving fast, and even I realize I can't chase him down.

He has too much of a head start already. I'm fit, but I'm not a fucking cheetah. My pace breaks down as I watch the cab get smaller, until I'm standing in the middle of the road, a broken man, completely and utterly fucking destroyed. "I know everything," I wheeze, my head dropping back and looking to the heavens. "I fucking know!" I slam my hands onto my head as I watch the woman I love run away from me.

Chapter Twenty-Eight

HANNAH

My face is stinging as I'm driven through the countryside, my tears relentless, my heart the heaviest it's ever been. Just get away. Run. It's my natural instinct, and I'm unable to stop it. I wish I could stop and face my fear. I wish I could tackle it head-on. But the truth is, I don't just fear for myself now. I fear for Ryan, too. I know what Jarrad is capable of. I can't put Ryan in the firing line. And I can't ruin his illusion. I'll be gone, but at least he'll remember me as I want to be remembered. Smiling. Happy. His Hannah.

I cover my face with my hands, my body jolting painfully from my racking sobs, my mind taking me back to places I thought I'd long escaped. To the times Jarrad played with my sanity. Made me feel stupid. Took a sick pleasure out of watching me tremble, when I was wondering whether he was going to punch me or kiss me. In the end, everything was a game to Jarrad. He played games in business. He played games with me. It made him feel more powerful to control people's fear. To control their lives. To know everything good that happened to someone was because of him. And he had the power to take it away.

He's here. And he's playing with me all over again.

"Whoa!" the taxi driver cries, slamming his brakes on and sending me flying forward in my seat. "Watch it, arsehole!"

My heart twists in my chest, my fear rocketing. I look out the windshield just as a truck swerves in front of us and slams on its brakes, tires screeching.

Ryan's truck.

He gets out, slams the door shut with force, and paces toward the cab, his face cut with anger.

I scramble to get out, to keep him from coming closer and making this harder than it needs to be. "Stop!" I yell.

He doesn't, he just keeps marching toward me. "You're not doing this to me, Hannah."

"I have no choice," I sob, reversing my steps as he keeps coming forward.

"You do!" he yells, reaching me and grabbing the tops of my arms, shaking me as my tears pour. "You do have a fucking choice because I'm giving you one!"

He doesn't understand. I've always wanted to shield him from my dirty past. "I can't," I murmur as I stare into his eyes, trying to disregard all the love I see in them. Unfathomable amounts. All for me.

"Then tell me why you're leaving. At least give me *that* before you disappear. Because if the reason is more powerful than how much I love you, then I want to fucking know what it is."

Shame eats at me from the inside out. Is my fear more powerful than his love? I glance around the countryside, seeing nothing for miles. Am I incapable of stopping myself from completely crumbling each time something reminds me of my past? I saw a truck and feared the worst, started building scary scenarios. I had some flowers delivered by a client and read past the blank card. Both triggered something in me, something I couldn't ignore, but is that good enough reason for me to spiral into meltdown? Is that a good enough reason for me to run away from a man who loves me? Is my paranoia out of control?

"What are you going to do?" Ryan asks. "Run your whole life?" He switches his hold, taking my jaw and holding it in his grasp, squeezing firmly. "Aren't I enough to make you stay?"

"Don't." I look away, but he shakes me, silently ordering me to look him in the eye.

His jaw pulses, his frustration and anger palpable. And his hope. "Aren't I?"

I close my eyes, feeling tears flow over and roll down my cheeks. "It's not that simple."

"It's very fucking simple from where I'm standing, Hannah. Am I enough?"

"Yes!" I yell, angered that he would believe otherwise. "Yes, you're enough!"

"Then fucking stay!" he roars back, yanking his hand away from my jaw. He seems to take a breather, seems to think and calm himself. "I know everything."

I step back on a sniffle, wiping at my nose with the back of my hand. "What?"

His eyes ping open, and I see a resolution and determination in them that I'm not sure I like. "I. Know. Everything." He doesn't need to say any more. His gaze spells it out letter for letter, word for word.

I lose my breath, stepping back away from him. "How?"

"Does it matter?"

"Yes!" Suddenly my reasoning—that I'm being paranoid, that I'm turning nothings into somethings—vanishes, and I look around us frantically. It prompts Ryan to do the same. There's still just acres of empty fields.

He must understand my sudden alarm. "I work in protection," he reminds me. "I have contacts."

"You had someone pry?" I ask.

"If I hadn't, would you have just left me in the fucking dark forever? Let me love a woman who isn't who she says she is?"

"The woman you love is the woman I am!" I scream. "That's the fucking point, Ryan! I'm not *her* anymore. I'm not a punching bag anymore. I'm not a trophy or an alibi." My voice quivers with so much emotion, I'm sure I could crumble under the weight of it at any moment. "That's the fucking point," I sob, pointing at him. "You love me." My hand lands on my chest, my shoulders jumping as I cry uncontrollably.

I know it enrages him to see me like this. It must tear his heart out, hearing my fear and my reason. And that's another fucking point. I know him well enough to know that it could push him over the edge of sanity. Could have him tracking down Jarrad and stabbing him in both eyes so he's physically unable to search for me.

"Hey!" The taxi driver leans out of the window, his face impatient. "Am I staying or going?"

"Going," Ryan grates, pulling my duffel bag from the backseat and throwing a twenty to the driver. He slings it over his shoulder and slams the door, and the taxi pulls away.

When I look back at Ryan, he's regarding me closely. "Why did you run today?" he asks. "I need to know, Hannah. No more secrets."

I take a breath, but I don't hold back telling him. Not now. "I saw a truck at the fete." I shake my head to myself, knowing, now I'm calmer and stable, that it was just an overreaction on my part. "It was a Mitsubishi. It was there, then it wasn't, then it was again. It was odd. I remembered you said it was a Mitsubishi that ran you off the road and my imagination ran away with me. Then he flashed his lights and I freaked out."

He closes his eyes, and I hate that it's an obvious attempt to gather patience. He thinks I'm overreacting, too.

"I'll have it looked into," he says, and I can't help but think he's trying to pacify me. "I'm sure it's nothing, but for peace of mind, I'll check it out."

"There's something else," I go on, needing him to hear the rest so maybe he might empathize and understand why I went off the deep end.

Ryan's instantly alert again. "What?"

"The guy who's bought some of my paintings. He sent me flowers," I say quietly, and Ryan's jaw immediately tics. It's not worry. It's anger. Annoyance. "And a picture of them hanging in his castle."

He swallows hard, nostrils flaring. "Right," he pretty much growls. "And that freaked you out, too?"

"With the truck, the flowers..." I shake my head again, realizing how unreasonable it sounds, but I reacted and I wasn't able to stop it. And I hate that.

Ryan drops my bag with a sigh and comes to me, hauling me forward with force, pinning me to his front. "I promise you, he can't touch you, Hannah. He can't find you. He can't hurt you." He kisses my hair and pulls me free, making sure I can see the purpose and sincerity in his eyes. "I. Promise. You." He wipes under each eye with the pad of his thumbs. "Please, don't run again. You don't have to anymore, because you have me." His palms frame my face. "Let me love you."

I cough on a sob, throwing my arms around him and clinging on like he is life. Like he can save me from my torment.

He can.

He will.

And I need to find the strength I've lost to continue to save myself.

*　*　*

I'm quiet as Ryan drives us back to town. With the fete still in full swing, he has to take the alley that runs parallel to the shops to get us to the other end of the street.

"I should go back," I say uncertainly, my sense of responsibility taking over. "The kids will be finishing their paintings by now. I'll have to oversee the judging."

Ryan pulls up outside the gate to the courtyard of my shop. "You're not going back," he tells me with enough assertiveness to make me think twice about protesting. "I need to lock up your store." He unclips his belt and then mine, his way of telling me I should go, too. I don't argue. I'm not leaving his side, and Ryan seems okay with that. He collects me from the passenger side and leads me through the gate into the kitchen. "Do you need anything while we're here?" he asks, going through to the store and securing the front door.

I shake my head, though he can't see it as he checks out onto the street. "No," I confirm when he comes back to me, claiming my hand again. He proceeds to check every window in my store and apartment with me in tow, silently being led by him. When we arrive in my bedroom, he scans the mess I left behind, and I sense his anger through the flexing of his hand. I remain quiet, watching him, and after doing a full sweep of my place, he takes me back downstairs and locks the back door behind us before putting me back in his truck.

As he pulls away, he makes a call, and a second later Alex's voice is filling the cab.

"I won the pageant!" she declares. "Where are you?"

"Of course you won." Ryan releases a small smile, and a horrible guilty feeling swoops through my tired body. "Hannah's not feeling too good. I'm taking her back to the cabin to rest up."

"Again?" she asks, and I close my eyes, hating that I'm forcing him to lie to his daughter. Ryan should have been there to see her win. Instead, he was chasing me down. Will she hold it against me?

"You know I wouldn't bail unless it was really important, Cabbage."

She's silent for a few seconds, obviously pondering the soft serious tone of her dad's voice. "Is she going to be okay?"

Ryan takes my hand again and places it in his lap. "She's going to be fine because I'm going to make sure of it." He flicks his gaze my way, his face straight, but his eyes are promising me. I squeeze his hand in acknowledgment. "Will you do me a favor?" he asks, returning his attention forward.

"Sure," Alex chirps.

"Will you make sure the painting competition is taken care of?"

"Of cour...wait. Does that mean I can't win?"

For the first time in what feels like years, I crack a smile. "You've already won in my eyes, Alex."

"Hey," she chirps, sounding pleased to hear me. "Guess what?"

"What?"

"Mum said my painting was the best of them all, so actually it doesn't matter if I don't win."

I look at Ryan and find him smiling at the road. "Then she's obviously got a good eye for good art," I say, feeling so warm inside.

"Will you let Molly know Hannah's gone home?" Ryan asks.

"Sure!"

"Call you in the morning, okay?"

"Okay. Must dash. I have a competition to fix." She chuckles but quickly stops. "Wait. You said *home*."

"What?" Ryan questions, his forehead creasing. I purse my lips. She doesn't miss a trick.

"You said, *Hannah's gone home* but she hasn't. She's going back to the cabin."

"Did I?"

"Yes, you did."

"Slip of the tongue." He looks at me out the corner of his eye, checking for my reaction. "Speak tomorrow."

"Yes, we will." She hangs up with that threat hanging in the air.

"Kids," Ryan mutters, pulling out at the top of the high street and driving away from town.

The rest of the short ride is silent, and although it isn't uncomfortable, it does give me thinking space to wonder, *What now?* We'll have to talk. I don't know if I'm up for that at the moment. All I want to do is curl up in Ryan's arms and return to my new tranquil world. But I know that isn't going to happen just yet. To get to that place again, I need to face my demons head-on. And most important, I need Ryan to understand.

He parks under the willow tree and collects my bag before collecting me. Just being here in his space offers me a little reprieve from my turbulence.

"Sit," he commands gently, taking me to one of the chairs by the fire. I lower and watch as he lights the fire and stabs at the wood with an iron poker, encouraging the flames. Then he sits in the chair opposite me, and I immediately hate the distance he's putting between us. I start to fold in on myself, fear of the impending talk we need to have bringing on an onslaught of unease. He's just looking at me, probably trying to fathom where to start.

The pressure gets the better of me, and I shoot up from my chair. "I need a drink," I blurt, turning and walking to the kitchen, feeling his eyes nailed to my back. Why is he being so cold all of a sudden? Has relief made way for anger again? Has he spent the journey back here gauging just how pissed off he is?

I pour myself a glass of wine, hoping it'll settle my nerves. How much is he going to make me explain? He says he knows *everything*. Does he want to hear it from my mouth, too? Confirmation?

I screw the cap back on the bottle and return it to the fridge, then claim my glass, and with a shaky hand I raise it to my lips, staring out the window, willing the courage I need to tackle it all. I see my bike propped up against the tree, the colors vibrant. It's a pretty accurate representation of me since I met Ryan. Will he look at me differently now?

As I feel his eyes drilling into my back, I hate the notion that he already does. For a fleeting moment, I damn him for chasing me down and stopping me leaving. Because this feeling is just another reason for me to go. This hopelessness. This shame.

I set the glass down on the counter and take a few controlled breaths. "How did you find out who I am?"

"I already told—"

"No," I snap, turning to face him. "I know you have connections. But don't tell me you called them up, gave them the name *Hannah Bright*, and they came back with an entire shitty story of a woman who's been dead for five years." I take more wine, but I'm sure to keep my eyes on Ryan. "Because if so, Ryan, I'm in serious trouble." I'm being sarcastic, spelling out loud and clear that there's more and he's not telling me.

He stiffens in his chair, flexing his strung muscles. "I followed you yesterday morning to Grange." He makes his confession with not one hint of remorse or shame, and my legs become heavy, holding me stock-still.

He followed me? Watched me? He saw every moment of my anguish?

"When you left Grange," he goes on, "I followed the women you were watching to a care home." Still no shame, and I reach back to the counter to steady myself. "I waited for the younger woman to leave and then checked the visitor log. That's how I got the name of your sister and your mother."

Stunned, I stare at him, unable to comprehend the lengths he's gone to. Just the mention of my mum and Pippa punches at my heart. Ryan collected me from the high street yesterday and brought me here. He took me to the lake. He told me he loved me. Our relationship shifted into top gear, and all that happened after he'd followed me? "Why didn't you say anything to me?"

"Because I decided it didn't matter. Because I talked myself into believing that as long as I have you and you're safe, I could let you keep your secrets and I'd deal with that. Maybe one day you'd trust me enough to tell me. But until that day, if it ever came, at least I knew enough to understand you." He pushes his palms into the arms of the chair and rises. "And I don't regret digging for that information, Hannah. I don't regret storing it. Because that is how I knew something wasn't right today." He walks forward slowly, like he's approaching a frightened animal. "That is how you are standing here in my cabin." He reaches me, taking my hands from behind me and resting them over his heart. "And that is how you are still mine, Hannah. So don't hold it against me. Don't be angry." He circles my neck with his hands. "I'm standing before you now *begging* you not to run again. All I want is you, Hannah." His hold of my neck tightens, to a point so firm, I should be freaking out. I should be panicking, fighting off relentless flashbacks and fear. Yet I'm numb to everything except the pleading in his eyes. "Because everything before you now seems half complete."

I have so much to say, but none of it seems adequate. So I take my hands to his face and hold him while I kiss him, breathing my appreciation and thanks into him. He sighs around my swirling tongue and lifts me onto the counter, knocking my glass of wine over behind me. It doesn't deter us, doesn't distract us from our reunion. Ryan moves between my thighs and returns my kiss with equal force and persistence. His kisses reveal his weakness. His kisses tell of his strength. His kisses speak of his love.

And I am forever consumed in every element of them.

He slows his lips, inhaling deeply, as if bringing himself around. Holding his mouth on mine, his eyes closed, he takes a moment for himself. "How did you do it, Hannah?" he asks as he opens his eyes, and I can tell, simply from the softness in his voice, that this is something burning his curiosity. "The fake papers, the death."

This is a secret, along with so many others, I never *ever* thought I would tell. "The dying part was easy," I begin. "The new identity, not so much. Jarrad thought I was as oblivious to his business dealings as he wanted me to be. I overheard a conversation between him and his associates discussing the downfall of one of Jarrad's biggest competitors."

"Quinton Brayfield?" Ryan asks.

I nod. "They wanted him gone so they could buy out his business. I also discovered that Brayfield had a spy in Jarrad's corporation. Jarrad found out, but Brayfield was one step ahead. The guy, the mole, was protected by a false identity, making it impossible for Jarrad to track him down and protect whatever data and information he'd stolen. My husband isn't the kind of man to risk being beaten. And he would never let anyone get one over on him. So..." I fade off, restocking on strength.

"Hannah, what did you do?" Ryan asks.

"I went to old man Brayfield," I say quietly, not surprised when I see Ryan's eyes widen. Because why would I do that? "I figured if he planted a ghost in my husband's company, he could help me become one."

"Fucking hell, wasn't that a bit risky?"

"Maybe." I shrug. "But I'd always been fond of the old man. He was ruthless, but he wasn't cruel. Loyalty meant a lot to him, and since I knew Jarrad was plotting a hostile takeover with his son, I figured he'd appreciate that information and help me." I'll never forget his face. His compassion. The fact that I was sitting in the chair opposite him at his desk sporting a broken nose and two black eyes probably helped. "I didn't ask him for anything other than the name of someone who could give me a new identity. He gave it to me. And a gun. I didn't see him again."

Ryan's cheeks puff out, his palm rubbing at the back of his neck. "But you know Jarrad killed him."

"He came home late one night. He told me if the police asked, he was home with me all night. The next morning news of Quinton Brayfield's suicide broke. He'd hung himself." I notice for the first time since I started talking that I sound a bit robotic. I've not replayed any of these events in over five years. And yet I recall every single detail as if it happened an hour ago.

"Hannah." Ryan rests his palms on either side of my waist, leaning in. "Why didn't you just go to the police? Have him locked up."

I smile, but it's in sympathy. He has no idea. "Do you think my husband's power and influence would shrivel up just because there were bars between us?"

"He wouldn't be able to hurt you."

"Jarrad always fell in shit and came out smelling of roses, Ryan. He would have gotten himself out of it in one way or another. I would have still been a prisoner. He would never let me go, Ryan. His ego would never allow it, and neither would his obsession with power. Jarrad didn't see me as his wife, he saw me as a possession. He never lost his possessions. He told me endlessly that only death would ever take me away from him." I swallow, feeling my throat thickening. "So I had to die."

Ryan turns away from me, as if he can't look at me anymore. "I want to kill him."

My head drops, the energy it's taking to keep it together waning. This is exactly what I feared. "I need you *not* to do that," I say, with almost humor in my voice. "It's taken me a long time to reach this point in my life, and I don't need you ruining it for me."

He swings around in utter disbelief. "This point in your life? Hannah, at this point in your life, you're being spooked by every little thing that reminds you of him. At this point in your life, you're constantly looking over your shoulder. You should let me kill that motherfucker slowly so you can have your life without those constant worries." He slings his arms into the air in frustration. "And then maybe I won't live in fucking fear that I'll wake up one morning and the woman I love will be gone because she saw a fucking Mitsubishi drive past." He takes his fingers to his temples and wedges them there, closing his eyes tightly. "So don't fucking tell me I shouldn't kill him."

"I didn't say you shouldn't. I asked you not to," I murmur timidly. "And I realize I have a way to go, Ryan. I realize I'm a work in progress, but I've been doing well. I'm proud of myself, and you should be proud of me, too. This is a blip, that's all. A minor relapse." I slide down from the counter, feeling a bit mad. Kill him. Problem solved. Except for the fact that Ryan will be locked up or face retribution, and, frankly, keeping Ryan is more important than inflicting pain on my husband. "So lose your damn ego and look a bit closer to home for what's important." I barge past him and get precisely nowhere, his arm shooting out and curling around my stomach, hauling me back. I'm picked up and set back on the counter, trapped by his hands on either side of me.

"No running," he grates, his face furious. "Never, ever run from me again."

"Then stop being such a pigheaded arsehole," I fire back.

His forehead falls onto my shoulder, resting there, and I watch his back roll with his deep breaths until he finds it in himself to look me in the eye again. "You said dying was easy. How did you do it?"

"Does it matter?"

"Yes, Hannah. It matters to me. I need all the pieces of the puzzle to stop me losing my fucking mind."

He's right. He's losing his mind, and I can't watch that happen. God knows what he'll do. "The caves," I confess, and Ryan frowns. "There are tunnels in the caves where we were on holiday in the Bahamas. One of them opens onto the rock face to the side of the waterfall. I crawled in and followed it to an opening on the beach."

"How did you know where it would lead?"

My lips purse, and I realize how ridiculous this is going to sound, but it's the truth, however crazy. "TripAdvisor," I murmur.

Ryan lets out a loud bout of laughter. It makes me flinch. He thinks I'm joking. I'm not. "Be serious," he chuckles.

"I am." My shoulders jump up on an awkward shrug. "A guy uploaded a video of him following the tunnel from a beach on the east of the island to the waterfall. It took him forty-three minutes." Another shrug. "It took me an hour and fifty minutes, and I was covered in cuts and grazes."

Ryan stares at me in utter disbelief, and my lips press together in something close to an awkward smile. "I don't know what to say," he murmurs quietly.

"You don't need to say anything."

"And then?"

"Then I stole a towel off the beach, went to a hotel and collected the stuff I'd sent there, and from there I flew to Tenerife."

"Why Tenerife?"

"Jarrad hated the place. Reminded him of the time he couldn't afford luxury holidays and he had to settle for cheap package deals." Those vacations were some of my favorites. Before everything went horribly wrong. Before Jarrad became more successful.

"And money?" Ryan asks. "I know you paid for your identity with a watch, but how have you survived? Did you siphon money off over time?"

I laugh. "Jarrad knew how much he made every second. I couldn't buy a tampon without producing a receipt." The man was controlling down to the penny.

"Then how?"

"My rings." I hold up my left hand. "Jarrad had them commissioned. My engagement ring was a heart-shaped yellow diamond. One of a kind and worth a fortune."

"Isn't that a huge risk?"

"I sold them to a private collector of precious stones. There's a reason he wanted to remain anonymous."

"Crook?"

"I guess so. I didn't ask. Brayfield put me in touch with him."

His head looks like it might pop off with the pressure of my secrets. Weirdly, I find myself smiling on the inside. I know he's not just shocked over it all because it's all pretty shocking, but because this is me. His cute, quirky Hannah. He didn't know me back then. He doesn't know of the things I faced. I had no choice but to play the game. I'm well aware that if Jarrad had gotten a sniff of my betrayal, I would have paid the ultimate price. It wouldn't have just been old man Brayfield dead. It would have been me, too. I hope Ryan sees that now. I hope he sees my world through my eyes.

My happiness hangs on the wire. Without anonymity, there is no freedom for me. And there is no me for Ryan to love.

He drops his head low, and it hangs heavily, the information weighing it down. "And you came back to England for your mother," he eventually says, looking up at me.

"She's dying, Ryan." I don't know how I keep my voice even. I feel hollow. "I needed to see her. And soon I won't be able to see her at all."

"What if you could?" he asks, throwing me for a hoop. "What if you could see her?"

I shake my head. I've considered it, of course, but ultimately, the risk is too great. I could never put my sister and her family in that position. I could never risk their safety for my need. I said goodbye years ago. They bought my lies and reassurance that all was well in my life. I became a good liar. The best. I couldn't allow them to worry. And I couldn't allow them to find out how weak and damaged I'd become. Jarrad knew how much they meant to me, and I had no doubt in my mind that he would use them against me. Everyone was safer if I was dead. And, painfully, I couldn't choose whom I was dead to. It was all or nothing. They've had time to heal. Time to mourn me. And Mum's mind isn't her own anymore. It's done. "You look like you could do with a beer."

Ryan laughs, digging his fingers into the sockets of his eyes. "Or for someone to pinch me and tell me that none of this is real."

I reach forward and squeeze the skin of his cheek. "I can't tell you none of this is real. But I can tell you I love you."

He softens before me, holding my hand on his face. "You look like you need a cuddle," he breathes.

"Can I have one?"

"Can she have one?" he whispers to himself, lifting me from the counter and squeezing me.

I settle into his hold, try to enjoy it as best I can, but I feel like every dirty little secret is stuck to my skin, staining me. Staining him. Staining us. "Can I take a shower?"

"Sure." He kisses my forehead and carries me through to his bathroom, holding me to his chest as he flips it on. He starts to remove my dungarees, and some of the uninvited feelings are replaced with feelings I want to feel forever. I inhale, and he growls brokenly as he rips himself away, and it's all I can do not to yank him back. "Soon," he promises, backing away into his bedroom. He slides my phone onto the nightstand before he heads out, and apprehension instantly sinks into every bone.

"Where are you going?" I blurt, and he stops at the door. Takes a breather. Then reverses his steps, coming straight back to me and holding my head in his hands, getting so close to my face.

"I'll never be far from you, Hannah, I promise you." He shakes me gently, as if trying to get that promise as far into my head as it can go. "Okay?" he asks, and I nod as best I can with my head restrained. "I just need a moment to process things with a beer in my hammock."

I blink up at him. He'll never be far. I wrap my hands around his wrists as he pushes his mouth to mine. And then he's tearing himself away again. He needs a moment. I should let him have that. Honestly, I should take one myself. It's been a tidal wave of emotions and truths. Ryan knows everything. My secrets are no longer secrets. And he still wants me.

I stand and stare at the closed door for a while, immobilized by relief, but I eventually talk life into my muscles and strip down. Stepping into the shower, I relish the warm spray as I wash my hair and scrub myself clean. By the time I'm done, my skin is tingling.

I rub myself down with a towel and slip some knickers on from my duffel bag, but instead of dressing in my own clothes, I snag my favorite of Ryan's shirts from the chair in the corner of his room—the gray plaid one—and pull it over my head instead of wasting time unfastening the buttons, only to refasten them. His scent wafts up to my nostrils, and I lift the fabric to my nose and inhale. So distinctive. So manly. So Ryan.

Padding out to the kitchen, I peek out the window, seeing him reclined on his hammock, swinging slowly, one leg draped over the side. He's staring into space, lost in thought, taking sips of his beer every now and then. I need a drink, too. Anything to further calm me.

I look down at my wineglass on its side on the counter where we left it, and reach for the stem, standing it up. I wipe up the pool of wine and go to the fridge, pull out the bottle of wine and pour myself a fresh glass.

I settle back at the window, watching him swinging peacefully, as I take my first sip. I freeze. *What the hell?*

I frown, the glass held at my lips, my gaze moving to the bottle on the side.

Chills.

They jump onto every inch of my skin as I stare at the label, swallowing hard.

Chapoutier Ermitage l'Ermite Blanc.

I set my glass down with a shaky hand, the wine I've always hated feeling like it's burning its way down my throat. I step back, continuing to stare at it, like it might speak up and offer me the perfectly reasonable explanation I'm hunting for. There is no explanation. There's only memories of Jarrad's insistence that this particular, outrageously expensive wine be served wherever we were.

One more step back. The chills sink past my skin and reach my veins, and I swallow, not anticipating my stomach to turn at the exact same time. My coughs come on thick and fast, choking me, and I run to the bathroom, smacking my shoulder on the doorframe in my haste to make it to the toilet in time. I throw myself over the bowl and bring up a mixture of bile and acidic liquid, my throat burning, my retches violent and uncontrollable. My eyes water, my body goes into spasm. I've lost control of every muscle and limb.

I fight to pull it together, reaching for a towel and bringing it to my mouth to wipe. "No, Hannah." I slam my fist on the edge of the sink, my freak-out stalling me from thinking clearly. I breathe in deep, let it out, in deep, and let it out. I'm just having a moment. Freaking out over nothing. I can't let Ryan see me like this again, over something so stupid.

I will my shakes away, bracing my hands on the edge of the sink and breathing my way through it. My imagination is running away with me. It has been all day. Ryan could have bought that wine. Just a coincidence. Surely?

I hear my mobile phone, and any progress I'd made on settling my nerves disappears. I edge toward the door tentatively, looking at the nightstand where Ryan left it. My phone glows, the ring seeming shrill, almost like a warning. Ignore it. And then what? Wonder who it was? Wonder if it was him? I can't go on like this. A prisoner to my fear.

I take slow, cautious steps toward my phone.

Chapter Twenty-Nine

RYAN

The motion of the hammock swinging is enough to send me into a trance. The beer is good. The quiet is good. Until it's no longer quiet. My mobile rings in my pocket, but I'll be damned if I can move my tired arse to retrieve it. It rings off, but immediately starts again. I groan and lift myself a bit to reach for it, sliding it out and spinning it the right way up to see the screen. "Luce," I mumble, relaxing back into my hammock as I answer. "It's been a long day. Are you going to make it longer?"

"You asked me to keep an eye on Knight."

I'm frozen still in a nanosecond. I don't like the sound of this. "And?"

"And he's apparently taken a leave of absence from his empire due to exhaustion. Jarrad Knight doesn't seem to be the kind of man who would take a leave of absence, especially because of exhaustion. The guy is propped up on cocaine and power."

"I agree. So where is he?"

"In between his London penthouse and Scotland. His pregnant wife, however, has joined her family in Prague while he recuperates. I mean, it's all a bit strange. If my husband—"

"Scotland?" I ask, pushing my way up from my hammock and sitting on the edge. "You said Scotland."

"Yeah, Scotland. He bought a derelict castle there a few years ago. Spent millions renovating it."

My bottle of beer starts to shake in my hand. "Hannah's been sending paintings to Scotland," I say mindlessly.

"What?" Lucinda sounds as confused as I would expect.

"Hannah. She's sold a few pieces to a man who owns a castle in Scotland."

"Are you joking me?"

"No." I stand and start pacing to the cabin. "He sent her flowers today. What else do you know?"

"Well, for a man who's apparently emotionally exhausted, Knight's been a busy boy. He recently spent a small fortune at a private auction."

"On what?"

"A rather spectacular one-of-a-kind, *very* rare heart-shaped yellow diamond ring."

"Fuck, no." I throw my beer to the ground and break into a sprint, running like a man possessed.

CHAPTER THIRTY

HANNAH

I don't recognize the number on the screen and it turns my blood to ice. I reach for my phone with trembling hands and answer, though I don't speak. And neither does the caller, leaving a stretched silence between us.

"Hello?" I somehow find the courage to say.

"Hannah?" The voice nearly makes me throw up again, but this time it's in relief.

"Molly?"

"Yes, are you okay? I found the flowers Ryan bought you on the street."

"I'm fine," I assure her. "I came over a bit funny. Dropped them. Ryan's brought me back to his cabin to lie down."

"Oh my God, he's actually making you light-headed with his swoony gesture."

I smile, though it's tight. "Whose phone is this?"

"Mrs. Heaven's. Mine's at the cottage. I just wanted to check up on you."

She's a good friend, and best of all, I now get to keep her. "I'll come back to help you clear up."

"Don't worry, I've got an army of children to help. Crap, gotta go.

Father Fitzroy has started country dancing." She hangs up, and I laugh, tossing my phone on the bed. "So stupid." I turn to go join Ryan—he's had enough time—but I make it only one pace before I jerk to a stop. I stare at the doorway in front of me, my heart thumping its way up to my throat. Ice glides across my skin. Blood pumps in my veins with such force I can hear it.

You're seeing things, Hannah!

I slowly turn on the spot until I'm looking at Ryan's bed, and I take fairy steps forward until I'm standing at the foot, staring at his pillow.

And my wedding rings.

"No," I breathe, grabbing my phone and backing up, banging into the wardrobe.

"How have you been, Katrina?" His voice cuts through my flesh, and I swing around, my scream building.

But his hand is over my mouth before I can release it.

Chapter Thirty-One

RYAN

Hannah!" I yell, flying through the door. I stop, listening, my eyes taking in every inch of my cabin. It's eerily silent. I sweep up one of my axes from beside the door and stalk on, my insides an inferno of anger and fear. When I reach my bedroom, I stop, staring at the closed door. I can't hear the shower. I can't hear movement at all. I push the door open with the head of my axe and scan the space. Empty. Except for her mobile phone lying in the middle of the floor.

My nostrils flare, my head set to explode with the pressure building, as I swing my axe in a rage, sinking it into the plaster. Soon that'll be Knight's head.

I turn and stride out, anger pumping through my veins. When I find him—and I will find him—I'm going to fucking kill him. I just get to the bottom step of the veranda when I hear something, and I still, lowering my foot gently on the brittle leaves, making them crack. My neck cricks as I look to my left into the trees, listening. I hear screeching tires in the distance.

Adrenaline pumping, I run to my truck, throw my axe into the cab and jump in. My phone rings, and I answer. "He's found her." I race toward the main road, my eyes scanning high and low.

"Fucking hell," Lucinda all but whispers. "Ryan, don't you do anything stupid, do you hear me? I know you. I know what idiotic shit you'll pull."

"What, like kill him?" I ask frankly. "Because that is what I'm going to do, Luce. Slowly. Painfully." I'm planning each and every torture tactic I'm going to adopt.

"Ryan—"

"Can you cover it up?"

"What?"

"If I kill him, can you cover it up?"

She inhales, falling silent. She knows as well as I do that no matter what road I take here, Hannah will be exposed to the media and world, and could possibly even go to prison for faking her death. And even if she came out the other side a free woman, the trauma would set her back years. I *refuse* to do that to her. Not only that, I can't put myself at risk of being sent down and leaving her alone.

"Fucking hell, Ryan," Lucinda eventually says.

"Answer the question, Luce." I need her to think quickly with me. Time is of the fucking essence. I get to the end of the track and turn right onto the main road out of town. The road that'll take me north.

"Only if you don't leave marks."

I laugh. "Are you joking me?"

"No, I mean it, Ryan. No marks on him whatsoever. He's taken a leave of absence. He's got connections with dealers to the rich and famous. His wife died tragically over five years ago, and his current wife is pregnant and currently taking refuge in another country. Things aren't looking too rosy for Jarrad Knight, catch my drift?"

It slams into me, so obvious, it's almost beautiful. No marks. How the fuck I'm going to manage that, I have no idea. I look at the axe on the seat next to me, imagining it sunk into Knight's head. "No marks," I assure her, returning my focus to the road. "He's in a Mitsubishi." The fucker. He was the one who ran me and Alex off the road. It was him earlier today on the high street watching Hannah. Jesus, how long has he been playing with her, playing with *me*? "I need to go." I hang up and call Darcy immediately, not giving her the chance to talk before I hit her with my order. "I need you to get Alex, get some things, and leave town."

She laughs. "Whatever are you talking about? Don't be silly!"

"Darcy, please, for once in your fucking life, do what I say, no questions asked."

She's silent for a moment, probably registering my deadly tone. "What's going on?"

"I said no questions," I snap, wincing as soon as I've bitten her head off. "I'm sorry. Just do it. Tell me you'll do it."

She's quiet again. But just for a beat. "I have a friend who lives an hour away. Alexandra is always nagging me about visiting. They have an assault course in the forest nearby."

"Sounds perfect."

"Ryan, are you okay?" she asks, a genuine concern in her tone that I'm not used to. It also speaks volumes for how I sound myself. Murderous? Worried? Dying on the inside?

All?

"You sound scared," she follows up quietly.

"You know me, Darcy." I blink, realigning my focus. "Nothing scares me." I hang up on that lie. Scared. That's exactly what I am. I'm scared to fucking death of losing Hannah.

My stiff hands loosen up around the wheel, my knuckles white. Scared and angry. So fucking angry.

The road goes on forever, my speed dangerous. It matches my mood. "Come on," I mutter, willing my truck to go faster, my eyes scanning the woods as I drive.

And then I get something.

As I'm swooping around a curve, I just catch sight of the back end of a truck off a concealed dirt track to my right, and I slam on my brakes. The stench of burning rubber is instant, and so is the smoke surrounding my truck. That was a Mitsubishi.

I sling my arm over the passenger seat and look back, reversing up the road. My heart is going wild as I yank the wheel clockwise, the back end of my truck swinging out. I pull onto the track, the divots and bumps slowing me down, as does my instinct. I find myself following the mud trail, scanning the dense overgrowth as I let down all the windows and listen for anything that'll lead me to her. A scream? I flinch, batting away the violent thoughts trying to worm their way into the deepest, darkest corners of my mind.

Impossible.

No marks? Lucinda will be lucky.

Chapter Thirty-Two

HANNAH

I'm restrained by terror.

He's slowed down now we're on the dirt road, but I'm still jolting around in my seat. My solid muscles are aching, my mind being blitzed by flashbacks of every time I was punished. They got progressively worse over the years. But this punishment is going to put them all to shame.

Jarrad is quiet in the seat beside me, but I'm not fooled by his silence. The few times I've dared look at him, I've sensed the storm building inside him, quietly contained until his temper explodes and he loses all control. I've seen it too many times. I gulp down my trepidation, glancing around the truck, frantically trying to think of a way out of this.

"Be a good girl, Katrina," he says finally, with a silkiness to his tone that makes my stomach turn. That voice. Always so smooth and calm, but loaded with threat. He reaches across to me as he negotiates the road, resting the handgun in his palm on my bare knee, his finger poised on the trigger. I sit back in my seat, my eyes fixed on it. "We wouldn't want any accidents, would we?"

"How did you find me?"

He laughs. The sound makes my skin crawl. "The collector you sold your rings to died." He sounds so angry, and I close my eyes on a gulp. "His wife put up much of his collection for auction." His light laugh is loaded with evil intent. "Can you imagine my surprise when Curtis emailed me the lot details?" Yes, I can imagine. But it was a rhetorical question. "I knew that if you were really alive, you would find your way back to your mother somehow." He casts a sick grin my way, and my jaw tics with anger. "You always were a mummy's girl. Shame she still thinks you're dead. And Pippa, who hasn't changed a bit, but you know that, don't you?" He laughs. "Two peas in a pod, isn't that what your mum used to say? She was right. Because you're as dumb as your sister." His tone drops at the end, carrying disgust. "You always looked so lonely on your little bench in the park, Katrina. So sad and desperate to join your mother and stupid sister."

I swallow, feeling so violated. He was there, watching me. And I had no idea. One of Jarrad's favorite pastimes was to tell me I was stupid or make me feel that way. He's as good at it as ever. Next he'll be giving me every reason why I need him and not them. Why he's good for me. Why he loves me. No. "What are you going to do, Jarrad?"

"Depends on you, beloved wife." He drags the barrel of the gun up my thigh, pushing back the tail of Ryan's shirt. My back pushes farther into the seat, my whole body racked by shakes. "This shirt doesn't suit you." He pulls the gun away and lifts it to my head, and my shakes intensify as I look out the corner of my eye at the tip of the gun sitting in my hair. "And this blond? I hate it."

"Then I'll change it," I say, forcing myself into the placating wife I used to naturally be. I'm in self-preservation mode. Buying myself time. "For you."

He pulls the gun away, but I don't relax. "For me? You mean you're coming back to me?"

"Yes, I'll come back to you," I whisper, hating the sound of those words.

Jarrad slowly casts his eyes to me. The glint in them is borderline evil. It's also a sign of his intention. "But you're dead, Katrina," he says calmly, before propelling his arm toward me and cracking me across the head with the butt of the gun. I cry out, pain radiating through me as my head starts to spin. "You took me for a fucking fool, Katrina!" he bellows, his temper now unleashed and ready to destroy anything in its path. The monster can't be contained anymore. This is it. "You of all people know I'm no fool."

My hand clenches the side of my head, the warmth of the blood soaking my palm. Everything is woozy, my head thumping. I can't think. Can't see. But I can hear.

"You left me, you scheming little bitch. Everything I gave you. All the hard work I did to make the perfect life for us. And now I learn that you were feeding Brayfield information? He helped you run away from me?" He sniffs his disgust. "I should have killed him slowly. I fucking loved you!"

Amid my chaos, I manage to believe that, yes, maybe Jarrad did think he loved me in his way—as long as I was the wife he wanted me to be. But when I disappointed him, nothing could contain his rage. Not me begging, not me promising to do better. I took what he dished out, and then I accepted the gift he would buy me to show his remorse. Every beautiful piece of jewelry I owned represented an injury I'd sustained at his hands. I would be holed up for weeks, unable to leave our mansion in case I was seen. Those weeks in solitary became more frequent. Until one day I stepped out to walk my beloved dog. I was careful. I wore huge shades to cover my black eyes. A hat pulled low to cover the graze on my forehead. A scarf pulled high to conceal my fat lip. No one saw me.

Until I got home and found Jarrad had returned from work early. That time, he broke my arm and my nose. My dog defended me. Growled at Jarrad as she stood guard by my broken body on the floor.

So he took her away.

I feel a tear trail down my cheek, mixing with the blood there, and I look at the madman next to me, knowing beyond all doubt that he will kill me. He won't risk me destroying him. He won't risk anyone else discovering that I'm still alive. His status and power are too precious to him. Even more precious than I was as his possession. I'm being driven to my death.

I look across to Jarrad, my fear mixing with hatred, and for the first time since he took me, I consider how rumpled he is. His hair isn't slick and neat, the black waves more haphazard, and his suit has been replaced with a pair of trousers and a bomber jacket. It doesn't suit him. This truck doesn't suit him, either. This truck would suit Ryan.

Ryan.

"I wonder how your boyfriend would feel if I told him you were dead," Jarrad says as if hearing my thoughts. He's composed again. The storm has calmed. But not for long.

He has my attention, and he knows it.

"Would he feel how I felt?" Jarrad muses, as if having a discussion with himself, his attention fixed on the dirt road. "Does he love you as much as I love you?" He gasps. It's over-the-top and intended to be. "Does he love you at all?" He flicks me a sick smirk. "I think he does." Nodding to himself, he turns the steering wheel. "I think when I break the news, I'll let it sink in for a while before I kill him."

"No!" I blurt, stupidly showing some emotion. I should have kept my mouth shut. I shouldn't have showed my hand. I see the realization in him, and I see the tightening of his jaw quickly after. He stares forward for a few moments. He's allowing the rage to take hold, and when he turns his eyes my way, I see the psychopath in him. The emotionless beast.

His hand swings out again, catching me clean on the cheekbone, my hands coming up to defend me too late. The dizziness returns, the pain intensifying. "You cheating, lying, betraying whore," he seethes. "You think I'm going to let—" He's cut off abruptly. "Fuck!" he curses, and I jolt in my seat, being thrown against the door. Through my hampered vision, I just catch sight of something flying across our path and disappearing into the overgrowth on the opposite side of the road.

Jarrad curses as the truck veers off into the bushes, shaking to a stop. I blink, fighting the blur and dizziness away, scanning the area, searching for…"Ryan," I whisper without thinking. He knows these woods like the back of his hand. I've no doubt he's gone off-road through the overgrowth to get ahead of us. No doubt at all.

"Your boyfriend is one determined fucker," Jarrad growls, grabbing me by the hair and yanking me across the cab of the truck. I hiss, scrambling as best I can, blood seeping into my eyes. I land on the ground with a thud, and he kicks me for my trouble, yanking me to my feet. I immediately feel the tip of his gun pushing into my temple, my back to his front.

Sticks and twigs dig into the bottoms of my bare feet as he walks me backward, moving away from whatever ran us off the road. Ryan? Was it him? I frantically search for him, silently begging him to stay away. "Maybe I'll kill him first," Jarrad whispers in my ear, making my skin crawl. His forearm is wrapped around my neck, my whole body covering his front, shielding him, as he drags me backward. His breathing is heavy. He's shaking against me. He's nervous.

I can barely see where we're going, my vision clouded by blood trickling into my eyes. "You'll *have* to kill him first," I whisper quietly, feeling Ryan close by. My senses are alert to him. I can feel his presence. Smell his rage. My tangled mind seems to unravel as I gain my composure. Jarrad jerks me in his hold angrily, tightening his grip around my neck. It forces me to reach up and cling onto his arm, trying to relieve the pressure on my windpipe. He stops moving. The leaves and twigs stop crunching beneath our feet. The sun is struggling to break through the branches above us, keeping us shadowed.

It's deathly quiet. No sound, no movement, for such a very long time.

Then Jarrad startles when a bird crows from behind, and he swings us around, his head snapping from side to side, searching. "Come on, where are you?" he whispers, turning us back the other way. "You want to watch me kill her?" he shouts to the trees. "You want to watch her bleed out?" The gun is wedged into my temple with force, and I whimper, my feet clumsily dragging against the ground as I'm hauled around again. Then he stills, and it falls eerily silent once more.

And I realize: Jarrad won't kill me first. It'll leave him exposed and without bargaining power. Has he realized he's out of his depth? Has he realized he's made a grave mistake?

Has he realized he's about to die?

A loud rustle sounds in the distance, and Jarrad spins us toward it, firing blindly into the trees. I flinch, the bang echoing around us. He's breathing heavily. Sniffing constantly. And then he jerks on a pained yelp, and I just catch sight of something in my peripheral vision. "Duck, Hannah." The sound of Ryan's voice has me whimpering my relief, yet my fear for his safety rockets, too. But I have to keep it together. Jarrad's hold of me loosens, and I wrench myself free, staggering a few paces before I land in the dirt a few feet away.

I hear Jarrad yell, and then see him hit the ground with a thud. He loses control of his gun, a shot sounds, and Ryan lands on top of him, launching his fist into his face with a deafening crack. He doesn't give his victim a moment to react.

I scramble back on my arse until my back meets a tree trunk, watching as Jarrad has holy hell rained all over him, Ryan's fists slamming into his face repeatedly as he straddles him. It goes on and on, pound after pound, and in this moment of complete, ferocious madness, I wonder if there are enough strikes being delivered to Jarrad's face to match those I received over the years.

Appallingly, probably not.

I'm shocked by the violence pouring out of Ryan. He's a machine, powered by a rage that doesn't look like it's going to end anytime soon. Only when Jarrad stops moving does Ryan halt his assault.

He leans back, his adrenaline ebbing. All I can see is blood. It's covering Jarrad's face and Ryan's fists, splattered on the ground around them. And now it's quiet again, though the sound of silence is more eerie. Somehow more unnerving. I see Ryan's muscles tense again, his arm drawing back. He's not done.

"Ryan!" I yell, my plea broken through a sob. I've seen enough. I can't see Jarrad breathing, his body unmoving and limp, his head lolled to the side. Ryan stills, looking back at me. His eyes are empty of the laughter I'm so used to. Now there is only vengeance. "No more," I plead, having to cling to the tree trunk to steady me as I pull myself up. I keep our eyes locked, make sure he sees only me. "No more." My whisper is hardly audible, but he hears it. I see his eyes clear. I register his body engaging to move.

And then I notice Jarrad jolt, catching Ryan off guard, and he's suddenly free from under Ryan's body, crawling through the dirt with urgency.

He reaches for something.

The gun.

And it's quickly aimed at Ryan.

"No!" I scream, but my cry is drowned out by the sound of the gun firing.

Ryan's body catapults back, landing nearby in a heap. He's still, lifeless, and I crumple to the ground again, watching as blood seeps through his jeans. "Oh my God," I wheeze as Jarrad clambers to his feet, his expression of pure hatred perfectly clear through the blood on his face. He stares down at Ryan's unmoving body, a sick smile ghosting his thin lips.

My sobs come on relentlessly, my heart cracking. "What have you done?" I murmur, taking my hands to my hair and pulling, praying death will take me, too. I'll never be able to live with myself. I'll never forgive myself for this.

Jarrad looks across at me with an abhorrence I feel for myself. My obvious grief seems to anger him further, the monster inside preparing to be unleashed again. He's going to kill me. Good. I hope he makes it quick.

My jaw tightens, and I square him with a determined stare that I know throws him off balance momentarily. He takes one step forward, raising the gun, aiming it at me. I don't flinch. Don't move. I make it easy for him, keep his target still.

I'm so focused on my intention, so determined. Any purpose I had, and happiness I found, it's all gone now. Ryan's dead. And it's my fault.

Not moving my eyes from Jarrad's, I sit, waiting for the sound that'll signify my end. My eyes drop to his finger on the trigger, watching closely as he squeezes.

And then he jerks, the gun fires, and I startle, instinctively ducking.

"I don't think so." Ryan's voice is like life after death, and I look up, seeing the two men rolling around on the ground. Jarrad aims his gun straight into Ryan's face, and my broken heart flies up to my throat, stripping me of the ability to scream. My brain hasn't had time to register what's going on; things are moving too fast.

And before I know what's happening, I'm up and running toward them. My leg catapults forward, kicking Jarrad's hand, and the gun goes flying into the air, landing a few yards away.

"You stupid bitch!" Jarrad yells, starting to get up off the ground urgently. But Ryan moves faster, expertly, straddling him and firing a few more punches into his mangled face.

I don't scream at him to stop this time. I lower, picking up the gun from the ground. And I aim it at my husband's head. "Ryan," I say, and he stops and looks up at me, while he holds Jarrad down by his throat. His gaze falls to the gun in my hand. And he nods.

I wait for Jarrad to look up and find me, wait for us to be eye-to-eye. Wait for him to see the strength and purpose in me. His stare widens, and I move forward, bending and pushing the barrel into the top of his head.

And I pull the trigger.

CHAPTER THIRTY-THREE

RYAN

Staring down at the mess of blood and guts beneath me, I curl my lip, wishing I could revive Knight and repeat. I flop to my back next to him, reaching for my leg to apply pressure. Fuck me, the pain. I start to take deep breaths, feeling a bit light-headed as I strain to lift my head. I find Hannah frozen, her impossibly big eyes even larger than usual. Shock. I get it. But she's going to have to pull herself together.

"Hannah," I say, the effort of calling her name taking everything out of me.

She slowly lowers her eyes to the gun hanging limply in her hand, and then drops it like it's a hot potato. I take in the mess of her face, blood staining the entire right side. My fists clench. If I had one more bullet, I'd crawl on my hands and knees and sink it into his dead heart.

"Hannah," I call again through my teeth, pulling her attention to me. She lifts her fingertips to the cut at her temple when she registers my glare rooted there, flinching.

"It's nothing," she whispers.

Nothing? I hope Knight is burning in hell. "You just gonna leave me here to die?" I rip my stare away and realign my focus on Hannah.

She snaps out of her inertness quickly, now completely panicked, and rushes around Jarrad's dead body to me on shaky legs.

Dropping to her knees, she scans me up and down, her hands held up in front of her, trembling. "Oh my God." Those shaking hands go to her face and cover it. "Please don't die," she begs. "Please."

I grab her wrist, yanking her hands down. "I'm not going to die."

"But you said—"

"I'm *not* going to die," I reiterate firmly.

"How do you know?" She takes another peek at the blood on my jeans, shaking her head mindlessly.

"If the bullet had hit anything fatal, I'd be dead by now." I grab her hands and put them over my wound, pushing them in hard. "Fuck," I breathe, blinking back the stars. "Just keep the pressure there." I feel my way to my pocket and pull out my phone.

"What are you doing?"

"Calling for help."

"Oh my God, they're going to lock you up. And me!"

"We're going nowhere," I say with grit, putting the phone to my ear. Lucinda's hello is calm. Unruffled. "I can't promise no marks," I say coolly, and she sighs. I imagine her forehead meeting her antique desk, rolling from side to side. "It was him or me, Luce." I flinch, sucking in air through my teeth as a nasty stab of pain shoots through my thigh.

"You're hurt," she says in response. "How bad?"

"I need medical attention, I know that much." I smile mildly when Hannah looks at me like I'm mad. And she *looks* mad, her lips straightening.

"How much attention?" Lucinda asks, trying to get a feel for what she's faced with.

"Enough to help dig a bullet out of my thigh."

"Oh, fucking hell."

"I'll live."

"And Knight? How bad?"

I drop my head to the side, looking at the malevolent motherfucker. "Suicide definitely isn't gonna wash."

"For the love of God," she yells. "I told you, make it clean!"

"Like I said, him or me. Are you going to help me or not?"

"Jesus, Ryan, this will be the end of us."

I hear her, loud and clear. I know what I'm asking. "I can do it on my own, Luce, but it'll take me a lot fucking longer without your help."

She's silent for a few beats, probably staring at her laptop in despair. "What do you need?" I hear her tapping away at the keyboard before she finishes speaking.

"A doctor, first and foremost. I'll send you the address of my cabin. I should be able to make it back there." I ignore Hannah's incredulous glare. "I need a cleanup. Discreet."

"Discreet?" Lucinda parrots. "No, I'll send them in with foghorns and carnival music. Fuck me, I'm gonna have to call in every fucking favor owed to me for crimes gone by."

I smile. Good old Luce. "Knight's Mitsubishi is here. I want concealed transportation to get it to his castle in Scotland."

Hannah releases some pressure from my leg, and I force it back down, seeing it all slowly sinking in.

"There are paintings by Hannah Bright hung somewhere in that castle. I don't know what rooms. There are three. Get rid of them."

"Anything else?" she fires sarcastically.

"Yes, a few kilos of cocaine." The pressure on my thigh lightens again, and I slam it down, giving Hannah a warning look.

"Piece of cake," she mutters. "For fuck's sake."

"Oh, and my truck's totally mangled. It needs to be destroyed," I add, and she groans. "I'll never give you a headache ever again, Luce."

"This isn't a headache, Ryan," she mutters. "This is a fucking brain tumor. And you don't damn well work for me anymore."

"I'll send you the coordinates of our location."

She sighs, and it's weary. "Okay."

"Thanks, Luce." My voice is quiet but loaded with appreciation.

"No sweat. I'm looking on the bright side."

"There's a bright side?"

"Yeah. I might lose all the favors I'm owed from every bent spy, cop, and politician I've ever scraped out from the shit, but at least I'll be owed by you."

I laugh, and immediately wince. "Shit."

"Get back to your cabin and sit tight," she murmurs, sounding concerned again. "There's no chance of the carnage you've caused being found before we get there?"

I look around, seeing nothing but trees and overgrowth. Hear nothing but wildlife. "We're a few miles outside town. Population zero for at least a four-mile radius."

"I'll have a cleanup team there by nightfall." She hangs up, and my hand flops to the ground, exhaustion sweeping in. But I can't flake out yet.

"The paintings," Hannah mumbles. "It really was him buying them."

I nod.

"I wasn't losing my mind." She swallows. "He's been tormenting me." She looks across to his dead body, a wave of anger crossing her pretty face, hardening it. "He's been fucking with my head."

I grab her arm, finding it rock-solid, her body tense. "Look at me," I order. Her eyes snap to mine, and I'm taken aback by the dilation of her pupils, her eyes virtually black. Hollow. I imagine she had this look about her many times in her previous life. A look of desolation mixed with anger. She had no way to exorcise those feelings. She had no way to escape. She lived on a knife-edge, could never have freedom.

Now she does.

I find some strength and reach for her neck, pulling her down. "Until the day I die, I will consume so much of your mind, there will be no room for anything else. I will be the shield between you and your memories, Hannah. There is only happiness in our future. Only tenderness and love."

Her lip wobbles, her face nuzzling into mine. I feel the wet warmth of her tears against my skin. They will be the last tears she ever sheds because of him. "Promise me," she whispers.

"I promise you."

CHAPTER THIRTY-FOUR

HANNAH

Six days later

I've been waiting for this day for what feels like centuries. I've been praying for all that time, too.

"I'm coming," Ryan declares, not for the first time, as he hisses and spits his way up to a seated position on the couch, panting when he finally makes it. "Fuck...me."

I exhale my exasperation and go to him, sitting on the sofa beside him. "You're not coming." Not because I don't want him to, but because he's far from ready to exert himself to that level. Since we made it back to the cabin last Sunday, he's been hobbling around the place, refusing to take it easy. I don't know much about what happened after we walked away from the woods. Well, I walked. Ryan limped, refusing to let me support him. He just wanted to hold my hand. The heroic move was stupid, and I told him so, though he didn't listen.

Then a woman showed up, a formidable-looking creature, with dark hair and a crisp suit. She didn't look happy, but I saw the wave of concern for Ryan past her steely exterior. A doctor followed shortly after. I wasn't the only one who was utterly dumbfounded when Ryan ordered him to check me over first. The stubborn mule wouldn't budge, either, not until I was cleaned and sewed up.

Jake followed in behind the doctor. His boots were covered with mud and leaves. I caught him shake his head at Ryan, not that Ryan paid much attention. And I heard him mumble a quiet, "All sorted."

Ryan seemed to relax in that moment, allowing the doctor to tend to him. Me? I couldn't even begin to comprehend the lengths Ryan has gone to in order to protect me. He drank half a bottle of scotch while the bullet was removed, fed to him by Jake. Then he slept for twelve hours straight. And the whole time he slept, I watched him, attempting to process everything that had happened. There was too much, and I scorned myself for even bothering to try. And when Ryan came around, he saw the worry I couldn't shake off. He said everything would be okay. He promised me.

I believe him.

Now he's plain grumpy, constantly getting annoyed with himself.

On an epic scowl—not at me, but at himself—he pushes his palms into the couch and starts to rise. "I'm coming," he repeats, struggling to his feet.

I shoot up, far faster than him. "Ryan, you—"

His move is quick, but not without discomfort, and he grabs my chin, leveling me with the kind of Ryan look that I know means business. "I. Am. Coming." He's so determined. And really, I want him to come. I think I'm going to need the support.

"Okay," I agree. "The taxi will be here in a minute." I look down at his bare torso and the sweats that cover his bandaged leg. "Promise me you'll be careful."

He takes my hand and kisses it, not saying anything. He just smiles, walking away slowly to change.

I wait until he's in the bedroom before I move across to the window, looking out for the taxi. I reach up and blindly tweak my hair, seeing the cab emerge through the trees. My stomach flips upside down. "Taxi's here!" I call.

* * *

My knee bobs up and down at a rapid rate until Ryan is forced to settle his hand there and apply pressure to push my adrenaline back. "I'm sorry." I pull at my blouse, looking down my front, wondering if the huge sunflowers splattered all over it is too much. Too bright? Too loud? Too...alive?

I fold in on myself, my hope fading. And I pray again, pray that last week was just a little blip, that my mother's fine and I'll see her today. When the cab pulls up by the park, I crane my neck, trying to see beyond the gates, despite it being a little early. Ryan pays the fare, and I jump out, thoughtlessly leaving him to struggle behind me. I come to my senses when I hear a sharp *"fuck"* and swing around, rushing back to him.

"I'm fine," he wheezes, his face bright red, pain etched over every inch of it.

"You're not fine!" I snap, not meaning to sound so harsh, but, give me strength, he's so fucking stubborn. "Why don't you do as you're damn well told for once in your *damn* life, Ryan Willis?"

He recoils, his face the epitome of *Who the hell is this woman?* "What exactly did you tell me to do?" he asks, pushing the door of the cab shut and unbending his body a little gingerly.

I falter for a beat, thinking. What did—? Oh yes. "I told you to stay at home."

"Yes, well, I didn't want to be away from you. So here I am. Every broken inch of me." He grimaces and lays his hand over his wound.

"Does it hurt?" I ask, pouting guiltily.

"Like a motherfucker." Releasing his thigh, he takes my hand and kisses my knuckles. "But I'll live."

And thank God for that. "Will you be grumpy forever, too?" I ask, letting him lead me to the gates. He's endearing when he's grumpy. Almost...sexy.

"Only when we're apart, baby," he says wistfully.

As we sit down together, he pulls me into his side and rests his mouth in my hair. And we wait for my sister, the world going by. I know he senses my growing despondency with each minute that passes and my mum and sister don't show up, because his hold becomes firmer and firmer, to the point he must be in pain. But he sustains it, not that I'm in any position to stop him. I'm becoming more dejected by the second.

"They're not coming," I murmur dismally, willing myself to keep it together. I saw my mother's face last week. It was ravaged, her complexion sallow and her eyes lifeless. I reach up to my heart when it twinges with pain, looking up to the heavens. Is she already there? I flinch, knowing that's the best place she could be, free from pain, but that tiny, selfish side of me hopes that she has held out for just one more week.

Ryan holds me close as we watch everyone going about their business. Every time I see someone enter the park, my back straightens, hoping it's them. And my heart splinters a little bit more when, each time, I register it isn't.

"Hannah," Ryan says eventually, feeling at my cheek, but keeping his chin resting on top of my head where it's lying against his chest. "Baby, we've been here for over an hour."

An hour? Where has that time gone? I nod into him, silently accepting that it is time to leave. To accept I won't see her. But what now? What am I expected to do, just read every obituary until I find her?

"Let's get a coffee," Ryan suggests, making the first move to get up. I'm so lost in my haze of grief, I barely hear his sounds of pain now, my focus rigidly set on my devastation. He walks us to a nearby coffeehouse, guiding me the entire way, being my eyes and ears. I'm sure if he could manage, he would have picked me up and carried me here.

I find myself at a table and stare blankly at the chair in front of me, vaguely hearing Ryan in the background talking. He didn't ask what I wanted to drink. Probably concluded there was no point.

A while later—I don't know how long—Ryan is back. But he has no coffee. "Come," he says, motioning for me to stand.

"I thought we were having coffee."

"We'll have coffee somewhere else."

He applies a light pressure to the small of my back and pushes me on until I'm on the street and he's leading me the wrong way. "Ryan?" I question, but he just keeps on walking, checking the road for traffic before he crosses us. "Ryan, please."

He says nothing, his silence infuriating, until I've been dragged around a few corners and down a few streets.

Finally, I can't stand it any longer. "Will you please just tell me where the hell we're going?"

He stops, turns to face me, and points upward. "Here."

I look up. And lose my breath. "What?" I shoot my stare back to him, looking for the confirmation I need that he's lost his mind.

"I couldn't sit by and do nothing."

"What did you do?" I ask, terrified for his answer. I know my family is safe now, but they don't need to be dragged into my mess. If the police ever ask questions, I don't want them involved, not on any level. I also don't want to ignite their pain. Or have to explain everything that I've been through. I'm better off dead to them.

"I called the home," he says, his eyes like laser beams on mine. I lean back, wary of what comes next. "And asked them to have your sister call me."

"Oh my God, Ryan." I turn away, panicked. "I told you I couldn't put them at risk. I told you they're better off not knowing." He didn't listen to me. He didn't respect my wishes.

"You have to trust me, Hannah. Your family are at no risk. But *you* are. If you don't have this closure, you'll never be able to move on. Not truly. You'll always wonder, *What if*. I can't let you do that to yourself." He turns me back around to face him. "It's the final bit of peace you need, Hannah. Let me give it to you, I beg you. You need it."

"You spoke to my sister," I mumble. "She knows I'm alive?"

He nods, and my mind blows further. I swing away from him, unable to think straight, and come face-to-face with... "Oh my God." My hands cover my mouth, my legs giving out, forcing Ryan to lunge to save me from collapsing.

"Katrina." My sister's eyes well with tears, her chin trembling, her whole body shaking.

I cough over my emotion, just staring at her, amazed to be this close. "Yes," I sob.

And at the exact same time, we move forward and crash into each other's arms, crying on each other uncontrollably. "I'm sorry," I weep. "So sorry." I feel her head shake into me, her body jerking against mine.

She pulls away, her hands feeling at me everywhere, her eyes following, like she can't quite believe I'm here and she has to keep touching me to convince herself. I feel the same. She makes it to my face, ghosting her finger across the stitches on my cheekbone. "Everything you've been through."

I pull her hand away. "I'm okay. Please," I plead, not wanting to taint this moment with everything ugly. "I've been watching you," I tell her, needing her to know I've been with her so much. "Every Saturday morning when you took Mum for a walk, I was there with you."

More tears fall down her cheeks, her disbelief evident. "You look so different. You look like when you were a teenager, all messy and chaotic." She says it over a laugh, holding my arms out to the sides so she has the best view of my outfit. "Oh God." We come together again, embracing each other fiercely, making up for years of missed hugs.

She looks past me, and I follow, finding Ryan back on the wall, just watching our reunion silently, letting us have our moment. I don't think I could love him any more than I do. "You must be Ryan." Pippa releases me and steps forward, holding her hand out. "I recognize you. You were here last week."

Ryan nods, flicking his eyes to me as he starts to rise.

"Please, don't get up," Pippa says.

Of course he ignores her, and my sister flinches with me when she sees Ryan's struggle. "Him?" she whispers, her eyes on his hand over his thigh.

"He came off a lot worse," Ryan tells her, steady and strong and with that hint of madness in his tone. "Trust me."

"Good," she says, dropping her hand and moving in on Ryan, carefully wrapping her arms around him. "Thank you."

"Don't thank me." He holds her with his one spare hand, his eyes darkening.

I move in, if only to distract Ryan from the anger I can see igniting again. "How's Mum?" I ask, hoping I've not read this wrong. If my sister is here, then surely Mum is still here, too?

"Hanging on in there," she tells me, releasing Ryan and motioning to the door. "You ready to see her?"

I stare at the doors to the care home, reaching for my throat to massage the lump away. And I nod, taking in air. "Yes."

"Come on, then," Pippa says, starting up the path.

I concentrate on putting one foot in front of the other, following her on unsteady legs. I don't need to look back for Ryan. I can feel him close by.

Pippa signs us in, and the receptionist smiles brightly at me, though I'll be damned if I can return it. We get let through the automatic doors. I'm led down a corridor, and I manage through my haze to recall the cozy décor. It's still cozy.

We reach a door. My sister takes the handle, looking back at me with a faint smile. She pushes her way in, while I remain on the threshold, scared to go any farther. I see a nurse by the sink in the corner. Flowers in a vase on the nightstand. And then my mum in her bed, tucked in tightly, her eyes closed. She looks so peaceful, and it offers me some respite from my pain.

"How is she?" Pippa asks the nurse, placing her bag on the chair in the corner.

The nurse smiles sadly. "I was just going to call you. I don't think she'll make it through the night."

I'm stunned when my sister laughs lightly. "You've said that for over a week." Pulling up a chair, she sits down. "And you're still refusing to let go, aren't you, Mum?" Taking Mum's hand to her lips, Pippa kisses the wedding ring that she still wears, though it's loose now.

I watch as my sister plumps our mother's pillow, changes her water glass, rearranges her flowers. She folds the sheets, tidies the room, and combs Mum's hair. She does all the things I wish I could have done. Standing here, I feel useless. Almost unneeded. But I can't feel disappointed. Pippa has had no choice but to get on without me. To deal with things. I'm not the only one who has suffered. Would she welcome my help? I don't want to tread on her toes, don't want to butt in where I'm not needed.

"Are you going to stand there all day or come help me change her?"

My head snaps up, and my sister gives me a smile I'm all too familiar with. It's the one she used to give me when she knew what I was thinking and wanted me to know she knew. I return it, thankful, and go to help, following her instructions as we wash our mother together, strip her down together, and put her in a clean nightie together.

It's only when we've settled her back on the pillow that I look to the door, seeing it's closed, no Ryan in sight. But he's out there. Waiting for me.

"Pull up a chair." Pippa points to one in the corner, and I drag it across the room to the other side of Mum's bed. And we sit. Me on one side, my sister on the other.

Mum in the middle of her girls.

I can't believe I'm here.

"Truth or lie?" Pippa asks, resting her elbows on the side of the bed and taking Mum's hand.

"What?" I glance at Mum.

"She can't hear you," she says on a laugh, and I realize quickly what she's doing. There will be no talk of what's happened in the past, though I'm sure Ryan's given her enough information during their phone call. There will be no questions or probing. She's taking us back to the time before it all went wrong.

"Okay," I agree, mirroring her pose, taking Mum's other hand, but being careful to avoid the syringe driver that's in her arm. Painkillers. They've made her as comfortable as possible in her final days. I breathe in shakily. "Fire away."

Pippa looks up to the ceiling, thoughtful. "On a night out with some girlfriends a few years ago, I'd had a few too many wines and wolf-whistled at a hottie crossing the road. A few weeks later, we had a home visit from the teacher of the preschool Bella was starting. Guess who the teacher was?"

"No," I gasp. "Oh my God, that is so truth. That could only happen to you."

"And it did! I nearly died. I had to leave the room to compose myself."

I chuckle across the bed, and Pippa joins me. It's like we've never been apart.

We spend the next hour telling our stories and guessing whether they're a truth or a lie. I learned long ago, the more outrageous my sister's stories are, the more likely they are to be true. She just had a habit of getting herself in some terrible scrapes, and it seems she still has that talent.

"One more," she says, wiping at the laughter tears in her eyes.

"Shoot."

"I fancy your boyfriend."

I snort. "Definitely true."

"Where did you find him, Katrina?" She looks to the door where Ryan is beyond. Where did I find him? I didn't. He found me. "Truth or lie," I say, and she nods, a grin on her face. "He ran me over," I tell her. "Then we kept seeing each other around town, and every time, I lost all mouth functionality."

"I hope not *all* mouth functionality," she says around a smirk.

"Pippa!"

"Bite me," she quips, rolling her eyes. "Go on."

I smile, in my element. "We nearly kissed a few times. It was awkward. Then I decided enough was enough and turned up at his cabin in the woods. It was raining. He was shirtless."

"Oh my God, it's like a romance novel."

I laugh, my eyes falling to the sheets keeping Mum warm. "And then we made love, right after he swept me off my feet and carried me inside. I fell in love with him and his daughter. Then the bad guy showed up and tried to destroy our happiness. He paid with his life."

"Truth," she whispers, her eyes gleaming with a mixture of happiness and sadness. "Don't tell me it's a lie, because *I'll* die of disappointment."

"Truth," I reply quietly, looking to the door.

"And now I fancy him even more," Pippa says on a breathy whisper.

I laugh lightly. "You're married and all things terrible."

"I can look." She flashes me a devilish grin, and then we both jump out of our chairs at the exact same time, each of us on a loud curse. I stare down at my mother, quickly grabbing for her hand again which I lost mid-jump. I see my sister do the same in the edge of my vision.

"Did you feel that?" I ask, my heart beating crazily.

"I don't know."

I lower back down to the chair, just as Ryan bursts through the door. "Everything okay?" he asks.

"She moved," I tell him. "She definitely moved."

"Get the nurse," Pippa orders gently, and Ryan obeys immediately, moving as fast as he can. "She's not stirred for nearly a week," she says, sitting back down, too, but moving to the edge of the chair, getting as close as possible to Mum's bed like me. "Not even woken up."

Oh my, has she listened to our terrible chatter? I smile, hoping she has. She would have laughed with us if she could.

Then I feel it again. A very light squeeze of my hand, and I nearly come out of my skin. "There," I say loudly. "She did it again."

"Oh my goodness." Pippa wraps Mum's one hand in her two, and I lean in some more, resting my chin on her arm. "I'm here, Mum," I tell her. "Me and Pippa. We're both here."

"Again!" Pippa blurts, making me jump. "I felt it again."

My throat clogs up, and I find my sister, seeing her face is a red blotchy mess like I'm certain mine is. I smile through my tears, feeling Mum's hand flex ever so lightly again.

"She knows you're here." Pippa's eyes overflow, her head shaking. "She's been waiting for you."

I convulse on a sob, hoping my sister is right, as I wait not so patiently for another sign of life from her.

The nurse enters the room, and I look at my mum, watching her, knowing another move won't come. Was she waiting to know I was okay? Just waiting for me to get here to say a proper goodbye?

I look at my sister as she looks at me, both of us smiling through our tears.

She was. She was waiting for her girls to be back together.

And now she's at peace.

Chapter Thirty-Five

RYAN

I'm a realist. Always have been. I know it's going to take time for Hannah to recover fully, and I will help her. Every step of the way, I will be here for her. Solid. Devoted. Madly and utterly in love with her.

As the two sisters embrace, I wait patiently, despite the fact that I'm fit to drop. But just seeing her face, watching her hold her mother's hand was worth every relentless stab of pain.

Hannah's eyes are puffy as she approaches me after saying goodbye to Pippa with a promise to call her tomorrow. I can feel the peace in her as if I'm feeling it myself. I made the right choice. I'm so glad I took the gamble to call. Bringing Hannah here was for the best.

She doesn't say anything when she comes to a stop before me. She just looks up at me with those big watery blue eyes and nods, so very mildly, I nearly don't catch it. But I do catch it.

No words are needed. I don't have to tell her how sorry I am for her loss. She knows it. She reads me. It's the most beautiful thing about our relationship. We say so much to each other without saying anything at all.

I pull her into me, kiss her with all the love I have, lingering a long time, before I lead her across to the taxi waiting on the other side of the road.

The journey is quiet. I let her have her time, content to be here. Just...be here. I always will be.

As we're driving up the high street in Hampton, I sit forward in my seat, seeing Alex outside Mr. Chaps's store, scuffing her Vans on the curb as she sucks on a lollipop. I haven't seen her for six days, and my heart is aching with her absence. Darcy kept our daughter at her friend's house, as she said she would, letting her run riot on the obstacle courses, getting messy beyond messy. My neck cranes to keep her in my sights as we drive past, and I smile, telling myself I'll see her soon. That I'll make up for lost time.

"Stop!" Hannah shouts, making me jerk when the taxi slams his brakes on.

I groan, falling back in my seat.

"Shit, I'm sorry." Hannah reaches across and pats at me pointlessly. "We should see Alex," she says, and I look back out the window, seeing my girl take off her cap and put it back on back-to-front.

"She thinks we were in a car accident, Hannah," I admit. "It was all I could come up with. Darcy was pressing me." I had no choice but to bullshit if I wanted to evade Alex's sharp mind. Her calls have been relentless, question after question—who, where, how?

"Well, you look more like you've been run over to me, but whatever," Hannah says with complete indifference, reaching across me and opening the door. "Get out."

I don't argue with her. Why the hell would I? Edging out of the car, I rise to find Hannah has already made it to me. She holds her hand out. I take it. And we move down the high street toward my daughter, constantly flicking glances to each other as we go. I can see Hannah's happiness. She's missed my stinky Cabbage, too.

We come to a stop outside the store a few feet away from Alex, who is still oblivious to our presence, and I feel Hannah squeeze my hand. But she's not looking at Alex. She's looking at the newspaper stand outside the store.

TECH GIANT FOUND DEAD
AT HIS SCOTTISH CASTLE

I don't need to move in to see the small print. Jake sent it to me last night. Poor Jarrad Knight got himself on the wrong side of some wrong people. I read the entire thing with a curled lip and then texted Lucinda a simple *thank you*. I didn't get a response.

I turn into Hannah, worried this might trigger something. "Ha—" I'm halted from trying to reassure her when I see she's expressionless as she looks down at the picture of her dead ex-husband. There's no anxiety. No fear. No anger. Nothing.

She breathes in, looks up at me, leans in and kisses my chin, and then redirects her attention down the road to Alex. "Hey, stinky Cabbage," she calls.

Alex quits with the scuffing of her Vans and spots us. "Dad!" she squeals. "Oh my days, Dad!" She races toward us fast, and I drop Hannah's hand, instinctively getting ready to catch my girl. But she stops abruptly before jumping into my arms, leaving me hanging. "You look like crap," she says, taking a long, drawn-out assessment of me.

I straighten, quite put out. "Thanks."

"Much damage to the truck?"

"Total write-off."

"And you look like hell, too," she says, looking across to Hannah, who then looks at me like I can offer some guidance. I can't. I don't know what to say or do. So I shrug. I only wanted a hug, for fuck's sake.

Hannah returns my shrug, and we watch together as Alex's smirk breaks, building and building until it's splitting her face. "I've missed you guys so much!" She grabs us both and pulls us in, one of her arms around each of our necks.

I swallow down the pain and look across her shoulder, seeing Hannah's eyes closed, her smile small but peaceful. "I've stocked up the fridge with beer and the freezer with Chunky Monkey," Alex declares. "We're having burgers tonight."

"Where did you buy beer?" I ask.

"I didn't. Mum did." She releases us and puts herself between our bodies, taking a hand in each of hers. Darcy bought me beers? "I'll cook," Alex goes on. "It's my treat. And I'll do breakfast in bed for you, too." She continues to reel off the plans for the evening, while Hannah and I remain silent, constantly glancing across at each other as Alex leads us on.

"Alexandra!"

We stop and turn, and I see Darcy outside the store with a bag of shopping. She takes me in, up and down, a small frown on her face. "Hey, Mum," Alex chirps. "I'm gonna hang with Dad and Hannah tonight."

I expect fireworks. There are none. "Okay, darling." Darcy carries on her way to her car, looking back at me before she drops into the seat. She gives me a huge beam, the most genuine and human smile I've ever seen grace her face. That's another bit of the peace I need slotting into place. I return her smile, hoping she sees how grateful I am.

I know she does when she nods mildly.

"So, I've told you my plans," Alex says, getting us back to walking, swinging both of our hands as we go. "Now tell me yours."

Fine by me. "Well, after you've fed and watered us, I'm going to ask Hannah if we can go to her place, pack all her stuff, and move it into the cabin."

Hannah looks at me, not in shock, but more in an *Oh?* kind of way. "Okay," she says with a smile.

"Sounds good to me," Alex agrees without a second thought.

"Then I'm going to ask her to marry me," I declare, loud and proud. "And I hope she says yes."

Hannah's head cocks, her blue eyes wide but definitely delighted. "Guess you'll have to ask and find out."

"Puh-lease," Alex scoffs, her stride turning into more of a skip. "You are *so* saying yes."

"We'll see," Hannah muses casually.

I let my smirk escape, my mind immediately racing with all the ways I could ask her. It's obvious. The lake. It has to be the lake. "Yes, we will," I agree.

"I like this plan so much," Alex sings, completely unfazed. "Then what?"

"Then," I say, forcing myself to start skipping with her, easily disregarding the pain. I'm too fucking happy for anything else to infiltrate my nerves. "I'm hoping one day we might have more kids, and we're all going to live happily ever after."

"I knew it!" Alex yells. "A baby brother or sister! I was hoping you'd say that."

Hannah starts laughing, breaking into a skip, too. "We'll need more space."

Fair point. I hadn't thought of that. "So I'll extend the cabin."

Hannah stops, tugging me and Alex to a stop with her. "Maybe we could use this to pay for the building work." She pulls something out of her pocket and holds it up. The heart-shaped yellow diamond ring.

"Oh my God, that's one huge rock." Alex reaches to pluck it from between her fingers, but Hannah quickly retracts her hand. "Hey, I want to see," Alex whines.

"We don't need that," I say quietly as I look at the ring, forcing my lip not to curl.

Hannah smiles, breathes in, and walks to the curbside. Looking down into the drain, she holds the ring above it and releases on a little rush of breath.

Alex gasps and dashes over, looking down the grate. "Why would you do that?"

"It's just a piece of junk," Hannah says, turning to face me. We gaze at each other for a few moments, both our smiles growing until we're grinning at each other.

"You two need to see another kind of doctor." Alex trudges over, shaking her head. "You nutters."

Hannah laughs as she runs at me, throwing herself into my waiting arms and wrapping every limb around me. I feel absolutely no pain. All I feel is untold happiness, contentment, and best of all, Hannah's peace radiating from every inch of her perfect form.

She squeezes me to death before pulling away and looking down at me, her smile dizzying. Then she gives me the kind of kiss that puts all our previous kisses to shame. Because this one...this one has acceptance in it.

And as ever, it leaves me breathless.

Acknowledgments

There are a few significant milestones I have when writing a new story. There's the initial rush of excitement because I'm about to create a whole new world with new characters. There's always a point when I question if I'm writing a pile of dog shit. There's the point when I have a mild panic attack because I'm already tens of thousands of words in, and I haven't even gotten started. There's a point when I smash my fist on my desk with a whoop because an unplanned plot twist just came out of nowhere and it's frigging brilliant. And then there's the end when I sit back, smile, and crack open a bottle of wine.

Okay, so if you know me, you'll know that I've probably drunk a few *crates* of wine in the time it's taken me to write a book. But that final bottle? That one's the best.

Leave Me Breathless followed my usual writing routine. It took me to all the places I usually go and then some. It manifested in my mind for months before making it to the page, and once I started, I couldn't stop. I hope when you start reading, you can't stop.

I can't tell you how much I adore letting my imagination play out on the page for you to read. It's the most incredible journey, from an idea to hearing your reactions when you read my words. So many people play a part in that journey, and they all deserve a brand new thank-you with each novel of mine that's published.

First and foremost, my gorgeous agent, Andy, who is an absolute rock. The amazing people at my publishing houses, Grand Central and Orion. My fabulous editors, Leah and Victoria, whose input is invaluable and makes my stories the best they can possibly be. My Rockstar publicist, Nina, who is there for me day and night. Literally. My social media team at Rocket, especially Joe, who is one adorable bundle of happiness and excitement. Love ya, Joe! The girls who look after the fan pages, Lisa P, Bongo, Patty, and Lisa S. I think you guys know more about me than I do! And finally my two girls, Zoe and Ava, who do all the things I cannot do when I'm lost in my imagination.

Without you all, I would still write my stories, yes, but I know for damn sure that no one would ever get to read them. Thank you all for everything you do to get my stories out there and keep the JEM world alive.

JEM x

About the Author

Jodi Ellen Malpas was born and raised in the Midlands town of Northampton, England, where she lives with her husband, boys, and a beagle. She is a self-professed daydreamer, a Converse and mojito addict, and she has a terrible weak spot for alpha males. Writing powerful love stories and creating addictive characters has become her passion— a passion she now shares with her devoted readers. Her novels have hit bestseller lists for the *New York Times*, *USA Today*, *Sunday Times*, and various other international publications and can be read in more than twenty-four languages around the world.

You can learn more at:
    JodiEllenMalpas.co.uk
    Facebook.com/JodiEllenMalpas
    Twitter @JodiEllenMalpas